BETTER
THAN ᴛʜᴇ BEST

AMABEL DANIELS

Happy reading! ♡ Amabel Daniels

Cover Design and Interior format by The Killion Group http://thekilliongroupinc.com

DEDICATION

Every time in my childhood that I asked, "Why do they, Mama?", you would smile and patiently think up an answer. You never hesitated to encourage my curiosity with the world around us, especially as I endlessly wondered what makes people tick. As my number one supporter, you've embraced my creativity, fostered my love for reading, and always assured me it was okay to run away with my imagination. This one's for you, Mom. Love you.

ACKNOWLEDGEMENTS

This work of fiction would not be possible without the encouragement and support from my friends and family. Endless thanks are due. Phil, for my very first critique. The dedicated and insightful critique partners and beta readers I've been so fortunate to find: JoAnn, Renee, Bruce, Carolyn, Christie, Emma, Tracey, Rhonda, and Liz. Amanda, you called dibs…you were my very first official "fan". For professional expertise: Coty Sparks, Dr. John Herman and Cynthia Cummings. Michelle Josette, for her professional care and editing savvy.

Last but not least, this novel would've never seen the light of day without the staunch faith and patience my husband has in my imagination and determination. Here's to you, for every time I said "just five more minutes" and typed away into the night.

CHAPTER 1

At three in the afternoon on Halloween Eve, Kelly should have been on duty on the ER floor, not sitting on the bathroom floor with a towel wrapped around her dripping-wet body. And her husband should have been at his actuary office, not humping another woman in their bed.

Eyes closed tight, she dialed her best friend. Heather picked up on the fourth ring.

"Seriously, Kel? You've got some nerve to call me after ducking out of work again. This better be good. I've got a teen with a severed digit who only speaks Portuguese, a toddler with 103 who won't stop screaming, and an old man who cut his nuts off, and as of two seconds ago, decided he has to poop."

Kelly winced and let her head fall back to the toilet lid. A new LPN was chattering away in the background of the hospital chaos that sounded from the other end.

"All the way off?"

"Nearly. He was getting ready for a hot date and the razor couldn't hold steady. Why are you whispering?"

Kelly grimaced. She should have known better than to call Heather in the middle of a shift. But the shock of what she had found in the bedroom rendered her numb to common sense.

"Kel? The dog die or something?" Heather's impatience calmed rather than annoyed. To hear her voice, anything, to mentally stave off the obscene noise filtering through the door from the master bedroom. Her bossy friend was a semblance of normalcy in her life.

"John's cheating on me."

After she gasped, Heather's voice shrilled. "What? Seriously? You finally hired someone to follow him?"

Kelly squinnied her eyes open. It was one thing to suspect infidelity. It was quite another to be caught in it. Caught in it as a non-participant. "Not really." She bit her lip.

"Huh?" Heather threw out a quick order to the LPN. "How long has he been cheating?"

This time or altogether? She glanced at the clock on the wall. Her not-so-relaxing bath had started a half hour earlier and Kelly was positive her husband wasn't in the bedroom when she came home. She didn't want to know how long his affair had been going on.

"Who is it? O.M.G. Kel! He's actually *cheating*? With who?"

"I don't know who she is. I need to get the hell out of here."

"Amen. I always thought you could do better."

Her jaw dropped. "That's not what you told me the night before I got married!"

"Well, duh. You were getting married. I had to stand behind you since you had your mind made up."

Kelly closed her eyes again, afraid to confess she'd never really made up her mind about John. Bad karma for marrying with doubts was certainly catching up to her.

"Besides, that was two years ago. He's never made you happy. A man is supposed to want sex more than once a month."

Yeah, he's been getting it elsewhere.

The lack of sex was only part of the problem. "You should have told me you didn't think he was right for me."

"Then what?" Heather scoffed. "You would have believed me and not gotten married?"

She shook her head. They were discussing the beginning of matrimony, not the closure, which appeared to be pending quite rapidly. What about the house? The furniture? Worries escalated and she took a deep breath. "We'll talk about this later. I need to get out of here."

"I'm done at seven. We'll go out to get you wasted. Maybe Donna can take your shift tomorrow. Not like you wouldn't call off again anyways."

"Shit. I'm scheduled for tomorrow?"

Heather snorted. "Look, Kel, I know you keep saying you've been in a funky mood about John. Looks like you're right on target about that asshole, but you've been acting weird about work for a while. Ever since—"

"I let Norbert die?"

"He had a heart attack, Kel. For the last time, it wasn't your fault."

She clenched her fist. "He suffered from a drug interaction. From the damn heparin Betsy gave him at the end of my damn shift. An elementary mistake I should have foreseen and prevented."

"You weren't responsible for her actions. You were her mentor, not her supervisor."

"But I should have been there to check it and—"

"Kel! It. Wasn't. Your. Fault."

It wasn't her fault. Those words were the mantra she fell back on whenever a patient's death weighed her down. A circle of life and death. Not everyone can be saved. She counted her breaths, scowling when a moan came from the bedroom. "I need to get out of here."

"You go tell that bastard you're leaving him. And come over to my place—"

"No. Not figuratively. I mean I literally need you to come over and get me out of here."

"Here where?"

"My bathroom."

Dings from a heart monitor clicked in an angry succession on the other end as Heather seemed to stall for a reply. Kelly's shoulder slumped with a renewed wave of guilt for calling Heather. People were hurt. People were dying. John cheated... Yes John's infidelity sucked in her world but there were people with bigger problems. Real problems. Life or death sorts of problems.

She couldn't call any of her four brothers. It was too mortifying and if family came over, there would be fists and injuries. John was cheating?

Good riddance. But he wouldn't stand a chance against her four over-protective older brothers. And then there was Dad…

"Why do you need me to get you out of the bathroom?"

"They're in the master. I came in to take a bath since I had a migraine and they must have thought I wasn't home since I parked in the garage. They're going at it like the plane's going down."

"In the bedroom?"

"Yes." Kelly opened her eyes and winced at the thumping sounds of the bed in the adjacent room. A scream? She rolled her eyes. Alright, so she wasn't good enough in bed for her husband, but John had never been spectacular enough to elicit a scream.

Yeah right. Hellooo, Johnny boy, she's faking it.

What about the dog? And the wedding gifts? It was two years ago, but they still hadn't even opened some of the boxes. There had to be some kind of official etiquette to follow. Her brows sank. Divorce was uncharted territory. And what the hell is the difference between divorce and annulment?

"They are having sex on your bed in your bedroom." It should have been a question.

"Yes!"

"You're in the bathroom while your husband is having sex in the bedroom."

"Yes!"

"Do they know you're in there?"

"What? No!" Kelly sighed at the obvious. "My iPod was so loud I couldn't hear a tornado. I turned off the lights to make it like a spa. Then I was trying to relax and not think about Norbert and Betsy, but I couldn't chill. I mean, baths are like sitting in a puddle of your own filth. I was about to get dressed and saw them in there. I'm trapped. I can't face him like this. I'm in a towel. I need an upper hand. I can't have an upper hand in a towel while he's in another woman!"

"Who's in what is beside the point. Kel. Go and face him. You can't put it off. Be cool. You can do this."

"I'd rather be in clothes. And I'd rather not be numb. I can't think, Heather. I don't think I can breathe. I'm shocked. I know he's scum but I'm so…"

"Deep breaths, Kel."

"Please, I need you to come over and make them leave. I need a diversion to escape."

Desperation annoyed her. Having to enlist help irritated her. *Where was a teletransporter when you needed one? Beam me up, Scottie!*

"Escape? It's your house, too!"

"Heather, please!"

Beeps and chatter were louder on the other line. "Girl, you know I'd do anything for you, but we're slammed. The floor's been a zoo all morning. I can't come over. Call your brothers."

"They'd kill him."

"You think I wouldn't?"

Kelly frowned at the closed door. "I can't face him like this. Not until I scream, or punch something or have alcohol or cry, or…" Tears fell down her cheeks as the stabs surfaced from under the shock of the discovery. Blunt discovery.

Infidelity was apparent when…what? A spouse has mysterious calls and credit card receipts. A trend of going out of town or staying out late. Lies that didn't add up. Maybe the extreme of someone witnessing a kiss or grope that fell outside the boundaries of matrimony. Someone tattling.

Not walking out of a bathroom and seeing it full-frontal like a low-budget porno.

"Kel, you can do this. Go out there and tell him—"

"I can't burst in there and—"

"For God's sake, Kelly, you don't need a damn invitation to go in your own bedroom."

"I don't want to get involved. I only want out."

"How long have they been going at it?"

"Probably close to an hour now."

"Damn."

Kelly's stomach clenched. Yeah, *ouch*.

"You can't be a wimp and hide in the bathroom. I mean, you're catching him red-handed. Can't be any clearer."

"I didn't plan on this!" Kelly stood quietly to pace. "I was caught."

"No. *He* was—" Shouts and rushed voices clashed in the background on Heather's end.

"Jesus, what did he say? Another stabbing victim? The third this week." Kelly pinched the bridge of her nose. "I can't believe I even called you. Look, I'm going to crash at your place. I'll figure something out."

Kelly hung up and called for a pizza delivery. She paced until the doorbell rang. After heavy footsteps sounded, she peeked through the slit of the door. John headed for the hallway. It was her only shot to escape and save face.

Without a second thought, Kelly tiptoed onto the navy blue carpet, wanting to scream as she looked for her clothes. Instead she found *her*—the other woman. She had a model-worthy body. Smooth skin, no fat, a slutty rose tattoo nearly on her ass. With a start, Kelly gasped in surprise at the woman still in the bed. *Her* bed. Frozen in place, she watched the woman lazily roll from her stomach to her back.

Kelly had no desire to scream and throw objects at her husband's lover's head. No escalating itch in her throat to become a crazed psycho spewing threats. No tears and sobs were ready to beg him for fidelity the next day. No impulse to create a fourth stabbing victim. What kind of wife was she if she couldn't fathom some kick ass retaliation?

Nerves paralyzed, Kelly couldn't compute a single thing to do or say. She could only stare at the woman who was stealing her husband. The brunette raised her brows, not in surprise, not in alarm, but in something resembling curiosity.

"Who the hell are you?" she said with ease. Sass, even.

Kelly's jaw dropped. Who was *she*? Her mouth flapped silently in a wordless stammer. Who was *she*? Who the hell else would she be? It was her house! She narrowed her eyes at the woman and flipped her off.

Kelly darted through the bedroom, grabbed her clothes and purse, and rushed for the second-floor balcony off the master suite. Curtains waved as she shut the door behind her, the inanimate farewell likely the only one she would get. She slipped her jeans and shirt on over the towel before tossing it to her feet. Her cheeks burned at the whistle from her elderly neighbor as he watered his garden. Wincing at her hurry to extract herself from the betrayal in the bedroom, she had no option but to shimmy down the column to the backyard.

Only when she fastened her seatbelt in her Subaru did she remember to inhale deeply. On the drive to Heather's apartment, her emotions clashed and butted in a fury. Numbing shock. Awkward sadness. Heartbreaking pain. Red-cheeked humiliation. Jaw-clenching anger. Most of all, though, what lurked beneath the raw feelings was the rational and solid notion of fear at what would come next.

Loneliness.

CHAPTER 2

Bright lights blinded Emily as she sat on the bed in the hospital, picking at the cuticle on her thumb. She closed her left eye to the throbbing burn and scanned the room. No cameras. A blood pressure cord hung from a hook, in case she needed to kill the nurse. Closest exit was down the hall to the right.

She had studied the facility enough to know. A true predator, Emily left nothing to chance in a hunt. In pursuit of confirming her power, always proving she was the best, Emily had hunted many people.

But not this hunt. Not this target. Instead of stalking a steal, Emily was preparing the chase for that bitch. The damned bitch who took her power.

Three hours ago, Emily had killed Steal Number Forty. At the memory, her nail lodged under her skin to send blood trickling. Killing usually calmed her, reminding her of her power, her finesse, her control.

She sucked the blood on her thumb.

Killing Forty had done nothing to abate her fury for Kelly. After stowing the body, she had maced her eye. In order to get information about Kelly, to start this unprecedented chase, Emily had to get close to Kelly's bimbo best friend, Heather. Stalking didn't seem like the appropriate technique. Stalking required waiting, and Emily had no patience to find Kelly. No time for a strategic and careful hunt. And it was risky being back at the hospital.

Kelly had to be punished for what she did to Forty. Kelly had screwed up Thirty-Nine, too, but it was revenge for Forty Emily sought.

Emily licked the pulsing cut on her thumb.

It would be too suspicious if she killed Heather for information, or tortured Daddy dearest for specifics. Macing her eye was a temporary injury, yet severe enough to concoct a way into the ER to get to Heather.

Emily avoided permanent damage to her body. Like a blank slate, she needed to be able to change it as she had many times in her life. Those many times when she had been unidentifiable.

Plastic surgery, reductions, implants, haircuts, dyes, tattoos, tattoo removals, piercings. Emily couldn't count the ways and times she had changed her identity.

She never left a trace. Ever careful to never leave a clue behind, Emily could come and go, never be remembered except for her current name and role. No one could follow her. But this time, she needed to follow Kelly.

Heather returned to the room and deposited instruments on the little table. Bottle of water, a salve, junk. Emily darted her gaze, following each of Heather's motions. Blue illumination of light flashed in the pocket of her scrubs. Cell phone.

Staggering and moaning, Emily stood up.

"Take it easy, now." Heather went to her as she struggled to her feet.

Leaning her weight into her, Emily slipped her hand down to take the phone. "I need to go to the bathroom." Emily groaned as Heather's pager buzzed at her hip.

"Okay. Okay." Heather guided her to the tiny bathroom space. "I'll be back in a second, okay? They need me down the hall for a minute. I'll be right back."

Emily nodded weakly and shut the door. One eye shut, she sniffled from the mustard oil and peered at the phone. She scrolled through texts from Kelly, learning where she was.

Finished, Emily tossed the phone to the floor and left the ER undetected.

"So when are you going home?" Randy asked Kelly as he slid into his seat across from her.

She wanted to scream. Go home to what? To whom? To the depressing and slightly freaky world of dating and being alone? What about when home wasn't about a house but a companion? Go back to the only place she'd ever lived and work the job she had cringed to think about as soon as she woke up?

Eating at the small diner in Churchston, she stuck out like a sore thumb. Kelly Newland, failure at love and life.

"I'm on vacation." She shrugged, then grabbed the ketchup bottle from the man sitting across from her. The expiration date was two years ago. She was tired of defending her decisions, and exhausted because she had no real answers. Perhaps her presence in Churchston didn't make much sense, but nothing in her life did anymore.

"I thought you said you quit your job," he said.

John's affair was the catalyst for her departure from Atlanta. In the wake of his infidelity, Kelly had let the other elements of her life dissipate as well. She said buh-bye to nursing, leased her house and tried to convince her family she wasn't crazy when she announced she was moving to Myrtle Beach. Confidence had evaporated across all fronts. In marriage. Home. Work.

Kelly sucked in her lips, then said, "Yeah. I did. I hated it. I was the most incompetent individual on the floor. Hey,"—she nudged the man next to her—"ask Edna for some ketchup packets."

Clay tipped his face up to prevent the food from falling from his mouth as he mumbled a reply. "The bottle's right there."

"This stuff expired years ago." Kelly slid it further away on the scuffed and worn tabletop.

"So if you quit your job, are you on a permanent vacation?" Randy said.

She faced the realtor opposite the booth she resided in with the local mechanic. "Why twenty questions?"

"Trying to figure out what your plans are," Randy said.

"Let me know when you do." Kelly leaned around Clay and waved down the waitress.

She really had meant to move to Myrtle Beach. If she was hunting for a change of scenery, peppy sunny beaches had to be the cure. But a storm had stalled her journey en route to the coast, and she had exited the ramp for Churchston. Edgy from driving, she had checked in to the hotel for a couple days and had taken respite walking her mutt, Eddie, along the lake. She hadn't intended on sticking around.

"Can I have some ketchup packets?" She smiled at the Dolly Parton with a bad hair job.

"Bottle right in front of you, hon." Edna jutted a hip out and filled the coffee cups like a sloth.

Kelly sighed at Edna's dismissal. *No shit there's a ketchup bottle on the table. I'm not blind.* "Haven't you ever heard of anaerobic fermentation? If this condiment container hasn't been in an adequate refrigerated environment, the organic compounds of the tomato puree will ferment in the absence of oxygen in the bottle. I don't particularly wish to suffer the side effects of food poisoning, such as nausea, vomiting—"

"Alright, alright. I'll get you some damn packets, Miss Smarty Pants." Edna trudged off.

"Don't you think the hotel is getting tired of Eddie barking in your room?" Randy wiped at his mouth. "And what about Alan?"

"You done with your burger?" Clay licked his lips.

Kelly opened and closed her mouth as she stalled for an answer. To Clay's, she slid her plate over. To Randy's she hesitated.

"I still want the fries," she told Clay.

With the impromptu decision to explore the tiny tourist town of Churchston, Kelly had met the goals of checking out the shops, admiring the water, and exercising her dog so he wouldn't whine the rest of the way to Myrtle Beach. But on her walk, she had accidentally gained employment.

On a lazy stroll she had passed an older man hurrying down Main, walking with a limp and juggling a dozen or so boxes. In the essence of being a Good Samaritan and possessing a deep sympathy for people in pain, she had righted the boxes and taken a couple as she walked with him.

Lonely old men were her weakness. She had never been able to escape the clutch of heartache at the thought of Dad, lonely and sad in his old age.

And Norbert. He'd been another lonely old man passing away by himself until Kelly found his estranged daughter.

Not my fault. I can't save everyone. Not my fault.

Alan, as the man had introduced himself, was the owner of the bowling alley which housed the single pizza joint in town. He seemed too flustered to accept her help in the delivery for his goods, so Kelly convinced him she might as well carry some of the boxes since she had been walking anyway.

The next day she had found him again, fumbling along with his deliveries. He had been too proud to welcome her offer of help, and Kelly assumed he would be humiliated to accept charity, so she developed a habit to meet him on Main as a friendly companion to walk with while he made deliveries. After a couple weeks, though, he asked her to carry more boxes. And maybe, would she mind coming back to the alley and run out a few more? How about tomorrow, he had said. How about you come back Monday at ten?

"He told me someone was going to be coming back to town soon. Someone who tended bar for him a couple years ago." Kelly grinned at the arrival of fresh ketchup.

"Probably Jaycee," Clay said.

"Maybe. I wasn't paying attention."

Clay nodded and stuffed his mouth with the last of her burger. "She was spending time for, uh, possession and dealing. Heard she was supposed to be coming back to town."

"Sounds like a stellar individual," Kelly said.

"So you're only sticking around to help out Alan and then you're gone?" Randy sipped his water.

Kelly almost smiled at him. So neat, so proper. Such the momma's boy. With a perfect haircut and good manners, he was about the nicest man she had ever met. The exact opposite of Clay's sloppier, leering, and womanizing self.

As Randy was Clay's old high school buddy, she had met the pleasant man after she became acquainted with Clay at the hotel, having seen him coming and going from multiple women's rooms on various nights. She befriended Clay once she started making routine deliveries to the garage where he worked.

"Maybe, maybe not," she said. "It's not like I live here."

"Well, what if you did?" Randy said.

"Here? Churchston?" Kelly took her check from Edna. She had been paying for her hotel room with the money Alan slipped her under the table and with some minor dips into her savings.

Clay slung his arm around her shoulders. "Why not?"

The thought hadn't crossed her mind.

Churchston. Home? She doubted it. It wouldn't have surprised her one bit if she grew tired and impatient with small-town life. Kelly didn't know what Churchston could have for her that she wouldn't find anywhere else in the world. But it was a start. A new beginning. Turning a leaf. All that crap.

"Here?" She wrinkled her nose at the thought.

"Yeah, why not?" Clay said again.

She had enjoyed her walks through the small 3,000-population town. Authentic woodwork scenic signs advertised Lake Moultron. Quaint buildings dotted the road across the linear public beach area. The diner, barbershop, little shops, Clay's garage, Alan's bowling alley, little odds and ends of small businesses to support the tourism which ran the small town. Trees and vines decorated the land from the lake bank. It was a polar change from the busier, bustier Atlanta.

Tapping her finger to the table, she weighed the possibilities. From the little she had learned from Randy and Clay, people left the small town to escape the slow pace. They didn't immigrate to it. But for Kelly, the anonymity of being a new face in town had its appeal. She was no longer defined by the labels of an ex-wife, or a nurse, or a baby sister. In Churchston, Kelly was, well, Kelly.

"I don't think walking food around will pay for a place." It was at least a practical reason not to move to the middle of nowhere.

"Burns is looking for help." Clay picked at his teeth. At her blank look he elaborated. "Kayak hut on the beach across from the garage. He always needs help in the summer."

Kelly studied Randy, sensing an ulterior motive as his small talk and genteel conversions had never bordered on persuasion before. Probably had a rotten house he wanted to load off on her. "What, you've got a listing you need off your hands? How bad is this place?"

He reddened. "Hey, it's not so bad." He exchanged sheepish glances with Clay. "It's not like I'm in a rush to get it off my hands, or anything… It's not to own. A spacious apartment to rent. Right next to Clay. It's, it's well, a little place where you could stay if you're planning on sticking around. You know?"

She didn't know. She bet the dump Randy had in mind was pathetic. She predicted her well-meaning family would freak if she called home to say she moved to an itty bitty town where everyone warned of the gators. She estimated that delivering food and manning a kayak hut would bore her as they were more fit as chores for a teenager than an almost thirty-year-old adult. She gambled having Clay for a true neighbor might be a bit too much to tolerate.

"What's the worst that can happen?" she said.

Clay patted her shoulder, then stood up. "You're staying?"

"Really? You want to look at it?" Randy couldn't hide the relief on his face. "No pressure, Miss Newland."

"For God's sake Randy, you're two days older than me. It's just Kelly already. I'll check it out tomorrow morning."

Randy slid out from his seat and scribbled directions on a napkin. They left her to finish her coffee and when she stood in line to pay at the register, the second thoughts clustered on her rash impulse.

Standing in line as an elderly couple argued the sales tax on a piece of pecan pie, she couldn't stop the emotional questions from bombarding her, filling the lack of anything better to concentrate on.

Was I bad in bed?

She frowned and tried to recall the last time she had even seen John's dick.

How long had he been seeing her*?*

Kelly sighed and squinted at the comb-over on the man in front of her. Length of time wasn't important. Cheating was cheating.

Maybe I wasn't good enough for him.

She hadn't forgotten how Sasha had looked back at her in the bedroom, confident, unruffled, and cool. Kelly's jaw clenched for a second. It was almost as if the woman had been gloating.

Why did I even marry him?

In the absence of an answer, she grimaced, called herself every kind of an idiot. Sure, there had been doubts, second thoughts. Every woman going into marriage had to experience some uneasiness. But staying two years after… That had made her the moron.

Why wasn't I there to save Norbert?

She kneaded her forehead with her fingers as her trivial woes suddenly changed to a heavier one. He'd been her patient. No matter what they said, the doctors, her charge nurse, the hospital's legal team—they had explained over and over again: it wasn't her fault. She hadn't been on duty. Her shift had ended. But Norbert had been *her* patient. And she hadn't saved him.

So her new intern LPN Betsy was the one who technically administered the drug in the last few minutes of Kelly's shift. The undeserved guilt would forever burden her.

I should have been there.

"Can you get the driver of the gray SUV?"

The roughly spoken description of her car broke her from remorse. She turned to see the man who had entered. He was tall and frighteningly huge. She tried to make out the details of his face under the navy cap and abundant facial hair. It wasn't quite ZZ Top yet, but the long hair and shaggy beard likened him to a long-lost, unkempt warrior.

"That you?" The waitress gaped. "Why—" She clutched her hand to her chest. "I didn't know you were back."

"Gray SUV?" he repeated curtly, scanning the room.

"Why, now, when did you get back?" The waitress all but cooed.

"What difference does it make? I'm here now." And he didn't sound pleased about it.

Past the windows of the diner, blinking orange lights of a tow-truck flickered with a weary rhythm in the darkness of the muggy night.

"Well now, how are you doing, hon?"

"I'll be doing better after the fucking SUV moves."

Kelly slanted a brow at him and the waitress huffed at his attitude. Impatience, she could relate to, but really, he was a jerk. His attitude was quite a contrast to the ho-hum hospitality of the bumbling diners, the superficially kind locals of Churchston. And a bit more human.

"Why do you need the SUV moved?" Kelly held out her money and bill to the waitress. "You can keep the change for Edna."

"What's it to you?" His retort was the only pause in his survey of the diners.

"Well, seeing the 'fucking SUV' is mine, I'd say its parking spot is nothing to me, but it seems like it's something to you."

He grunted and nodded his head to the front door. "Can you move it?" Without a look at her, he moved to leave.

"I parked it there. I'm sure I can un-park it, too."

She didn't follow him out. She waited for him to exit and storm back in when he realized she wasn't in tow.

"What the hell are you waiting for? It's going to deluge any minute now."

"I don't melt."

"Then can you move the fucking car or not?"

She nodded but didn't budge except to cross her arms.

He brandished his hands out as if to say 'anytime, cupcake.'

"What?"

"You going to move it or not?"

"If you ask me to."

"I just did! Twice!" His bellowing had silenced the easy-going local chatter. All eyes were on them with the instinctive eager anticipation of a good fight.

"You asked me if I *can* move it. Try again without your head up your ass."

Snickers rose in the diner.

He grit his teeth and stepped closer to her, his shaded face likely emitting tangible rays of hatred at her.

Someday she'd remember to watch her tongue. She couldn't sass back at any man like she could her brothers. His face said murder. She didn't know him to tell if it was honest. "Will you *please* move your car?"

The way he clenched his jaw and spoke through his teeth had Kelly imagining he had a vise grip clamped onto his balls. She tucked a strand of hair behind her ear and strode past him out of the diner. She had no idea who he was, or what his problem was, but she wasn't taking shit from anyone. Especially not some random local yokel.

"Not enough room to pull it out from the other side?" She went for her car, noticing an old clunker was backed in to the spot in front of hers.

Thunder growled softly in the night and drizzle tapped at the bill of her hat.

"Rear-wheel drive," he said and strode behind her.

"I can wait. No need for you to get wet," an older man called out from the driver's window of the immobile vehicle. Kelly recognized the elderly man from the ice cream stand on the public beach.

The tow-trucker sighed deeply at her side. "No. It's okay. Sit tight," he said.

She raised a brow. While his tone was still curt and direct, it was magically gentler for the elderly. He was a respectful jerk, if such an oxymoron existed. Eddie barked at her coming near.

"Quiet, Eddie." He whined louder. Thunder cracked from above and the man pounced. He clutched her arm and shoved her behind him as he crouched to the pavement.

What the hell...?

She hadn't the time to ask him what was wrong. His movements had been too sudden, shoving her down so forcefully. She frowned, and the contents of her purse spilled and spread in a puddle on the pavement. She couldn't see much of his face from his nomadic facial hair and the low bill of his hat, but from the death grip on her arm and his sharp intake of air, he had to have been terrified. Coupling his reaction to the noise with the fact he "protected" her behind him, she clamped her mouth shut.

Thunder. Not a gunshot. Kelly hadn't had many post-trauma victims during her unsatisfactory career of nursing in Atlanta, but she wasn't stupid. With a tense swallow at the adrenaline rush, she wanted to look away as he closed his eyes—in relief, in embarrassment, maybe both. As much as he was an arrogant asshole, she rationalized he was hurting. He was skittish, more like a rabid dog than a man, and she fought the pity she always felt when her heart bled for her patients.

As suddenly as he had struck her down, the man jumped to his feet. With trembling fingers, he rubbed at his face. She sat on the wet pavement, letting her shorts dampen as he paced back and forth.

"You going to sit there all day or move the car?"

She smirked at his sharp question. *All bite and no bark after a scare, I bet.* "You're not going to help me up?"

Dependence on someone for something as simple as standing up seemed brainless to her, but she wanted to piss him off. Nothing like a dose of petty anger to chase away the fear he had experienced.

He swore under his breath as he stopped and looked to the sky, then came back toward her, his face still covered in the depth of his hat.

In a thrust of impatience, he stuck his hand out to help her up. Kelly ignored the extension and stood on her own. He glared at her.

"Principle of it." She crouched to the ground to gather her stuff. She tore her gaze from his unsteady hands.

"Goddammit, my candy's getting wet." She whined, hoping her petty bitching would distract him from his panic attack and hide the pity he might catch on her face.

On her haunches, she picked up the loose scattered articles, and he squatted to help her after taking a deep calming breath. She shook the water from the soaked Junior Mints, then tossed them back in her purse. He studied her well-worn copy of *Grapes of Wrath* before shoving it at her and she scooped up her loose change.

"Well, lookie what we have here."

They both turned at the slow, exaggerated drawl from the driver's side of the car that pulled to a stop at Kelly's rear bumper. The patrol car shifted to park, cleanly blocking her in.

The man's scowl deepened momentarily and then he looked at the birth control package in one hand and the tampon in the other. Kelly bit her lip. Stranger or not, it was weird to see her feminine belongings in the dirty rough hands of a man. She snatched them back.

"He giving you trouble, ma'am?" The cop exited and looked the man over carefully.

Eddie started yapping again.

Hon. Ma'am. The staple endearments were already getting on her nerves. "Ma'am? Please. I'm probably hardly older than you." Kelly scoffed.

"He giving you trouble?"

"What do you want?" Irritation sparked from the man's question. "She's moving her car."

"No need to lose your temper, now." The cop strode for the diner.

"What the hell are you doing?" The rain came down harder, dimming the man's yell.

"Getting my coffee and piece a' pecan pie." He was nearly inside the shelter of the diner.

"Move your—" A crack of thunder silenced his shout. Kelly winced at the following swear.

"Mr. Parker…" The feeble old man's voice called under the drone of the rain.

"Eddie, shut up," Kelly said at the nonstop barking.

"Sit tight, Jared. Only take a second." The man turned and wiped at his mouth, swore some more, then slammed a clenched fist on the car next to them. The car alarm beeped ominously.

He flinched at the commotion. "Goddammit!"

She couldn't help it. Small laughs tickled from her lips.

He glared at her. "You think this is funny?"

Shaking her head, she tried to stop. "Lighten up."

"Shut up," he said to Eddie.

"Hey, I'll tell my own dog to shut up!" She pointed to the patrol car. "He left the window cracked."

"Brilliant observation. Now he'll have a wet ass."

She shook her head as she approached the cruiser. It wasn't like she was enjoying the rain either. She squeezed her arm in the crack, popped the lock, then opened the door. After shoving the gear into neutral, she slammed the door shut and gestured to the car as though she was a *Price is Right* model.

"What the hell are you doing?" He glanced up at the windows in the diner.

The big badass is afraid of the dinky little cop? "You're not going to make me push it too, are you?"

He licked his lips, tempted yet hesitant. After another glance at the diner, he jogged toward the hood, then pushed the car out of the way. Seeing no need to saturate her clothes with more rainwater, Kelly drove away, wondering how long she'd last in Churchston.

CHAPTER 3

"It's not as bad as it looks." Randy's greeting was more of an excuse when Kelly met him at the apartment the next morning.

"I could only hope." She let Eddie out of the car and set her hands at her hips as she examined her future residence. It was a little drive from town, past the vintage streetlights and pointless boutique shops. A sad-looking two-story house was turned into twin townhouse apartments. And it was uglier than hell. Even in the early dawning sun. She hesitated to know what it could look like in full daylight. "Never judge a book by its cover, right?"

"It's a solid structure."

"Uh huh."

"Rent can be due the first of the month." He stepped up on the porch and Kelly gave a discerning eye at the yard. It was out in the country. Lakefront. There was a remote feel to the place and she couldn't argue the solitude. The only other building in sight an older stone house behind them, tucked close to the woods. Instead of the isolation reminding her of *Friday the 13th*, she cherished it in the form of what could be peace and quiet.

Randy gave her a hopeful smile and opened the door. The hallway was narrow and there was a door to the left and a door to the right. Right it was.

"Clay's on the left. It's a bit empty in here." Empty was an understatement. There were no divisions to rooms. No furniture. Nothing.

At least it didn't smell like mold or BO.

"You don't say." Kelly stepped in to look closer. There was a small bathroom. Small kitchen. Potential? "What about the storage space out back?"

"Locked. Nothing out there. Guy who lived here before was going to turn it into a studio but, uh, it's locked now.

Kelly nodded slowly. "No problem about my dog?"

Randy shook his head.

She held out her hand. The place didn't emit a warm welcoming sense of homecoming, but her need to hurry compelled her to take the place in the manner of, why not?

"Where do I sign? I've got to meet Burns at the kayak hut in ten minutes. Without checking with me, the dumbass next door told him I'd start today."

Kelly was reluctant to consider working in a kayak hut a career because it was too damn close to minimum wage, and because she had no idea how long she was going to stay in Churchston. Nonetheless, she intended to diligently put her best effort forward. Not much would be needed. It was bound to be mindless busywork and would give her the time to reflect what she might want to really do with her life, because she felt no more destined to deliver food and rent out kayaks than she had been to be a nurse.

If nothing else, it would give her distance from Atlanta to properly accept and move on from her failures—as a spouse and a nurse.

Gingerly sipping coffee as she walked across the sand to Burns' kayak hut, she appreciated the sleeping beach, much more picturesque with a beautiful sunrise, the sand devoid of pasty bodies with skin the sun should never see. It was nothing more than a ten-by-ten shed. With the wooden and bamboo trim, Burns had probably been trying for a Beach Boy's theme but seemed to have settled for tiki. His little hut was positioned conveniently next to the small lazy river where the boats could float further into Churchston and out towards the woods.

Main Street had been developed with the beach as the central point. The mechanic garage where Clay worked was practically across the street from the kayak hut. From her vantage point, she could see almost all of the town. With a hint of claustrophobia, it reminded her of a snow globe, and she was partially glad she had taken the apartment out of town.

No one was in the hut when she stepped in. The beach was hardly populated and she wondered if her new boss had forgotten to come in to show her the ropes.

"Hello?" *Perfect. I wake up early and he doesn't?*

"Huh?" A teenager poked his head through the door to the hut.

Kelly sipped and checked out the kid. He couldn't be more than a teen with the acne rampant on his cheeks, but he had a boyish cuteness nonetheless.

"Might you know where Roger Burns is?"

He blushed then shook the bangs off his forehead. "Oh. You're the new girl."

Girl? She had at least ten years on him. "Kelly Newland." She offered her hand to make it a complete introduction and he blushed. Such a skittish little guy, like Harry Potter minus the glasses.

"We just got here. Dad's talking to Stella." He nodded toward the door. Roger, it seemed, was the balding man, stomping his foot and waving his hands, apparently arguing with a thirty-something woman at the yet-to-be-opened lemonade stand.

She turned back to the kid and found his gaze glued to her chest. Caught, he blushed even redder.

"Too old for you, kid." She gave him a deadpan stare. "Got a name?"

"Uh, everyone calls me Junior."

Junior-sized, she was sure. "Aren't you supposed to be in school?"

"I stay home with Dad. Home school." He did the hair sweep head jerk again. In the distance, Stella hollered about scriptures and virgins.

"What's with the crazy lady?"

Junior sighed and leaned against the door to the hut. "She wanted to know if he hired Sandra back this year for the busy season. She was trampy. Dad doesn't like trampy girls, but he needed someone to run the hut. Stella likes to think she's a virgin. Holier-than-thou."

She blinked. "Who's Sandra?"

"Sandra ran the hut last summer. She moved out of town for a job. Does every winter. Lot of the girls your age do. Daisy gets too cool and leaves. Jaycee comes and goes to spend time. The guys take gigs in the winter in the city."

"How would *you* know if crazy lady's a virgin?"

If he blushed any more his cheeks would have turned maroon. "*I* don't know Stella's not a virgin. Everyone does. Common knowledge. She had a baby last year and claimed it was divine conception."

Kelly gave a discerning eye to Junior. She hadn't met him or his dad in her adventures as Alan's deliverer. Neither had she experienced the pleasure of the aforementioned women. Junior seemed wise in his small world but she imagined his kind of gossip was girly for a teen dude. Then again, what else is there for small-town folks to do than small talk and gossip?

"So how does this work?"

Junior sat on an upturned cooler which had seen better days, and Kelly took the bar stool. "You open the hut in the morning, get the kayaks in the river, and tie 'em up to the dock. You stay at the counter and run the register. Once it gets warmer out, I'll probably close the hut at night. Or you would. Dad doesn't like me working a lot when I have to study."

Kelly frowned. He kept shaking his head, the bangs toss. *Either cut the damn hair or get screened for Tourette's.* "Where do they get off at downriver?"

"Our house. It's about three miles out of town."

"I pick them up?"

"We all do. Well, I do. Or Dad. He runs an online baseball card-trading site. You call when customers are coming our way. If Dad's busy, I'll stand out there to help them, or he will. Most times it's me. Then I drive them back here to the beach."

"People, or you bring the boats, too?" She had seen a dilapidated truck with a trailer and a van parked behind the hut.

He shrugged. "Sometimes we wait until there are enough boats to load the whole trailer and rack on the truck, and then run them back here all in one trip. Sometimes I'll bring it, sometimes you'll pick it up and I'll take the hut. Like, I'll bring the van back with the people while you drive the truck out to our house for the boats. We all kind of move around. It can get boring in here sometimes."

Easy enough. The kid must be pretty smart if he could juggle school and kayaks. He exhibited another damn bangs jerk and Kelly bit her cheek. She sipped her coffee to avoid the awkward silence.

"So are you venturing on to college somewhere, or does everyone kind of stay imprisoned here?" she asked.

He raised his brow. "Uh, someday I want a scholarship for MUSC."

She couldn't hold back the scoff. "Pre-med?"

He nodded and she studied him. Ironic. Damn adolescent was more confident in his life choices than she was.

"How the hell can you want to do that?" She crossed her arms, morbidly curious at his choice.

"I want to help people."

"What about the ones you can't? What about the ones who won't make it?"

He cocked his head and crossed his arms. "Well, we've all got to die someday, right?"

She almost smiled. Kid already had a steadier mindset than she ever had in the medical world. He was lucky.

Another hair flip. She cringed.

"Are you depressed or something?" he said.

Kelly raised her brows. Depressed was a strong label. Commercials for drugs and cartoon animations of frowning people who couldn't get out of bed or eat food played in her mind. Eddie made her smile and she loved candy, so by her diagnosis, no, she wasn't clinically depressed. She might not be a morning person but she was always eager to start the day. Problem was, she didn't know what the hell to do once she got out of bed. Restless, perhaps, but they didn't make fix-all remedies for it.

"Who the hell knows," she said bitterly. *How's that for some pathetic downward social comparison?*

"Dad said you're from Atlanta."

She nodded.

"Why'd you move here?"

"I honestly have no fucking clue." She gave him a polite smile.

The wrinkles of his forehead held her obligated to explain.

"Just signed my divorce papers. I headed to Myrtle Beach, but I kind of stopped here."

"Clay said you were a nurse."

"ER."

"Man, that's so cool. Why'd you leave?"

Kelly licked her lips. "A patient died on me. I can't say it wasn't my fault. His daughter threatened to kill me because I didn't save him. The LPN who administered the drug that killed him…" She paused. "She hung herself the same night."

Junior swallowed.

"Let's say I wasn't fit for the job."

"Okay…" By the creases on his forehead, he didn't seem convinced.

Stella hollered an unkind farewell as Roger headed for them.

"Damn women." Roger's grumble announced his entrance into the hut. "Oh, hey. You came."

"Hired me, didn't you?" Kelly ignored his sexist remark. Like he was a real prize as an almighty male.

He gave her a once-over with doubt written on his scowling face. "You ain't going to give me any trouble are you?"

"I'm a perfect angel."

"Hey, Dad, can I take the truck to see Allison later? We won't be busy today."

Roger shook his head at Junior. "No. She's in school." He straightened the pile of brochures on the counter.

"Nut uh. President's Day. They're off."

Roger's sigh seemed painful, as though he was pronouncing the woes of parenthood. "Alright. I don't care. Go get the disinfectant out of the truck first. Put it out on the dock. Kathy can wash off the life jackets since we're not busy yet." He turned to Kelly and clapped once as his son left. "He tell you how it works 'round here?"

She nodded. "Kelly, not Kathy."

"Right. Sorry. I gotta hire a young face every season, I can't keep track anymore. I'm pretty laid-back. Not like it's a difficult job anyhow. Oh, watch out for the gators." He demonstrated the register and how to fill out the liability forms. "You got a boyfriend in town here? You with Clay?"

She crossed her arms. "No." She narrowed her eyes. "And this is your business because…?"

"Well, he's the one who told me to expect you this morning. I assumed you were one of his girls."

She opened her mouth, but he rambled on.

"I came down here one afternoon checking on the register and saw Sandra fucking some man behind the counter. Didn't know the stool could take the weight."

Kelly shot to her feet and raised her hands up like a surgeon gloving up. *Alrighty then. Note to self: disinfect wood hut.* "Lovely."

Roger shook his head. "I got my boy coming down here. He's a good boy. Smart. Doing the best I can since his mom left when he was two. It's the last thing I need for him to see. I thank God he's smarter than the next, but they don't need to be doing nasty sort of stuff in my hut. On the beach at all!"

"How old is Junior?" Kelly spied hand sanitizer and squirted some on her palms.

"Sixteen."

"None of my business, but he probably—"

"Don't want to hear it." Roger shook his head. "Yesterday he was a little boy. Now he's got a *girlfriend*. I've always hired a seasonal hand. Getting harder to find a trustworthy help. Year before, I hired the governor's daughter. Or stepdaughter. I don't know. Alice or something. Caught her making out with some black chick."

Kelly raised her brows. Her new boss didn't like promiscuous women *and* he was racist? *My, my, no mystery Churchston was sheltered.*

"No wonder Stella's flipping out. Young crowd's always rowdy on the beach." He gave her another once-over. "You look alright, though."

'Alright' as in she wasn't good-looking enough to warrant sex in the hut, or alright as in she wasn't a tramp?

"So you aren't working for Alan, anymore?" he asked.

"He said he'd work around my shifts here."

He nodded, then jerked a thumb at her ball cap. "Braves ain't going to make it, city girl."

She flipped him off and he grinned.

CHAPTER 4

On her first day of manning the hut, it didn't take Kelly long to appreciate the father-and-son duo's business. It *was* laid-back. Totally opposite of nursing. Before he left her alone in the hut, Roger had explained business would pick up when the tourist season bloomed into full swing. In the meantime, she was at liberty to read, bounce a ball off the wall, people watch, ponder—as long as customers got boats when they wanted.

Truthfully, she enjoyed Junior's company when he wasn't staring at her ass or boobs. Even his adolescent ogles were tolerable. Although they worked on a beach, she wasn't wearing the bathing suit to advertise her assets—not that she believed she had many to begin with. She had decided to interpret Roger's assessment of being 'alright' as one of trustworthiness, and his approval had to stand for something. In the sandy land of plastically-enhanced women in thongs and itty-bitty bikinis, eyes were surely roving elsewhere before they bothered with her.

In the lull of brooding over her marital and career failures, Kelly didn't stop her absent-minded rhythm of tossing the ball against the wall as people passed on the beach. As Junior had prophesized, more and more Churchston natives returned to the beach town as the warm weather approached. Peering out onto the public beach from the hut, Kelly discovered a wide variety of faces she hadn't met on her deliveries for Alan.

At the open bay of the garage across the street, she watched as Clay worked his magic on what had to be an underage vacationer. Then she returned her gaze to the sidewalk and saw him. The beach-running guy. Kelly frowned at him, matching his expression.

Since the first day she had set foot in town, she had seen this guy running on the beach. It had to be the arrogant tow-truck operator. Same hoodie, same cap. Every day, he'd run on the beach. He was hauling. Like a locomotive machine, not a vacation jog, but seriously speeding. And every time she caught the blur of him in the background, she had the same impression. Angry. Strong. Big. Fiery. *Can you say bad-boy?*

She didn't know his name and didn't think it mattered. He never smiled, his lean angles tanned and stuck in a scowl or an indifferent mask of nothing. Like a robot. She'd seen him walking down Main. In and out of the bar. At the town's sole gas station. Once he was behind her in line at the grocery store. He would drive by on his Harley or in a battered truck. She was grateful to never have delivered to him before.

They never met eyes and Kelly believed he was a man who kept to himself. Angry at the world and antisocial the rest of the time. She wouldn't want to be on his bad side, which, of course, had to be always since he never seemed happy. It was irritating how she couldn't resist looking at him.

"Something catch your eye out there?"

Kelly jerked up from her slumped position over the counter and smiled at Clay. He had his mechanic jeans on and no shirt. Eye-candy for the womenfolk. With a smug grin and a grease-stained sack in his hand, he sauntered to the hut and hopped onto the counter.

"Lunch break?" Kelly asked.

"Coming to see my new roomie."

"There's a wall between us. That makes us neighbors. Who's the hulk who always runs on the beach?" She sat up straight and Clay settled in to eat, leaning his powerful arms on the counter.

He dismissed her question with a wave. "Eh, the local drunk. He's an asshole. How come you don't stay with me instead of renting your own place?"

She smiled. "You don't really want me, Clay. I told you when you introduced yourself at the hotel the first night. Not interested."

"Give me one good reason why not." He took his sunglasses off and peered closely at her with a mischievous grin.

"Because then we couldn't be friends."

"Sure we could."

Kelly stared at him. Casual sex did happen, but she felt no heat around him. Perplexing. The

Channing Tatum lookalike in front of her was like a humping bunny. Humping bunny with the determination of the Energizer Bunny. Not her goal. But if she didn't want a sinfully sexy man like Clay, was she really as frigid as John always told her? Her self-esteem crawled a little lower. She shook her head as he bit into his burger.

"Do you even know what this stuff does to your LDL?"

"My what?"

She squinted to the sky. "Cholesterol."

"I'm barely past thirty. I'll worry about it when I'm an old man. Right now, I'm a growing man. I need my nourishment, baby."

"In the form of lard."

"This here is beef, baby. What are you, some kind of hypochondriac?"

"Well, I was a nurse." She turned a brochure over to start a list. "Randy said I could fix up some stuff at the apartment and take it out of my rent. Wanna help me on the porch tomorrow?"

"Sure," he said. "Aren't you going to be busy working here and for Alan?"

"I like to stay busy. It'll be a DIY quickie. They keep saying this place will be swarming with more tourists, but I've only rented out two boats all day."

"It will be. Give it a week and it'll be packed. You left nursing to come here? What were you making up there in the city?"

"Isn't that kind of a personal question?"

He hopped off the counter. "I'll tell you how much I make and then we'll be even." He entered the hut to throw his trash away.

No. Please no. She assumed the obvious. He had to be making diddly squat in a petty small town. She didn't want to embarrass him. "You're not supposed to discuss income among friends."

"Are we friends now?" He bumped his shoulder to hers.

"We could be if you stop looking at my boobs."

"I pulled in sixty-eight last year. Now what did you leave behind?"

"Sixty-eight? Here?"

"Supply and demand. We're the only garage in town, smack in the middle on Main. Where else are they going to go?"

Her eyes widened. "Huh." Not shabby for a mechanic. Maybe Clay wasn't a doofus to stay local after all. "Eighty-five. I was ER."

"You gave up eighty-five a year to work for Roger?"

She didn't want to rejuvenate the defense of why she chose to do whatever the hell she chose to do. She didn't know why herself, but for the blood, guts, tumors, poop, pee, pus, attitudes and criticism. The sorrow of patients dying, family members worrying and grieving. Nursing had fit like a wrong shoe. Knowledgeable and skilled, she still loathed those harshly lit hallways of the ER department. And after Norbert, she knew she didn't belong.

"Yes. I can say it absolutely made me unhappy." Hell, if her best friend hadn't also been her coworker, she would have quit years ago.

"Everybody hates their job at some point." He cleared his throat. "Junior says somebody died on you."

She looked to the water. "A lot of people did."

"And someone came after you?"

She slapped her hands to the counter and straightened. The questions were only going to keep coming. "We admitted an older man. A basket-case of medical issues, a workaholic. His girlfriend was trying to act as a will of power, but his estranged daughter still had the say. I contacted the daughter and convinced her to stop by to see her dad. They reconciled, everyone was happy. He was recovering a bit. At our shift turnover, my intern gave him a drug which interacted with his blood thinner. He died. His daughter came and approached me with a knife. The intern hung herself after the shift."

She faced Clay's stare. "I should have been there to check the meds. They kept saying I did nothing wrong. I wasn't negligent. I know the next shift had just come on, but if I had checked a minute earlier, then…"

"No one's perfect, baby. Mistakes happen."

Heather's exact words. She cracked a bitter laugh. "I'm far from perfect. I wasn't even good enough for my husband."

"What happened with him?"

"Divorced."

"Couples therapy couldn't patch it?"

"I didn't even want to try. I know myself well enough that I'd never forgive and forget."

"You came down here heartbroken?" He grabbed her free hand as she continued to write a list with her other. "I can make you forget all about him."

She shook his hand off without looking up. "I don't need your help in that department. I figure you can fit all this stuff in your truck better than I could in my car, right? I mean you may as well be the one to pick up supplies. I don't even know where a store would be."

"Haven't found a boyfriend in town yet?" He smoothed his thumb over her knuckles.

She shook her head. "I thought we could do the railings. Nothing major. I only gave Randy a couple months upfront, and he said I could make a dog door for Eddie."

"So is there a girlfriend?"

She focused as she added to her list. "And some cleaning supplies. I didn't notice any mold in there, but better safe than sorry. Get the antimicrobial disinfectant. The other stuff is useless."

"I don't believe it. You're too sexy to be so hurting and sad, baby." He spread his palm further up her forearm.

Kelly sighed and set the pen on the counter. "For the last goddamn time, stop calling me baby. You're not Austin Powers. And I'm not going to be a broken record. Not interested. Take a note, will you?"

"Trying to help you out," he murmured.

"Look. You're decent company most of the time. We might be friends. Really, I think I can manage to not want to strangle you in the middle of the night. But I'm not sleeping with you."

"Why stop at friends? I can take care of you, ba—sugar."

"Treat me like a sister, okay? I don't want to have to hunt for another apartment already. This one is conveniently cheap."

"I'm an only child. I don't know how sisterly stuff works."

She shook her head and he caressed her palm. It would have pissed her off but he'd been harmless so far. Persistent, but he seemed to catch on to her boundaries once he pushed enough buttons. "Aren't you supposed to be sated?" she asked. "The reincarnation of Anna Nicole Smith dropped you off at the garage this morning."

He grinned. "She was hours ago. You can't blame a man for trying. I'm partial to beautiful women."

"Do you drink catalytic fluid at the garage to turbo-charge your balls or something?"

He snorted. "You need to get laid."

"Thanks. I'm hardly taking advice from you."

"Get laid and get wasted. You'll be whole again in the morning." He finished it off with a wink.

"Wow. Is that truly all you guys do down here? What, are you sixteen?"

Clay smirked at her, finally losing the bedroom eyes. "No. But I like to let loose and have fun. Nothing wrong with living a little. You should try it sometime."

Simple pleasures for a simple mind. Like Eddie. "Does anyone have ambitions down here? Goals?"

"Just because you're some smartass city girl doesn't mean we're all idiots. I might be small-town but I'm not a small man."

She pursed her lips for a beat. "That's another reference to your dick, isn't it?"

He gave her a smile dripping of seduction. "Want to check?"

She smacked his shoulder. "Look, I'll make a promise to you, alright? I promise I will never, ever want to have sex with you. Case closed."

"Never say never."

"When I'm the last woman and you're the last man on Earth"—she said and held her hand up when he opened his mouth—"in the universe, I still won't have sex with you."

"What are you, a prude?"

She didn't know why she was wasting her time arguing with him. Cognizant of the fact she would be seeing him often, she took one last stab at an explanation.

"Clay. What's the last book you've read?"

His raised his brows. "Is this an interview?"

"Answer."

"My *Sports Illustrated* came in yesterday."

She gave him a condescending smile. "I can't have sex with someone I'm not intellectually drawn to."

His eyes widened she hoped she was getting across to him. "Nobody said we'd have to discuss philosophy."

"Forget philosophy. There's no chemistry here, Clay. You, horny. Me, uninterested. Bide your time patiently for the next loose woman who walks by. You'll survive the momentary drought."

"You can come along."

"You're disgusting."

"And you're pretty bitchy. Who are you to judge the way I live my life?" He shoved off the counter and returned to the garage.

With a deep sigh she set her elbows on the counter and her face in her hands. Massaging her forehead, she groaned.

And this is what happens when I open my big mouth.

He was right, of course. Who the hell was she to judge him? She had never been a snob to judge and scold others and the fact she just had depressed her. No matter to whom it was, no matter where she was, she would always be caustic.

Is that why John didn't want me anymore?

After a moment of commiserating, she sat up and opened her eyes. She blinked at the brightness and raised her brows at Clay's return.

"Want a hug?" He pulled his hands out of his pockets and came into the hut.

"Are you going to cop a feel?"

"Do I have permission?" He stood behind her and wrapped her in a tight bear hug.

"Over my dead body."

"I told you I was an only child."

"You did fine." She patted his crossed arms. "Bickering is one of the things I do best with my brothers."

"So we're working on the porch tomorrow?" He nodded at the list in front of them.

"Are you available?" She smiled at the resumption of her plans.

"Now we're talking. Your place or mine?"

She elbowed his ribs and he let go with a grunt.

"Yeah. He's got his head up his ass again." Clay took the list from the counter and rubbed his side.

Kelly assumed the person in reference was Clay's boss. Judging by the frequency of his complaints, Clay was not on good terms with his employer.

"Well, good thing he's human enough to let you have a day off."

"Human?" He shook his head. "Not anymore, he isn't. This is it?" He waved the list at her.

"Yeah. Don't forget to ask for pressure-treated wood. Let me write it down." She reached for the list.

"Pressure-treated. I'll remember." He shoved the list in his pocket. "I'm going to love taking orders from you."

CHAPTER 5

It had been a long time since Emily had flitted from town to town, from steal to steal. Before Number Thirty-Nine, she had limited herself to simple steals. Every steal had the sole purpose of proving she was the best. She would be chosen. But sometimes she'd make a steal with a bonus of drugs. An escape from boredom. Spite. The thrill. But when she found Thirty-Nine, she saw dollar signs.

She'd nearly had all the easy money. Emily hadn't anticipated bitch Kelly to fuck it up, though. No one ever usurped her plans.

"Well, they always hire seasonal people." The blonde in line in front of her gabbed on her phone. "I don't know. Probably boring. Churchston? It's a lame little town." Giggles. "At least this way I'll have room and board, right?"

Emily perked at the name. She studied the new identity. Heels could meet the difference in height. Protein would fatten her to the other's build.

Emily leaned over and snatched a hair dye kit. Brown-colored contacts. Makeup.

A single young woman expected in town. No one would question her arrival. No one would suspect why she moved to town. No one would have reason to doubt her, to speculate about her presence, to analyze her actions. Most importantly, no one would wonder what happened to her.

Emily was the transient variable. No one could follow her. But invisibility posed a difficulty for her to convince an established community. People would notice. People would question. It had always been a pain in the ass to keep her head up above her lies and make sure she was untraceable. Years ago she had learned identities were easier to maintain when she took a body and kept the name.

Exiting the gas station, Emily followed the young woman down the highway. Staying behind until traffic thinned, Emily waited for the opportune scene to hide the woman's car. All she needed was her name. Ditch the body. Ditch the car.

Murky dark water reflected the rising moon's shine in the coming dusk. With a calculated calm, Emily sped up and smashed the woman's car off the road, sending it careening off the pavement.

Blood trickled from Emily's forehead and she hastened before someone drove by. She shouldered her door open and rushed to the woman's door. The identity gasped for air, her face smothered in the air bag.

"What, what happened—?"

Yanking on her collar, Emily pulled her out of the car.

"Who—? What is—?" The woman staggered on her feet, confused, maybe due to a concussion from the impact. Emily needed her info, needed her to answer questions. She smacked her up the face and sent her sprawling to the grass. Emily grabbed the purse from the passenger's seat, then led the woman to her car. The other car slipped down the slope.

Coming to, the woman started to panic. "Let go of me! Who are you—? What is—?"

Emily opened the trunk to her car and considered the face she was going to make her own. "I'm you." A head-butt knocked the woman out and Emily shoved her in. Back in the driver's seat, she reversed and rammed into the identity's car a few times until the pond water hid it.

Emily wiped the blood from her vision as she drove into the next nameless town. With the skill of a seasoned pro, she stole a new car after wiping down the last. After transferring the woman's body into the trunk, Emily riffled through the purse as she drove for a motel.

When she returned to the car after paying for a room, the woman woke up in the trunk, screaming, crying for help.

Emily kept her in the trunk until she quieted to a sob at the realization she had been abducted. To Emily, it signaled her surrender. She had met and accepted her fate.

Emily allowed a small smile. A hopeless body was easier to torture information from.

Will regretted his decision to finish his run downtown the second his shoes hit the raked sand of the public beach. Claws of fear and worry scraped at his spine, escalating to a full-blown panic attack. Laughter, chatter and playful squeals clashed into a roar of distraction to the point he couldn't even hear the waves which typically calmed him. And it wasn't even tourist season yet.

Aware he wasn't ready or willing to reenter society, he had kept his runs close to home and his interactions with townsfolk to the level of a hermit.

Deciding to run on the beach at noon was the most idiotic choice he'd made in a long time. People were everywhere. Strangers who were visiting and the locals who were permanent fixtures. He could feel their stares on his back, their judgments hovering over their heads. Will knew he wasn't welcome and didn't wish he could be. He had never fit in, and never would.

"Oh my God! He's drowning. Someone's drowning!"

He couldn't tamp the instinct to look up at the scene around him, the happy peppy people suddenly concerned with a commotion at the water's edge. Beneath the shade of his hat, he squinted at the blonde who ran past him, sprinting for an older man bending over at his knees and grabbing at his neck—assuming he had a neck somewhere under the rolls of fat.

"Someone call 9-1-1!"

Will found it ironic the white-painted tower of the lifeguard stand was vacant. Past its vertical presence, he saw Clay shoveling his tongue down the throat of a scantily-clothed lifeguard. So much for his mechanic catching up on cleaning the garage. Will trotted closer to the foamy slop, remnants of the last wave.

"My husband's drowning!" A waif of a woman wailed next to him as he stopped completely to catch his breath.

In a blue bikini, a petite blonde stood behind the man and tried to wrap her arms around the wide girth of his chest. "He's not drowning," she protested as she struggled to hug him from behind.

"What are you doing?" The wife shrilled and wrung her hands. "He needs CPR! Don't you know what you're doing?"

"Please shut up." The woman winced while she tried to connect her hands around the blubber.

"You're going to kill him." The wife wheezed in a desperate breath from her yells. "He needs CPR."

"Oh, for fuck's sake," Will muttered and strode the couple feet into the water. He shoved the blonde away from the man, who was obviously choking, wrapped his arms around him, and tried to perform the Heimlich maneuver.

"Is that—Will? Will Parker? No." The wife slapped at his shoulder. "Don't you touch my husband, you…you murderer!"

"What the hell are you doing?" The blonde pulled the wife away as he jerked the man to his chest, like hoisting a buffalo.

He scowled at the blonde. "What do they even hire you for if you can't do the job?"

"My job? This isn't my job! It's not my fault he's morbidly obese." She adjusted her baseball cap and held the wife back.

"What is he doing?" The wife carried on. "Can't you people see he needs CPR?"

"He doesn't need CPR because his head wasn't in the goddamn water! He's suffering from acute aspiration of a foreign object in his trachea."

Will grunted at another jerk toward his chest, then turned to face the blonde. *Haven't I seen that hat before?* Blue bathing suit and tank top, not the standard lifeguard red. She was simply a diligent bystander. Her elaborate jargon had stalled the wife, as she gaped like someone trying to understand a foreign language.

"A cute what?" the wife asked.

Blondie rolled her eyes and threw her hands up. "He was choking on a damn hot dog while he waded in."

"Don't you swear at me." The wife put her hands on her hips.

Will felt the man gasp after the obstacle flew into the lake. Heaving for precious air, he wobbled forward on his own pudgy legs. Will straightened his cap and stepped back to let the spouse baby the Moby Dick as he recovered his breath.

Still red in the face, with blubbery cheeks wheezing, the man faced his savior.

"What, what the hell are you doing here? Get away from me!"

The scorn in his voice told Will it was past time to leave. He might be a jerk, but he wasn't so inhumane to let someone die. Even a Churchston asshole who hated his guts. A bitter scoff tickled at the back of his throat. Who was he kidding? He was no lifesaver. He had let his best friend die.

"He saved your life!" The blonde seemed surprised at the lack of gratitude and Will guessed she was a vacationer, not privy to why he was the chosen black sheep of town.

"What? No. No, he likes to watch 'em die." The man straightened, clearing his throat. "Don't you, boy? You couldn't stand to see him better than you."

Will had had enough. No one on Earth could understand the raw pain he lived through every day, the ache of the failure when he hadn't been able to save the one person in the world who had meant something to him. With no energy to defend himself, he let people crowd around him to get close to see the action.

"Where's the lifeguard?" The man's wife fussed as she wiped her husband's sweaty hair from his forehead. "Maybe you should go to the hospital."

"I don't need no damn lifeguard."

Will dunked his hands in the water. Since he had shaved and cut his hair, he felt even more exposed. He wiped at his hoodie in an attempt to chase the man's sweat off and the crowd parted for one of Churchston's officers. Fred marshalled forward with a blank expression of authority, followed by a lifeguard clad in the tiniest bathing suit possible.

"What's going on here?" Fred asked.

"My husband was drowning."

He nodded to the woman and smoothed his mustache, then directed his deep monotone to the blonde. "Why wasn't this called in to dispatch?"

Will met her gaze as he caught her staring at him. *That damn Braves hat. I know I've seen it before.*

She faced Fred, her concentration on Will seeming to delay her realization that the cop was holding her accountable. "What are you looking at me for? I work for Burns. And for the last damn time, he was choking, not drowning!"

Fred acknowledged the lifeguard next to him. "Where the hell were you?"

She flipped her hair, then scratched at her nose. "Out here."

"Why didn't you see him?" Fred cast a brief eye over the choking victim.

"There are a lot of people out here, okay?" The lifeguard sneered at Fred. "I can't watch all of them."

"You couldn't see a group of people in a crowd and a lunatic screaming 'he's drowning'?" the blonde said.

"Lunatic? I'm not a lunatic." The man's wife reddened deeper than her sunburn.

"What, you think you can do my job better than I can? You ugly little bitch—" The lifeguard clenched her jaw as the blonde walked off without a glance back. Junior trailed away with her, his face turning back and forth between the blonde and the lifeguard, his attention bouncing to and fro like a tennis match spectator.

"I don't think you even know how to do your job." The blonde backpedaled for the kayak hut.

"To lifeguard means to guard life, right? What the hell were you looking at if you could miss so much commotion?"

"I don't need some two-bit bitch telling me how to do my job! You think you're better than me? Huh?" The lifeguard fisted her hands and chased after the kayak employees. Before her hair could be yanked back, the blonde ducked down and the lifeguard stumbled into Junior.

"For crying out loud…" Fred trotted forward to restrain the lifeguard. "Kendra, take it easy. I'll need to report this to your supervisor. Break it up, everyone. Show's over."

Besides lingering glares at Will, people started to scamper off. With the almost catfight anticipation in the atmosphere, they had completely forgotten his presence. He was thankful for the easy distraction as he headed to the garage to finish past-due jobs.

CHAPTER 6

Late in the afternoon, Clay came back to the garage with sand on his knees, lip balm on his neck, and a cocky smugness in his eyes. Miracle his dick wasn't sprung out like a flagpole, too.

"Where the hell have you been?" Metallica roared on the radio as Will slammed drawers shut. He might not be in touch with society, but it didn't mean he didn't see. He might not care about the functions and events of the real normal world surrounding him, but like the man choking on the beach, it was natural instinct to want to know what was going on.

First his mechanic had gone to flirt with the blonde at the kayak booth. Then he had walked over to play with the lifeguards. All was fun and grand in the world of Clay. Will saw it all. The whole world could testify Clay was a player. It wasn't any business of Will's who he slept with, but it was his concern it took Clay an hour to return. Especially when the pastor's wife wanted her car back pronto. Customers waiting for their vehicles put him in the position to handle small talk. He didn't do small talk. He didn't even do talk anymore.

"Lunch break." Clay rolled his eyes at Will as he passed and went to the workbench for his shirt.

"The lady for the Prius came back. Her AC should have been done a half hour ago. Some crazy bitch keeps calling for you on line two. And I need to get this engine in the Ram before the man comes back at four."

Clay sighed and nodded like a sullen teenager. Will remembered when he would smile and goof off with him, when there wasn't constant nagging and tension and annoyance. He could remember the way a lot of things used to be. He didn't have time for memories and had no regrets but one. He should have died instead of Matt.

Ever since he had bought the garage right out of tech college, they had always worked together, really Clay for Will, but they were a team. Partners almost, if he could have ever trusted Clay with numbers. Frankly, he had thought then and still thought now—Clay didn't want the responsibility of being a partner.

"I'll do the AC then I'll help with the Ram."

Will slammed another drawer of sockets shut in the cabinet and went off to resume working. "I just finished the AC."

"Why the fuck did you bother telling me about it then?"

Clenching his jaw, Will went into the next bay for an oil change. Simple, stupid, fast. Then he'd take a break. Sighing in the muggy air of his garage, he wiped the sweat off his forehead and winced in pain. His damn scar was going stiff on him again. And his knee. Worse because of the anatomy-literate bimbo needing his help to free the hot dog from fatso.

Some days he could take the pain, others, he barely got by. Last thing he needed was Clay acting like a punk when he was hurting so badly. But Will knew he didn't matter in the world and the world didn't matter to him anymore either.

He was overdoing it. If he followed up with VA docs, they'd pump him with drugs, tell him he's drinking too much, he's being too hard on his body.

It was all he could do. There was the bodily pain. The nerve-stinging stiffness in his knee which sometimes it took an hour in the morning to break it in. Not often, but sometimes. He didn't limp. He didn't break his gait or stride. The runs. The weights. He couldn't stop, and he wouldn't. Breaking his body was all that kept him going. If he stopped pushing, he would break his promise to Matt. He had already let him down so much.

Clay dropped something in the other bay and Will barely flinched. Ozzy on the radio smoothed the corruption before the sound frayed his nerves and whatever calm he thought he had.

Maybe he'd go for a run at night. He'd pay in pain the next morning, but it would soothe him. Dull the other harsher pain of missing his best friend.

"Will. The woman for the Prius is here," Clay called out.

"Then give it to her." His answering yell was toneless.

Will had stopped caring about the little details. How much money he was making. Even before hell broke loose, before Matt died, before his injuries, Will had never worried about his garage. As far as he was concerned, cars weren't a fad and there would always be a demand for repairs. If he was making less money than he potentially could, it didn't make him lose sleep.

Sleep was already a joke. He couldn't bring himself to drink like his dad, all the while knowing sleep would be easier and without nightmares if he took to the bottle more often. It's what he pushed his body for. Maybe one day he'd push his body too far and that'd be the end of it.

Will didn't bother with such thoughts. He tried to survive the day. The absences were hardest to acclimate to. No more Matt to go for a ride with. No more enemies trying to blow his head off. No more looking for bombs. No more making plans. No more relaxing. Real world after the war had been harsh for him.

After Clay left without a good-bye, Will closed down the garage to go home. He stopped at the stoplight in front of Elmer's bar and considered it a moment. Lights flashed from the TVs inside and he felt the tension in his chest. Too much noise, too many people, too many lights. He swallowed and waited for the light to change.

As he wound his way to the lake, he passed the Burns' property and saw the blonde picking the kayaks up. Probably the last run of the day for her. At home he saw smoke coming from behind the townhouse duplex. Clay was cooking out again. On cue, Will's stomach growled and a faint memory of past cookouts with his friends almost itched into his mind before he shut it out.

Exhausted, he slumped on the couch and ran his hands over his face as the answering machine played. A message from the VA doctor for a missed follow-up appointment for his knee. Some ditz from the bank. Randy had called a couple times. A couple hang-ups which he guessed were Randy's as well. Then a couple clients about engine rebuilds.

The bank and Randy. It couldn't be a coincidence. He had more money than he knew what to do with. Since he'd returned to Churchston, Randy did his bookwork for him. But Will never told Randy about the savings account. How his best friend had made him the sole recipient in his will. How before Will left him to die, Matt had decided to give him the townhouse and adjacent stone lodging. Never saw any reason for anyone to know.

Before he could stop it, he was asleep and drowning in nightmares.

He dreaded waking up, the sun harsh on his eyes from fitful sleep, knowing he had to make it through another day. First thoughts ran with remembering where he was, in the territory of enemies or the base. Then he'd recall he wasn't in the service anymore. He gave up trying to find a reason to get up, but the training ingrained in him and the memory of his friend forced him to stand and work movement into his knee.

In the morning, Will ran hard on the beach, the humidity sending rivulets of sweat streaming down his skin under the hoodie. His knee was unforgiving and he thought of the VA doctors. Grunting a moment, he focused on his labored breathing and the lapping waves on the lake.

The garage was supposed to be closed on Sundays. Since the prospect of going home with nothing to do but avoid thinking and feeling, Will came in to the garage to keep his hands busy. To put shit away Clay never would. Clean up spills. Mop his office. Organize the workbench. With the radio blaring, it was as close to peace as he could get. Not as soothing as running, but it was better than being at the stone house. The house wasn't home. Matt had been. Now he had nowhere and no one.

Between his knee and the mess Clay had left in the garage, Will was in a sour mood. His thoughts ran between the war, Matt, responsibility, and alcohol. He had half a bottle of rum at home but then the memories of his father came fast. And remembering his father reminded him of his mother. So when Randy came knocking on the windows on the garage door of bay three, Will was pissed.

"Hey." He opened the door reluctantly for his old friend. Will was no one's friend anymore. It was his own fault. Randy used to be cheerful and relaxed and always responsible. He still was responsible, and that's why Will suspected he had an argument coming.

"Long time no see." Randy was dressed down in jeans and a polo shirt, probably not showing any houses today.

Will resumed sweeping up broken glass from a windshield Clay had replaced.

"How's it going?" Randy's question was an awkward one. As far back as Will could remember, Randy had been borderline shy. Will was sure it was the Downs' influence. The prestigious pampered precious family of Churchston. Matt's family. Will cringed. He gave a blunt raise of his eyebrows to Randy.

"Stupid question. Right." Randy leaned his hip on the workbench stool. "Your leg doing okay? Still running, I see."

"It's doing as well as it ever will." Will wished he could snap out of it. He was a jerk and Randy most likely had good intentions. But Will was sick of everyone's good intentions. Not many people even cared about him.

His father had been a neglecting drunk when he hadn't been an abusive one. Hardly a father. His mother had left before his first birthday. In a lifetime of hardening and shutting down, there wasn't a long list of people he considered close.

The problem with other people's good intentions was he had to live up to them, he had to meet and exceed these well-caring people, please them he was doing okay because he'd only be an asshole to let them down and have them burdening their heads with worrying about him. He had never been skilled at meeting people's expectations and he had lost the desire to try before he hit puberty.

The two men endured a long uncomfortable silence as the Black Keys blared from the radio. In a perverse way, Will hoped he could cram enough decibels in his head so he really would go deaf sooner than later. His strategy would save him the heart-pounding adrenaline rush of jumping at every sound which resembled a bomb detonating.

Randy scoffed, the lack of communication too tense to ignore. "Jerome Larkey said he saw you trying to jump off the bridge again. Looks like you're back on the suicide story."

"Uh huh." Will inhaled deeply. The stupid shit people wanted to believe. To fill the gaps when gossip ran low, they switched from his tragic hero image to the troubled suicidal veteran. Jump a bridge? He had been a fucking Marine. And the water was only five feet below the damn road. It'd be more like a nice soak on a hot day than a personal termination.

Randy stood, then paced some, clearing his throat like a lifelong smoker. "Guess this brings us to the last thing I can say. I called a few times."

Will passed him to dump the dustpan of shards, his face still devoid of emotion.

"I'm worried about the garage. It's going under."

Will crossed his arms and leaned against the workbench. He waited for the lecture to take its course.

"Bills are getting paid, but not for long. You might need to advertise or cut down on services, or…"

"Or?"

"Or not be an asshole to everyone who comes in here!" Randy lost his temper, something not easily achieved. "Mrs. Ronaldson was livid at the diner. Said you barely listened to her and called her stupid."

Lack of parental units had left Will empty-handed for manners and grace for most of his life. The Marines, however, had turned the rowdy bad-boy into a man. He gave Randy the expression of bored skepticism.

"And if you didn't say the words, you implied it."

"You try explaining the difference between a carburetor and a piston to a pastor's wife."

"You can't blow off customer service. You have a service business. You can be an ass to everyone in the world, but you have to pretend to be nice if you don't want to go bankrupt."

Will twitched his mouth. "Don't tell me how to run my business," he finally said. "Do the books. I don't care."

"You don't care." Randy swore under his breath and resumed his nervous pacing. He had never been one for confrontations. "You don't care about anything."

Randy wouldn't understand. No one would. Will grabbed his thermos and got ready to leave. The clock told him it wasn't even noon yet. He'd have a whole damn day of nothing. Another run? He didn't know if he could test his knee.

"There you go. Walk away. Can't face your problems. Don't want to hear it."

Will spun back and grabbed Randy's shirt at the neck. "Don't." He was provoked, but he had nothing to add. He released the shirt and stormed off, hoping the garage locked behind him.

In his truck, he sped faster than he should have in town, daring the dipshit cop Eric to pull him over. He was spoiling for a fight, the temper coursing his blood, his knuckles white on the steering wheel. When he came onto the road home, his gaze pulled to the duplex which had once been his and Matt's home. The sight on the porch chilled his blood at the same time it boiled his body.

CHAPTER 7

"What the fuck?" Will worked his jaw as a woman took a sledgehammer to the wooden rail. Matt's rail. The first woodwork he had ever done. Back in senior year, both of them had been ambitious and eager to take on the world. Matt in a carpentry shop. Will in his garage. Big dreams that had died too young. He slammed on the brakes, then drove up to the porch and ripped his truck door open.

"What the hell are you doing?" His yell was unheard over the music blasting from speakers. Why ask, when it was obvious? Clay pissed off the wrong woman. Again. And she was taking it out on the porch. Damn idiot.

He reached the steps before she swung and he pulled the sledgehammer from her hands. Her lips parted in an 'O'. It didn't take her long to react. First she narrowed her eyes. Then she shoved him and he fell. While he was down, she took the sledgehammer back, turned the radio down a little, then stood back.

Her Braves hat had fallen to the ground in the brief struggle.

It was the kayak girl. The little beach blondie. Blue, no, green, wait, blue-green eyes. High cheeks. Mussed hair. Will couldn't stop staring. Sleek arms, her breasts heaving from rapid breathing under a little tank top, her hips, her legs, and legs and legs. He shut his mouth and squinted a closer look.

That damn hat. The woman with the gray SUV? *She* landed him on his ass?

"You can't fucking destroy my house." He stood quickly and took the sledgehammer back, furious he had been so dumbstruck by her to let her retrieve it in the first place.

"Porch. We're standing on a pathetic porch. *That*'s the house. And it's called demolition, not destruction." She stuck her hand on her hip and held the other out. "Give it back."

Will threw it into the yard. "I don't care how much he screwed you, whatever bullshit he said or how much he cheated on you. You can't attack a fucking house!"

He couldn't believe it, but at the same time he could. He'd seen Clay hitting on her at the beach just before he'd moved on to Daisy and the others. Right in front of her eyes. Sure, she was pissed because Clay had moved on. He was a player. But she had to be the craziest woman he'd met yet.

She studied the distance with confusion. Probably off her meds.

"You know John?" She almost whispered it.

"Who the fuck is John?"

Randy pulled up and the alarmed expression on his face was unique. Confusion, fear, and concern. Will clenched his fists with his muscles nearly shaking. This stupid woman was going to smash Matt's first woodwork because she was dumped?

"Who the hell *are* you?" She stepped closer. Will looked down at her, puzzled at her bravado. Last he checked he was six feet and two inches of 210 pounds of hard lean muscle. She couldn't be more than five-four and a hundred pounds. He looked at her breasts again. Okay. Hundred ten. He wasn't barbaric enough to personally harass a woman, but did she really think she had anything on him? Talk about naïve.

She glared right back at Will as he got stuck in her eyes. Blue-green. Not green enough to be common, not blue enough to be pretty. Something more like breathtaking. They grabbed him.

"Will. Hey. What's going on?" Randy jumped out of his car.

"Who's this?" she demanded of Randy as he raced up the steps. "Is he…" She crossed her arms, nodding her head. "You were the jerk at the diner."

"Like you were any nicer—"

"Got too hot running with all the hair?" She cocked her head to the side, studying his shaven face.

He clamped his mouth shut, disliking her close scrutiny as much as her sass. "Where is he?" Will directed his yell at Randy. "That dumbass brings this crazy woman here and pisses her off because he found something better and now she's ripping apart the fucking porch!"

"What do you care about the porch?" Blue-not-quite-green sparked at him. "And go get the sledgehammer."

"What?"

"You threw it out there. Go get it. Randy, what's going on? Is he drunk? Clay said he's the town drunk."

Drunk? Will's mind reeled, but he hadn't had anything for almost two days.

"Will, she's living here," Randy said. "We're going to—"

"Why's he freaking out? What's it to him?" She narrowed her eyes at Will when she caught him glaring at her.

"She's been renting the apartment." Randy tried again to explain.

"What?"

"You're in the hole, man. I had to get you some more money in the account. The apartment was sitting there and you weren't doing anything with it. I thought it would be easy cash to help you out."

Will wished he'd told Randy about the savings account. Now this woman was living in Matt's place. His stomach turned to stone. He and Matt playing games in the front room. Parties. Poker. Memories hit him hard. It was the closest he had come to the house since he returned to Churchston. Pain kept him from even looking at the building when he drove home some days.

"Let me guess. *You're* the landlord."

He faced her. Well, at least she caught on fast.

"Will, this is Kelly Newland." Randy began his introduction as they stared each other down. "Kelly, this is Will Parker."

"Did I ask you to rent the place?" Will ran a hand through his hair, not wanting to look at her or Randy. Her eyes, he couldn't stop. Eyes the portal to the soul? It was a scary thought because her soul seemed to want to kick his soul's ass.

"No. Jesus Christ, Will, you need the money."

He stepped away and leaned his fists on the railing.

"Don't." She stepped forward and Will eyed her with fury. How could this pint-size woman come in here and take over the last of Matt...

She held her hands up in truce and shut up, and he leaned down on the railing only for it to give way. He caught himself and slowly walked back to her. Strangle? Choke?

"Not like you would have listened to me." She didn't budge. Crossed her arms. Chin up defiantly. "The wood's all rotten. It's a safety hazard. Seeing you're an absentee landlord, you haven't known the difference."

A motor sounded on the drive and Clay's truck pulled up.

"You had no right renting the place out," Will yelled at Randy over Green Day on the radio. He imagined she had changed it all. The memories of Matt, gone forever.

He turned and pointed at Kelly. "You can't demo anything on the house."

"Clay!" She threw her gloves to the rotten porch floor, her attention past him, not giving him a second of her time. "Dammit. I knew you'd screw it up."

"Sugar, you wanna talk about screwing—"

"Shove it, Clay." Kelly stepped to the edge of the porch. "I told you to write it down."

"What?" Clay came up toward the steps and cast a disapproving frown at Will. "How do you know I screwed up? I gave the attendant the list of lengths you wrote down."

She crossed her arms and shook her head.

Will tuned out Randy's explanation about renting the apartment, finding Kelly to be more intriguing.

"Was she sexy?" Kelly said.

Clay grinned. "Oh yeah, sugar. Almost as hot as you in this little tool-belt get up." He landed on the top step and reached out to pull her by her pocket. "You're still my favorite, though."

Kelly smacked his forehead. "Pressure-treated. Pressure-treated." She had cupped her hands around her mouth to enunciate. "Pressure-treated." Clay's face fell.

"You're a sorry little fool. One whiff of a woman and you're stupid. Dammit, Clay."

Speechless, Will followed her as she went to the truck for a closer inspection of the wood. Women cooed to his former friend and only employee. Clay had women kissing, smiling, begging, pleading. Never had Will witnessed a female scolding him.

"Wood's wood, sugar," Clay argued. "It doesn't make a difference."

Biting back a smile, Will remembered Matt's exact mistake. He had made the same erroneous purchase, hence, the rotten wood now.

"Yesterday it was baby, now you're on to sugar. Leave it at my name or I'll tell everyone I meet you've got the smallest dick in the world." She paused and concentrated with a hand up.

"Then again, half the world has already seen it to know. Please, no. *I* don't want to know. This will rot. If we use this, we'll have to prime it and paint it to protect it. More work than I planned on. Hawks play at seven."

Clay set his forearms on the wood hanging out the bed. He gave her a sad pout. "How the hell do you know all this?" he asked as if he could win back her favor.

"My brother." She rubbed the back of her neck.

"I thought he wrote for a magazine."

"Also known as a journalist. That's Wade. Sean's the contractor."

"How many brothers do you have?"

"Enough to kick your ass if you piss me off." She smirked and Clay sighed.

"Oh, don't waste your puppy face on me. I'm immune. Come on. It'll take longer now since we have to do all the finish work." She started back for the house and stopped halfway to spin and face the men. "Of course, if we have the landlord's permission."

Will matched the challenge in her eyes, admiring her at the same time he despised her. With a blank face, he shoved his hands in his pockets.

"The sledgehammer?"

She wanted him to fetch for her? When hell froze over. Will walked to his truck and drove home.

With a new person living in Matt's old space, Will recalled his solo homecoming.

After the explosion, he had been stabilized and shipped to Landstuhl. He endured one week of pain in Germany before he was dismissed to San Antonio. His time in the Marines had been officially complete with his injuries. It had been another seven months until he left SAMMC for a VA rehab hospital in Columbia. He hadn't been able to even fathom living in the duplex he once shared with Matt, and had moved into the stone house by the woods instead.

The stone house was an abandoned work-in-progress, a mess from years of neglect and decay. He had confined his living space to one bedroom, the living room, the kitchen, and a bathroom. Two-thirds of the house had never been touched. It had been his only option since he owned the land courtesy of Matt's will.

Will had known Delores was upset her son had left the duplex and stone house to him. Matt had bought the land with his trust money and Delores was never pleased her precious son wanted outskirt land. Salt in the wound that Matt had given the despicable land to the one person Delores would always deem despicable himself.

Will hadn't planned to make the rest of the house habitable since such goals fell under long-term ideas. He was stuck on day-to-day survival until he was stronger.

Never before had he even cared about the land. He had the stone house, which was nothing more than shelter. He had the beach for runs. And the duplex, he had noticed on his return Clay had moved in there. He had never given another thought to what happened otherwise.

But that day, he did think. And for the first time in over a year, he discovered he had a clear vantage of the duplex's front porch. As he waxed his bike in his drive, he had a hard time refraining from casting a glance to the group working on the rails. For the first time in over a year, he realized his curiosity in his new neighbor dimmed his constant brooding and depression.

A further distraction from his sour mood came with a call from Fred. Towing vehicles wasn't his primary service, but since he had the means to do it, he occasionally accepted the assignment.

"Where at?" He cradled his cell in the nook of his shoulder and screwed the wax tin shut.

"Alley coming off of Dixie." Fred yawned on the other end.

"Whose vehicle?" Will pushed his bike into his garage. If it had been Eric calling in the favor, he would have hung up. He never minded Fred. A common sense and no-nonsense man, Fred was a decent sort of law enforcement and as a Churchston local, he had never displayed frank hatred at him since the war.

"Bartender at Alan's. Jaycee."

Will scratched his chin as he entered his truck. "Wasn't she busted for possession?"

"And selling. Got out last season but she just came back in town. You gonna come pick it up?"

"Nothing else to do."

"I'm heading to urgent care with the victim. She's a tourist and doesn't know where to go. Whiplash. Her car can stay there since it ain't in the way."

Will didn't check the progress on the porch as he drove by to the garage. After he parked his personal truck and revved the tow-truck, he headed for the scene of the accident.

In a bad mood and too-tight denim that suffocated and spilled over her fake tanned muffin-top, Jaycee didn't acknowledge his arrival other than to bitch at the fact he took too long. At her side, Daisy sympathized her woes.

"So he goes, 'I didn't know you were coming back.'" Jaycee stuck a cigarette on her lower lip. "Fucking dipshit. I told him I was gonna come back to this hellhole after I was out."

Daisy shook her head. "He's a fucking old moron."

"So I say, 'Alan, what the fuck.'" Jaycee sucked in a deep hit. "I mean, I told him I was coming back someday. He goes, 'I heard you had a job in the city.' Well, yeah, I thought dancing was gonna be it. Make a shit-ton of cash and stuff, you know."

"What happened with that?" Daisy studied a zit with her compact.

"Oh, they had it out for me. Damn bitches lied to the manager. Said I was stealing their tips. I wasn't stealing. They were taking my dances. Fucking hoes would lure my clients away, so it was technically my money in the first place, you know whadamean?"

Will left them yammering on the sidewalk as he backed the truck up. In the peace and quiet of the driver's seat, he inhaled deeply. The air in the cab was stale with remnants of exhaust and WD-40, but it was better than the funky perfume the women had polluted the alley with. When he exited the truck, they were still griping.

"That sucks." Daisy grimaced as Will released the chain on the bed.

"And then the one ho jumped me after work and, you know." Jaycee hitched up her too-small shorts. "I had to watch my back. I didn't need no more violence bein' on my record again, but she was a mean ho."

Daisy shook her head. Metallic clinks chipped as the chain lugged Jaycee's car onto the truck. Will wished the whine of the winch could have been loud enough to drone out the whine of the wench.

"So, anyhoo, I asked him who he hired. He points out some blonde bitch who was carrying out some deliveries." Jaycee stubbed the cigarette out. "So I go after her and tell her she ain't needed no more. Mick still works there, I'm back in town now. Alan don't need no more help than us."

"She's working for Burns, too. Some big-city girl. Her husband dumped her or something other," Daisy said.

"Oh yeah? Huh. So she asked Alan if he wants her help and he nods like a pathetic old dirt bag. I tell her nut-uh, fat ass, I'm taking my job back. Tell Alan he better let me back or else. So new girl sets the boxes down on the ground and gears up like some Jackie Chan, holds her fists up like some motherfucking kung fu freak. Says she don't take shit from deadbeats. Tells me I ain't gonna threaten old fart Alan when she's around. Now old Alan gets all fussy and scaredy-cat about it all and he says I can work part-time. Only in the bar. Blonde bitch will do the deliveries."

With Jaycee's car on his truck, Will scribbled the essentials on the form and shoved it at her.

Jaycee snatched the paper from his hands without a glance at him, continuing her complaints to her pal. "Mick tells me she's some black-belt shit. Black belt, gold belt, I don't give a rat's ass. I'll tell you what, girlfriend, blonde bitch better watch her back."

CHAPTER 8

"Penny for your thoughts." Randy nudged Kelly's elbow as she sat on the hut countertop. He had stopped by for small talk and Clay had stopped by to window-shop the bikini-wearers on the sand. As Junior played hacky sack with his teeny-bopper girlfriend, Allison, Kelly's mind wandered. For a change, it wasn't the sadness claiming her brain.

"Why did he freak out?" Three days after Will had exploded on the porch, she still didn't understand the intensity of his reaction. Sure, he had some anger management issues, one of those alpha males who had to be consulted for permission for everything in life. But over a porch rail?

Randy took a deep breath, then cleared his throat. Kelly grimaced. There was a high probability she wasn't going to like what he'd say.

"He was close friends with our old buddy, Matt Downs. Will, Matt, Clay, me, we all hung together. Since we could walk. Well, Matt and Will figured out in high school they were best friends. They lived there together before they went into the Marines. Both went in and only Will came back. He didn't take Matt's death well."

Kelly nodded. And post-trauma, too. It didn't escape her notice he almost jumped when Clay had slammed the wood-laden tailgate. "It was just a porch railing."

"Matt went to school for carpentry. He made those railings before the first semester started. They put them up when Matt bought the townhouse. Will must have had some sentiment in them." Randy kicked the stray ball back to the teens. "I'm sorry, Kelly. I should have told him I rented Matt's half. I didn't mean to go behind his back, but he's not easy to deal with."

"You don't say."

"He's having a rough time of it."

"Bullshit," Clay said. "He's an asshole. Plain and simple."

Kelly finally understood why Clay had scowled near Will. He must get the brunt of it all, having to see his former friend was gone and a jerk replaced him.

"Anyway. I should have told him you were living there."

"Not like he's noticed for near three months now," she said.

"True. But that way he could have come to terms with it and not blown up at you."

Kelly bet Will would have blown up at her in some capacity or another. He was simply an angry man. Post-trauma or not, he had anger in his genes. If not anger, something else equally fierce.

"And I'm sorry I didn't explain your landlord is kind of—"

"An asshole," Clay finished for him.

Kelly stood up and stretched her legs. She retrieved a disinfectant spray bottle and headed for the used kayaks. "It's alright, Randy. I grew up with wrestlers and quarterbacks and they drank, too. I'm not scared easily."

"He'd never hurt you. He's not…" Randy held a zoned-out gaze across the street.

"He's not mean." Junior spoke up. "He's an asshole. But he's not mean. More secluded. He doesn't want anything to do with anyone, is all."

"Was he hurt in the war?"

Randy nodded, but didn't go into detail. Kelly pursed her lips and sprayed the first kayak. "Sounds like you guys lost two friends."

"We care about him. But there's nothing we can do." Randy dug his hands in his chino pockets and studied the sand.

"What about his family?"

Junior choked on a cough and no one answered. She checked their faces with curiosity.

"He doesn't really have any," Allison said.

Kelly frowned. "Orphan?"

Randy cleared his throat. "His dad was a drunk and died when Will graduated high school. He wasn't really there much."

"His mom?"

"His mom's Delores Downs."

Kelly squinted in surprise and faced Randy. "The former governor's wife? How?"

"She was engaged to Dennis Parker, Will's dad. After he was born, she left. Didn't want to be married to a drunk. Then she married Bruce Downs."

"So she took Will?"

Randy shook his head. Kelly was speechless. What kind of a woman leaves an infant with a drunk? "So Will never lived with his mom?" she said.

"She never acknowledged Will after she left," Clay said. "Be smart to never mention her name around him."

"Wait, wait." Kelly crouched to wipe at the tip of another kayak. "I know this is a small town, but this kind of stuff doesn't happen. Children's Services, school, cops. Someone had to have taken care of him if the drunk dad didn't."

Clay flipped a coin. "You know the old ice cream dude, Jared? His sister was something like Churchston's first whore. She stayed with Dennis a bit since people in town hated her. I've always figured she was the one who made sure he ate some meals and give him Tylenol when he was sick." He pocketed the coin and walked off with a nod to Randy. "See ya'll later. Hey man, I gotta finish a car across the street."

Silence spanned before curiosity got the better of her again. "So, like father, like son? The drinking, I mean?" Since she'd been in town, Kelly had witnessed Will going into Elmer's, his bike in the parking lot frequently. But when he ran, he moved like a determined, powerful animal, not a weak, sloppy drunk. He seemed too strong and independent of a man to surrender to something like alcoholism.

Randy cleared his throat. "He's given up on life. There are rumors about him trying to commit suicide, but I never believed it." He waved good-bye and followed Clay across the street.

Kelly shook her head. She could understand life sucked, but Will had an awful lot of strikes. "So people really think he's the big bad wolf and that's that?"

"What, he isn't mean enough for you?" Allison laughed.

"He saved the fat guy choking on the beach and people practically spat on him. I don't get why the whole town would collectively hate him. Drunks aren't exactly monumental sinners."

Allison shrugged. "Because he killed Matt."

"Allison!" Junior threw the ball at her. "You know that's not true."

"Well, it's what they say." She glared at Junior as she fixed her hair.

"He did what?" Kelly said.

Junior walked closer. "Everyone thinks he killed Matt. In the war. Delores hated how they were friends. Hated how Matt wanted to be a carpenter. Hated that Matt wanted to go in the Marines. She blamed it on Will, said he was a bad influence on her son."

"But Will *is* her son!"

Allison shook her head. "Not according to her."

"Delores convinced people it was Will's idea to go in the Marines. He pressured Matt to enlist. Then when Will came home and Matt didn't...." Junior frowned. "She got everyone to believe Will deliberately set him up to die overseas."

Kelly crossed her arms. "Right. And everyone's gullible enough to buy such bull. Will was in the war, too. He was injured in the same explosion."

"It's not too far-fetched. Will and Matt were always one-upping each other," Allison said.

Junior shook his head. "They were both punks. But they were best friends."

Kelly studied Junior. "How come you never believed it?"

"I'm not the only one. I was at the diner the day Matt bugged Will to enlist. It was his idea to go, not Will's. Matt wanted a way to escape Delores. He'd bought the townhouse land and she tried to take it from him. Something about having it re-zoned. It wasn't fit for him."

Allison tossed the ball back to Junior, seeming bored with the old news. "And she's wacko. Only the old farts in town believe her. When she found out about Matt's death she set up a contractor to bulldoze the property. Clay was living in his apartment when the workers showed up."

"She's crazy..." Kelly said.

"Fred had to arrest her," Junior said. "She started attacking Clay, demanding he get off the property. Fred patrolled the stone house when Will came back in town, worried she was going to hurt him. My turn or yours?" Junior nodded at the customers approaching the hut.

"Yours," she told him and after he left, she absorbed the drama.

Later, she sprayed the boats in comfortable silence as Junior and Allison played ball in the sand next to her. Every time she stood to prop another boat against the wall, she caught Allison's cold glares.

It was no hidden mystery her younger coworker had an innocent crush. Junior's adoration had tapered off to the point it didn't bother Kelly anymore, but his outspoken girlfriend clearly didn't trust her.

Honey, relax, he's too young for me.

"So you're a lesbian." Allison broke the silence of their game with a stab of immature smugness.

"I am?" Kelly wiped the grit from a seat and sprayed more disinfectant.

"Allison!" Junior hushed back with a blush.

"Well, that's what Jaycee said. Your husband left you because you prefer women." Allison grimaced as Eddie tried to lick her hand.

Kelly had yet to understand how everyone she met in town relied on assumption and gossip. Why was everyone's business everyone else's business? At moments like this, Kelly missed a more civilized home.

"Funny Jaycee could know I'm a lesbian when *I* didn't even know. I'll have to thank her for clearing it up." Kelly patted her thigh for Eddie to leave Allison alone. "Not that there's anything wrong with that."

Allison rolled her eyes. "Well, you don't like guys."

"I don't?"

In defense of his new friend, Junior threw the ball at Allison's forehead, likely to shut her up.

She gasped at Junior. "You only hang out with Clay and Randy." She hurled the ball back at his balls.

A couple of college beach boys whistled as Kelly bent over to pick up the roll of paper towels at her feet. "Yeah, so? They don't talk about makeup and hair and losing weight."

"And you never even talk to them." Allison nodded to the lifeguard stand.

"Because they talk about makeup and hair and losing weight."

"You don't have a boyfriend. You don't even like it when guys hit on you."

"Allison!" Junior tried to hush her again.

Kelly raised her brows but didn't really mind the girl's nosiness. At least Allison was young enough to be blunt and tell it to her face rather than talk behind her back. In a small way, it was more amusing than annoying. Kelly had no motivation to give a damn what Allison thought. They were all trivial matters of the teenage mind.

"I don't have a boyfriend because I'm freshly divorced. Call it heartbreak. And I don't care if they hit on me because all they want is a piece of ass. Call it wise judgment."

The answers seemed to shut Allison up and the teens tossed the ball some more while Kelly worked. Her boredom must have been obvious.

Allison's nosiness hadn't been exhausted. "Are you ever happy?"

Kelly cast her gaze skyward. "All the time. Every single moment of the day."

"Dad only washes the bottoms of the boats, Kelly," Junior said, tossing the ball from hand to hand.

"Uh huh."

"I'm just saying, you don't need to wash the seats. They're plastic. We only hose them down sometimes."

"Do you realize HPV is transmissible on solid surfaces for up to twenty four hours?"

Allison snorted. "You sound like a nerdy freak when you say stuff like that. *That*'s why your husband left you."

Kelly paused her trigger finger on the bottle, slightly irritated at the teen's judgment. *What the hell would a juvie know about married life?* She quirked a brow behind her sunglasses. Did anyone ever stop to consider sanitation on the plastic surfaces which hundreds of barely-there bathing suits sat on? Really, did they?

Kelly was mature enough to know her pedantic, medically accurate speech wasn't her being snotty. Or patronizing. Or freakish. It was her being Kelly. It didn't matter if she was in Atlanta, Churchston, the North Pole, or the pits of hell. She was sarcastic and blunt no matter where she was or who was around. And if she wanted to consider the ethical ramifications of spreading possible diseases, she damn well would.

But the stab still stung. *Is that why John had left me? Do I really sound like a walking Dorland's Dictionary?*

She worked her mouth a couple times, in hunt for a proper comeback, but lost the enthusiasm.

Junior must have been aware of the awkwardness. He suggested they head home and Kelly relished the solitude they left behind. After she finished housekeeping on the boats, she took shelter in the hut for the remainder of the afternoon.

CHAPTER 9

A couple strolled down to the dock where their kayaks were waiting and Kelly harbored a glimmer of jealousy at the young pair. So in love. She didn't know why she believed in it anymore.

"Oh give me a break," she said to herself as the young couple tickled each other in the kayak. The ring of her cell phone saved her from her sad envy.

"Hello."

"What's with you?" Heather said.

"Eh, depressed." Kelly forced a smile and stood up to the register as a couple men came to the booth to sign up for a kayak.

"What else is new?"

"Ha. I'm not depressed. Depressing maybe, but not depressed." Kelly took the cash from the guys and pointed to the dock. "Number thirty-four. Yep. Thanks. Have fun."

"What's wrong?"

She threw the ball out in the sand for Eddie to fetch. "Saw a couple who made me wonder why I'm fooling myself to think I'll ever be in love again."

"Again? I doubt you ever even loved John."

Kelly winced. "Come on, you tell me. Why should I believe in it anymore?"

Heather sighed. "Because despite the fact you're jaded, you're a romantic." Heather sighed. "It's who you are. You'll find someone someday."

Kelly took a sip of her iced tea, then stepped into the sunlight in front of the booth to stretch. Uniform consisted of her bikini, and whatever clothes she wore on top that she didn't mind getting wet when she got the kayaks out of the river. Sometimes, she barely got wet. On warm days, she wanted to dip in. In a Burns' tank top and her bottoms, she stretched her hamstrings and watched the pedestrian traffic on Main. Promiscuous, no. But it sure as hell beat wearing scrubs.

"Why bother?" She didn't really mean it. Eddie plopped down to gut the ball and she resorted to people watching. On the sidewalk in front of the garage, Clay talked to Randy. Two perfect specimens. Her gaze roved over the skin and muscles of the men on the beach. Fine eye-candy. But her heart wouldn't let her body lie to her mind. Kelly wanted more.

"Because," Heather said.

Kelly grimaced at the phone.

"What? You're getting horny and want some casual sex? Go for it."

"I'm not shallow," Kelly said.

"Never said you were."

"I was cheated out of love before. I want one good shot at it."

"You'll get it."

"It does exist, right?"

"Of course. It's been a while for you. Go hook up with the stud muffin next door. It's not going to hurt you."

"Clay? I don't think they make condoms heavy-duty enough to protect against his kind of popularity."

"I have good news!" Heather exclaimed with an abrupt change of topic.

"Yeah?"

"John broke up with Sasha!"

Kelly frowned in the sunlight and returned to the hut to close the shutters. "Okay..."

"That's it. He broke up with her."

"Damn." Kelly put equal lack of emotion into twisting the lock on the shutter.

"You don't care?"

"Why would I care? We got divorced. Too bad for him."

"Too bad for him?"

Kelly held the phone on her shoulder as she stepped out into the setting sunlight and yanked the hut door closed. "Yeah."

"You're not supposed to not care. He cheated on you!"

"Yeah, I do remember that bit. Am I supposed to be a spiteful bitch and never want him to be happy? I don't care who he's with. All I know is he and I never made each other happy."

"You're like a generous saint or something."

"What? You think I'd want him back?"

"I don't know. He was such a dickhead. And now since we hate him it'd be hard to play nice if you got back together."

"I don't hate him. I hate what he did but I don't hate him."

"Oh." Heather stalled.

"All I want to know is why he cheated. Why wasn't I good enough for him?"

"Let me get this straight. He's never made you happy and that's a write-off for you. But you want to know why you didn't make *him* happy? He cheated. Why should you care?"

"Well, why did he cheat? Was I not good enough for—?"

"Kel, why are you even asking? He wasn't good enough for you, why do you care if you were good enough for him?"

Kelly frowned, unable to explain how his infidelity had hurt. "Never mind. How'd you hear this, anyways?"

"What? They broke up? Jean's niece works at the bank and she saw them fighting, like a couple months ago. Then the night LPN said she saw he'd been living at the condos where her brother lives. Without Sasha."

Kelly couldn't put herself into the gossipy spirit. "Well, shit happens."

"Yeah. I guess he quit the office, too. Maybe he's doing some kind of midlife crisis deal like you are."

"I'm not having a midlife crisis. I needed a break from nursing. And a change of scenery."

"Yeah, yeah. I know. I just miss my best friend—"

"Hey, I miss you, too. Wait, what? He quit his job?" Resignation seemed too impulsive for a conservative planner like John.

"Sounds like it." Heather's brother was an assistant to the HR department at John's office. Small world, indeed. "He emailed them about suffering from stress. With the divorce and whatever. Said he was going to take a job at some company in Denver."

"Stress? Bull. He wanted the divorce. Asked for it. He wanted to propose to his little stripper."

"It's what I heard."

Kelly scratched her hair. "Denver?"

"Yeah."

Denver? The Mile High City? John hated high elevations. He killed the mood on their honeymoon in the Smoky Mountains, whining he was too dizzy to even leave their cabin. Denver was the last place she thought he'd go.

Since Heather needed to head to work, they hung up. Kelly walked across the street to see if Clay wanted to split funds for some meat to cook out at home. Men's voices sounded from the garage as she neared.

"So you're really not interested in her?" Randy asked as he watched Clay work on a car.

"When did I say such nonsense? First time I saw her...that ass. Those tits. Like a walking wet dream." Clay reached in to tighten a bolt.

"She seems so sad all the time."

"Yeah, why don't you go after her, then?"

Randy rubbed the back of his neck. "She's, uh... She's not really my type."

Clay chuckled. "Mine neither. She's too fucking smart."

"Kind of seems she'd be perfect for..."

Clay scoffed. "Yeah, what I thought, too. But he's too much of an asshole to even notice her."

She walked over to the hood and leaned in, the guys too close to the metal to notice her arrival.

"Hand me a wrench," Clay said and held his hand out. Randy straightened and froze at the sight of Kelly with her forearms leaning overhead on the hood as she watched Clay work. He swallowed and blushed. It was almost adorable. He was the mama's boy, alright. All manners and polite etiquette. Randy would never understand Kelly was used to the guy talk. It still was annoying and sexist, but she had four brothers. What else could she expect? She had always been one of the guys.

She picked up the tool and handed it to him.

"Come on, man. I've got some sweet pussy to catch tonight. Can't stall with this piece of crap all day."

Randy elbowed Clay sharply.

"Ah shit." Clay wiped at his jaw.

Damn, if he wasn't such a playing idiot. She admired how gorgeous he was, then crinkled her nose. There was not even the slightest primal feeling of wanting him.

"You were there the whole time, weren't you?" Clay stood to face her and leaned his hip against the car.

"Certainly was." She pretended to study the engine.

"Why didn't you say something, moron?" Clay directed his whine to Randy. He wiped his hands and slid closer to Kelly.

"If you had a brain you wouldn't talk so filthy all the time." Randy tended to his ringing phone.

"Baby, you can't sneak up on a man like that," Clay said.

Kelly no longer had any question as to why he was such a successful player. The smooth husky crooning of his voice was panty-wetting.

"Dirty, dirty mind." She shook her head. "Dirt. Not Clay. You're Dirt."

"Being around you makes me so dirty, baby." He wedged himself closer and snaked his arms around her waist to hug her to his body.

"Is this how the infamous player scores? Lamest line I've ever heard."

"What kinda lines you like, baby?"

Kelly met his bedroom eyes and gave him a wry smile. "Are you talking about seduction?"

"Yeah." He tried to lean closer and she let her arms rest on his shoulders.

She traced his jaw softly. "Touching is enough."

"Don't tease." Clay lowered his voice. "Don't you get lonely being next door?"

"Lonely indeed, but not for you."

"Give me a chance," he whispered playfully.

"Nothing doing."

"Gimme one good reason why."

There were plenty but she wanted to sting him. "You have bad breath."

He grimaced and gently shoved her back.

She bit back a smile, then paid attention to the car once Clay resumed working.

"How exactly did Matt die?" Kelly asked. They fell quiet at her question.

Randy spoke first after gazing to the sky for a moment. "Car bomb. Afghanistan."

"He must have been a great guy."

"He was." Randy rubbed the back of his neck. "He was my cousin. Delores married Bruce and they had Matt. He was two years younger than Will. And my mom is Bruce's sister. So Matt was my cousin and Will was kind of my cousin."

She shook her head, but thought she had the hang of Randy's ancestry lesson. "There isn't a lot of incest and stuff down here, is there?"

They sneered.

Not only did Will lose his best friend, he lost his only sibling, too. *No wonder he's an ogre.* She hugged herself, not wanting to imagine how someone could stomach the pain of losing a sibling.

They stood in an awkward silence in the muggy garage. Clay wiped his hands and Randy stepped away to answer his phone again. From the corner of her eye, Kelly caught the blur of Will running like hell was loose. For him, it probably was.

"Hey." She elbowed Clay as he stepped out on the sidewalk for a break. He loped his arm around her shoulders.

"Yeah, baby?"

"Stop calling me baby." She punched his stomach and he winced. "*He*'s a drunk?" She pointed to Will running further from town.

"Who?"

"The guy who's always running. That's Will?"

Clay smirked with a strange expression. "You asked me before. Yeah. He's the local drunk now.

We tried to help him after he got back, but he pushed us away. He used to be one of my best friends. But there's no way to get in his head now."

She wasn't convinced. Yeah, he was rough around the edges, but he had to be hurting. She imagined how Clay would react to not having a mother, losing his best friend and brother. *Probably bury his sorrows in a stranger's vagina.*

If she lost one of her brothers, she'd probably be running on the beach too. With that kind of loss...she wouldn't want Heather trying to get in her head. She'd be trying to escape it herself.

"And he's a drunk," she said.

"Yeah. He's always got a bottle around. He's made Elmer's his second home."

Kelly slanted her brow. The residual lagging drag of alcohol intoxication would put him at a jogging pace, not record-setting Olympian speed. Even as he widened his distance from town, she could sense the furious power of his body, tearing strides down the beach. In a hoodie in the summer sun.

Clay tugged her closer, tearing her attention from Will's routine.

"Why do you always have to invade my personal space?"

"You always look so upset."

She flashed him her best false peppy smile.

"Or pissed."

She nodded.

"You don't like hugs?" He dug his finger into her side, tickling her. Kelly fought the smile at her mouth.

"You smell like exhaust." She hugged him back.

"You smell like river water."

"What the fuck are you doing?"

Kelly spun her head to the side where the feminine demand had sounded from. Clay sighed against her, not releasing her.

"Hey Daisy," Clay said.

"What the fuck are you doing?" she repeated.

Kelly slid out of the hug. She wasn't going to let some country bumpkin tell her who she could be friends with. At the same time, she didn't want to welcome crazy wrath. Jaycee had some kind of a history of violence and Kelly didn't need Daisy to sic her friend on her.

Holding Clay's hand, she pulled him close to Daisy. She thrust his left hand up to the woman's face. "No ring, Daisy. No ring," Kelly said.

"So you want her now?" Daisy demanded of Clay.

"No. We're friends, Daisy."

"Friends my ass." She snorted.

"Daisy, we never said we were exclusive. We talked about this when you came back in town, 'member?" Clay rubbed his palms over his face.

"So you want her now? She didn't even know how to fuck her husband!" Daisy trilled with a temper-fueled jealousy.

Kelly looked to the sky and wished Will had a jinrikisha to get her away from the meddling minds downtown. Her divorce wasn't any of Daisy's business. And even if she could lower her standards and seek a quickie with Clay, it still wouldn't be any of Daisy's business. The catty remark struck a nerve, but instead of feeling pissed at Daisy, Kelly felt pissed at herself, feeling the weight of doubt and low self-esteem sinking her down to the cracked cement of the sidewalk.

"What the hell is wrong with you, Daisy?" Clay lost his temper. "It's not like that. We're only friends, goddammit!"

Kelly didn't even bother to open her mouth. She walked back for the kayak hut to get in her SUV and head home. Defending herself to Daisy wasn't important. She'd rather extract herself from the situation.

"Yeah, you walk away. That's it. You stay away from him." Daisy's cocky threats called from across the street.

Working her jaw, Kelly stopped mid-step and counted to ten. *Nope, no patience.* Sometimes she saw the merit in turning the other cheek, but Clay was her neighbor and she wasn't going to have Daisy assuming she was stealing her man.

Kelly kept her face neutral and cracked her knuckles as she crossed the street again.

"Didn't you hear me, big-city bitch?" Daisy crossed her arms like a guard in front of Clay.

"Daisy—" Clay pulled her arm in restraint, but she slapped him off. She took two steps toward Kelly, arms swinging like she was readying for a fight. With the same confidence as she had had to wrestle drugged or mental patients in Atlanta, Kelly took hold of her, spun her, and locked her in a tight head lock.

"What the fuck?" Daisy gasped and struggled to claw at Kelly's arms. Pedestrians and window-shoppers clustered around the commotion.

"I heard you, Daisy. Now shut up and listen to me. It's none of your business who I sleep with. If I ever want him, you'll know the moment I do, because I don't share. In the meantime, pay attention and back the fuck off. He's my damn neighbor." She held her for a moment more. "Got it?"

When Daisy didn't answer, Kelly tightened her grip. "I said, do you understand me?"

"Whatever." Daisy wriggled and Kelly released her.

Daisy rubbed her neck and mumbled to herself.

Kelly whistled for Eddie, then called back as she walked away, "Wasn't the coffee bar guy satisfying enough?"

"Shut the hell up!" Daisy said.

Clay wasn't happy either. "Brent? You're fucking him, too?"

"She's making it up."

Kelly shook her head as she walked further away. "You only had the whole beach to witness at lunchtime. Get a room next time if it's not for public knowledge."

CHAPTER 10

After she pulled the gloves inside-out, Emily threw the last bit of evidence into the fire. She stood back, cracking the kinks out of her neck as the flames hissed, erasing the decayed flesh of the identity's body.

The Buick's trunk reeked of the sweetly sour funk of death. It had been a challenge to find the time and opportunity to dispose of the corpse. No quick and easy stash in the freezer like she had done to Forty.

Emily stoked the fire as she rehashed the details of her thwarted plans. She'd nearly had Thirty-Nine. Then Kelly threw in the complication of the other daughter. And then Thirty-Nine had to die on her.

"Fucking bitch," Emily said.

Bent on revenge, Emily had planned and researched how to get back at Kelly with Forty. But Forty had brought no true revenge because Emily had failed to *keep* Forty. And because of that failure, Forty-One was going to be an unprecedented accomplishment. Never before had Emily needed to steal from the same person *twice*.

A flame slid over the neck of the woman on the ground. Emily cocked her head and crouched closer, remembering the details of her last kill. Forty had lasted only seconds after she cracked the neck. The crunch so definite and satisfying.

Emily was testing her patience, controlling herself, to let Kelly make the move. And as soon as she did, as soon as Forty-One came along, Emily was going to teach Kelly a very important lesson.

She was the best. Everyone always chose her. Always.

Between running Burns' kayak hut and helping Alan at the bowling alley, Kelly was happily preoccupied and didn't brood as often. Only when she was alone at night. Or when she saw pairs like the old eighty-five-year-old couple who came in every Friday night for a pizza, holding hands and smiling at each other. Senile or still in love, Kelly hoped for the latter.

Having grown up with four older brothers and no mom, Kelly was no stranger to the close proximity of men. Almost every night, she would try to ignore the sounds of Clay's love life through the oh-so-thin walls. Content with the influx of vacationers who didn't mind an out-of-town romp in the bed, he had decreased his pointless flirting. But his constant presence was still aggravating.

One morning as she let Eddie out to pee before she went to the kayak hut, Clay exited his apartment. Tiptoeing in his boxers, he clutched his clothes in his arms and teethed his lower lip as he creaked his door shut.

Kelly sipped coffee as she stood at the screen door of the hallway which divided the townhouse. She paid no further attention to her neighbor as she absentmindedly waited for the dog to find a spot. Randy had given her permission to cut out a dog door, but as finicky as Will had reacted to the porch work, Kelly wondered if he would care.

Then again, Burns hadn't cared if she brought the mutt to the kayak hut in the day. Eddie was mostly obedient after all. Catch was, Eddie couldn't exactly fit in at Alan's. Sometimes Clay would watch the dog at the garage and then take him back to the townhouse while she worked nights at the bowling alley. She had even caught glimpses of Will petting Eddie in between jobs. There was hope, she supposed, that even a sad, mad, supposedly suicidal jerk could still enjoy a dog's company. Maybe he was human after all.

"Morning." She yawned.

"Shhh." Clay tiptoed closer and cast a glance back at his door. "I need you to take me to work."

She raised her brows at him, then checked through the screen door. His ancient sans muffler truck was parked in the driveway.

"She'll wake up at the sound of my truck starting."

"For the love of God." Her brain was slow to react to the infusion of caffeine. Mornings were not her best time. And he bobbled between annoying and amusing.

"Shhh. Come on."

She relented with a shake of her head and got ready for work. On the way into town, Clay explained his dilemma. Melissa, last night's conquest, was Daisy's out-of town stepsister who was visiting on a college break. Kelly had already gathered Daisy was still a semi-regular between his sheets. Melissa, despite her status as a vacationer, had seemed convinced she was the one and only. For a quick escape, there was good old Kelly for the rescue.

"You're pathetic," she said as she stopped on Main in front of the garage.

"Pick me up at eight?"

Her jaw dropped.

"Come on," he said. "I've got some things to catch up on at the garage and you'll be getting done at Alan's by then, won't you?"

"You owe me." Who was she kidding? It wasn't like she had anything better to do.

"I don't know what I'd do without you." He pecked a chaste kiss on her forehead.

"You'd find another gullible woman to be at your beck and call," she said dryly.

"Thought we were friends. You're not gullible. If you were, I wouldn't have to work this hard to get into your pants." He grinned like the cocky idiot he was and went inside.

After her shift at the kayak hut, then a shift at the bowling alley, Kelly was tired on her feet when Clay called.

"You said eight." She tallied the register at Alan's and propped the phone on her shoulder.

"I know. Bring me the usual. Put it on the tab for the garage."

"I'm ringing out the register now. You're lucky. What's the magic word?"

"Please, sugar honey baby sexy mama?"

"You're pathetic." *Or I am.* She hated the thought she might really be a pushover. But he did watch Eddie for her. And he promised to someday check out the rattle in her SUV. When she hung up and turned around, Jaycee gave her a dubious look. Another woman-hater.

It hadn't taken long after her official move into the townhouse for many of the women in Churchston to detest her. More so, detest her nearness to the town's stud. It wasn't a foreign feeling. Always preferring the company of males over females, Kelly had learned long ago girls don't trust the girl with guy friends.

"Alan!" The clash of bowling balls striking pins roared over her voice. She took a deep breath to holler to the old man. "I need a pizza sub and a ham grinder for the garage." Waiting at the counter adjacent to the bar, Kelly stretched her back.

"I'm out of here in a few minutes. Anything else you want me to do?"

At no reply, Kelly finished checking the cash register, ignoring Jaycee. After the night Kelly had told Jaycee she wasn't leaving Alan, Jaycee sulked like a grudging cat. Kelly wasn't enamored with her job of setting pins and delivering subs for Alan. It certainly wasn't out of long-term career ambitions she had wanted to keep the job. She hadn't trusted the woman to refrain from taking advantage of Alan. Kelly had a soft spot for lonely old men, likely due to the sadness she had always felt for her dad who hadn't remarried until recently. She avoided the bartender as much as she could, which wasn't too difficult as the Jerry Springer candidate occupied the space behind the bar for the most part.

"Ya know Daisy's engaged to him." Jaycee's sneer broke the peace. Her dyed black hair draped like a screen covering her smoky caked eyes and barely contained cleavage. No one would cheat on *her*. She was the definition of an eager bedtime partner.

"Who?"

"Clay."

Kelly was surprised she didn't actually hear a 'duh', too. "Well, congrats to them." It was a threat. A warning to back off from Clay. And it warranted a laugh. For as much as Churchston spread assumptions and gossip, it was ironic they neglected to accept the reality that Kelly was, apparently, the first female to turn down his offer of sexual ecstasy.

At the garage, a fuzzy-haired frantic redhead screamed at Clay in the middle bay. She either had a perm from hell, or her tresses didn't agree with the South Carolina humidity. Kelly entered with the subs and raised her brows at the chaos. Blues raged from the radio and Kelly stepped over the tires and oil pans to lean against the workbench.

"You told me you loved me!" the redhead shrieked.

"Honey, I do love you." Clay held his hands in surrender.

"Fucking liar! Don't lie to me."

"Holy hell, it's Medusa PMS-ing," Kelly mumbled, assuming the snaky redhead had to be the naïve Melissa. *How long is this going to take? Should I leave?* If Clay took the risk to two-time, he could figure his way out of it and how to get home. But she didn't have a hard heart to leave him stranded. She sighed with patience.

"Clay!" Kelly turned her head to the left at an almost familiar angry rumble. "Get the hell over here and help me with this!"

"Hang on. Baby, calm down." Clay tried to step away.

"I'm not going to calm down, you mother fucking liar. You lied to me. Why'd you lie to me?"

"Baby, I didn't lie—"

"Clay!"

Kelly rolled her eyes and crouched down to tousle Eddie's ears and hug him close. "Why did he lie to Medusa Melissa? Because she's a crazy bitch, that's why."

"Clay!"

"I'm coming." Medusa had Clay backed up against the wall and he gave Kelly an expression of desperation. "Can you give him a hand?"

Kelly groaned and walked to the car where the voice came from. Grease-stained jean-clad legs stuck out from underneath.

"What do you want?" she asked the mechanic.

"Hold the radiator hoses up," the voice commanded from below. Kelly reached for them.

"No. Not those. The radiator hoses."

She made a face to herself and searched again. Radiator. Hoses. Ah ha. She held them out of the way. Clay and Medusa were arguing at the caliber of a domestic dispute in the worst neighborhoods of Atlanta, and Kelly considered intervening. Medusa was one angry lady.

"Go to the bench and get some zip ties."

Kelly obeyed and then the mechanic instructed her to tie hoses out of the way.

"Now go to the wall and hit the green button."

She did and the car rose. From below the lift, the man stood up, still under the car, and turned to face her.

"Mr. Landlord. What a pleasant surprise."

Will rolled his eyes. "Hold this out of the way." He wiggled a chuck of metal.

Kelly came close and held it to the side. She had to stand nearly on her tiptoes. "Can't say please?"

"I can but I didn't. Missed my chance. What the hell are you doing here?" He resumed unscrewing bolts, wincing at the tight fit.

She scowled right back at him. "I brought the subs."

"He's got you sleeping with him, bringing him food. Why are you even renting the apartment? You could be his resident bitch."

Her jaw dropped. "I'm *not* sleeping with him and I'll never be anyone's *resident bitch*. I deliver for Alan!"

Will glanced down at her as she fidgeted to stand tall enough to hold the harness above her head and out of his way. The dried pizza stains on her chest stretched against her breasts and she was acutely aware she was sticking her girls out. She frowned and wished he'd hurry up because Clay's banshee screamed even louder in the next bay.

"Why are you still here then?"

"Short-term memory loss? You demanded I help you."

"Clay is supposed to be working now." He was quick to avoid her eyes.

"Yeah, well, he seems preoccupied. He asked me to give you a hand. The faster he's done here, the faster we can go home."

"Still trying for a place in his bed?" He couldn't help asking, could he? Kelly bit on her lower lip, tired of the assumptions that she was hooking up with Clay.

"No. A place in my own bed. The weasel asked me to take him home to avoid confronting Medusa. And now since she caught up to him, looks like I'll be waiting to go home as well."

Will fumbled with the air conditioner.

"I don't know what's worse. He's trying to coo and baby her so he'll still have the option of sleeping with her again or she's so berserk over a one-night stand that she should have known better than to believe a word he said." Kelly shook her foot from the awkward position of standing tiptoe for so long.

Will glanced at the couple bickering. "She's a woman. They're all crazy."

Kelly narrowed her eyes. "Not all women are crazy."

"Every one of them. Emotional and not worth a damn."

She kicked his shin.

"Son of a bitch!" Will dropped the wrench to the ground and worked his jaw. "What the hell did you do that for?"

"What's wrong?" She tapped her foot, still holding the stupid harness above her head.

"You just fucking kicked me for no reason."

"Don't swear. You're not in the Marines anymore. You going to finish this or what?" She shook the harness in her hands.

"Can't take the Marines out of 'em." He rubbed his knee as he moved to stand.

"It's vulgar."

"See, you're crazy too. You kicked me for no reason."

"Aren't you supposed to be finishing something up there?" She nodded her head to the car above as he paused in his ascent. She cleared her throat at his blunt glare. "And I'm not crazy. I was proving you wrong."

"About?"

"Your stereotype. Why didn't you want me to kick you?"

He grit his teeth as he stood straight. "Because it fucking hurt."

"Hurt? You mean pain? Gee, sounds like a feeling to me."

He rolled his eyes.

"I'd bet with those charming welcoming smiles you're sending my way you're angry at me, too. Two emotions in one night."

"Try annoyed."

"Three. My, how you're brimming with feelings. Guess our genders aren't so different after all, landlord. You really *are* human."

Medusa and Clay were still yelling at each other. It had taken a while, but after Medusa screamed at him for ten minutes, he finally lost his cool, too.

Blood drained in Kelly's arms. "Are you almost done?"

Will dropped the wrench as though her voice had startled him. "I would be if that woman would shut up." He wiped the sweat from his brow.

"Why can't he give up and tell her what she wants to hear so she'll go away?" Kelly studied the pipes and pans and hardware above his head.

He grunted in amusement.

"What?"

"Screw what she wants to hear him say. It'd be a lie one way or another. She should move on." He twisted the wrench and his elbow chucked her in the chin.

"I swear, the next time he brings home a lunatic I won't feel sorry for him." She felt his gaze on her as she followed the maze of parts above them.

"Jealous?"

"Of what? A one-night stand with something recycled ten times over?"

"What are you, a virgin?"

"No. I choose to not be stupid. One-night stands are pointless."

"How so?"

She broke her absent-minded stare to watch him struggle to free something in his hands. It confused her they had carried on this much of a conversation.

"What do you mean?" he asked. "You're saying sex is pointless?"

Kelly watched his bicep bulge as he tried with a wrench. "No, a one-night stand is."

"Never had one?"

"It's nothing I want to repeat."

"You're going celibate."

Kelly groaned. "One-night stands aren't synonymous with sex in general."

"Sex. Copulation. Reproduction," he said. "What's the difference?"

"There are differences," she said.

"You stick a dick in a vagina and there you go."

She bit her lips. He was mocking her and she laughed at herself. She expected the jerk to understand the concepts of loving someone versus scoring? She was a ninny after all.

Medusa threw something at Clay. Will and Kelly both whipped their heads to the side at the commotion. By ducking his head lower, Will's face was inches from hers. She held her breath.

Up close for the first time, she studied him. The rugged face. His scowl. The weathered lines of hard work and sun. His nearly black hair still in a crew cut. Muscles. Hard, tanned skin. She averted her eyes to the ground. Heat soared through her body in waves, a warmth she hadn't felt since before she met John.

Whoa. "Why are you standing on one foot?"

He gave a heavy pause before he answered. "Because." He cleared his throat.

"Where is the manager? The owner? Your boss?" Kelly looked around and pulled at her collar. "He lets you guys work late whenever you want? Couldn't he get rid of Medusa?"

Thinking back, she realized she had never seen anyone but Clay and Will work at the garage. She often delivered food fit for multiple people and she assumed it was for a few mechanics. And thinking even further back, she wondered who Clay's boss was, the man who was stud competition before Matt died.

"Medusa is Clay's problem so he can handle it like a man," he said.

Her attention caught on the flex of his biceps again. Kelly frowned and focused to not stare. Or drool. If Clay's voice was panty-wetting, Will's was a premonition she should invest in a morning-after pill.

"Come on, landlord, don't kid. Clay's not a man. He thinks he is. That and God's gift to women."

He coughed. Not even the hint of a smile. He really was a robot. "Believe it or not, I have a name. Stop calling me 'landlord'. It makes me feel like I'm Fred Mertz or something."

"You feel? Damn, Will, I thought you said only women have emotions."

He deadpanned.

"Who owns this place?" she said.

He let the air conditioner come down in his hands. Finally. He set it on the ground and exhaled tiredly before he reached up to take the harness from her. He shoved it into the myriad of parts.

"I do."

"You?" She rubbed her arms.

"Yeah." He walked to the bench for a towel to wipe his hands. He ripped paper towels down to wipe the sweat from his forehead.

Him? He avoided her and busied himself with his work, going in and out of a little office. She wrangled her brain and tried to remember everything the guys had said. Will?

So much for pegging Will as a common brainless mechanic.

Clay came over sans Medusa. "Crazy bitch."

Kelly stood up. "Serves you right."

"Don't bring your women here anymore," Will said as he moved around them, putting tools away. "No more screaming whores. And I don't want her tagging around here either." He pointed at Kelly then opened his sub.

"I delivered the food!"

"Then don't stick around after." He opened a jar of pickles and put a few in the middle of the sub. "Find some other way to get into his bed."

"Pickles on a pizza sub?" To each his own, she figured. She crinkled her nose before his words hit.

Clay was faster. "Fuck you. She's not like that!"

"I came to give him a ride!"

"She's not like that?" Will smirked. "She's just another woman. They're all like that."

"Go to hell." Kelly flipped him off.

"Already there."

"You're such an asshole. You used to be cool and now you're an asshole." Clay spoke as though he had acid in his mouth.

Kelly had never seen Clay so peeved. After a few rounds with Medusa, though, she could be sympathetic.

"I had to ask her for a ride home because you're too twisted and pissed off at the universe to give me a ride when you live right next to us!"

"You need a ride home because you don't know when to keep your dick in your pants and your mouth shut," Will said. He ate his sub as he went around shutting down lights.

"Asshole!" Clay pounded his fist on the workbench. "You're nothing but an asshole. Go on. Take a piss on your friends. Go to Elmer's and drink like your dad. But don't take it out on her!"

"Soft on her already?" Will said without a flicker of emotion on his face. He glanced at Kelly. "You work fast."

"He's a friend."

"Men and women aren't friends. They fuck. What they're made for."

"Well, it's not what I'm made for," Kelly said and went for her purse.

"You're frigid?" Will said.

"No. I'm not another easy piece of ass."

"Leave her alone," Clay warned Will.

"Then what are you hanging around him for? Go on, Clay, have mercy on her and give her what she wants."

"He's a friend," Kelly crossed her arms, irritated at his jab. "When I let someone in my life for sexual pleasure, it will be to someone who matters. Someone to make love with me."

Will looked to the ceiling and scoffed. "There's no such thing as love. It's a myth. Can I lock up now?" At the door, he held his sub in one hand and his keys in the other.

Kelly and Clay went for her car.

"I'm sorry what he said," Clay told her.

"I'm not. It doesn't matter to me. He's angry and had to vent."

He turned to her as she drove, confusion and anger in his eyes.

"It's hard for me to walk away from an argument. Call it my weakness. I never know when to shut up."

He raised his brows.

"Oh jeez, why should I care what he thinks? Stick and stones…"

He had no answer. As she pulled up in the drive, he patted her thigh. "You're right. I think you are the coolest neighbor I've ever had."

CHAPTER 11

The next morning, to avoid the boredom of slow business at the kayak hut, Kelly tutored Junior.

"Like this." She beckoned him to come at her. He reached for her arm and she spun him into a headlock. "No. You're not twisting fast enough." Since she had deflected not one but a few catfights, it seemed Junior had developed the exaggerated idea she was the expert of all kinds of martial arts.

"I did!"

"If you did, you wouldn't be caught." She squeezed her arm tighter to tease him, then released him. She waved him to try again.

"How did you learn this?" Junior wiped the sweat from his forehead.

"My brothers. They figured I should know how to defend myself. Finn was a boxer, so he taught me the basics. Wade got me into Judo. Grant took Maga classes with me. I played around with Tae Kwan Do. Good exercise. Sometimes people would get physical in the ER, so it paid off." She blocked his arm and encouraged him to try again.

Despite Will's hostile attitude at the garage, Kelly couldn't chase away her fascination with the man. "You were saying he got a medal?"

"Huh?"

"You said Will got the Medal of Honor?"

Junior grunted when she slammed him down to the sand. "Yeah. Some kind of service award."

"Was he always an asshole?" She helped him up.

"No, not really. I dunno. He was gruff, but always gave a hand when it was needed. He helped Dad one time. You mean people would threaten you? Like the guy who died and made you quit?" He readied to tackle her.

Kelly sighed at the doubled conversation they were dancing through. He wanted to know how she knew self-defense. She wanted to learn more about Will.

"The guy didn't make me quit. I was already in a rough spot. I wasn't cut for watching people suffer."

"But you said his daughter came after you."

She sighed. "After he died, she went hysterical. He'd disowned her years ago because she was a starving artist drug addict. When I contacted her, I had to coax her into seeing her dad, to give him a chance. And she did. They seemed to have mended their differences. After he died, she blamed me. Blamed me for contacting her. Blamed me for letting her think she had a future with him. Blamed me for not looking out for him."

She hadn't realized she had stood still for a moment until he cleared his throat. "You didn't kill him, Kelly. I mean, not deliberately."

She scoffed and waved him to come forward. "Yeah. That's what they all say. But it doesn't change the fact it's on my conscience. Betsy gave him the heparin. I told her to check all his meds with me. I would have spotted the problem immediately if she had done it a minute earlier. It's done now. Nothing I can do about it." She spun him to the ground. "You have to duck more. Will helped your dad how?"

Junior twitched his head to shake back his bangs. "Will was like ten, or something. Dad's truck stalled coming in to town and his leg was in a cast. So Will pushed the truck to the garage."

She nodded. "Why does he—"

"So she…" Junior slipped on the sand before he could grab her arm. On his back, he squinted at the sky. "So she tried to attack you and then she killed herself?"

"She ambushed me in the parking lot. Landed in a psych ward. Last I ever heard of her. The LPN, Betsy, hung herself the same night. Couldn't handle his death on her conscience. Come on, it's getting too sunny out here. We'll practice another time." A customer approached the hut. "You want to get them a boat? I'll grab your bag."

Junior trotted off to take care of business and Kelly lugged his backpack into the hut. He often studied when he worked the hut.

"What the hell do you have in here?" She slapped it on the counter and peeked through.

"I gotta prep for the entrance exam," he said as Kelly riffled through the texts.

She nodded. "Mechanical memorization and caffeine. Best advice I've got."

"I'm mostly nervous about the USMLE."

She smiled as she flipped through the pages of a familiar text. "It's not bad if you study."

"You took the USMLE for your RN license? I thought it was for MD."

"It is for MD. I took Step 1 of the exam for the hell of it. Wondering if I wanted to do something more."

"How'd you do?"

"Ninety-eighth percentile. Only one person scored higher in my section."

Junior gave her an incredulous look of awe so she poked his side as a tickle. He wasn't so bad to be around when she reminded him to give up hope. She was too old for him. Junior was like a kid brother with kindred career interests. Well, her former career, at least.

He wrestled her away with a smile. "Holy shit!"

She shrugged.

"How can you stand working here?" Junior laughed. "It's boring as hell. You're like a genius! You don't belong here."

"I don't think I belong anywhere anymore, Junior." She frowned at him. She hadn't been fit to be a nurse, a wife. At least she was still a good daughter and sister.

"Why don't you go back to school?"

"For what? I don't want to watch people suffer and die. I can't."

He shook his head. "You're wasting your talent. You were like, awesome with Todd on the beach."

"Who the hell is Todd?"

"The man who was choking on the beach. You saved him. You were right there—"

"Will saved him. I couldn't get my arms around him."

"You could be helping people."

She shook her head.

He hurried to his bag and rifled through it. "Here." He thrust out a flyer. "What about this?" It was an advertisement for a paramedic program.

"I can't handle it anymore—"

"Think about it. You wouldn't have to be there to *save* people. You would be there to *stabilize* them. I bet you could transfer your credits and bypass the technician program. Go straight in for paramedic."

She flicked the paper from his hand. He grinned. Not wanting to stomp on his good intentions, she gave in an inch. "It's not a completely bad idea. Come on, let's grab some Chinese at the end of town. I'm tired of eating subs."

Junior slapped the counter window shutter closed and she led him towards her car, her arm around his lanky shoulder.

Since her Subaru wouldn't start—dead battery, they deduced—Kelly took Burns' truck instead. She'd be coming right back to the hut anyway.

Checking her appearance in the grimy mirror, Emily nodded approval to herself. The wig's shiny, ebony strands reminded her of when she had killed Mama—her first kill. She was only ten. Mama had been whoring then, and collecting extra revenue selling Emily as a plus. Sometimes she'd be the sidekick assistant.

Never better than Mama, of course.

Mama had presented the first steal that night. The man who paid fifty bucks for an orgasm from the whore and her ten-year-old daughter. He hadn't even noticed when Mama didn't come back in the room. Emily finished his blow job and left Mama's body in the tub.

Staring at the depth of her pupils in the mirror, Emily relived the details of stabbing Mama in the face, blood streaking through the black wig she had been wearing. Her first adult kill. Steal Number One.

With a steady breath, Emily focused on the present.

At Jared's ice cream stand, she spoke in an accent as she ordered a drink from the clerk on duty, Allison. Emily took her drink to a bistro table on the patio in front of the stand and pretended to text on her phone, a prop while she eavesdropped and spied. Brent got in line and flirted with Allison's coworker. He hadn't even recognized Emily and she'd been sucking his cock every other day on the public beach. Emily gambled Allison wouldn't even have recognized the single person who was listening to her. A perfect identity.

Positioned between the kayak hut and the ice cream stand, Emily listened to Allison's woes and watched Kelly goof off with Junior. She analyzed. Measured.

Junior with Kelly... Emily weighed the possibilities. It was obvious he was in love with her, and Emily had seen Kelly playing around with the boy. Everyone on the beach did. He was younger than Kelly. But did she really want him? Is Junior Forty-One? Emily had to know. Was dying to know. If Kelly wanted Junior, then Emily would take him.

It would take time...and energy. Junior wasn't a man. She was more used to stealing adults. Not juveniles. They weren't so trusting in the game of sex. Some hadn't even been introduced to the game of sex yet. Sometimes that innocence was an advantage for her, other times, it was an extra obstacle.

Oh, she had stolen her share of adolescents. Number Twenty-Four had been a twelve-year-old who lost his virginity with her. It was Emily's revenge on the mother. Taking her little boy from precious youth to the reality of manhood. It was a sweet steal. To steal a parent's child's virginity— no returns on innocence. Emily was a master of her craft. But there was no denying it would take time to accomplish the theft of Junior from Kelly. Emily was too ripe for the satisfaction of ruining Kelly.

Her decision was made easier. She'd kill the boy. Or kill Kelly? Emily walked back to her car in the parking lot, coaching herself again to resist killing Kelly. How easy it would be, to sneak in the townhouse and kill the woman. Such notions teased her, taunted her. *Kill her!* Her mind screamed the thought, but Emily resisted. It would be too simple. Too fast.

With a smile, she drove home to expedite an online purchase.

CHAPTER 12

Glancing up from a thick tome of philosophy which wasn't telling her much about the real mysteries of life, Kelly listened to Clay come home next door that night. Different book? She checked the stack on the coffee table. *Classical Electromagnetism* by Jerrold Franklin. Her dorky curiosity wasn't quite in the mood.

Digital slashes on the cable box told her he was home a little later than usual. *Is he going to be imposingly social, knocking on my door with an invitation for a late cookout, or is he going to be tipsy and horny with a date on his arm?*

Giggles and laughter sounded on the front porch and Kelly rolled her eyes. Definitely the latter. It took them some time to get inside his half of the townhouse because from the sounds of moaning and raspy breathing from the front, Clay was either getting inside his date on the porch or she had advanced asthma.

Moaning turned to erotic cries, and Bertrand Russell's *History of Western Philosophy* forgotten, Kelly slammed the book to the coffee table and buried her face in her hands on her knees. It would be another sleepless night.

"Why does he have to be so loud and obvious?" she asked Eddie next to her on the couch. His brown tail lazily flapped twice in a wag.

She followed the sounds of the couple making their way through the front door. Shuffle of feet, giddy giggles, husky whispers, and the slam of the door. Not wasting a moment, Kelly took her cue and slipped her tennis shoes on, grabbed a sweatshirt, and headed outside.

It was getting to be a pathetic habit, having to escape her apartment to avoid the sounds of normal people like her neighbor getting it on, a stark reminder she wasn't. Not that Clay could really be normal, though. He'd have to leave his balls to science when he died.

Darkness spanned the lakefront, not a cloud to mar the blanket of navy blue. No moon, but she found her way to the sandy beach anyway.

Peace? She stood on the edge of land before water and stuffed her fists in her pockets. The water was peaceful but she couldn't agree the sentiment suited her.

Calm? She stared at the horizon, a blend of dark blues in the distance, with short, frothy waves striping in the slow wind. She might not have her peace, but she couldn't completely deny calmness. It was soothing in a way, to start fresh in a new place as she had been for the past few months. Even if she still felt lost in a large sense.

She scanned the beach and sky, darkness and solitude surrounding her like a vast sheet. Aside from the gentle laps of waves at her feet, all was silent. No headboard thumping next door. No television. No animals. No cars. No worried phone calls from Atlanta. No townspeople gossiping. A deep breath left her lips, stretching the void which ached in her chest.

Alone? A familiar sting burned her eyes and she slumped to sit in the sand. Alone. It was what she had wanted, she reminded herself. Her therapy. Her recovery from a blunt divorce and unloving relationship. Alone. She had wanted her space to accept some forced truth that she wasn't at fault for Norbert's death, for his daughter's anguish at losing him. To sink in guilt when she read all those editorials about Atlanta's shabby healthcare killing off a promising governor candidate.

As she leaned back in the sand, crossing her arms behind her head for a pillow, she wallowed in the emptiness of the wide-open space around her. No peace, some calm, and a lot of alone.

Warmth tickled her skin as the tears flowed freely. Too routine to cause a sob or noise anymore, Kelly let the tears fall, hoping someday they would cease. Memories tugged at the ache in her ribs, thoughts and illusions that had once made her giddy and giggling and smiling.

Pain of her ex's rejection broke down her esteem, scars of the betrayal stabbed at her pride. Kelly lost track of time as she leaned back in the sand, watching the lightless sky give her no answers or signs of hope. Drowned in her sadness, in her heartbreak, in her guilt, she lay and waited for a resolve of peace to claim her darkest thoughts.

She'd give Clay a few hours. God forbid if he had found another Medusa. It wouldn't serve well to return to her apartment when a rejuvenated love-fest was bound to commence. Her neighbor had quite the stamina for his lady friends.

Breathing in the balmy lake air, she shoved aside the pain of her broken marriage and considered Junior's idea.

Go back to school? Sure, she loved to learn. Return to the medical field? She winced. Not to save people, but to stabilize them... She had always been praised for her take-charge attitude, her infallible grip to keep cool when chaos broke out on the floor.

It was much later when she thought she heard a car coming down the drive. She wondered who it was. The next moment, she heard the motor clearly. Will's Harley. She inhaled deeply, confident he wouldn't see her past the bank of grass leading to the drop-off to the beach. Hidden from his view, she stared at the sky, listening to the roar of his bike coming from town toward his home behind the townhouse. Throaty puttering drifted past her and she could imagine him pulling into his garage. A slight crash sounded and Kelly winced. Knocked the trash cans over. Drunk. She shook her head slightly. It was a miracle he didn't kill himself.

Annoyance turned to anger at the thought of her landlord. Drunk again and it was a miracle he didn't kill himself? It was a miracle he didn't kill someone else. Everyone had their problems, but his irresponsibility rubbed her the wrong way. Hypocritical it may be, but she judged Will's rude and sullen behavior just the same, she was sure, as everyone in town judged her edgy, shy, sad behavior. But her moping wasn't a danger to anyone else. His recklessness was.

One moment she was admiring the depth of the blue and the quiet of the outdoors, the next, a leather jacket and jeans tripped over her. A squeak of alarm left her lips as a harsh curse came from his.

"Fuck." Will rolled with the fall, then caught himself on his elbow. Leaning in the sand, he squinted at her.

On his hands and knees, he wiped the sand from his eyes and screwed up his expression at her. Kelly frowned at him and rubbed her shoulder, no doubt where his boot found its obstacle. Not that he had been walking straight anyway. A sudden flash of headlights shone on his face, lighting from near the drive to the townhouse. Oh great, nympho Clay must be in the mood for an orgy if another visitor was arriving.

With a grunt, Will fell back to the sand and sat next to her. He craned his neck to face the sky. His blurry gaze went back to her face and he blinked more of the sand from his face. Masked with a drunken scowl, his attention had settled on her eyes. She wiped her tears away.

"What the hell are you doing out here?" he asked.

Kelly dragged her gaze from the water as she leaned up on her elbows to face him.

He frowned more at her silence.

"You're bleeding," she said.

His hand went up to his forehead, touching the sticky ooze. "Wouldn't be if you hadn't been lying out here like a booby trap for me to fall over."

Her attention returned to the lake. "Trust me. You would have fallen on your ass without my help. You're drunk."

He ignored her comment. "What the hell are you doing out here?"

"Clay brought home another woman. I didn't really want to hear them go at it." She sat up. "You might want to clean off the cut. It could get infected."

He shrugged.

"Right. You're the sad drunk veteran. Why would you care about a stupid little cut?"

His eyes were cold when he faced her. "Look who's talking."

She gave him a dry stare and he scowled even more.

"You're the one who's bawling like a baby out here."

At his harsh words, her shoulders moved a little and the movement revealed some of her neck. His stare seemed to burn into the exposed flesh. For the first in a long time, Kelly opted for silence, lacking anything flippant to say to his observation of her tears.

"I don't give a shit if I bleed to death," he said. "Not much worth living for."

"Now it's the sad, drunk, suicidal veteran."

His jaw twitched.

She sat up straighter and wiped sand from her sleeves. "Do me a favor. If I interrupted your journey to the water for a fatal swim, which" — she cleared her throat— "if you're not suicidal, swimming right now might kill you since you're so damn drunk."

His fist clenched as she continued.

"Reconsider. Sleep off your bad night instead, okay? I've had enough drama for one day." Suicide was no joking matter. She recalled the hysterical edge to Norbert's daughter when she was informed of her father's death. Will might have his problems, but Kelly doubted he'd ever been suicidal. She wouldn't leave him alone.

"Touching."

"Seriously. I've got a hard enough time getting sleep as it is."

"Yeah. You've got a rough life. Your man left you for something better. Tough shit."

"I'm not going to compare my problems to yours," she said, her patience tested.

"You don't have a fucking clue what my problems are." It was more of a growling snarl than a retort.

"I've heard." She twirled circles in the sand with her finger, avoided his eyes. "Not the same since the war. Sad. Mad. Drinks all the time. His best buddy died."

Will stilled.

"Never married. Didn't have a good dad. Mom left him. Sad stuff." She dared a glance at him and cleared her throat. "Used to be the stud of the town. Women loved him. Men envied him. Was such a sweet boy when he didn't misbehave.

Always courageous and strong and ready to give a hand."

She met his eyes then. "What they say in town. But I've always been one to make my own judgments and it's clear to me they've got it all wrong."

Will scoffed. Written on his grim lips was the expectation she was going to say something lame.

"I mean, that's what they say, but I only know what I see. Maybe they want to think you're a big tough sad war hero who had a tough childhood, but all I see is a wimp."

His glare shot to her like he had been stung. Whipped. Shocked with live wires.

"A wimp," she repeated and for an instant, she feared what she was doing. Past the alcohol, past the anger and hostility, she could see his pain. Having learned from four brothers, she knew men weren't always receptive to being babied. Those times called for other measures of communication.

"What?" he asked.

"A wimp. I don't know why everyone thinks you're so special and fearsome. All I see in front of me right now is a large, irresponsible, heartless, cruel, self-serving weenie who needs a shower." Her mouth went dry at his harsh expression. She was walking on thin ice as she continued. "A wimp. Wuss. You know what I mean."

"What did you call me?"

She licked her lips, hoping to God reverse psychology worked on even the most temperamental assholes in the world. All she wanted was to goad him back to being human, but his expression of murder had her second-guessing. It was none of her business, but she couldn't deny she was drawn to him. She wanted to help him. Second nature had her wanting to help everything living and breathing. Will's pain drew to her with steel tentacles.

Why can't I ignore him?

She swallowed thickly.

He moved too quickly for her to register what was happening. Besides her bias that he was nothing but sloppily, slurry drunk at the moment, she wasn't prepared for him to launch himself at her. In seconds, he had her solidly pinned to the sand.

"You don't know what the hell you're talking about." He bit the words out, with his face dangerously angry above her. His arms were taut, the muscles seeming to rip his sleeves.

A fleeting instance of fear paralyzed her. Just as irritating, a hibernating heat swelled in her blood. Drunk, angry, tired or not, Will wasn't a bad sight on top. Why did he do this to her? She cringed. Hormones. Hormones and a lack of release.

She tried to sit up—not easy with his grips harsh on her arms above her head.

"I'm not an expert, but if your life was so damn bad, you would have faced your problems. I mean, it's not like it's hard. Grow up and deal. Move on and all."

"You don't know what the hell you're talking about!"

"It's probably none of my business. I'm a random tenant. Hell, if you're content to mope

about the war and your friend and your dark
morbid little world, I'll leave you to it. Like I said,
I'm not comparing my problems to yours. It's—"

"You've never killed anyone, have you?" He
tightened his grip on her arms. It was a brief
squeeze, more of a side effect of energy as he
exploded. "Huh? You don't know what it feels
like to watch someone die in your fucking hands!
I should have died. Not him. He had people
waiting for him to come home. It should have
been Matt getting off the plane, not me. He had a
life, a future, a family!"

Kelly bit her cheek as Will's outburst
simmered and then cooled. His glare was intense
and his weight was no longer imposing but steady
on top of her.

"Golly." She was surprised at the neutral calm
in her voice. "Sounds like a breakthrough."
Returning his gaze, she dared not to smile and
hoped she appeared bored, indifferent to the
confession which likely hurt him to share. "I've
got to tell you, Will, I wonder how long it's been
since you've gotten those thoughts off your
chest."

He blinked dumbly.

"Speaking of, mind getting off mine now?"

His brows furrowed almost in confusion,
maybe from the grim humiliation.

Kelly worried while Will seemed to struggle to
get his words in order. His lean face was etched in
pain when she shoved at his rock-hard abs.

She squirmed to sit up as he got off of her. His
retching had a painful note to it. She crouched
next to him as he puked the alcohol out of his

system. "Oh Christ. You're not even a drunk. Not a real drunk." A real alcoholic wouldn't vomit his night's accomplishments. And he wouldn't be able to do all his running with hangovers. Will was still weaning. The realization turned her lips up in a slight smile. Alcoholic schmalcoholic. He wasn't fooling her.

Rubbing his strong back, she shook her head. "Now you'll really hate me. First, I bully you into acting like a human. And then you're going to have a bitch of a hangover regretting you said anything to me." With a final pat on his back, Kelly stood up and went home.

Never watched anyone die? Oh the stories I could tell you. As she left Will on the beach, Kelly couldn't help but criticize his false accusations. She'd seen plenty of people die. Norbert, she watched him take his last breath.

She stopped in her step and turned back to see him. He sat there, his head hanging low.

Despite everyone's insistence, Kelly couldn't shake the guilt that she had killed Norbert. If she really was a perfect nurse and she was magically in the right place at the right time…

She sighed and resumed her walk home. Maybe she'd never seen a family member or a personal friend die, but she was no stranger to death. As inaccurate as Will was, he still proved her wrong on one count. She had tricked him into speaking his mind about losing Matt, putting his thoughts and fears to speech. How much of a coward could she continue to be, if she wallowed and refused to move on past the misplaced responsibility of one stranger's death?

CHAPTER 13

Kelly soon learned Clay could not only piss off the ladies, but their men as well.

The night after Will had encountered her on the beach, an angry pounding woke her late at night.

She opened the door with a frown and the man in front of her winced as though he'd been duped into taking a bite of fat-free food.

"You're not Nikki."

"No shit. Who the fuck are you?" She wasn't fond of his attitude or the whiskey on his breath. She had never seen him before.

He turned around to pound on Clay's door. "Nikki! Where are you, you little bitch? I know she's with you, you motherfucking asshole. Don't you dare touch my wife."

Kelly started to shut her door with the realization that Clay had taken someone's wife for the night.

"Don't shut the door." As he retreated back for her, she slammed it shut. Fists banged loud enough to wake the dead and Kelly eyed the frame with skepticism.

"Open the door, bitch! Where is he? Nikki! Get your ass out here!"

Furious now, Kelly retrieved her largest kitchen knife. She wasn't stupid enough to believe her petite weight could stand a chance to his bulk. "Eddie. Come on boy. Help."

She opened the door to see the angry biker reaching to grab her and Will slamming him to the opposite wall.

"What" —Will stood slowly, speaking in a menacingly angry demand—"is going on?"

When the hell did he get here? She swallowed and the weight of the dinky weapon in her hand reminded her of how foolish she must look. And some guard dog. Eddie wagged his way to Will.

She'd seen men fight. Her brothers especially. Boys will be boys. But she had never seen one move with as much ruthless strength and intimidation as Will had. Nor as quickly. Working her brain from a muddle of daze, she tore her gaze from his powerfully lean body in nothing but boxers.

Oh God.

The hallway was dark but she had gotten an eyeful enough. Taut skin, pure muscle, an interesting rugged scar. She looked down at her pajamas. Neither of them wore enough clothes to stop her X-rated thoughts.

He snapped his fingers and she flinched. The angry set of his lips jolted her to reality. Hormones. He was a man. A good-looking man. With crap of a personality. *Don't even go there.*

"Clay's with his wife," Kelly said and returned to her side of the townhouse, scolding her heart to slow down from the sight of him.

Morning came too quickly. Clay knocked on the door. "Kelly, baby, come on."

She had dressed after an un-soothing shower and flung the door open.

"I haven't had coffee yet," she warned. "Do *not* call me baby."

"Damn you're pissy in the mornings."

"Too bad." She scanned the hallway for Mr. Nikki as Eddie went for the front lawn.

"I need a ride," he said and Kelly went back to pour coffee in her thermos. He followed.

"Have Nikki take you."

"She left after her husband did. Called her sister to pick her up."

"Seriously, Clay? She was married? Aren't you afraid you'll piss off the wrong husband or boyfriend and lose your nuts?"

He shrugged. "So, what happened?"

His careless and self-centered behavior irritated her. He probably assumed she'd take care of the problems for him. "I don't know. All I know is he's gone now. You're a crappy neighbor."

Clay threw his arm around her shoulders and grinned. "See, if you were waking up every morning in my bed, you wouldn't be so cranky."

She punched his shoulder and jumped into the driver's seat of Burns' kayak truck.

"Dammit." He rubbed his shoulder. "Girls aren't supposed to know how to punch."

"Have Nikki kiss it." Kelly drove toward town. "Why am I taking you to work?"

"Maybe you should be my bodyguard," Clay said. "He slashed my tires."

Kelly smirked. "Better your tires than your balls, right?"

"Why are you still driving Burns' truck?"

She quirked her brows. "What, you want me to punch you again?"

"No, why—" He smiled without a leer, a wince lining his usual grin. "Fuck. I forgot. I'll get your battery today."

Her car had been at the garage for three days now. "Uh huh."

Luckily for Clay, there was enough to do at the garage that Will was too busy to berate him for the last night's disruption. Sleep had eluded Will with nightmares of the war. If he hadn't been sitting on his front porch in the dark of the night, he wouldn't have noticed any commotion at the townhouse. It was unusual to see so many headlights coming their way so late at night. And the drunk's yells had been loud enough to alert him since he was already awake. He didn't really care if Clay was screwing with some other guy's wife. Clay was a big boy, he knew what he was doing. But Kelly was scared.

With a groan, Will concentrated on the brake pads in his hands. He couldn't afford to waste concern on a woman. At the sight of her tear-streaked face, on that night he'd tripped over her, something primitive had ripped at him. It had been a long time since a woman could get under his skin. It was a power he didn't want to relinquish. But instead of moping in an intoxicated blur on Matt's birthday, he wanted to pull her from his sadness even though he couldn't escape his own.

He had watched from the garage as Kelly dropped Clay off in the morning and he didn't blame her expression of annoyance. And later, when Clay browsed the shop computer, Will inferred he needed four tires.

In the lull of the humid afternoon, Clay strolled over to him in the middle bay. "Hey man, I've got to pick up some parts in the next town."

Will tossed his empty water bottle in the bin. "And four tires?"

Clay smirked. "Sobering up so early?"

"Take my truck. I've got to drop off the Jeep to the house in Point Place." It had been a collision job, and the owner still sported a full length leg cast. Will empathized with the handicap.

"How are you gonna get back?"

Will hadn't planned far ahead. Normally he and Clay could handle drop-offs and pick-ups. Clay's truck was at the townhouse, but Will typically had his pickup or bike handy. Vehicles were abundant—it was a garage, after all, sometimes with half-alive cars people abandoned or, like Clay's truck, clunkers that customers bartered with for service. If he put a little elbow grease and money into it, the dying truck Clay recently collected would operate like semi-new. "I'll figure something out."

"I've got to get the parts in the next hour," Clay insisted. "Ask Kelly."

"What?"

"Ask Kelly. I need to go pick up the parts before someone else takes them. She can take the Jeep and you can follow her on your bike."

Kelly? Will scowled, regretting his verbal slip on the beach. His words had been thoughts he'd kept guarded under lock and key. Humiliation tickled him like a feverish rash spreading under his skin. He didn't want her pity. But of what he remembered, she hadn't pitied him, though. He grit his teeth, recalling how calm and cool she'd been, bored even, as she cajoled him to losing his control.

"Ask Kelly," Clay repeated, and waved his hand toward the beach to coach him on.

Will kinked the stiffness in his neck. No. She hadn't coaxed him either. And she hadn't dismissed his problems. She wasn't the pitying kind of woman who would beg him to be happy, and she wasn't the hateful malicious kind of local who would wish him dead. Instead, she had simply forced him to speak his mind. Will squeezed his eyes to slits, hating that someone had cracked his walls even slightly.

"Isn't she working the kayak hut?" Clay nodded. "She'll probably be leaving to go to the bowling alley soon. And Junior can watch for her while she's gone. Go ask."

"You go ask. She's your friend." Will started to put the tire back on the car.

"Don't be an asshole. She's nice. We'll go over there and ask her after I finish this oil change."

CHAPTER 14

A half hour later, Will walked across the beach with Clay at his side.

"Hey Kelly." Clay smiled at her.

Will froze. She wore a Burns tank top over her bikini top and her bottoms. He had never actually intended to watch her from the garage all day. But as Burns' hut was the only thing blocking the view of the beach from the garage, how could he *not* have seen from the distance? Playing catch with Junior in their downtime. Fetching with her dog when she brought him along. Chatting with Burns and customers. Reading as she sat on the counter. Helping kids in the boats at the little dock. Maybe her rack wasn't spectacular, but it wasn't her true beauty.

Kelly's real attraction was the challenge in her smirk. Intelligence behind her eyes. Wit. She had some strange kind of humor and impatience that had him fighting smiles. She wouldn't back down from him and it was a novel experience. He scratched his chin, the annoyance at his stubble matching the irritation he still held at her for forcing him to talk to her on the beach.

But up close? Her eyes were steady on him. Not a local's sneer of hatred, not a stranger's casual glance of interest, not an easy woman's measurement of his body. Those blue-greens...he couldn't peg what was on her mind. Being near her had him fidgeting. The Braves hat on her messy blonde hair hid her face enough to make it teasing.

How does she always look like she belongs in a bedroom?

"Clay. Will." She smiled with surprise. "Kayaking today?"

"What's up man?" Clay leaned around her and punched Junior on the shoulder. In his signature pleading and wheedling tone, he explained they needed a favor.

She glanced at both men before answering. "Sure. I don't care. I have to be back before two to get to the bowling alley, though."

"Won't take long." Will cracked his knuckles, aware people were watching him. Anxiety escalated in his blood. Noises jerked at his nerves every which way. Crowds were still an issue, and he bet they always would be.

"It hasn't been busy so I've only used the first ten today, the others are still on the rack," Kelly told Junior as she stepped out of the booth. "And the ones out there will need picked up in about fifteen. I haven't taken the truck out since this morning, but you'll probably need gas if you go for them."

Junior dismissed her with an adolescent wave.

"Can I stop and get ice cream first?" she asked Clay, tucking her hair behind her ear. "For some reason there was too much commotion this morning to eat breakfast or pack a lunch."

The three of them walked for Jared's ice cream stand before crossing the street for the garage.

"Why's everyone staring at us?" she asked Clay.

Will glanced at the beachgoers and found their nosy attentive gazes staring right back. He gnawed on the inside of his cheek, then checked a cautious glance at Kelly. *Well, look at her. Who wouldn't be staring?* If he wasn't so convinced Churchston despised him, he imagined the beachgoers could have been watching her. He found it endearing she seemed so clueless of her raw beauty instead of flaunting it like other women did.

"Because the Grinch is out." Clay nodded his head to Will.

Kelly's eyes sparked with amusement and he narrowed his eyes at her, daring her to test him. They ordered their ice cream and Will focused on breathing. Impatience, anxiety, shame. They tossed and tumbled in his stomach. He wanted to return to his garage.

"It's on Mr. Parker today," Kelly calmly explained to Jared. "He's taken enough time leering at my ass for one morning. He owes me."

Will avoided Jared's shocked expression. The old man didn't need to hear such gibberish. Jared was likely the one person in town who didn't wish him dead. He licked his lips and fought the urge to tell her to shut up. He had a bad enough reputation already.

The jab had lowered him to Clay's level. But he didn't care for long because he was easily preoccupied at the sight of her licking her cone.

"Don't blame you, man," Clay said as they walked for the garage.

Kelly punched Clay. "Shut up, Clay. You should be playing nice to me after all the noise last night."

Clay grinned. "Was she screaming in ecstasy?"

Another punch and Clay flinched like it hurt. "Her husband. Don't pull crap like that anymore or I won't want to be your neighbor." She licked her cone, and glanced at Will. "What is it?" Turning her head side to side, she scanned the sidewalks and studied him.

Will clenched his fist, irritated she could read him so well. She could detect the instant he was uncomfortable beyond usual. But more than irritated, he didn't want to hash out the details of why.

"What the hell is wrong with you?" Kelly hurried to keep up.

"Nothing."

"What do you have, a switch to your personality disorder? One minute you're almost human, and then you shut down like you're—"

"Come on, let's get back." Will shoved Clay to walk faster.

Instead, Clay surveyed the sidewalk and frowned. "Oh."

"Oh what?"

"The woman up there? She's uh, that's Delores. His—"

"Mom. Right," Kelly filled in.

"They don't get along."

"And this entire town has nothing better to do than watch? Don't they have TVs for entertainment? Why do they even care?"

Clay opened and closed his mouth a couple times, seeming to search for words.

Will ground his molars and hoped Clay would stay quiet, gulping air like a guppy. It had been his harebrained stupid idea to fetch Kelly in the first place. He never should have left the safety of the garage. Never should have followed along to get ice cream. Never should have come back to Churchston.

"What—" Will caught himself from falling to the ground. He had tripped over Kelly's foot. Kelly's perfectly shaped ankle that she had stuck in front of his feet.

Kelly backpedaled in front of him. "Well since they're staring, you may as well give them something to talk about." She twisted her lips to hide a smile, but lost. Clay choked on his ice cream and broke into laughter.

It didn't matter if Delores was watching. If every single Churchston resident was watching. Will couldn't believe she had actually tripped him. What was she, ten? His knee had gone through extensive… "You little…" He let his ice cream fall to the sidewalk as he turned to chase her.

Her smile turned to amused surprise at his pursuit and she shrieked as she ran off. Two ice cream cones on the sidewalk stayed with Clay as Will chased her. He picked her up at the waist and carried her unceremoniously to the water.

She giggled and protested. "Come on. Put me down!"

Holding her over his shoulder, Will kept his face frozen. He resisted the instinct to stroke her skin, to feel her warmth and softness. He clamped his tongue between his teeth to tamp down the urge to smile at her gumption.

He hadn't touched a woman since before Matt died. Hadn't held one. Hadn't wanted one. He dumped her in the water. She spat out the lake water in her mouth and sat in the waves. Will didn't notice the wet tank top clinging to her. He tried not to. "You asked for it."

Her hat floated away and she smirked up at him. "And you're not overreacting?" She shook her head, seeming to like the water as he stood with the waves splashing his calves.

His boots were soaked, now his jeans, too. His filthy sweaty garage garb wasn't exactly swimwear. "Don't play games with me," he warned.

"Chill out, tough guy." She searched the water by splashing her hands. "Where's my hat?"

"Floating away." *Walk away. Walk the fuck away.* Will tried to abandon her in the water. She had tried to humiliate him. She had almost smashed his fragile pathetic knee to the cement. She had almost made him a laughingstock in front of Delores. But he couldn't walk away.

She frowned. "What? I love my hat."

Jesus, a pout? "Why? They don't have a chance for the wild card this year."

"They could," she insisted and stuck her hand through the waves again. "My brother gave me that hat."

"Too lazy to get up and get it your—" He stepped further in the water to reach for the hat. He felt her foot find his calf and he joined her in the water, falling on his ass.

Fury simmered his skin hotter than the sun. Twice in five minutes she had made him fall. In moody silence, he watched as she stood, and he'd be a liar to say he didn't enjoy the smooth wet skin of her legs showcased at eye level. Damned if he'd let her leave him in the water, he hurried to his feet to follow her as she dismissed him, putting the wet cap on her head as she led the way back.

Water sluiced from his soaked clothes as he followed her to the sidewalk where Clay laughed.

She wiped water off her cheek. "You owe me another ice cream."

"You got a fetish for making men fall on their face?" Will asked.

She glanced at him. His clothes clung to his frame, detailing exactly how masculine he was, and she forced herself to avoid falling on her own face. *Hormones.* All physical, she reminded herself. They called him Will? He was the Hulk. He-Man. Conan. He was the embodiment of every possible action figure in the world. How can he have so many muscles? So much strength in one body? *Fit?* Will wasn't fit. He was so ruggedly powerful he needed a new word to kick *fit*'s ass down the road.

Simmer down, girl, simmer down. She took a deep breath.

"You caught yourself. And you should have seen the second one coming. A Marine?" she said. "I'd think you'd be faster on your feet."

"Don't ever try me again."

She winked at him. With a dark susurration to himself, he ripped his shirt off. As he wrung the water from it, Kelly stumbled on her feet.

If he didn't want anyone looking at him, then he's doomed shirtless.

Hormones. Physical. He was still a jerk. She kept those thoughts as a mantra. *Right foot. Left foot. God, I can't even walk straight.*

"You're lucky I have extra clothes in my office." He clenched the shirt in his fist.

Right foot. Left— What? Kelly couldn't help but envision him stripping the rest of the wet clothes off. She winced at the delectable vision in her mind, reminding herself she couldn't possibly want him.

Hormones, woman. Nothing but hormones.

"What the hell do you know Judo for?" He wiped the water from his chest.

She shrugged, pretending she wasn't attracted to him. She couldn't be attracted to *him*.

She gave him a watered-down explanation of her overprotective brothers forcing her to take defense classes. And it still had never been enough. Ever the baby sister, they called her daily to check in if she didn't call them first.

"Paid off, though. Psych patients were never easy to handle."

"Patients?"

"Eight years in the ER."

"You left a steady career to run a boat stand?"

She chose not to answer, not having the energy to defend her decision of leaving her job after she had just given the spiel to Junior.

They waited at the light signal at Main among the tourists and locals. Commotion split through the cluster of people and they parted as Allison rushed up to Kelly. The teen cast a glance over her shoulder.

"Kelly, I need your help." The girl's cheeks shone red from embarrassment and not the sun. After a glance at Will soaking-wet in his clothes, she did a double-take and raised her brows before turning to Kelly.

Kelly pursed her lips, thinking fast. It had to be one of two things.

"Uh." Allison looked between Will and Clay. "Look, I'd get it myself but I'm grounded. My mom flipped out. She thought Junior snuck out with me last night but I went over to my friend's house. She even went to his house and saw his truck wasn't there! She's so paranoid."

"I had the truck. My car needs a battery." Kelly smacked Clay's arm.

"I'm picking it up in an hour!" Clay rubbed his arm.

"Well, she thought he was hiding out with me somewhere so I'm grounded. I'm only allowed to go to work today."

"How late are you?" Kelly cut the chase. Clearly the girl couldn't go to the pharmacy for a pregnancy test while she was grounded.

"Huh?" Allison's eyes widened. "Oh, no! Not that. But his birthday is coming up and—"

Kelly nudged Clay's arm. "Gimme your wallet." He handed it over and she pulled out the condoms. Two blues. She ripped one off and gave it to Allison. *Hey, at least she was thinking ahead.* "On second thought." She gave the second one to her, too. Smiling a thank-you, the teen took off as quickly as she had come.

"Hey, I was saving those for you, baby," Clay teased.

"They'll disintegrate in your pocket before anything happens between us." She tossed his wallet back.

At the garage, Kelly took off her useless tank top and shook the water from it. She tried not to think of Will changing in his office. On the workbench, she found a shop rag that wasn't covered in grease and figured she could sit on it to not get the seat wet.

With a sixth sense telling her she was no longer alone, she whipped around from placing the rag on the seat of the Jeep. Will immediately faced the garage door and rubbed at his neck, avoiding her.

"Clay," Will called out, coughing at something stuck in his throat. "Keys are on the bench." He walked over to the Jeep as Kelly shut the door and put her seatbelt on.

"Do you know how to drive a clutch?"

"Baby sister to four boys. Of course I do."

"We're going to the blue house in Point Place," he said.

She turned the radio up, head-banging to Nazareth. "The one with the fountain in the front yard?" She started to back up. There wasn't much time before she had to clock in at the bowling alley. "See you there."

"The brakes are kind of stiff," he yelled out as she sped out in a reverse on Main. It wasn't a long drive to the house. After Will handed the keys over to the owner, he came back to his bike.

Kelly buttoned one of his dirty work shirts over her bikini. "You left this in the Jeep," she said.

Will's attention was glued to his nametag stitched over her breast.

The shirt was huge, dirty and gross, and felt like a dress as the hem tickled her thighs.

"Thought it might get windy on the bike." She raised her brows at his rigid grim face. Yet again, he had evolved from pissed-off to uncomfortable, but there wasn't anyone around this time. Whatever.

Will mumbled to himself and straddled the bike. She hopped on behind him and held on since it seemed she wasn't the only one who liked to drive fast.

CHAPTER 15

Slowing his bike on Main, Will wiped his forehead with his wrist. The clutch of her arms around his torso warmed his skin with a foreign heat.

"Stop!" She fisted his shirt with one hand and pointed to the kayak hut. He sped over.

The door to the kayak truck hung open as Junior lay on the sand. On his side, he tugged his leg to his chest.

Kelly slid off the bike before Will came to a stop. She pushed through the few bystanders, running to her coworker's aid.

Will flipped his kickstand down and jogged over to the commotion as Eric parked his cruiser.

"What the hell is this?" He got out of the car, dusting his shirt. "Hey, hey Parker, you can't park your bike on the beach. You want a tick—"

"Call life support," Kelly called out.

"Life support? Hell for?" Eric pushed through to them.

Junior wheezed as he clawed at his knee, seeming to pull his leg up. Rocking in the sand, he gasped for air. People murmured in a circle around them, closing them in. Will tensed at the crowd.

"His airway's constricted." Kelly frowned as she felt his pulse. "His heart's slow. Junior. Hey, buddy, it's going to be okay." She tipped his eyelids up. "Pupils are dilated. He's anaphylactic."

Will took Junior's hand from his knee. "What's he allergic to?"

"Hell if I know," Kelly whispered. "He's passing out." She tipped Junior's head back, ready for CPR. "Allison, go get my purse out of the hut."

"What in the hell is—" Eric leaned over Will's shoulder to see.

"Eric, call a squad out here! He's anaphylactic." Kelly said. "His heart rate is—"

"Don't tell me how to do my job. He's ana what?"

Will felt down Junior's leg. Heat bloomed at the swelling near his ankle. He whistled at Kelly. She turned to him as he pulled Junior's sock down. Two fang marks glistened with blood.

"Snake bite." Will searched the sand around them.

"Aw, shit. A snake?" Eric backed up for the sidewalk. Bystanders retreated, dancing and checking their steps.

Allison returned with Kelly's bag. "Here."

Kelly dug through and pulled out a tube. She bit the cap off and jammed the plastic in Junior's thigh. "Keep his leg down," she said to Will.

"Hell you doing to him?" Eric asked as he stood on top of a bench.

"EpiPen. Did you call a squad yet?"

"Yeah, yeah. They'll get here when they get here. Aren't you supposed to cut his leg and suck the poison out?"

Kelly stood, scanning the sand. "No. And it's venom, not poison. Stand back!"

Will pulled Allison down to the sand. "Hold his leg down, like this. We need to find the snake." He shot to his feet to help Kelly search.

"You don't go hunting for a damn snake. Leave it be, Miss Newland," Eric called from his perch. "You're gonna provoke it."

"We need it to ID." Kelly squatted to see under the truck.

"Bite's a bite." Eric waved at the ambulance coming near.

Will checked in front of the truck as Kelly searched underneath. Passing the open door, he spotted the mound of scaly flesh, partially hidden by the floor mat. "Whoa." He grabbed the back of Kelly's shirt—his shirt—yanking her to her feet. "By the brake."

She nodded. "Cottonmouth?"

He squinted for a closer look. "They're common here. Those and diamondbacks." He grabbed a shovel from the bed of the truck. "EMT should know."

"I administered a 25mg of epinephrine three minutes ago," Kelly stated to the EMT who tended to Junior. "It seems to be a Cottonmouth. Do you have Confab in your unit?"

"Yeah, we do." The EMT turned to Will. Half of the scaly body was scooped into the blade of the shovel. "Whoa, whoa." The EMT jerked his head at his partner. "Do we have any SAPV?"

"South African Polyvalent?" Kelly shook her head. "Confab's for cottonmouth or the diamondback."

Will wielded the shovel to pull the snake out of the truck. Sweat dripped at his brow. A woman screamed at the reptile. In a swift tug, the scales slipped from the shovel as it slithered away onto the sand.

"Shit!" He backed up, arms up to usher people away. "Get back!"

Kelly dropped to the ground and grabbed the shovel. Running after the snake, she swung the shovel to the ground. Once. Twice. She lowered to the ground and then ran back to the EMT.

"Well, what is it? Which antivenin does he need?"

"Damn, lady." The EMT pushed Junior's stretcher into the ambulance as Kelly held up the bloodied half of the snake's body. The mouth showcased slick fangs as it jerked its head in death.

"Adder. Puff adder." The second technician took the snake from her, dropping the carcass in an evidence bag. "We've got SAPV at the hospital."

Allison was on the phone with Roger as she climbed in to ride with Junior to the hospital. As soon as they left, the crowd dispersed.

"I hope no one ever calls *you* for help," Kelly said as Eric stepped off the bench.

He straightened his pants. "I don't take unnecessary risks."

"I bet you don't take…" Will said under his breath, rubbing at his knee.

"What's that, Parker? Huh?" Eric set his hands on his hips. "And you gonna move your bike, or what?"

"You okay?" Kelly nodded at Will's knee.

He shrugged as he walked off for his bike.

"Where'd it come from?"

Both men faced Kelly.

"The snake," she said. "Where'd it come from?"

Will frowned at her. "Adders aren't native. Maybe it was an exotic pet someone tossed out."

"But how did it get there?"

"Look, Miss Newland, the drunk here just said. Somebody musta tossed out a fancy pet. Being a city girl and all, you ain't used to the bugs and crawlers, but out here we got all kinds of creatures. It must have come from the wood line by the river and—"

"No shit. But the last time I checked snakes don't stand up and walk. How the hell did it get up into the truck?"

CHAPTER 16

Emily picked at her food at Elmer's. She speared her fork with tense jabs as she tried to mask her fury. The damn snake had backfired. And listening to Clay and the rest of the crowd, she had produced the opposite of her intended effect.

Instead of Kelly squirming in pain from venom, or Junior tragically dying as her young lover, Kelly the fucking hero had found Junior in the truck and rescued him. What was she, some kind of superwoman? Who carries a goddamn EpiPen around? And how the fuck would she know to save the damn snake?

"Pretty smart, if you ask me," Randy said to Clay.

Smart? Emily tongued the fork tines, wondering as she had many times, how Kelly had screwed up Forty. Kelly had screwed up Thirty-Nine without realizing it. She had been doing her job as a nurse, maybe doing too good of a job for her to bring the daughter into the picture. But how did she manage to keep Forty? Thirty-Nine had taken two long years to win over. Stealing Forty had been almost too easy. Emily had gotten Forty in under a month.

After eavesdropping on the whiny brat on the sidewalk, Emily learned Junior hadn't even been with Kelly. She tapped her foot at her own miscalculation. There had only been the kayak truck and Clay's truck in the drive at night. Feminine moans of delight had sounded loud and clear as she crouched in the darkness outside the townhouse. Why wouldn't she have put one and two together and figured Junior was paying Kelly a late-night booty call?

It had been risky enough spying at night. The damn dog had started barking as it frequently did in her nocturnal visits.

Emily didn't allow mistakes. She sipped her drink, clenching her incisors on the straw to cut clean through the plastic.

"I never would have thought to keep the snake," Randy said with his mouth full of food.

"He was lucky she found him when she did." Clay finished his drink.

Breathing in deeply, Emily focused on the conversation. Kelly was lucky Emily hadn't lost her temper enough to take the shovel upside her head. *Patience. I'll always be better than her.*

Eyeing Clay, Emily devised another tactic. Maybe those feminine orgasmic squeals had been from Kelly after all. If not from Junior, maybe from Clay? Would Clay be Forty-One? Emily sensed an advantage to getting a closer watch on Kelly than stalking outside the townhouse at night. What better Trojan horse than Kelly's neighbor? Emily had already fucked him out of boredom.

Clay told them he wasn't interested in bowling later. He insisted he didn't want to go. He had promised Kelly he'd change her transmission fluid. Didn't want to break his promise.

Clay was a flirt. Of course he'd been hitting on Kelly on the beach. But was he more than a neighbor to her? He was so adamant on not letting Kelly down. She was waiting for him. Expecting him.

Emily debated whether or not Clay was a target. Weighing the risks of her strategy, she devised the steps she would need to take. In desperation and impatience, she decided it didn't matter anymore. She was tired of elaborate plans. She was out for blood. She had to trust her instincts on this one.

"Come on, Clay, hang out for a bit," Emily said and squeezed his thigh. She left him no gray area to confuse her motivation. She slid her palm closer to his crotch, to nonverbally clarify her message: 'Fuck me now.'

"No." He chuckled and stood. "Later, baby. We'll hang out another night."

Emily clenched her jaw in the dark bar. He rejected her. Clay rejected her to go for Kelly. Brilliant fucking Kelly.

Clay elbowed his buddy. "Yo, Randy, I've got to take a leak. Tell them I want my tab, will you?"

As soon as Clay turned for the bathroom, Emily eased her way to the parking lot. It was the last time Clay would reject her for Kelly.

Kelly swore as she lay under her SUV and wondered for the nth time where Clay was. He'd said he was going to help. Help. She shot out an inpatient huff. She was reluctant to ever admit she needed his help, anyone's help. But she did need the transmission fluid and filter he was supposed to bring her. And his help wouldn't hurt because she couldn't get the damn nuts loose. It seemed her routine yoga wasn't good enough for manual labor.

"Dammit." She puffed out another breath of frustration. He was two hours late. She'd been surprised he had even gotten the battery earlier. Probably jinxed it. With a growl, she stuck the wrench back on the nut and pried. Shook at it. At the sight of dirty boots at her side, she turned her head.

"About time, Clay."

Will got down on his good knee and faced her under the SUV.

She narrowed her eyes at him. "What are you doing here?"

"It's my property. What are you doing under there?"

"Playing hide and seek." She wished he wasn't so damn masculine. It screwed with her head. At the lack of a response, she hated how he waited her out and won. "I'm changing the tranny fluid."

"You mean Clay was supposed to and you're impatient enough to think you'll do it without him?"

She let her arms fall to the ground. "I think I might be the first woman you've ever met who isn't helpless. Just because we don't have dicks doesn't mean we can't figure out dirty work."

He deadpanned.

"He was supposed to bring the stuff two hours ago," she said.

Will checked the tools she had strewn on the ground. "So what do you think you're doing now?"

"I thought I could take the pan off until he gets here. Be ready to put the new stuff in."

"But?"

She bit her lower lip. "Look, my dad showed me how to do this before. I'm not stupid."

"But?"

He won again and she hated it. "I can't get the nuts off."

He gave a small shake of his head and what could have passed as a smile. "Move over."

"What? I didn't ask for your help." But she had to move over as he slid under the car next to her.

"No, you didn't."

She couldn't believe his body would fit in the small space. The little quirk of his lip had her melting. *Will? Smile? Impossible.* It was much easier to accept the ready impression he was an unlikeable asshole. Much easier than analyzing her visceral reaction to him.

"Then go away. Clay's going to help me." She pushed at his shoulder as he settled next to her, reaching up to fiddle with stuff. Her hand stilled on his arm. Like the instinctive reaction to palming a stovetop, she yanked her hand back.

"He probably forgot about you. Seeing as you don't put out for him, he's probably getting it somewhere else." Will fit the wrench to the nuts.

She had come to the same conclusion. Musky smells scented the close air they shared. *Mmm, Old Spice.* She warmed and doubted it was a fever of medical reasons. It was ridiculous. "Well. I'm not that impatient. He can do this when he's got it out of his system for the night."

Will faced her for a brief study. He started to screw everything back together. "Bring it to the garage when you're done working sometime. It'd be easier to do it there."

She nodded. "Okay."

"Why'd you move to Churchston?" he asked.

Instead of regretting the need to explain herself to another nosy local, she appreciated he had actually asked a question, had actually initiated communication. He didn't seem like a gossip. She absently traced the lines of the metal above her and let him work. "Change of scenery."

"From?"

"Atlanta. I grew up there."

"You left a prosperous city and a career for this little hellhole?" He let out a hybrid of a snort and laugh.

"I got divorced over the winter. I sucked at my job—hated my job." She lifted a shoulder. "I wanted a fresh start." Communication ceased again, and this time, Kelly couldn't stand it. "Why a mechanic?" she asked, figuring work was a safe enough topic.

"I like working with my hands." He finished and let his arms drop, studying the engine while he answered. "The old man who owned the garage in town sold it to me when I got out of high school. Clay's been here since day one. When I went to tech college, I had someone part time 'til I got back. Same for the war." His shoulders jerked. "It's what I've always wanted to do. I like fixing things."

"Wh—"

"You've got a leak in the exhaust."

She nodded. He was closing up. She sucked in her lips, stopping herself from saying something soothing and pitying. Stopping herself from reassuring him it was okay to talk to her. That she loved it when he talked to her. "I overheard you arguing with Roger yesterday. Why can't the Braves make the wild card this year?"

Her heart raced when it seemed the corner of his mouth tipped up again.

"Because they can't bat if their lives depended on it." He slid out from under the car suddenly and effortlessly. Kelly frowned, missing his closeness. She crawled out and was surprised he leaned against the car with his arms crossed. Well, not at his gruff, annoyed, too-strong and sexy appearance, but the fact he hadn't walked away yet.

"Didn't seem like you lacked any first-aid skills earlier," he said.

Kelly leaned next to him. "Habits are hard to break." What did he say before? Can't take the Marine out of a man? *Well, you can't take the nurse out of a woman, either.*

"Any word on Junior?"

She nodded. "He'll be fine with an overnight of observation. With the antivenin, hydration and rest, he'll be back to normal. It's a good thing the snake was still there. It wouldn't have helped a bit if they used the wrong antivenin. There's a slight risk of infection at the bite wound, but with…"

He was silent. She grimaced, hating her tendency to babble medical mumble-jumble.

"Kind of odd it wasn't a native snake. I looked up adders on my break. They're pretty easy to buy online."

Still nothing. Kelly admired the sunset and worried if she had rambled too much.

"In a selfish way, I'm glad it wasn't busy this morning." Kelly sighed. "Heck, I've been driving the truck for days now until Clay finally remembered to get my battery. Otherwise I would have been the one to get in the truck first. Junior wouldn't have even been there if he wasn't so bored."

"He's infatuated with you." Will pushed off the Subaru.

"He's sixteen."

"Maybe he's hoping you'll be a cougar."

A joke. Kelly smiled. *He made a joke!* "Everyone always goes on and on about watching for gators." She turned on the hood and looked at the lake behind them. "I never even thought about watching for snakes."

Will leaned his forearms on the hood next to hers and furrowed his brows at the lake.

"What?"

"Still doesn't make sense how it climbed into the cab." He glanced at her. "I checked the carriage. There weren't any rusted-out holes or gaps it could have slid through." He pulled his ringing phone from his hip. "It could have climbed up through an opening if it had been sitting there for weeks. But you'd been using it." He stepped away to answer his phone.

By the confusion etched on his face as he hung up, she assumed it wasn't good news. "What?" she said, intrigued at the shadows which crossed his face. He was generally irritated, but he was awfully expressive at the same time.

"Clay was in an accident." He started for his truck, rubbing the back of his neck. At the driver's door he paused with his hand on the handle and turned back to her. "Want to come?"

Much later, Clay sat between them on the way back to the townhouse. He glanced at Kelly, then Will, then her again with a lopsided smile.

"What?" she said. "The meds are wearing off already?"

"No. It's not so bad."

When they arrived at the hospital, Clay had been making out with a nurse's aide. Kelly had collected discharge instructions and Will listened to Eric whine about car insurance and citations. Clay had been lucky to be under the limit.

On the way home, Will stopped at the wreckage still in the ditch where Clay had lost his brakes. Since they shared the only tow-truck in town, Clay's truck had remained in situ, its crumpled hood intact. As Will inspected the damage, Kelly listened to Clay's story again. It wasn't an epic tale. His brakes went out as he slowed for the stop sign fifty feet up the road.

"You want me to tow it to the garage tomorrow?" Will lowered to a plank to study beneath the vehicle.

"Yeah." Clay sighed. "I'll work on it when the cast is off. Guess I should have done the brakes before the power steering on Larkey's castoff." He elbowed Kelly. "I can mooch off you for rides, right?"

She nodded and lowered to the ground to see what had caught Will's attention. He said nothing, and stood up. Curious what he had noticed, she scrambled to her feet to follow the men back into the cab of Will's truck.

For the rest of the trip home, they fell silent. Kelly felt like a sardine. A half-fried one. She fidgeted at Will's warm presence on her left. Clay's slumped body cramped her on the right, the hard cast on his left arm forcing her to sit closer to Will. There simply wasn't enough room. Not enough air, either. Will's thigh brushed hers as he shifted and Kelly sucked in her breath. *Not. Enough. Air.* Exile's *Kiss You All Over* came on the radio and her hand bolted forward to silence it.

A torpedo of chaos tore at her thoughts. First, she was peeved Clay had in fact forgotten about her and had been driving home from Elmer's, last seen with Daisy and Kendra and the 'gang'. She thought they were friends. Friends stood by friends. But it seemed Clay's punctuality only worked with his balls. Of course, the accident was a significant delay, but he'd told her he would come straight home to help her.

Secondly, she recalled the sight of Will shirtless.

"Sorry about your tranny, Kelly."

She flinched at Clay's interruption. "It's not going anywhere. Burns doesn't seem to mind if I use his truck." *I'll only have to check for snakes first.*

"I had the stuff in the bed." Clay fingered the cut on his cheek. "It might have flown out when I crashed."

"I picked it up," Will muttered.

Clay bobbed his head in a small acknowledgement and kept his face trained to the window.

Was he upset because his arm was in a cast and temporarily useless so he wouldn't be able to perform his job well, or perform between the sheets well? Nonetheless, her nurturing instinct tugged at her heart. "You know, if it scars, it could be kind of sexy…in a rugged way."

Clay smiled and Kelly was glad to amuse him. He cared more about his sexual appeal than the fact he could have died if the shards of the windshield had come closer to his jugular than his cheek when he flew head-first out of the cab. *Simple comfort for a simple man.*

CHAPTER 17

Rain poured from the sky the next morning and despite how late she had been at the hospital, Kelly woke up early. She nursed coffee on the porch and caught the blur of Will running through the torrential precipitation. For dedication, or from demons?

Due to inclement weather and for Junior's stay in the hospital, Burns closed the hut for the day. Instead of taking the morning off, Kelly took Clay to the garage and went in for a double shift at the bowling alley. They were never busy in the daytime, but Kelly accepted the offer from Alan to earn extra and deep-clean the lanes.

With the unforgivable and ceaseless rain, the deliveries were in high demand. No one wanted to get out in the rain and pick up food. With an umbrella in hand, Kelly was busy. On her walks back and forth on Main, she noticed Clay was taking advantage of his injuries, getting the poor-baby pamper treatment from everyone.

Daisy, Jaycee, Kendra, even the loner Alyssa were constant visitors to the garage to coo over

Clay. Kelly wondered if Will was annoyed or pleased with the female company.

At noon, she left Alan's with Clay and Will's subs, but not before she went in the kitchen and put pickles on Will's. She noticed he never ordered it with the pickles, but he clearly liked them. She had yet to see him take a bite without adding them.

Clay and Kendra swapped spit in the first bay. Kelly doubted Daisy knew about their development. She waved Clay's sub box and put it down on the hood of the car. They didn't look up.

She walked over chunks of metal and hoses and headed for Will. Nirvana blared from the radio and Will glanced at her from under a car on the lift.

"Thanks." He nodded to the workbench.

She set the sub down and joined him under the car. She inspected the conglomerate of parts over her head. The shower of rain still fell from the sky past the window. Why not stall? "What's all this?"

"People call it a car." He tossed his rag down and went to wash his hands. Opening the sub box, he watched her study the belly of the car. "Want to do the tranny tonight?"

She faced him. "You're going to do it?"

"Thought you said you were the expert." He took a bite.

She smirked.

He stopped chewing and faced her with a ghost of a smile. "Bring it when you're done at Alan's.

Won't take long. I'll be here late since I'm doing his work on top of mine now."

Kelly peeked at Clay and Kendra. Her shirt was sort of missing and his pants were sort of off. "Don't you always?"

He gave her the almost smile, but she still frowned.

"His brake lines were cut, weren't they? That's what you saw under his car."

He nodded, still eating with his eyes sharp on her.

"He really has enemies?"

"You already forgot about the moron who was hunting for his wife the other night?"

"The one you pulverized?"

"What the hell were you going to do with the knife?"

She shrugged. "It was better than nothing. Did you always have to look out for him?"

"We kind of all looked out for each other." His tone was neutral but it seemed like a painful confession.

She started for the door, already too mesmerized at the sight of him and concerned about the hurt in his eyes. Her freaking bleeding heart would be wasted on the man who despised the whole world. "You're sure you won't be too busy for my car?"

"No. Drive up to the middle bay."

When Kelly returned at the end of her night at Alan's, she actually witnessed Clay working. He browsed the computer for parts and explained Will was doing a brake job. Guilt tickled her and she knew she should come back another time. He was so busy he hadn't even known she had pulled up to the middle bay.

"How's the arm?" she asked Clay.

He grinned. "Fine."

Kendra, Alyssa, and Daisy entered through the side door.

"You going to need a ride home?" Kelly asked him.

"Nah." He gave his girls the bedroom eyes and Kelly nodded. How did it not get complicated? Was it a competition or an orgy? Regardless, she deduced this was going to be another night to escape to the beach.

"Hey," she called out for Will over the roar of the radio. He stood under a car, on one foot again. He didn't answer and gave no move to show he'd heard her.

"Acrobatic, are we?" She stood in front of him. His face was grim with creases of pain.

"Oh. Hey." He let go of the brake drum and took a deep breath. "You're here to take Lothario home?"

She began to frown, but caught herself. He had forgotten about her. Surprisingly, it hurt. "No. Looks like he's got an orgy lined up along with a chauffeur service. See you around."

"Shit." He reached out and grabbed her arm. "Your tranny. I forgot." He shifted his weight onto his other foot. "Let me finish this and then I'll do it. Been kind of busy."

"What exactly is wrong with your leg?"

"Knee. Busted in the war."

She checked the scars. "Reconstructed patella?"

"They actually saved it. Mostly it's the tendons."

"You run—"

"All that helps." He winced in pain as he wrestled with the drum again.

"Do you want help?"

"From you?"

She cocked her head to the side, feeling small. It was a hypocritical realization that he seemed to hate offers of help as much as she did. But her assistance wasn't out of pity. "I'll come back."

"Are you always this impatient?"

Kendra and Daisy giggled loudly from the distant bay and Will went to turn up The Offspring on the radio. "Pull in behind the convertible on the lift," he ordered to Kelly, yelling over the music.

"You don't want to put it on a lift?"

"They're all taken. Come on."

Once she was parked inside, she lowered to the stained cement floor to follow him under the car.

"I said it won't take long." He barred her from getting under the car with his hand.

She smacked it away. "My car. I'll help if I want to. I'm not worthless."

He opted for silence but Kelly couldn't handle it. They passed the time arguing about sports and debating appropriate condiments on Italian food. He asked questions about her brothers and when she explained Sean was a commercial contractor, he participated in the conversation less and less. It was only when he seemed too absent-minded, misplacing tools, when she remembered his pal had been a carpenter.

"Here." She handed him a wrench, regretting she had reminded him of his loss.

"How long are you staying in town?"

"Have another tenant ready to take my place?" He didn't answer.

"I don't know. It can be kind of idyllic down here. Nice little summer town," she said.

"You're so afraid of your ex to leave town for good?"

Afraid. Ha. "No. It made me miserable. He betrayed me, humiliated me. It still hurts. I'm a stickler on loyalty."

"What are you going to do after the season? Find another hospital to work at?"

"I doubt it." She sighed. "A patient died on me—"

"I heard Clay talking about it with Randy."

She scratched her forehead. "You know, it wasn't really him that did it. I'm not sappy. I've seen a lot of death. But…"

"Yeah?"

"His daughter. She was so destroyed over his death. But it's Betsy who sticks with me. She hung herself over the guilt. I remember going back in his room, trying to revive him. She broke down. Shocked."

"And the daughter came after you? Why? You didn't give him the medicine."

"She looked upon me as being in charge."

"So that's it? You give up and work in a boat shack for the rest of your life? Because of one old man and his crazy kid?"

"Excuse me?" She slapped the next bolt and nut in his hand.

"Since you've been in town I've seen you attempt the Heimlich on a whale, save Junior, behead a snake. Doesn't seem like you scare easily. Sure, your assistant hanging herself will drag you down if you've got a big heart. Obviously she wasn't cut out for the work. You are." He glanced at her. "You working for Roger doesn't make much sense."

"Nothing makes sense anymore," she said. "Trying to get rid of me already?"

He took a deep breath. "No. You're not half bad company a quarter of the time. Give me the socket."

She raised her brows.

"Please," he said.

She reached to her right for the socket, then handed it to him.

"No. Other one. Half inch." He handed it back to her and she reached again for the right size. As soon as she let go, it fell out of his hands and rolled on the cement past their heads. He slapped his hand back to catch it and dinged his elbow on the car. She leaned up to twist back and reach for it, forgetting where they were.

"Watch your—"

She winced as she smacked her temple on a pipe. Will caught her back. With narrowed eyes, she silently warned him not to laugh. Crouching lower, she leaned over him and stretched her arm out to grab the socket.

His hand pressed to her back and Kelly was acutely aware of her breaths, bringing her chest closer to his. Their bodies were pressed together, length to length, her soft curves and his hard angles. Practically on top of him, she couldn't distinguish if it was her heart racing or his.

Socket in hand, she inched her way back down him, enduring a personal private torture. His hand was still there. Like a plate of fire, it scorched her skin.

Kelly stopped when her face was above his. Her forearm scratched with grit as she leaned on the cement floor. The socket felt greasy in her hand as she braced it on the floor next to his head. *Swing Swing* by the All American Rejects blared from the radio and she was barely aware of the other people in the garage.

But she was completely attuned to Will. His nearness. His warmth. His hand burning the skin on her back. She felt heavy and lost in his gaze. She imagined it was desire in his eyes and she lowered her face to his, hardly rationalizing her actions.

His brown gaze locked on hers as he watched her lower her lips over his and she considered the intensity of his expression. She hesitated, second-guessing and blushing. *He doesn't want me. He doesn't want anyone. No one would want me.*

She blinked a couple times, hoping to clear her head and save face.

Abort! Abort! You're not good enough, Kelly. Your own husband didn't even want you.

Retreating, she leaned away, but his hand on her back held her. Antsy at their staring contest, she couldn't resist him and brushed her lips against his. It was a soft, gentle, barely-there touch, a skim across his mouth. Kelly frowned at his lack of response. She tried again because she couldn't imagine not doing so. Harder, firmer, hungrier.

In an explosion of action, he pulled her down hard against his chest. He slanted his mouth to kiss her back, spreading his other palm over her back. She gasped and hummed as she deepened her kiss. The socket fell out of her hand as she felt his cheek, then slid her fingers into his hair.

Murmurs, groans, and little noises came from her throat. He held her closer, gripping her shirt at her shoulder blade, clutching her ass through her shorts. He pulled her to lie on top of him.

She caressed his cheek and he turned on his shoulder, trying to reverse the position. His knee and shoulder hit the car and he grunted in pain. She broke the kiss with a light laugh and snuggled closer against his body as he lay back down.

Sucking on his lower lip, Kelly felt his erection. She couldn't wake up from the reality of what they were doing. Like animals. Under her car. She whimpered and slid her tongue next to his in her mouth, feeling trapped and comfortably secure in his grip. Like she belonged there. It was an intoxication she'd never experienced. His thigh spread her legs apart and she was draped over him, not close enough.

"Yeah, let me tell him I'm taking off."

Clay's approaching voice broke through the mist and Kelly leaned up suddenly, smacking her head again.

Oh my God.

Holding the lump on the back of her head, she lay back down on the cold cement as Will scooted out from under the car. Eyes closed, she swallowed hard, still tasting his lips. Breathing harshly, she winced, regretting the torture. *What was I thinking?* She hadn't been. *Holy moly.*

"You alright, man?" Above the car, Clay's voice held a teasing tone. Kelly cringed as she rubbed the goose egg on her head. He had to have seen their legs together.

"Yeah." Will spoke roughly, still catching his breath. "My knee's been bothering me."

"Where's Kelly?" Clay asked.

Kelly bit her lip as she screwed the last nut in the pan. The asshole knew and was rubbing it in!

"Changing her tranny fluid," Will said as she started to crawl out from under the car.

They avoided each other's eyes, guilty like a first crush. Kelly let her hair out of her ponytail to hide the evidence of Will's hand musing it up. She gave a crooked nod to Clay. "Hey."

"How's the tranny coming along?" Clay grinned.

"It's done." She wiped her hands on her shorts and went for the bench to look for her keys. Daring a glance at Will, she found him raising a brow.

Done? Was she done? *What the hell has he done to me?* Kissing? That wasn't kissing. It was like a drug. The withdrawal from him had her aching and wondering as she got in her car with a small smile and drove away.

Emily slithered off of Clay in his bed, aggravated.

Her last mistake had been verified. Clay really wasn't sleeping with Kelly.

Emily was. Clay chucked her chin as he got up to go to the bathroom, leaving her in the sheets.

Over there, on the other side of the wall. She was so close to Kelly, to her prey.

Kill her. Smother her in her sleep. Do it, just DO IT!

Emily flinched at the thoughts in her head. She had to even the score. Killing her wouldn't serve justice and would rob Emily of the satisfaction. She had to reclaim the power Kelly had over her. Kelly couldn't be better.

Emily had screwed up. Kelly didn't want Junior. Kelly didn't want Clay. Men looked at the blonde, wanted her. Emily saw that as plainly as the sky was blue. But Kelly was either clueless or uninterested. Kelly didn't want anyone, it seemed.

Emily smiled at Clay as he returned. No more mistakes. When Kelly found interest in someone, Emily would know. She wasn't going to miss Forty-One when he came along.

Patience would only make the revenge sweeter.

CHAPTER 18

Kelly smiled politely at the groups of tourists window-shopping as she walked the short distance through town. Will's sub in hand, she neared the garage and sighed with anticipation, not knowing which end of the swing his mood would be in. Hopefully, only a hungry one. And most especially, a forgetful one. She didn't need Will to remember what happened a week ago when she was in the garage with him.

Lapse. That's all it was. Right?

Kelly had never felt a kiss like his before. Kissing had always grossed her out before it made sense as a prerequisite to sex. And even then, it had been like a chore. All the spit, and guys could have really bad breath, or not know what to do with their tongue. It was anatomically challenging if one considered it, sizes and fullness of lips, and the length of mouths. Or tongues. A world of physiological oral variety which coupled with the man's experience presented a hit-or-miss gamble of a tolerable kiss or a labor before getting on to the good stuff.

John had been like a guppy.

Will? His lips seemed to have been made for hers.

A sparkling clean Cadillac stood in the first bay and Clay cowered in front of a pant-suited older woman.

"Look, lady, I'm sure—"

Kelly crinkled her forehead at his irritable tone. It was foreign. If anything, he was slick with the ladies. Old, young, fat, thin. He was a ladies' man through and through.

"*Lady*? Don't you talk to me like that. I'm not one of your little sluts. You've got no respect—"

"Only giving you the same courtesy you've ever given me, Mrs. Downs." Clay leaned right back in her face. "I'm sure—"

"I don't care if you're sure of anything. Can you fix my car or not?" Mrs. Downs smoothed the hem of her jacket and flipped her hair. She seemed to be going for a Sharon Osbourne look. Pissy, money and impatient.

Kelly hadn't seen the woman up close before. Mrs. Downs? The name seemed familiar.

"No, not me. I mean, I—"

"This is ridiculous." Mrs. Downs shook her hands at Clay. "Where is Mr. Parker?"

Kelly noticed the flat tire on the car.

Clay crumpled his features. "*Mr. Parker*?"

"Mr. Parker," she repeated. "Your employer. The owner of this garage. Unless he's gone bankrupt already."

"You mean your *son*?" Clay lost the irritable edge to his voice and his yell was an adverse reaction for the woman, someone likely accustomed to being revered in Churchston, never questioned. Kelly stood speechless with the sub in her hand, too mesmerized by the conversation to intercept.

"My son is dead," Mrs. Downs clarified with a stern expression. "Dead!" Her voice shrilled and Kelly jumped at the thud from Will's office. No doubt something thrown at the wall. Kelly realized what the showdown was. Mrs. Downs was Will's mother. And it was an understatement to think she only disowned him.

Psycho.

Clay twitched his mouth and ran his free hand through his hair. "Mrs. Downs—"

"Can you fix my car or not?" she demanded coolly.

"I could, but—"

Kelly cleared her throat as Clay figured his response. Appalled and angry, and she was tired of standing there awkwardly with the sub. *Who does this woman think she is?* "Are you blind? How the hell is he supposed to fix your car with his arm in a cast?"

Clay spun to face her in surprise. Mrs. Downs turned slowly and stared at her like royalty weighing the peon. Kelly pursed her lips, daring the woman to judge her.

"Excuse me?" She eyed Kelly from head to toe and with the downturn of her mouth, she wasn't impressed.

"I've stated the obvious." Kelly took a deep breath of the grimy garage air. "Will here?" She waved the sub box in her hand.

"He's—" Clay started.

"Who is this?" Mrs. Downs demanded.

"Uh, Kelly. She delivers for Alan. Runs Roger's boat hut."

Kelly didn't care for the prim woman's obvious disapproval of her attire. Most of her hair was in a ponytail. Her shorts hadn't been stained with pizza sauce yet and her tank top was mostly clean, one little tear from the kayak earlier. *Go to hell, Mrs. Ralph Lauren Sharon Osbourne, I'll dress however I want. Tomboys are people, too.* "Where's Will?"

Clay pointed to the office.

"I'll tell you where Mr. Parker is," Mrs. Downs said. "He's no doubt drunk. Drunk and filthy and disgusting like his father was. He's wasting away in his little office, no doubt drinking and being nothing but a bum."

Crashes sounded in the office again. Kelly's face fell expressionless and Clay winced. It sounded like Will had punched the wall.

Talk about dysfunctional.

"He can't even run his own garage. His employees are as insolent and lazy as he—" She glared at Clay as he opened his mouth. "Mr. Parker?" Mrs. Downs faced Kelly. "Mr. Parker should be in hell, young lady. He's wasting away like his good-for-nothing father when he should be dead."

Kelly clenched her jaw as her pulse throbbed faster. Having heard the stories of Delores Downs, she couldn't have been prepared for the wrath of this Cruella DeVille. She wished her own son in hell? Stunned and enraged, Kelly fought to keep her patience, mind her own business.

Mrs. Downs tapped her heart dramatically. "My son should be alive."

"Shoulda woulda coulda." Kelly was nonplused. Not so much as a tease but a blunt reminder that nothing could change the past. "He's in the office then?"

Mrs. Downs glared and Clay shook his head with alarm.

"How dare you sass me," she sputtered.

"How dare I?" Kelly smiled without mirth. "I open my mouth and out come words. Tell him I'll get the change later."

Moving to set the sub on the desk behind Clay, Kelly only had thoughts of escaping the chaos. Dad had raised the Newland offspring to turn the other cheek, be the bigger person. But Kelly knew herself better and the old Botox woman was only an instigator for losing her patience. She didn't want to make enemies in town, but the woman was asking for it. *Someone* was bound to put her in her place someday, but she didn't feel it was her duty.

"This is like his father. Can't even run a business," Mrs. Downs said as Kelly came nearer to deposit the food. "I come here to have my car fixed and he can't even appreciate the revenue from performing his services."

"Looks to me it's your tire needs fixing, not the car. You'd rather see your son rot in hell but you'd expect him to work on your vehicle?" Kelly couldn't hide the dark humor in her comment.

"No, oh, no. Of course not. He doesn't even have the nerve to face me after he let my Matthew die. No, he'll hide and drink and waste away like his father."

A couple of thuds and a swearing from the office sounded.

"Then why are you here?" That did it. Kelly did *not* like this woman.

"Kelly…" Clay stepped closer to intercept Mrs. Downs' escalating fury.

"It's thirteen miles from my mechanic's garage. I wouldn't come to this filthy place if I didn't have to."

"Get someone to push it to the fancy place then."

Mrs. Downs glared at Kelly. "Of course. Because he's too much of a wasted coward to do his job. And him." Her red-clawed finger stabbed at Clay. "He—"

"Has a goddamn cast on his arm," Kelly said. "A flat?" She looked at the car again. "All this bitching for a flat tire?" Her eyes went skyward. "Clay, you owe me." She went to the car and slid the lift pads under the carriage with her sneakered foot.

"What is she doing?" Mrs. Downs said.

"Kelly?" Clay followed her.

"I'm fixing her flat. Plugs are in the second drawer, right?" She pushed the button to raise the lift.

"What is she doing?" Mrs. Downs said again. "She's going to scratch it. Does she even know what she's doing? I thought you said she delivers for Alan."

Kelly cranked the radio louder, letting Santana drone out the woman. Pop off the wheel and stick in a rod of rubber. Not rocket science. She'd seen the guys do it plenty of times. It couldn't have taken more than five minutes, but it had been five minutes too long for Kelly to endure Mrs. Downs' presence in the garage. She wiped her hands on her shorts and grinned at Clay as the Cadillac left the garage.

"I'm going to buy you diamonds and candy and sugar you like a princess. Perfect timing. I was about to wring her neck. He went straight in the office to kill something and left me out here to get rid of her," Clay said.

"Ha ha. Anytime." She was moved. Even though Will and Clay weren't the friends they once were, Clay still had his back.

"I can't believe she actually came here. I would have done it and gotten her out of here if I could have. So he wouldn't have seen her."

A few more punches at the wall sounded from the office and Kelly winced.

"His sub will be cold," she said and turned the radio down to its usual loudness.

"I can't believe she had the balls to even come here. She's wicked, Kel. Evil. A bitch from—"

Will burst from the office. Except for the scant few moments under her car when she had kissed him, Will had a default ogre hatred look. She was sure it was residue from the Marines. Kelly never wanted to witness the fury he emitted as he exited his office.

"What the fuck were you thinking?" he roared at Clay.

"Hey man—"

"Don't 'hey man' me! What were you thinking?"

"What was I supposed to do?" Clay offered his hands in a truce. "I'm in a fucking cast. I came back from a break and it was parked in here. She wouldn't even let me tell her—"

"Why the hell did you let her in here?" Will swore and punched at the air. "You got shits for brains?" He grabbed Clay's shirt at the neck and pulled him closer. Kelly was mesmerized by his force, the tension in his neck as he clenched his teeth. Yet she wasn't afraid. Rather, she worried about him, like watching a bomb swell and rattle before detonation.

CHAPTER 19

Kelly walked toward the front door of the garage after Will came out from his office. "Sub's on the desk," she called back quietly to let Will vent to Clay.

"You." It could have been a bear's growl. Will let go of Clay and went after her. He clutched her arm in a vise grip and pulled her back to his office.

"Yo, Will. Hey man. Don't take it out on her. She was trying to help. Hey man, she didn't—"

Will slammed the door in Clay's face. In the office, Kelly smacked at Will's hand gripping her shoulder. He swore and let go of her forcefully.

"Get the hell out of my way." She went for the door to leave.

"You had no right to do that!" He stopped her at the door with the bulk of his strong body.

"Get out of my way," Kelly repeated, guessing his temper wouldn't simmer for a few months. She had never seen him so mad and wanted nothing to do with it.

"You had no right to get in my business!" he yelled and put his hands on her shoulders again.

"Get your hands off me." Kelly slapped him when he pushed. In a whirl, his face twisted with rage. He grabbed her hand and spun her to slam her back against the door.

"Will!" Clay pounded on the other side of the door. "Will, let her go!"

The thudding competed with the throbbing in her head from Will's force and the adrenaline racing in her blood.

"You had no right to do that." Will's voice growled with fury.

"To do what?" she snapped back. "Fix her flat? I did you a favor. He's in a cast. You're back here brooding. I saved your day." Someday, she swore, someone was going to teach him he couldn't explode. But it wasn't going to be her.

"Saved my day." He scoffed. "Saved my day. She doesn't belong here. Never. She doesn't belong anywhere near me. She doesn't have the right to say my name. To think of me. I won't allow her to come near me. And I'll be goddamned if she comes to my goddamned garage for me to fix her tire!"

"*I* fixed her tire." Kelly shoved his grip from her and rubbed her wrist.

"She doesn't belong in my life. You had no right to fix her tire here."

"Boo hoo. I didn't see Clay getting rid of her. No way you were going to tell her to leave."

Will paced the office, his chiseled features still twisted in anger. "Tell her to leave? I'll never speak to her until the day I die." His big hand connected with a cup of pens and it went flying. "Which won't come fast enough for her!"

Kelly braced herself against the door as he got in front of her face.

"You wanted me to go out there and speak to her?"

Beneath the anger in his hooded eyes, Kelly could feel his pain, and wished she could stop it for him, put it away. Like a wounded bear, he was all bark and no bite.

"If you weren't a wimp you would. Make you the bigger person. Other than physically, of course, but that's probably obvious. I mean, she's what? Five-two, one-twenty? A little poodle of a person."

He punched the door above her head. Miracle alone it didn't shatter the glass. "*Wimp*? You don't have a clue what you're talking about."

She swallowed and fought the need to reach out and stroke his cheek. Instead, she feigned boredom. "She gave birth to you. Now she has a mental defect and doesn't like the fact you're alive. There are all kinds of crazy people in the world. Get over it."

"Get over it?"

Kelly raised her brows. "There an echo in here?"

"You think you're so goddamn smart. Let me tell you something. You've got no fucking idea what it's like to not have a mother. Even an evil bitch like her. You've got no idea what it's like to have your own parent wishing you were dead."

Stunned, she blinked a couple times. "No idea, huh? No idea. My mom died giving birth to me. I know exactly what it's like to not have a mother."

"That's different. That doesn't count." He pounded his fist once on the door next to her head.

"Doesn't count?" Kelly shoved him back without moving him. "My mom dying doesn't count?"

"You couldn't control that."

"And you could control her leaving your dad?"

Will rubbed at his mouth.

My God, he must have always thought she left because of him.

He paced again. "She wishes I was dead! Matt was supposed to live and I wasn't. She hates me because it was him, not me. She hates me, they all do, for letting Matt die.

"You can't change it now!" she yelled. "Why would you spend the rest of your time worrying about why she hates you? What's it to you? Cut your losses. You don't need her." Kelly watched the play of angry emotions on his face, knowing deep down, he needed something, someone. Everyone did.

"I don't need anyone." He kicked a plastic chair and it cracked against the wall.

"Yeah. There's the spirit. Brood. Mope. Be a damn idiot. You don't need anybody." She gave him a cheesy sneer and thumbs-up. "I said you don't need *her.*"

He grimaced at her sarcasm and looked around the room wildly. He locked his attention on the bottle of whiskey on the shelf next to her.

"Oops." Her elbow tipped it and he punched the door above her head.

"You little smartass…"

She looked to the ceiling.

"You enjoy pissing me off, don't you? You get a sick kick out of pissing me off." His face bent closer to hers, anger spewing like heat. "You've got nothing better to do than to—"

"Cut the crap. We both know you'd rather take a run to vent than drink."

His lips twisted like he wanted to scream. She almost wished he would—his face, his body, all of him, shook with such tension she thought he would burst.

"You are the most wicked, manipulative person I've ever met."

"At least I'm good at it."

He clutched her shoulder.

"Isn't it easier when you're mad at me instead of missing Matt?" She had an urge again to reach to him, hug him, touch him. A heavy cracking in her heart made her care more than she could afford to.

Anger sparkled in his eyes as though he wanted to rip something into a million pieces. He searched her face and seemed to defuse.

At his silence, she raised her brows. "What the heck, Will. Arguing with you can take my mind off how miserable my life can be."

He wrinkled his forehead in disbelief. "You think *your* life is miserable? What, because your husband found a better piece of ass? Cry me a goddamn river."

She failed to move him as she shoved, her sympathy and honest concern for his suffering switching to blistering defense. "That's not— that's none of your business!"

"What's the matter, don't like the taste of your own medicine? You had no right to get involved with my mother. She wants me to rot in hell!"

Miserable? She took a deep breath and bit her lip. *Am I really miserable?* Will clenched his fists and she traced the taut lines of his muscles flexing. Maybe he was calling her on it. Miserable? No, she wasn't fooling him, and she realized she should stop trying to fool herself. She might be confused and lost, but she wasn't miserable.

Not around him, at least.

Guilt lingered around the memories of Norbert's death, his daughter's rage, and Betsy's suicide. Anger flitted at the image of John cheating on her. She was too strong to linger in the past. Shoulda woulda coulda, she'd told Delores. She couldn't change anything that happened in Atlanta, and reflecting on her own advice, she resolved to move on.

Kelly took the roll of paper towels off his desk and grabbed his hand. As she wiped the blood off his knuckles from punching the wall, he tried to escape her grip. She tugged his hand back. Did he know how it easy it was to get an infection? Silly man.

She cleared her throat. "You know, scientifically, I don't think that's possible. Hell's supposed to be these hot flaming pits of fire, right? If something's going to *rot* in hell, it couldn't be too hot, only warm. And you need moisture for the decomposers to actually *rot* anything which was once alive. All the moisture would have evaporated."

She glanced up to see his attention was fixated on her hands cleaning his.

"If anything, you could incinerate in hell, if there is such a place. But it doesn't sound as demeaning as *rot in hell*."

He gave her a blank look as she finished cleaning his knuckles.

"My bad. You were saying?" She waved her hand permissively as if he had forgotten his cue. "She wants you to rot in hell."

"You just said I couldn't say that." He studied the cuts she had tended to.

"It's still America, isn't it? You can say anything you want. It sounds stupid. How about burn in hell? Has a nice ring to it."

"She can go to hell. Better?"

Kelly gave him an iffy look. "If you think you *aren't* going to hell, then yeah. But if you're not convinced you could go to some kind of heaven, then you'll be in some kind of hell. So then you're wishing her to be near you again. I thought you wanted to *avoid* her."

She bit her lip. *What the hell did I just say?* She was reaching for a distraction. True, she had a habit of rambling, especially when aggravated. But she usually made some sense. Maybe a kiss would help. He seemed to like it before. The heat they had generated would definitely be a distraction. Or maybe she'd kiss him for herself. She licked her lower lip in hesitation. Why she was so intent on distracting him out of his sadness madness, she didn't want to know. But she couldn't stand to see him hurting.

His gaze drifted to a picture on the desk of him and Matt fishing from Randy's boat, and with the flash of an eye he left the anger and fell into a pit of sadness again. "Why are you even here?"

"Brought the sub you ordered. You owe me seven fifty," she said. Hot and cold, hot and cold. It went back and forth, her feisty and yelling back and then calming and smartass. All of it raw and angry, giving her a strange thrill to be with him.

He reached in his pocket and gave her eight ones without looking at her.

Kelly took the bills and watched him gaze at the picture. It was quite the contrast. He stood there, angry and upset. His every muscle was taut, the tanned skin stretched in bulges of his strength. But she could only see and feel the pain and loneliness in his expression, those damnable feelings he fought to bottle and lock.

"What, no tip?" She stood with her back leaning against the wall next to the door and waited for his smoky eyes to burn at her.

"You think you deserve a tip?"

"Why not? I delivered on time *and* fixed a flat for you. I didn't think you were this cheap." She had to glance away, his steeled eyes searing her.

"You've got some nerve. You barge in here, get in the middle of my business and have the nerve to want a tip from me like you're something special."

"Common courtesy." Kelly chanced a brief look at him as he approached her. Playing with fire, she tried not to bite her lip.

"No wonder he left you. You think you're something special but you're nothing but a loud-mouthed, smartass, annoying pain in the dick."

"Yeah, well, no wonder your mom didn't want you either." Her heart hammered against her ribs as she glared back at him, his words stinging too much to censor her thoughts. "You're nothing but a despicable heartless bastard!"

Will closed the space between them and shoved her against the wall again, squeezing his hand on her shoulder, the other in a fist above her head. "What did you say?"

"Will! Open up!" Clay rattled the doorknob to open the door a crack as Will leaned over Kelly as though he'd like to choke her. "Will!"

He slammed the door shut in Clay's face. "What did you say?" It was a fueled whisper.

"You're a despicable heartless bastard." Kelly spoke the words slowly with a matching expression of hatred at his face inches from hers. His fingers tightened on her skin and she felt her heart race. Tingles shot her flesh where his calloused hands lingered. Looking down, she noticed the exotic difference between her smooth, clean skin to his tanner rougher hide. She felt small next to him.

So close to him, she was frozen in his power. The anger, the hurt, the testosterone calling at her body, the masculinity overwhelming in his grease- and dirt-grimed shirt, stretched at his muscular frame. It was then, with him trapping her to the wall, that Kelly wanted to whimper. Desire and sympathy collided in her mind and she fought the heat and need to touch him.

"You never know when to shut up, do you?"

Her mouth opened then shut quickly, regretting her harsh words. Bastard? *Did I really call him a* bastard? Guilt tickled at her mind, but he had berated her unjustly as well. She concentrated on maintaining a solemn mask of annoyance, hoping her treasonous need for him to be closer wouldn't show. Of all times, of all men for her to desire, Kelly didn't want it to be then, when she was most vulnerable. She didn't want it to be Will.

She refused to raise her eyes to his and winced when he sighed heavily.

"Well don't start now," he said and covered her lips with his. Her mouth parted in surprise as he demanded her response, holding her shoulder and leaning her back to the wall.

She kissed him back, his lips too insistent for her to resist. He slanted his mouth closer to hers, sliding his tongue next to hers and pressing the length of his body against hers to the wall.

Shocked and lost in thought at the feel of him on her, Kelly matched his forceful want. She pressed her palms to his chest, felt his heart racing in tempo with her own. When his hand left her shoulder to snake around her waist and pull her closer, his elbow knocked the empty whiskey bottle on the shelf to crash on the floor.

"Will!" Clay yelled after the tinkles of the breaking glass. He opened the door an inch and Will slapped it shut without pausing the kiss. He reached to grab the hair at the back of her head and held her closer.

His leg slid between hers and she sucked on his lower lip, reveling in the feel of his body intimately strong against the center of her heat. Wrapping her leg around his, her knee sent the pile of wrenches on the chair clanging to the floor.

"Will!" Clay pounded on the door and the doorknob rattled, but Will's hand shot from her head to brace the door shut, and he deepened the kiss.

"Open the door!" It was Randy, now, outside the office, alarm in his tone.

"Kelly's in there. He's pissed," Clay explained. "I think he's being rough on her—"

"Will!" Randy pounded on the door and Kelly gasped for air as Will held her closer, almost crushing her chest. She didn't want to be anywhere else but in his hold.

"Open the door, Will!"

Kelly groped one hand backwards to feel for the doorknob and twisted the lock shut. Free now, she slipped her arms around his neck and clung to him as he picked her up, holding her against his erection.

He struggled to stand steady and stumbled to the closest filing cabinet to set her on the edge. A box of wheel bearings knocked over and emptied. The pieces fell one by one, the heavy metal thumping to the floor as he pillaged her lips and slipped his palm under her shirt.

"Will!" Clay pounded on the door. "He's going to hurt her."

Kelly moaned as Will toyed with her lips. *Hurt me? He'd never hurt me.* He was strong and tough but his hands were only gentle and reverent on her. Gentle and hungry. She kissed him harder.

"No. He won't." Randy that time. "What happened?"

"The bitch came in."

"Kelly?"

"No. His mom."

Will's throat rumbled in pleasure as Kelly thread her fingers through his hair.

"His mom came in and he went nuts and he's taking it out on her." Clay pounded again. "Will!"

"He wouldn't hurt her," Randy said, though and he seemed unconvinced and rattled the door knob.

"The way they're always arguing? He's an asshole. He's going to hurt her," Clay said.

Kelly smiled in the kiss as she felt Will's hand inch up the bare skin of her back. She felt safe and wanted. Right where she belonged. *He wouldn't hurt me.*

Hurt. She let the word bounce in her mind, trying to remember why it mattered so much. *How could he hurt me?* she worried, nervous she was going too fast.

He framed her face and she lost the nagging doubt. So gentle and loving.

Loving. *Love?*

Will had said love was a myth. He didn't think women were anything but bedmates. His words came rushing back to her and her heart cracked even as he stoked the fire in it.

He would only hurt me. Kelly put her hands to his chest, almost in disbelief she was going to stop him. *He could only hurt me if he breaks my heart.* And he wouldn't break it if he never had it. It was the hardest thing she'd ever done, but she pulled back from him.

Will frowned.

"I can't," she whispered.

He shook his head. In doubt more than in protest.

"I'm, I'm…" She lost momentum as he kissed her softly, sending the blanket of desire over her mind.

She pushed him back. "I can't do this. It's not fair."

"What?" Will's eyes were intense on hers.

"It's physical. Hormones." Kelly stood up, torn between wanting him and knowing it would be doomed. Doom on her end because she would care. It'd be another bout of sex for him. A pastime. "I'm not thinking."

"I am!" Will whispered harshly as she backed away in the tiny office.

She shook her head. "I'm not looking for a one-night stand. I'm not an easy piece of ass."

"You want me to propose or something?" he mocked.

She glared at him. "No. I want to matter. I'm…I'm looking for love."

He threw his arms in the air.

"I'm sorry. Obviously I'm attracted to you." She doubted he'd ever heard a woman apologize for such a phenomenon before.

"You lead me on and tease me… And—"

"I said I was sorry. That should ease your ego! I didn't mean to want you. Or like you. You're so freaking infuriating!"

"You are the most confusing and irritating woman I've ever met."

"I didn't plan this!" Kelly never felt like such a fool. "I got carried away. It was physical. And I want more. This would be a rebound. I can't."

"Yeah?" Will turned to glower at her. "What do you want?"

"Someone to love me." It was a quiet, sheepish, timid declaration. "And you've made it perfectly clear you think it's bullshit."

"Because it is."

"Well." Kelly crossed her arms to guard off her vulnerability, missing his kisses and feeling like a coward. "That settles that. You only want a casual piece of ass and I'm not one. See you around."

Will stepped forward as if to reach out to her but shook his head. He ripped the office door open and stormed into the garage. Clay and Randy followed him, then turned to Kelly in the office. Speechless, they fumbled in silence for a second, then went off looking for something to busy themselves with.

Good riddance? Kelly held her chin up despite feeling like a fool. She was the idiot. She had to be at fault because it had been her own delusion Will was thinking with something other than his dick. Without another word, she walked out of the garage.

CHAPTER 20

A couple weeks later, not far from the townhouse, Will dismissed Randy from the stone house.

"See you tomorrow?" Randy called from the front door.

Will sighed. "Sure."

Boat ride on the lake. Why not? He had nothing better to do. It wasn't too late to go for a run but he sat on the couch instead.

Cause and effect. It was all her fault.

Will sat in front of the infomercial on TV and let his mind wander. Kelly had snapped him out of his zombie status. She had ignited him. She had annoyed him while she had warmed him. And she wanted to be loved.

He rolled his eyes, irritated she wanted nothing to do with him because he wasn't sappy and stupid and he didn't believe in such an idiotic thing as love. As soon as someone said those words, it was ammunition to leave. No one had ever loved him before. Except Matt, in a brotherly-friend way. And he was gone. To give a part of himself to someone, only meant that part would die when the other was gone. The pain wasn't worth it.

He had never felt so alive than when he had been with her. Even to argue with her. *It was for sex*. What'd she say? Hormones? Physical? Yeah, it was. And it was great. No reason to get stupid and pretend about love. So he had tried to find it again. Kelly was another ordinary average woman. He didn't see why she had to be so special.

He had tried. He started talking to women again, engaging in conversations, flirting. And it had been so tiring. They laughed too giddily. Some of them were so uneducated it was scary. Yeah, they were hot and promiscuous, every bachelor's dream. But it wasn't working for him.

He hadn't even been interested. Or turned on. And he hadn't felt alive and free like he did with Kelly. He'd been bored or annoyed. Too exposed. Like a chore to prove a point to himself. The couple women who tried to kiss him, he had fought to not run away, and had made lame excuses to escape.

But he'd been repairing the friendships he had let fester. Clay and Randy, they were bonding. He had Kelly to thank for them. It was slow and still hard, but he was easing a little, trying to care about the world again. Baby steps.

The following day, Kelly smiled at Randy and Clay as they came by the kayak hut at lunchtime.

"Hey." She waved them into the hut to hide from the sun.

"We already talked to Alan. You can come," Clay said, scanning the beach for babes.

She looked to Randy for clarification.

"Boat ride. Skiing. Tonight on the lake."

"Oh." *Would Will be there?* She forced herself to smile despite such a depressing thought. *Why the hell should I think about him?* "Okay, I guess."

It was a decision she regretted until the last kayak was on the rack at the end of her shift. It would be torture to see him with another woman on a boat. Rubbing it in when he had no idea what he did to her. Oh, it was stupid.

"Why do I have to care?" Kelly said to Heather on the way home to change before Clay took her to the marina. With frequent calls and texts, she had kept her friend apprised of her woes. "Two kisses. Groping. And I'm an idiot about him."

"Casual sex, Kel. Not the end of the world."

Kelly shook her head. "It would be a rebound."

"It sounds like you are already."

"What do you mean?"

"Well, you obviously have feelings for him. I bet you don't even think about John. You fell kinda fast. Except Will's not on the same boat with you. Find someone else to fall for."

Fall for? Had it come to that? Already? She groaned. Did she think about him all day long? Check. Did she find simple petty things which reminded her of him? Check. She had fallen for him like a tree crashing to the floor of a forest.

Damn, I'm pathetic. And he thought she was a body to poke like any other female in the world.

"But he'll be on the same boat with me tonight."

"That's the spirit!" Heather said.

"No. Literally. We're going on a boat ride with a group."

"Kelly, you're worrying about nothing. It's a crush. You'll survive."

Kelly didn't doubt she would survive the boat ride. And it started out well. Joking and goofing off with the guys. Ignoring Will as much as she could without seeming like a brat. The girls had given her snotty looks but they were expected since she was the girl who was also one of the guys. She might have been shyer and quieter than her usual quiet and shy but she had dissected it enough to be calm about it.

A boat ride. With the sunset. On the lake. Water skiing. She had always loved water skiing. From the corner of her eye she watched Jaycee stand close to Will.

Serve you well, Will Parker. Kelly imagined Jaycee had a whole slew of STDs to share.

And with such thoughts, Kelly knew she had no right to act so immature. It was the smartest thing she had done in a long time, to cut him loose before it went any further.

In the cabin of Randy's boat, Will stared mutely at the wall in front of him. Boredom was the runner-up to his irritation. Jaycee snuggled at his side like a leech. His temper itched at him. Claustrophobia swelled in the cabin. And he was pissed.

Randy hugging Kelly so tight. It felt a lot like jealousy and he detested himself for it. Will had gotten used to Clay's behavior around Kelly. He knew Clay didn't matter to her.

Neither do I. Not enough, anyway.

Will fidgeted on the couch, recalling how Kelly's body was so lean in her bathing suit instead of obese like Daisy's, or too plump like Jaycee's.

"Why don't you take your shirt off?" Jaycee said and traced her finger down his arm.

Because there's an ugly scar that will freak you out. On second thought, maybe she'd leave him alone if he showed her the scar. It wasn't pretty. Jaycee was probably a squeamish girl. Kelly hadn't been. She hardly noticed it when he had taken his shirt off, had hardly flinched when she cleaned up the cuts on his knuckles. Blood, gore, she could handle it.

Jaycee stood up. "I'll be back in a sec. I'm going to get a couple more beers."

Take a couple hours.

As he regretted coming on the boat, they lurched to a sudden stop. He wasn't sure who was driving. They had all been taking turns. But whoever had been at the wheel last was speeding, slowing, turning sharply, and speeding again. Joy riding. Goofing off. Everything stilled from the whiplash of the jerky stop and yells shouted overhead. Will climbed up top.

"What the fuck?" Clay yelled from the speedboat idling next to them. Will looked out from Randy's boat and wondered what the commotion was about. Clay had been driving for whoever had wanted to ski. Randy's boat was the limping-along yacht Matt had willed to him. They had a group of twenty or so peers drinking and mingling on the crowded deck.

"Where is she?" Clay sounded sick and Will scanned the surface of the water.

"What's going on?" Randy said as he came out of the bathroom.

"Who the fuck was driving?" Clay's face was taut in fear and fury and worry.

"What's going on?" Will's instincts sent his heart racing. Clay had been pulling the skis. Everyone else was on the yacht, drinking and relaxing. Everyone except one sweet little sassy face…

Will's pulse thudded with adrenaline at the stress written on the men's faces.

"I don't know." Clay's voice strained and he started to turn the boat around, away from Randy's. "I don't fucking know! Who was driving?" he shouted again at Will on the yacht's deck.

"I don't know. We all were. I was down below. What's going on?" Randy's confusion was a duplicate to Will's as he came to stand next to him.

Clay shook his head furiously. "You went right for her."

"Clay!" Will stepped to the edge of the boat. "What happened?"

Clay swore and shook his head as he started the cruiser away slowly. "She fell off the skis. You went right for her."

Someone quieted the music and a nervous apprehension claimed the atmosphere of the party. Heads pivoted as people viewed the water.

Will didn't bother to take a head count. With the queasy uneasiness in his stomach, he knew who before he noticed her absence. "Kelly!" he yelled out to the water and strained his eyes to see, his lungs not pumping fast enough.

Randy turned the boat around, the engine low and the propellers off as they searched. Everyone called out for her as the sun set.

"Bastard." Kelly clenched her teeth as she swam. "No wonder his mom left him. He's the spawn of the devil."

She didn't mean it but she had to focus on something before the shock and fear took the better of her.

"Asshole. Selfish, womanizing, irresponsible imbecile." Her teeth chattered every syllable.

Arm after arm, she stroked for the shore, ignoring the pain in her leg as she tried to survive. She'd be damned if she went near the boats again. Drunken stupid idiots. Every one of them. She'd never make it to shore but she wasn't going near the boat. It was getting darker, but it wasn't night yet. She was still visible. Maybe another boater would find her.

Are there really gators out here?

She fell off the skis and what did they do? Drove right for her. Thoughts sprouted in her mind, reminding her how close it had been. What if she hadn't reacted fast enough? What if she hadn't dived deep enough? What if…

Shaking, the shock started to take over and she tried to focus.

Marine, my ass. She didn't really know if Will had been driving. Didn't know who'd been driving. Since he was a Marine and should know the ways of the water, she doubted he had been. He wouldn't drive like an old lady on speed. And he wasn't drunk. In fact, she had hardly ever seen him drink. It was amazing how half the town was convinced he was a raging drunk. His label most likely constructed on the usual gossip and heavy assumption on account of his dad.

But he had been on the boat. He could have been watching the drunk idiots and be responsible. But no, he had been too busy getting his precious casual sex with a slut somewhere.

Kelly didn't know who had been driving. She didn't want to know. She blamed Will and tried to hate him for it because if she didn't, she would have to imagine who had accidentally almost killed her. And whoever he or she was, well, she'd have her brothers kick his ass after she did.

"Cock-serving, arrogant, angry, ego maniac bastard!" Her teeth chattered like a wind-up toy. Water stung at the slash on her leg. *How bad is it?*

"Kelly!" Will's voice bellowed from a distance.

"Go to hell," she whispered, shaking again. Her eyes rolled at the irony. "*Incinerate* in hell."

She turned around and experienced a sensation of déjà vu as Randy's boat approached her, everyone on the deck yelling her name.

"Idiots." She spat the lake water out of her mouth and checked how far away the shore was. Hours of swimming. She wasn't strong enough. And if she didn't make herself known, the drunks would run over her again. *No.* She tried to stop shaking, annoyed that she couldn't. I *am the idiot for coming along.*

Kelly knew when to fight her fights and admit her losses and she was never going to make it to shore by herself.

"Kelly!" It was Clay.

She didn't want to face Will. "Over here, Clay!" Even though he was a doofus, *he* had had the common sense to not run her over.

Randy's yacht drifted closer than the cruiser. Increasingly closer. Too close for her comfort.

"Coming back for the kill?" she yelled back.

"Shut the fucking boat off," Will ordered Randy. They pulled up to her and she glowered at Will leaning over the edge. If he hadn't looked so worried, she would have thought he was smiling.

"Hang on."

"To what, dumbass? I'm treading water."

He hoisted his leg over the edge of the boat, ready to jump in.

"Don't be stupid. It'll hurt your knee. Throw the ladder over."

"Kelly!" Clay said as he rounded the cruiser close.

"Are you okay?" Will asked after he tossed the ladder down. Brent, the barista from the coffee shop, leaned over to watch the commotion and Will shoved him out of the way.

She climbed up the ladder and took consolation in the fact her limbs still worked.

"Marine my ass," Kelly said as she stood up on the boat. She still shook. A bold slash of red streaked her calf, the diluted blood streaming steadily from the gash.

"Fuck." Will wiped his hand over her mouth.

Kelly realized her lips were trembling. "Drive for shore," she said to Randy. He paled and went to do so.

"Ah, come on. It was an accident. We're having a party out here," Jaycee whined.

"Shut up," Will and Kelly said in unison. He stepped forward, eyeing her cut.

She pointed at him angrily. "Back. Off."

"Oh my God. That's disgusting." Alyssa grabbed her stomach as though she was going to puke.

"Kelly, take it easy," Will said and followed her.

She had a slight limp as she made for the mini bar. She left a slick trail of blood in her wake on the old wood decking. "Take it easy? Piece of cake, asshole. You get run over by a boat and tell me how easy it is."

"Eww." Kendra squirmed at the blood.

"Don't be a baby now," Kelly said. "Some Marine you are." She glowered at Will.

"I wasn't driving!" Will reached out to steady her.

"Just as bad," she mumbled and poked her hand in the cooler.

"What'd you say?" He came to her side.

"Nothing. Don't touch me."

"Maybe you should sit down," Randy said from the wheel.

Kelly ignored him.

"You're going to have to get amputated now." Daisy winced at the blood on the floor.

"What happened?" Brent came closer before Will pushed him back.

"I can see your bone." Jaycee ogled the cut.

"The hell you can." Kelly rooted through the ice. "It's a superficial compound laceration which will only need a first-degree closure." With vodka in hand, she leaned over to inspect the wound. "I'm lucky it didn't hit the tendon." She stuck her foot on the table and opened the bottle with her teeth.

"What are you doing?" Daisy jumped up with alarm.

Kelly trickled the alcohol on the cut, and winced with a hiss at the sting.

"You're going to infect it!" Jaycee shrieked.

"Eww." Alyssa again.

"It's to prevent infection." She tied a decorative scarf from the cushions at her knee as a tourniquet. "I worked in the fucking ER. Leave it to me, huh?" She put her foot down and took a healthy drink from the bottle. Coughing at the burn of the liquor, she screwed the bottle shut then faced Randy at the wheel.

"This is close enough." She shoved the vodka bottle in her bikini bottom at the small of her back.

Will frowned. "What the hell are you doing?"

"Oh. The *drunk* wants his vodka? I'll reimburse." She limped to the edge of the deck. "Don't want to end the party."

"What the hell are you doing?" He grabbed her arm and she twisted free.

"I'm going home. Far away from you IDIOTS! You could have killed me!"

"Kelly—"

"Oh, don't be such a baby," Jaycee said. "It was an accident. Kinda dark out now, if ya'll hadn't noticed."

Kelly glared at her. Will took her arm again, and she yanked it away. "Don't touch me! I said I don't want to end the party. Go back to screwing with your little, your little, whatever. Don't mind my inconvenient near-death experience, which"— she leaned around him to smirk at Jaycee—"was only a mere accident."

"We're done?" Kendra pouted from Brent's lap. He was high and she was whiny. "Because she can't figure out how to ski we're done for the night?"

"This is my fault?" Will focused on Kelly.

"More or less."

"I wasn't even at the wheel!" Which was something Kelly didn't want him to elaborate on.

"We were kind of preoccupied." Jaycee licked her lips.

"Precisely." She met Will's eyes before stepping on the edge. "Pardon the interruption."

"Kelly!" Will said with his jaw clenched.

She jumped in and started swimming the remainder of the distance to shore.

"Can we go back out now?" Alyssa asked Randy.

"What the hell are you doing?" Will yelled at Kelly.

"Funny. I never noticed you were slow before," she yelled back. "I'm going home."

"You think you can swim the way back?"

"As long you idiots keep the props and anchors away from me!" She stroked further from them as the sound of hip hop resumed on the radio. Minutes later came the patterned splashes of Will swimming toward her. *It would have kicked ass if I made it all the way without him catching up. Bruise his ego. It would have been the highlight of the night.* But her arms were tired. And she hadn't stopped shaking. The booze helped, but she couldn't stop.

She appreciated he at least seemed smart enough to not say anything when he met her stroke for stroke. *He gets me.* Will was intelligent enough to give her space to vent in silence as she swam and worked out her shock and anger.

Kelly rejoiced when she finally touched sand and slimy algae with her toes, relieved to be on the ground again. She walked in the direction for the duplex, some, oh, four miles away. *What a hell of a night.*

"Stop." Will rushed around to stand in front of her, not even out of breath.

She stepped around him.

"Stop!"

She stepped around him again, but he caught her at the waist. She squirmed out. "Go away. I'm walking home."

"Don't be stupid."

"*I'm* stupid?" She smacked her hand on his chest. "YOU were stupid. Too busy getting some to care if you killed someone!" Her eyes burned. "I was this close, you moron." She held her thumb and finger apart as her voice broke. "This close. If I had been any slower the anchor would have killed me."

"I'm sorry." While he showed little emotion on his granite features, it seemed as though he meant it.

"No, you're not. You wouldn't have even known." She punched him without moving him. "You wouldn't have even known or given a damn!"

He wrapped his arms around her in a bear grip. It wasn't gentle or fun or romantic or nice. Nothing like a hug. More like a containment.

"Let go of me." She wriggled to get free.

"Easy."

"No." Stubborn to the end, she eventually stopped fighting him, realizing there was no point. He was stronger. Maybe more stubborn. *What a scary thought.*

Will held her until she stopped shaking, her breathing calmer. "I'm sorry. I should have paid attention to who was driving."

"Anyone could have gotten killed out there." Even if he didn't care about her personally, she hated to think of the troop of drunk Churchston fools killing anyone.

He didn't answer for a moment, agreeing with silence. "Are you okay?

"If you put me down I will be."

"Are you going to kick me?"

"Maybe your nuts."

He put her down and looked her over.

"I was a nurse. I can do my own inventory."

"Nothing bruised? You didn't hit the bottom of the boat?" He held her elbow as she put a hand on his shoulder.

She leaned to pour more vodka on the cut then tossed the empty bottle into a nearby trash can. "No. I was fast enough to be away from the props. But the idiots had the anchor half-down while they were speeding all over. That's what caught me."

"Come on." He started in the opposite direction, toward the marina.

She didn't move.

He swore and turned back. "You're not walking. I'll drive you home."

Kelly shook her head. She wasn't taking the knight-in-shining-armor crap from him. How easy it would be to cower, surrender to his strength and commanding presence. *Nope.* He didn't believe in love, she recalled. One thing would turn into another, she'd probably start stripping because of a heated glance, he'd respond, then... No. Nip it in the bud, she instructed herself. *Heed your distance.*

"We both know I'll end up picking you up and carrying you over my shoulder if I have to."

She scowled at him. His hold would be too close for comfort. All those muscles. His chest felt pretty damn good on her cheek when he had held her. She sighed and followed him to the bike.

"Didn't think you'd be able to swim so far with your knee."

CHAPTER 21

The same gang was at the bowling alley the next night, much to Kelly's annoyance. She still didn't know who had been driving. Did they even know? Were they too drunk to keep track of who had been driving? It had been a close call and she was guarded by nature. Yeah, she'd enjoy a drink or two every now and then. But mature while still youthful, Kelly appreciated a fine line between "accidents" and stupidity. Drunk-driving a boat when people were skiing nearby fell under the category of *really* stupid.

Shutting it out of her mind, she focused on her chores. Not on the fact that Will had come to the bowling alley. She'd never seen him there before.

It was a busy night, with some kind of a class reunion going on. She had opted for jeans so people wouldn't stare at her leg like motorists slowing down to gawk at car collisions for the hope of a head rolling on pavement. And it wasn't a horrendous wound. She had decided she didn't even need stitches, only some bandages. Heather agreed after Kelly had texted her a picture, and it was the extent of medical reasoning she deemed pertinent. But it still would have been nice to stay off her feet for the night.

"How you doing, Kel?" Clay asked as she dropped off a pizza to them. Another first, she actually saw Will drinking. They all were. But Will seemed doubly cranky.

"Good as I get," she said and took off, ignoring Jaycee's glare as they passed. She assumed they despised her for interrupting their party time. As Will had been with Jaycee before he had jumped in the lake after her, it was no wonder Jaycee seemed miffed.

Drinking seemed to be the number one attraction of the night, not the bowling. Kelly didn't know if it was because Jaycee kept slacking to hang out with the guys, but Alan was behind the bar and in the kitchen.

Her feet took her everywhere. Pizzas to this lane. Beers to that one. Lane three was jammed. Pins were stuck in lane seven. Mick had somehow gotten his foot stuck in the gutter of lane two. Busy was an understatement.

She was refilling beers at the bar when Will approached her. He sat on the stool and studied her. Staring contest? She gave him a cool gaze right back, not letting him know how much his brown eyes melted her.

"How's your leg?" he finally said.

"Fine." Kelly knocked the tap off and put another glass up. Jaycee hurried back to the bar, opting for Will's attention since he was done hiding from society for the time being. He was a single available man on the market, and Jaycee seemed determined to get first dibs. "As fine as it can be since I can see the bone."

Her resolve weakened at his almost smile.

"Ha. Ha." Jaycee sneered. Then she turned her seduction act on Will. "How are you doing, honey?"

Kelly shook her head as she took off with the drinks.

Will couldn't keep his gaze off Kelly. It had been stupid to come. He wasn't even bowling.

Someone had run over Kelly. Pissed, he wanted to know who. Possessive, he wanted to see she was alright. Protective, he ground his teeth when anyone looked at her.

The men in the lane next to him took their shots. They were jerks, punks in the grade above him in high school. He remembered the tall bald one especially, Pete. He liked hurting women, Will recalled.

"Look what the cat dragged in," Pete drawled at Will.

Will could remember a few fist fights with him way back to first grade. He didn't move.

"Thought you were going to kill yourself," Pete said and his cronies laughed.

"You want another drink?" Jaycee said next to Will, leaning at his side like a stray cat who wouldn't scram. He hadn't encouraged her. He shook his head.

"Come kiss up to me and get me a drink," Pete said as Jaycee stood. He smacked her ass. Acting like the bad girl she was, she giggled and shook her head.

"Three Jägers." Kelly came up and plopped the shots on Pete's table then walked up to his. "Sam Adams. Bud Light and rum and Coke." She rattled the orders off in a bored tone. Will caught Pete eyeing her.

"What's your name, honey?" Pete set his boot on the plastic chair and leaned his elbow on his knee.

"I wanted a rum and Diet Coke," Alyssa said.

Kelly barely glanced at Pete. "Randy, we're out of Coors. Want a Bud Light instead?" She grabbed Alyssa's drink.

"Sure," Randy said before he stood to bowl and Kelly walked away.

In a small way, Will was happy she was wearing pants instead of shorts. Especially around Pete.

"Who was that?" Pete asked, his eyes tracking after her every move.

Jaycee snickered. "The assistant."

"What's her name?"

"Kelly." Jaycee forced a smile empty of glee. "She's a prude."

"She don't like men?" Pete smiled at Will.

"It wouldn't matter if she did." She studied her nails, unaware Kelly had returned with the drinks. "She'll never get laid the way she looks like a frumpy fat-ass."

Kendra laughed and Daisy looked away to hide her giggles.

"Bud Light, Randy. Rum and Diet." Kelly maintained a rigid face, but Will knew she had to have heard. She walked away as calmly as she had come.

"Her ass ain't so bad." Pete grinned as he watched Kelly go for the door where the lanes' maintenance area started. "Don't matter. I'll show her how to like a real man tonight."

Kelly turned from resetting the pin chamber for lane five and walked back through the crowded narrow hallway where the balls ended their spins. Will stood before the door. She jumped with surprise. She had not been expecting company in the clustered clanging pit of the lanes.

"What are you doing back here?" she said. She had work to do. And she really didn't want to face him after Jaycee's comment.

He shrugged. "Too noisy out there."

"Post-trauma much?"

Another shrug. "They said it would fade."

"Time heals all." She leaned against the opposite wall.

He avoided her eyes, taking in the mechanics of the room. "Learn that line in nursing school?"

"Common sense, I guess."

They were quiet and Kelly lost in the mute contest. "I'm busy out there, Will. What's on your mind?"

He contemplated with an intensity which warmed her blood. He closed the gap between them with two steps and kissed her.

She pressed him back, but not too hard. At the lack of force in her resistance, he must have taken hope because he picked her up and held her against the wall.

She gasped and broke the kiss. "Stop."

He gazed at her, as though he was wishing her to give permission.

"Stop. Please." She made it firmer. Not as breathless. Reluctant determination and sadness raged a battled in her mind.

She slid down from his arms and left the hallway. Before she reached the kitchen, her phone buzzed in her pocket. Unknown number.

"Hello?" she answered.

"Kelly White, how are you doing?"

She smiled, despite the use of the wrong name. She'd recognize the drawl anywhere. "Actually, it's Kelly Newland now, Gannon."

"Right, right. Had to hunt your new number down from your brother."

She leaned her butt on the rack of bowling balls. "Easier said than done, huh?"

"You know, there isn't much that has intimidated me in my career with the federal government, but Grant tops the list."

Half of a smile graced her lips. No, Grant wouldn't go easy on the FBI agent who she'd met from Norbert's death. Norbert's death by drug interaction wasn't a stellar case. He had been a preliminary gubernatorial candidate, so his death had warranted the attention of federal law enforcement. Gannon had really been pulled into the case because of Betsy's suicide, though, since her death had crossed state lines.

"Be happy he's the only brother you met."

Kip Gannon struck her as a sharp man, always one step ahead and keen on details. He'd been a polite and laid-back man to answer questions for.

"I was surprised to hear you'd left Atlanta, gotten divorced."

"Not as surprised as I am to get a call from you." Norbert's death was half a year ago. While she respected the detective, she had no clue why he'd be calling her now.

"I told you I'd stay in touch. I was going through some files and something snagged me. Got a minute?"

"Sure."

"We found Betsy in the Alabama state woods, barely over the border. Remember?"

She scoffed. She'd never forget the day. Kelly tried to revive Norbert, and Betsy had stood there, shocked. As soon as she left the hospital, she drove to the Talladega National Park and hung herself in the forest. "Of course."

"Forensics found nothing unusual. Typical suicide. Except for the toll ticket. It was paid for by a credit card registered to the name of R. Denner. Ever hear her mention it?"

"No. I hardly knew her. She started at the hospital a week before Norbert came in. We didn't talk about much other than work."

"Hmm."

"Maybe it was a friend of hers?"

"I can't see her picking up a pal on her way to hang herself. Video in the parking lot showed her tearful, distraught."

"She was shocked. Maybe she wanted a shoulder to cry on."

"Maybe. There wasn't much of a trail past the card. Billing address went to a vacant apartment in Miami. I wanted to run it by you," Gannon said. "Why the divorce?"

His question seemed personal, not professional, but she wasn't offended. "Caught him cheating."

"Foolish man."

"To get caught red-handed?"

"That too."

She rolled her eyes.

"Didn't surprise me much. You leaving your job didn't make sense. You excelled at it. But the husband? Ha."

"I'll take the liberty to consider you a friend rather than an acquaintance, but I didn't excel at—"

"Still haven't learned how to take a compliment, I see."

She sighed. "Why'd you expect a divorce?"

"I'm not the most thoughtful man in the world. I may never understand the female mind. But *I* could tell you were in a rough spot. Guilty even though it wasn't on your shoulders to begin with, sad the daughter wanted her father again, stress about your coworker not handling it all. The old man dying hit you hard. Now if I'd been married, if my wife had been moping and frowning like you'd been? I'd at least have gone to the funeral with her."

Kelly let the breath out of the corner of her mouth. She'd been the only one from the hospital to go to Betsy's funeral. When she had asked John to go with her, so she didn't have to go alone, he claimed he was swamped at work.

Mick ran past her with a toilet plunger and she snapped back to the present. Busy night at the bowling alley.

"Look, Gannon, I'm kind of busy. If there's anything else you need to know—"

"We'll stay in touch. Seeing as we're friends and all." He hung up with a chuckle and Kelly returned to her tasks.

For the rest of the night, she ignored their lane for as much as she could while still doing her job. She brought the guys their drinks and food but it was a test to her patience to not meet Will's eyes every time she came near him. As if she needed another reason to avoid them, the freaky drunk guy in the adjacent lane made her feel like he was a wolf after a lamb.

At the end of the night Randy came to her and said his good-bye. "Make sure he gets home alright."

She peered around his shoulder. Jaycee clung on Will's arm and it stung against her wishes. Daisy provided a much too detailed display of affection on Clay's lips. Kelly's neighbors seemed to have their nights arranged already, so she frowned in confusion at Randy's comment.

CHAPTER 22

After Kelly helped close down the kitchen later that night, she and Alan were the only ones left. She pitied the owner and told him she'd lock up. He had to have been bone weary from the exceptionally busy night.

She shut off the lights and locked the rear door behind her before she made some sense of who Randy had referred to. But not why. On the pavement behind the bowling alley, she found Will on the ground with a fist in his eye. The wolf from lane five had delivered the punch.

"Will!" She ran to him. A fight was not an alien situation to her. She couldn't count the number of times she had broken up her siblings from beating someone to a pulp.

Will landed a few hits and managed his way on top, but then he was kicked in the knee.

"Hey!" She reached in to pull him away and his face contorted in pain.

"Get away from him!" Will slammed the guy to the ground as frantic red and blue lights bounced off the sleeping brick walls.

Fred came first. The wolf man lobbed a drunken punch at the officer.

"Get 'im outta here," Eric said, nodding at the wolf. The younger cop stepped with a lazy pace and nodded toward the car.

Kelly crouched to the pavement as Will struggled to sit up. "Will, what the hell are you doing?" She checked over his bloodied face.

"What's he doing?" Eric said in the darkness as he approached.

Not him again. Kelly never had a problem with members of law enforcement. She'd worked with plenty who came in the ER. She'd definitely dealt with a couple when Norbert's daughter ambushed her. Gannon was a great man. But Eric's incompetency and lack of ethics had her grudging his presence.

"What's he doing?" His shiny boot kicked Will's foot. "He's getting drunk and mean. Like his daddy did."

"Will?" She tried to help him up.

"Gonna drink and drive, huh?" Eric spat on the ground near Will's hip and kicked at his foot again.

Kelly stood up and gave him all of her five feet and three inches worth of guts. "You touch him one more time, it's police brutality. My brother will kill you in court."

Eric held his hands up, grinning at her defensive tone. In mockery. "Here you are again. Trying to tell me how to do my job. He's drunk. And he was violent. He's going in."

"Will?" She returned to the ground when he moaned in pain, holding his knee, ignoring Eric. If anything she guessed Eric had been picked on all his life and was a bully cop now because he was authority.

Kelly noticed the blood on Will's lip, smelled the alcohol on his breath, and gently fingered the swelling at his eye.

"No wonder your mama didn't want you," Eric went on. "You're like Dennis. A good-for-nothing drunk."

Kelly considered Eric, scheming how she could hurt him without getting arrested. Her attention flew back to Will, his head hanging down. All she could see was a boy, abandoned and unwanted. Churchston had practically spat on him because of his association to his father. Never wanted and never welcomed. *No wonder he doesn't believe in love. He's never been on the receiving end of it.* Eric was a living testament. Churchston thought one thing of Will. All brawn and balls and no brains nor bravery.

Heart cracking, Kelly was wise enough not to feel sorry for him. He wasn't a boy anymore. He was a man with a lot of baggage. He wouldn't want her pity or her heart, but she could still have his back.

"Come on." She helped him to his feet, no easy going since he had the physique of the Hulk.

He winced on his knee and Kelly worried it might be worse than she imagined.

"Now, Kelly. You leave him be." Eric stood back some as though Will was a threat. "I'll take it from here."

"Take it to hell. We're going home." She grunted under the weight of Will at her shoulder.

"He's under arrest, Kelly. Public intoxication and assault. You shouldn't be messing with him. He's dangerous. He's good for nothing."

Kelly continued toward her car.

"Now wait a minute." Eric trotted after her. "You can't leave. You put him down and I'll—"

"You okay?" she asked. Will's breathing was labored. Cracked rib? Internal bleeding? What did the wolf do to him? And why? Medical training insisted she check him out before moving him, but she wasn't about to leave him for Eric.

"Kelly. In the name of the law, I'm telling you to stop." Eric held his hand up.

She ignored him and helped Will into her car. He didn't speak on the way home and to her relief, Eric must have been too chicken-shit to follow them to the stone house. He and Fred would have had their hands busy with the wolf man anyway.

"Here." She patted Will's pockets for his keys when she parked at his house, "Sit tight and I'll go open the door." He was still uncoordinated, but she managed him inside. She eyed the outline of the couch and let him slide down to it as gently as she could. His descent was like an elephant plopping down. She winced and sought the light switch.

She studied the room as she moved through it. There were hardly any furnishings. TV, couch, table. That was it for the living room. It was sort of empty, but clean.

She went to the kitchen and found it tidy, unused. In the fridge she discovered packaged microwave dinners and protein shakes. *No wonder he eats from Alan's so much.* The thought brought another twist in her gut. *Probably never learned to cook. Because no one was there to teach him.* She began to understand his view of the world. Accepting it, no, understanding it, yes.

She took a bag of peas and a tray of ice. Before returning to him, she went in the bathroom and collected necessities from another empty but clean room.

"Will?" She sat on the edge of the couch since he had stretched out long-ways. Pulling his shirt up, she felt his chest for swollen lumps, any cuts and scratches to clean. He must have taken a couple hits on his right side because he inhaled sharply at her touch.

He hadn't said anything, but groaned. She felt his arms and legs. Her hand didn't even cover half his biceps. She slowed her palms on his arms, and swallowed, trying to be professional, not thinking about the desire he caused from contact. He needed her help and she wouldn't let him down. A flare of heat burned from her, head to toes. She stilled her hands.

Men, women, babies, children, adults and elders. Nursing gave her the experience of feeling many people's bodies in the duty of her work. Some sinfully attractive, some utterly hideous. Cushiony fat, taut muscles, wrinkly leather, and smooth satin. She had felt a wide range, but she had never lost her heart with a simple caring touch.

"Hey, Will, can you hear me?" She took off his shoes, then scooted to examine his face. Pressing ice to his lip, she wiped the blood away. She whistled and slapped his cheek. "Come on. Open your eyes."

His chest rose and fell in a steadier rate and he cracked one eye open. The other was too swollen to open much.

She crinkled her nose as she checked his pupils with the penlight on her keychain. *Survivable.* "Speak, Will. Speak."

"Woof," he whispered and tried to sit up.

"Get down."

"Now I really feel like a dog," he mumbled.

Kelly cleaned his cuts, relieved he was conscious and talking. She gently demonstrated for him to hold the ice to his eye while she rolled his pant leg up.

"Will ice help on the knee or is it too temperamental?"

He sat up. "Let me do it."

She pushed him back down, all business. He accepted her offer of ibuprofen and drank some water while she carefully laid the peas over his knee.

He's breathing. Ice. Painkiller. Rest. Her medical prognosis was Will would live. Her own? She was in heat.

His deep gaze was a physical burn as she spread antiseptic on the scrape on his elbow, then his stomach. Their silence lingered on the edge of awkwardness and she cleared her throat before speaking. "Was there any reason for the fight or was that just testosterone?"

His frown deepened.

"Did you know him?"

"He was watching you all night. He's done time for beating women." He adjusted himself on the couch.

He had her back, she realized. It touched. It mattered too much. She tried not to analyze it.

Men had fought over her before. Boys too. But it typically had been her brothers defending her because she was their precious baby sister. Which was why she had all four of them sign a notarized contract, vowing they wouldn't lay a finger on John before she told them he had cheated. They would die for her, she figured. And she always had to tell them not to use their fists. Dad had raised them to value family and honor. She always cringed when they used a fight as a solution to a problem. *How unoriginal.* It kicked ass to beat someone with words and wit because anyone could fight.

But Will… Kelly couldn't meet his gaze as she hypothesized why he had protected her. She appreciated it, but knew he couldn't care. He certainly didn't love her. She concluded the only logical possibility. He was being macho like a hero. Military man, hero complex. It made sense.

"So what's the deal with the knee?" She spread the antibiotic cream over the antiseptic, trying her hardest to ignore the contours of his abs. Tight, tense muscles. Skin she wanted to lick. She narrowed her eyes to focus on the task at hand.

He inhaled deeply. "Walked into a bomb. Tore the ligaments. Three surgeries."

Kelly nodded.

"They said I wouldn't walk again."

She slowly traced her finger over the scar on his chest. "It got you here, too?"

He nodded. "Debris from the explosion."

She moved her hands to his knee. Her fingers massaged the end of his thigh, above his scar, and he choked on air.

"Shit. I'm sorry. Too rough?"

He coughed as he moved her hands away. "Uh, it's sensitive."

Kelly arranged the ice again for the lack of having something to say.

"And you quit your job because…?"

Kelly relaxed and started to smile. She shook her head. "I have too big of a heart. It wore me out, wanting to save everybody." She lifted her face to find his deep gaze on her. "You going to be okay?"

He jerked his head in a curt nod.

"Thanks for looking out for me." She stood and crammed her hands in her pockets before she rationalized another excuse to touch him. "It means a lot."

"I was drunk. Lost my temper."

"Nice try. I know exactly how many drinks you had. I was serving them. You knew what you were doing."

Will stared at her, communicating something powerful she couldn't handle. She twisted to the coffee table and turned the TV on mute with the remote.

"Don't go."

Kelly couldn't face him. He was hurt and vulnerable. In a way, so was she. "I should."

"Sorry to keep you up." His voice was gruff.

"Hey. You're not half-bad company a quarter of the time," she teased. He seemed so lost and alone and sad, she knew if she didn't run she wasn't going to have the guts to leave. And it would only hurt both of them if she swayed to pity for him. She pressed a soft kiss on his forehead on her way to the door before she did something stupid.

Like admit she was in love with him.

CHAPTER 23

"*You going to be okay?*"

Will had replayed Kelly's question in his mind for the next day and into the next night. He hadn't known how to respond before she left and he still didn't have an answer as he sat at Elmer's bar at the end of a day's work.

He couldn't get the image of Kelly out of his mind. Her hair hiding her serious face as she tended to him. *Well, shit, she* was *a nurse*. No one had ever nursed him before. Is that what it felt like to be pampered?

Nodding his head, he pretended to listen to the woman on the barstool in front of him. He wasn't in the mood to meet a woman, or talk to a date. He wanted Kelly. Her sweetness and tenderness had cracked at his guarded soul. She was smart, witty, sharp, and sweet.

Why does she have to be silly and get worked up about love?

He grimaced as he drank his beer. He wanted her on so many levels it hurt him more than Pete's lucky punches had.

Don't go.

He had begged her to stay with him. Pled with her. She was screwing with his mind. Disgusted with himself, he checked the score on the TV overhead and choked on his beer at his date's last comment.

"Knicks?" he said and wiped his chin.

She was cute, he gave her credit. Prim and eager and attentive. But God, so stupid. "Knicks are basketball," he explained. They had been talking about last year's World Series. He was initially impressed with their topic of small talk, as he had been glad to prove Kelly wasn't the only woman in the world who knew anything about sports. He had been so smug in his discovery of another woman who could talk baseball. It was like walking into a brick wall when he realized she had no clue what she was saying.

Will opened his mouth to explain, but gave up, knowing it was useless. His aches and pains from the night before hadn't bothered him at work. But as soon as his knee throbbed, he recalled the image of Kelly placing the peas.

He straightened from his slump. His knee had reminded him of Kelly, how she hadn't been afraid to touch it, hadn't been grossed-out by the scars on his skin. His knee had made him think of *her*. Not another memory of Matt dying in his arms.

"Nothing." He forced a smile at the airhead, as he was trying hard to fit in at the bar. His new jeans were stiff, too clean and unbroken. And the stupid shirt he'd found in the back of his closet wasn't fitted to the muscles he'd gained. Lights flickered faster than at Alan's bowling alley. Women were giggling and shrieking all over and it reminded him of being stuck in a hen house with uncontrollable strobes. Claustrophobia neared.

"I love this shirt." She ran her hands up his forearm, a seductive smile on her painted lips.

What an idiotic thing to say. He sighed. He couldn't relax, couldn't flow with it like he used to. He was too annoyed with everyone, too irritated with the bimbo in front of him, an eager brainless twit who he would have been taking home to screw in his younger days.

She tickled her fingers at his collar. "How about we get out of here?"

He resisted the urge to swat her hand away like a fly. Her nails felt like talons and he wanted to snap.

Sex. She's offering sex. Sex is good. He frowned instead. *She doesn't know baseball. How can I sleep with someone who thinks the Knicks are a baseball team?* Before, baseball hadn't been a prerequisite. Talking hadn't been a prerequisite. He blamed Kelly. Kelly and her damn kisses. She had ignited him and now she didn't want him.

"We just got here." He patted her shoulder. "Let's finish our drinks." *And have a few more.* Because there was no way he could see himself putting up with her sober.

Three hours later, Will adjusted the seat belts, both the factory-made and human arm variety. He settled the drunk and very horny girl on her side of the truck bench seat and paid attention to the road.

"You're so sex-ee." She actually squealed. "Turn it up. Turn it up!" She reached for the radio and blared the country pop to drunkenly sing along.

Wincing, Will maneuvered his truck down the drive past the rental house. He couldn't help but notice Kelly's lights were out. Humidity stuck his shirt to his back. It stretched over his bulky frame and he tugged the collar. Rain was bound to come any minute.

No sooner than he had parked the truck and silenced the grating whining music, she had launched herself at him. If he hadn't been dually fighting her off and limping her feet along as he helped her into the stone house, she would have been left outside in the rain.

The first patters started slowly on the roof as he deposited her at the bathroom door. Long past desiring her company at all, something he wasn't sure he had even wanted in the first place, Will hoped she would pass out quickly so he could get a few hours of sleep on the couch. It wasn't until he stepped outside to pee in the front garden under the soft slow drizzle of rain when he realized his biggest mistake of the night.

"Fuck." Zipping up, he went for the front door and tried the knob. Locked. He had forgotten it locked behind him. He patted the empty pocket at his thigh. The keys were inside the house. He wouldn't even be able to find refuge in his truck.

A crash sounded inside the house and he worried what the girl—whose name he couldn't remember—had broken. Jumping to peer through the hallway window, he spotted her lying on the floor, sleeping, it seemed, and snoring quite loudly.

Shaking his head, he stuffed his hands in his stiff jeans and cursed the wasted night. Wasted night? Waste of what? If Clay wasn't hung up on some woman from the beach, they could have played poker or tinkered with something at the garage. Or Randy was always up for some fishing. And if Matt was alive…

His boot sent a rock flying.

He walked toward the townhouse. Clay would probably let him take the couch, but after knocking on the door and hearing muffled sex noises, Will didn't want to be a third wheel. He glanced at Kelly's closed door and something funny folded in his stomach. No, she had made it clear. She didn't want him. At the same time, she did. *Women. They were a headache.* With a sigh, he went out to the beach and let the rain fall on him.

Kelly didn't want to be a one-night-stand.

She wanted something more.

She was waiting for a big disappointment from whatever guy she ever let into her life. The thought of her with someone else burned like acid in his throat.

He could play nice. He could keep his cool. She wouldn't be too scared to lend him her couch. She could be civil. Somewhere under the smartass, there was sweetheart.

Will returned to the townhouse and knocked on her door.

"Oh come on!" Kelly groaned from inside before she opened the door. In a sweatshirt and shorts, she cracked one eye open at him.

He stood there speechless and gazed into her drowsy blue-green eyes, powerful magnets to his soul which trapped his attention. Heavy and heated tension sizzled as silence waited between them. Drips of water plopped to the floor from his drenched clothes. The corners of her lips turned down and he found her impatience cute rather than irksome.

She raised her brows in question.

He shook the water from his head and wiped his eyes, tonguing his teeth as he tried to find something to say. Anything to say. He crunched his forehead with concentration, thinking of how he could explain she wasn't a pain in the ass. Stupefied and intimidated, he reached in and shut the door. With his hands on his hips, he waited until he heard the lock slide.

Will walked toward the beach as the rain let up. Waves rushed to the shore, their crashes more ominous than soothing. It instantly reminded him of the last time he had gone swimming and why. His chewed on his cheek. No one had owned up to driving the boat, and it still sat uncomfortably on his conscience. He crossed his arms and studied a wave. He ceased wondering who and instead imagined the ungodly what-ifs. *What if I never get to see her again? What if I never get the chance to see her put Delores in her place again? What if I never get to feel her hands on mine again? What if...* He steeled his resolve to face her, no matter how much she intimidated him. He had never met a woman of her caliber and he was at loss how to approach her, but approach her he would.

Ten minutes later he pounded on her door again.

Shuffling footsteps sounded to the door and she flung it open. In a cami and panties, she groaned, then leaned her forearm on the doorframe and her cheek in the nook of her elbow. Her brows raised again in silent inquiry.

He took a deep breath and stepped inside the apartment, then locked the door behind him. With his back to her, he closed his eyes to commit her to memory. *I'm a dead man.* He faced her and exhaled slowly.

"Problem?" She blinked the sleep away.

"I'm locked out." He took his shoes off at the door, leaning on the doorknob.

"And?"

"It's raining. I'm crashing on your couch."

"What? Why?" She averted her attention from his chest as he took his shirt off.

"What, I'm sleeping on your couch. Why, I was locked out. It's raining. Have a heart."

"Stay with Clay."

"He's busy." He started on his zipper.

"Oh God. Stop!" She held her hands out like she was stopping an animal from running to her. A pink glow spread on her face. "You can't barge in here and invite yourself in."

"I own the house."

"I'm renting it!"

He shrugged. "My property."

"You can only stay here if I invite you. I was sleeping." She brushed the hair from her face and held her hand out again. "Stop taking your clothes off."

"They're wet."

She crossed her arms. "You can't sleep on the couch."

"Bed then?"

She smacked his shoulder. "I told you, I'm not a casual piece of ass."

"Sleep. Kelly. I know the thought of sex freaks you out. Calm down."

"It doesn't freak me out. This is ridiculous." She shook her head and he let his pants drop to the ground. Her mouth nearly followed suit. "Put those back on."

"I can't sleep in them. They're wet."

She groaned. "It's indecent."

"And you're not?" He scanned her body and hid a smile.

She crossed her arms over her chest. "I live here. I can wear what I want." She uncrossed her arms and held her hands together in front of her panties. Then crossed her arms again.

"I'm not complaining." Down to his boxers, Will went to the kitchen and helped himself to a bottle of water from the fridge.

"How did you get locked out?"

"I helped Jamie into the house, she sort of struggled and I stepped outside. Maybe it was Jessica? I don't know."

Her jaw dropped. "You come over here to sleep with me while you have another woman at your house?"

"Thought you said you weren't interested in sleeping with me." He set the bottle on the counter. Too tempted to watch her, he rediscovered Matt's old apartment. She had painted, he noticed. Put some shelves up, added some plants here and there. He was relieved to see the space, alive with color and purpose, not a mournful reminder of what he missed.

"You're despicable."

"And tired." He went for the couch and swatted Eddie off. He lay down and his feet extended over the armrest and dangled in the air. He shot her a blunt glare.

"Dammit. Fine. Take the bed. I'll fit on the couch," she said and looked to the ceiling.

He sat up and studied her. He had thought he was stronger than this. But his dick had other ideas. And she was arguing with him. *Since when could fighting be such a turn-on?*

When he had first knocked and saw her with sleep in her eyes, he knew he wouldn't be able to resist her. The second time he knocked, she had answered in practically nothing. He was playing with fire. He wasn't a saint, but if she didn't want him, then she didn't want him. He wasn't one to force anything, much less, beg—again.

The strap of her cami slipped off her shoulder. *Shoot me now.*

"We'll share." He stood and picked her up and carried her to the bed. Her fists pounded at his back and her knees jabbed at his chest as she tried to squirm free. In the same manner as he had dumped her in the lake water, he indelicately dropped her on the mattress. He pulled the sheet aside and got in the bed.

"Are you insane?"

"Shut up and go to sleep," he mumbled. He turned on his side before falling asleep.

Kelly couldn't, of course. She had shut up because she suspected anything she said would have gone in one ear and out the other. Glaring at his back as his chest rose and fell, she loathed him as he dozed like the dead. Sleep wasn't happening for her. And he didn't even seem interested in her at all. He had wanted her for sex that one day at the garage. He had already gotten it from Jamie Jessica until she had tossed him out of his own house. So he had come to crash at her house.

Never before had she felt so undesired. So pathetic. It sucked to be 'one of the guys'. Viewed as a pal, not respected as a breathing feeling woman. Heat radiated from his body and she bit her lip to not reach for him. As much as he infuriated her, she couldn't deny her attraction. Turning her back to his, she waited angrily and impatiently for sleep.

Kelly woke up in his arms and felt his smile on her scalp. They had fallen into a natural fit, him spooning her. Maybe their limbs had figured it out as they had slept because he took up most of the space on the mattress and she was so petite and small compared to him.

Knocking blasted the early morning silence. She groaned and elbowed Will away from her. He tightened his arms around her, reluctant to wake. She squirmed out of his arms, humiliated she had let him envelop her. Shoving hair back from her face, she squinted at the clock. It was hardly dawn and she flipped off the digital numbers that told her so.

Staggering to the door, she yawned as she pulled it open.

A young woman faced her. "Where is he? Bill? Will? I think his name was Will."

Oh Christ. Will's lover of the night. Kelly accepted the truth she really must be completely lame. She didn't want to get in the middle of it so she said nothing.

The girl smoothed her hair into a ponytail. "I need a ride to my boyfriend's house. He's going to freak I was cheating. Will can't dump me in the middle of nowhere without a ride."

Kelly whimpered, only wanting more sleep.

Will came to the door in his boxers, and by his slit-eyed scowl, he was missing sleep as much as Kelly was. "Sorry Jamie. I'm an ass. Figure out a ride yourself."

The younger brunette gasped dramatically as though she couldn't believe he dared to brush her off.

Heat seared the tips of Kelly's ears. *Now I'm going to look like a slut for having him here. And I didn't even sleep with him!*

"My name's Jane!" the brunette said.

Will slammed the door in her face, then retreated for the bed.

Dumbstruck, Kelly stared at her door, unable to compute a reaction. After a moment, Will returned, picked her up and carried her back to bed. He dumped her on the sheets, crawled in and reached to hold her.

Coming to, Kelly smacked his hand. "She thinks I stole you and slept with you!"

"Shh." He closed his eyes and reached for her again.

"You're an ass."

He sat up and glared at her. "Tell me something I don't know. How about this? I'm tired. You're tired. She doesn't matter to me and she doesn't matter to you. Go back to sleep." He gave her his back.

She flipped him off, then flopped back down.

A half hour later, the knocking returned. They had mysteriously gotten into the spoon position again and Kelly flung his arm from her. She growled as she went to the door.

Clay stood on the other side. He was probably used to her morning cranky face, but he'd never seen what she slept in. "Damn, baby."

She started to shut the door.

"Hey, hey. Hang on. Some girl's on the porch whining about Will. Says he took her home and left her there."

Kelly tried to pull together some words.

"Can you get rid of her?"

She pursed her lips.

He yawned. "Come on. I've got someone over."

No surprise there.

"And I don't know where he is."

Her lips didn't move.

"Come on," he pleaded. Kelly wasn't sure what was more annoying: his conviction *she* would never have anyone over, or how she had to get involved with his problem because she was too nice for her own good.

She opened her mouth to say, what, she didn't know, but Will's yell from the bedroom beat her.

"Shut the door!"

Clay's eyes widened in recognition and the furnace at her ear tips flared. Burned. Embarrassed was the mild version of what she experienced. And all she had done was let Will crash for the night. *Pathetic. Idiot. Pushover.*

"Kel?"

She shook her head, not liking the smile on Clay's face. "No. No, no, no, no. It's not what you're thinking. He's—we— No." She pointed at him sternly. "It's not what it looks like, Clay."

He grinned like a Cheshire cat as Will came out from the bedroom. Without a word, he picked Kelly up, put her over his shoulder, and shut the door in Clay's face.

"You jackass!" She tried without avail to escape his grip.

"Stop fidgeting." He dropped her on the mattress.

"You realize this caveman crap is really—" Kelly jumped out of bed with the urge to strangle him.

He reached up and grabbed her at the waist, then sat down in bed and pulled her to his lap. His arms strapped her with her back to his chest and she struggled to get free, her arms locked under his.

"He— You—"

"Calm down." His breath blew at the hair on the back of her head.

"Let me go." She wiggled and he hardly budged. Kelly tried silence, counted to ten and tried again. *Fine!* "He thinks we slept together." She bit the words out.

"I don't care."

"I do."

Will leaned to his side to look at her profile. "Why?"

"Because. I'm not a piece of ass."

"I know. He knows."

"But—"

"So why do you care?"

"Because it will take two seconds for everyone in this gossipy little town to know we slept together, when we didn't, and everyone will think I'm a piece of ass."

"Clay won't say a word."

She turned to face him. "How do you know?" Moving was a mistake, she realized as his lips were inches from hers, his breath tickling her cheek. Her heart neared cardiac arrest. *Kiss him.* She slammed the brakes on the thought.

"He won't." Will's expression conveyed sincerity she could believe in.

She inhaled deeply. "Why are you doing this?"

"What?"

"The caveman hauling around deal."

His chest heaved against her back like a slow warm tickle. "I came here because I needed to sleep. Apparently Jane wanted to use me to piss off her boyfriend. I took her home last night because she was too drunk to drive home herself. She passed out at the bathroom and I stayed outside to pee. So I was locked out."

Still doesn't explain why he's holding me on his lap.

"And I didn't know the boat was going after you. I still don't know who the hell was driving and I hate it."

She pursed her lips as her skin mapped out the comforting details of his body under hers. "Why haven't you let go of me yet?" She pushed to test her arms against his grip.

His cheek rose in his almost smile against her temple. "You have a violent temper. I can't trust you to settle down. I want some peace and quiet before I have to bust my ass at work."

Sounded simple. But it still didn't explain why he wouldn't let her go. She had stopped 'fidgeting', as he had called it.

They sat there, in peace and quiet with tension and chaos. Will's chest moved in a lullaby rhythm at her back and she relaxed enough to lean back on him. She guessed she wasn't going to get out of his arms until he was good and ready to let go of her, but she couldn't lie and say she didn't like it. There was nowhere else she wanted to be. He was strong and warm and it was like a comforting cocoon.

His lips brushed her shoulder and she shivered.

She cleared her throat. "Will…"

"You say stop and I'll stop."

It was a wicked tease. He had to know she wanted him, putting her on the spot to make the call. *Damn him.*

He spread kisses on her shoulder then up her neck, nuzzling the skin below her ear.

Her breaths came faster and deeper as he pulled her cami strap down with his teeth, kissing and licking her skin.

She swallowed, suddenly parched from the building burn inside her body. Shivers almost turned to shudders and she gasped when his lips found her ear and he nipped and tugged. Her cheek, the corner of her mouth, along her jaw, her shoulder, her collarbone, her neck. She relished the slow exploration of his lips.

Too slow. Leaning back against him, Kelly turned her face toward him and he caught her with a soft kiss. She melted at the faint touch. It was hot and gentle, screaming of his hunger. Gasping, she tilted her face up to his, reaching for more of his lips and heated caresses.

One of his arms left her waist. He smoothed his palm over her skin then cupped her jaw, turning her closer to his mouth.

She pulled her arms from his grip at her waist and snaked them up, over her head and back to grip his hair. Her chest arched back to him and he spread his palm under her cami, smoothing her breasts, teasing her nipples.

Will's hand made its way down to her panties to stroke her, and she whimpered at his slow and agonizing touch.

He clutched the flimsy material in a fist and ripped it off of her. Uninhibited, his fingers brought her close to a climax.

She gasped with impatience and lifted off his lap, onto her knees, while she pulled his boxers down. He slipped her cami off. Sitting down again, she sat above his erection and stroked him while he kissed her and teased her nipples.

"Will," she whispered his name at his lips and smoothed her hand over his cheek. She lifted her hips, then slid down over him to the hilt.

He gripped her hip, his arm over her waist possessively as she trembled. She rode him, the smooth skin of her back sliding up and down his chest. Both her hands roped above and behind her head. She threaded her fingers into his hair without breaking the kiss.

He smoothed his calloused palms down her thighs as she moved on him. He pulled her knees apart, bringing her intimately closer and deeper on him.

In a tight grip, she came and melted against him with a mind-shattering heat, sending him to thrust once up into her and fill her.

Sitting on his lap, she relaxed her cheek on his chest and he held her until they both fell asleep.

If Eddie hadn't licked her hand and woke her up an hour later, she wouldn't have been able to escape. Slowly and lightly, she moved off of Will's lap and sat next to him as he slept.

I can't believe I caved. He was irresistible in the most damning ways, but it was wrong. She knew it had to be. The sex, phenomenal. But the aftermath?

She traced his lips with her finger and planned to run away. She was in love with him. No more guessing. No more pondering. It was a fact to her as she watched him sleep. She loved him. Gruff attitude, depressing baggage, almost smiles, gentle touches and all. She loved a man who would never return the sentiment, and with a heavy breath, she left before he woke.

CHAPTER 24

Will wasn't surprised he was alone when he woke up. He smiled at the ceiling and turned to see Eddie lying next to him with his tongue lolling. It was the first morning in a long time he felt alive and with purpose. He had a reason to get out of bed. Something about a certain messy-haired blonde who was both sweetly submissive and damningly dominant in bed. Reaching out to rub the dog's head, he sat up and studied the apartment.

He showered and stalled in her apartment before heading to Clay's apartment for a ride to the garage where he kept his spare key in his desk. She had even taken the time to drape his wet clothes by the window. With a shake of his head, he tried to stop smiling. It was an overdose.

"Morning, boss." Clay grinned with an abundance of enthusiasm. Will glanced at him, daring him to comment. Either the man had gotten exceptionally pampered the night before, or he was teasing.

Clay chuckled at his non-answer. "Knew it."

Will didn't know everything about Kelly, but he figured he knew her well enough to assume she would be edgy, standoffish and shy since they had actually engaged in intercourse. He expected it. And he'd give her time to wrap her head around the idea. One-night-stand wasn't going to cut it. They'd survived it and Will missed her as soon as he saw the kayak hut on the way to his garage that morning.

But nothing could have prepared him to be cut out of her life in the following weeks. She'd walk Eddie on the beach, run the kayak hut, deliver for Alan. She was everywhere he looked. Even when he was sleeping.

But she hadn't talked to him. Hadn't acknowledged him. Hadn't looked his way. Hadn't met his eyes. It was as though he didn't exist. In the first week after he had slept with her, he had decided to let her come to him, reasoning if he approached her, she might still give him the cold shoulder.

But she never came to him.

There was no joking in the garage. No more small smiles she reserved for him. He didn't have the pleasure of meeting her gaze. Debating silly stupid mysteries of life. Discussing baseball.

It was over.

After three weeks, he resembled the world-hating monster he had been after Matt died. The realization irritated him. One woman? One simple ordinary blonde from Atlanta had rendered him more morose and angry than losing his best friend had? In brief moments of introspection, he wondered if this was another of her tricks.

Another of her games where she would break his walls. But she still never came.

He grew angrier with her with every passing day. He'd ordered from Alan's twice a day, to force her to physically enter the garage. But she always left the subs with Clay when he wasn't looking.

Sex. It was sex. He grew furious she was acting so childish, so immature. Taking the whole thing out of proportion. Wasn't he her friend, too? That idea enraged him even more. He had tried to let her in his life and she had cut him out.

Impatient and tired of it, Will ordered from Alan's, nothing unusual about it. But this time, instead of his own pizza sub, he ordered Clay's ham grinder.

Kelly counted the cracks of the sidewalk as she delivered Clay's sub.

Yesterday Alan had seen her putting pickles on Will's sub and laughed. He said he'd told the mechanic years ago pickles don't belong on pizza. She'd done it anyways.

In the garage, the music was low and she considered it a sign of Will's absence. She inhaled deeply with relief.

"Clay?" she called out and stepped around to find him. "Food's here."

Will walked out from the rear bay.

Dammit. She tensed at the frustration which sparkled from his eyes.

"Hiding's over, Kelly. It was sex. Not the end of the world."

She crossed her arms. "I'm not hiding."

"You've been acting like I don't exist for almost a month."

"That's what I'm supposed to do! One-night-stand means one night, right? You got what you wanted."

He came close and glowered at her. "Don't you dare tell me you didn't want it. And don't even think about saying I forced you."

"Oh, I wanted it." She licked her lips, readying herself for the argument. "I wanted you. There. Did I cushion your ego?" She stabbed her finger at his chest. "You should be thanking me for graciously giving you a wide berth, Will. I wouldn't dare to stand in the way of the next woman in line."

"What's the matter with you? One minute you're intelligent and sexy and now you're crazy. Do you get like this with anyone you sleep with? What, you want to get married now? You want me to tell you lies about how you're the only woman in the world who can make me happy?"

Kelly bit her tongue and ordered the tears to stop in her eyes. She turned away. He could never understand how much it hurt to love him.

"Yeah, walk away. Be a coward." He scoffed as she left.

Walk away. She cringed at his words. He was angry she was leaving him? She wasn't like his parents, or anyone else in Churchston. She wanted him. All of him. She loved him because he was strong and brave and didn't litter. She was attracted to his curiosity and intelligence and rough patience. She enjoyed his wit and gruff tolerance of the world. Kelly didn't want to leave him or walk away. But since he thought love, the very thing she was looking for, was a myth, he was making her walk away. And breaking her heart. She wasn't deserting him. She loved him, and that was the crime.

Turning, she looked back at him. "Why are you so upset?" Her voice cracked and she cleared her throat. "You could go through women like the days on a calendar. Commitment is a foreign word for you. Why are you pretending to care?" She faced him and threw her arms up in exasperation. "You don't believe in love. You got exactly what you wanted from me. It was sex. Not the end of the world, right?"

He stormed toward her. "What if it wasn't just sex?"

She laughed a single noise of disbelief. "Yeah. Which will explain why after you got in my pants you didn't want me around anymore."

"I knew you'd be edgy like this. I was waiting for you to calm down and come to me. You're so damned independent I thought I'd give you space."

"I'm not mad, Will. I knew what I was getting into. You explained yourself before. We want different things."

Will crossed his arms and ducked his head down to her eye level. "How? Tell me how it's different. You wanted me and I wanted you. Clean-cut math."

"You want sex. I need something more."

Once Will had taken care of the confrontation bit, Kelly could manage her days easier. The storm had passed. Contrary to his belief, she had known damn well he existed, working and living day in and day out so tantalizingly close to her. She hadn't hid, per se, but she hadn't tried to cross his path either. She'd said what she needed to and he had made himself perfectly clear. Crusading to change him seemed stupid and she wasn't *that* pathetic.

Like a bright spotlight in her dark days of missing Will, Heather came to visit.

"Kels!"

Kelly turned to her friend's yell. Heather had parked her car on Main at the beach and was running to her at the kayak hut. They hugged in a giggling display of friendship.

"Look at you!" Heather gripped Kelly's shoulders and held her arms out to see. "You're like a Baywatch babe!"

Kelly smiled and shook her head. Heather played at her waving blonde tresses like a mother fussing over her daughter. "Look at you. All tanned and sun-bleached and toned. You look great!"

"You do remember there's no such thing as a good tan, right? Skin cancer's the most common—"

"Oh, Kel. You haven't changed a bit!" She draped her arm around her shoulder.

Heather had only secured time off to stay for a couple days, so Kelly crammed in everything she could. They kayaked and bowled. Walked Eddie on the beach. She introduced her to the guys, staying away from any mention of Will's name. She hadn't needed to worry Heather would meet him because he had gone back to his reclusive ways.

It was too soon before her friend had to leave. They sat on the kayak hut counter, killing time before Heather drove home.

"You're happy now? Doing this?" Heather said.

"I'm happier," Kelly admitted. Despite her heartache at Will, she had grown to accept what had happened to Norbert. In fact, he had pushed her to accept it. How could she preach to him to move on past Matt's death, without taking her own advice? She cleared her throat. "I've been thinking."

"Oh boy."

"What if I went back to school?"

"For?"

"Paramedic."

Heather faced her with a smile. "Seriously?"

"What do you think? I could transfer a lot of my credits and bypass a lot of EMS-1."

"I think it would be awesome!" Heather pulled her into a one-sided hug. "I was so worried I was going to come down here and find you all depressed. New job. New man…"

"Uh, no. No new man."

Heather shook her head. "The mechanic hunk always running on the beach, that's Will?"

Kelly winced at Heather's question.

"It has to be. He's always watching you."

Kelly squinted at the waves on the shore ahead.

"And only I could know how hard you're trying *not* to look at him," Heather said and elbowed her.

Kelly pushed off the counter.

"I know. I know. It hurts," Heather said. She stood and played with her keys. "I still don't get it though."

Kelly faced her and waited.

"John was a handsome guy. A loser, but he looked nice. And he played nice, polite in public." She held her hand up as Kelly opened her mouth. "Now the neighbor, Clay? He's hot. Sexy fuck-me-now hot. Like a model. Then the curly-haired blond? Randy? Adorable. So sweet and nice. Like the All-American boy next door. Those are your types, Kelly. Those are the kind of guys you used to like. Will? I know you didn't go out looking for him."

Kelly struggled for a wise word to say. "What's the punchline, then?"

Heather paused. "Fate?" She walked for her car.

"Fate?" Kelly called out. "My fricking fate is a broken heart?"

Kelly was helping Randy rip out carpet at his house. Will knew this but didn't want to. It seemed he was always informed of her whereabouts because Randy and Clay wouldn't shut up about her. He was thankful they didn't ask him any questions.

At night he tried to watch the waves from the front porch of the stone house but stared at the townhouse instead. *Has she moved on to Randy?* He took a drink of beer. It burned. She had been spending a lot of time with Randy, but Will wondered if he was trying to distract her.

Randy would be a nice mushy guy for her. He'd coo and shower her with crap about love and destiny and all that bullshit. But Randy wasn't right for her. *Can't she see?* She needed tough, not mushy, and he couldn't imagine how Randy would handle her damn sarcasm.

Earlier in the day, Randy had borrowed Clay's truck to haul away carpet from his house, and left his car at the townhouse.

Will took a swig of beer and studied the moon's reflection in her bedroom window.

Clay worried she was sad. Randy worried she might be crying, wished she wouldn't mope so much.

Sure she had been divorced, and had a rough time at her job. But Will couldn't understand why she seemed so sad. He Googled her a few nights ago, curious about the patient who had died on her. After browsing the articles about Norbert, he still didn't understand why it affected her so much. Part of the job, right?

The obituary stated the demise of one Norbert King, age sixty-five. He had been worth a few million. One deceased daughter. One ex-wife. Please leave contributions to St. Joe's Hospital.

Nothing about the estranged daughter threatening hospital staff afterwards.

He finished the beer, rocked on his chair.

Someone walked around Randy's car in the drive, then onto the porch in the dark, heading for the front door.

Will snorted with jealousy. Another one for Clay.

Eddie barked and the person left. *Maybe they should put a light over there for the traffic at night.*

Not drunk enough to sleep, Will opened another beer and tried not to think of Kelly.

Standing in front of the kayak hut the next afternoon, Kelly watched Delores Downs walk on the sidewalk with a couple prim old ladies. They paused at the deli and had a sandwich to eat on the bistro tables out front. None of them ate more than a couple bites. The starvation diet of the vain.

The Governor's wife. Kelly scoffed. It turned out Mr. Downs had been the previous governor, not even in office anymore. But the family was like royalty in Churchston. The townsfolk still called him "the governor".

"You're not fond of her, are you?"

She turned to Randy, who stood next to her. "Is anyone? Other than 'the governor' and the people she pisses money on?"

He leaned his elbows back on the counter, mimicking her. It was a busy day, but a slow hour. "She's always been full of herself."

"Aren't you supposed to talk nice about her? Relative and all?"

"Distant relative. My mom is Bruce's sister. We've never liked her much. She's always been about power and money. Why she left Dennis and snatched up Bruce. She wanted authority and prestige."

Kelly sighed and gazed at the water.

"Looks like you're stuck on something," Randy said.

Will.

Perplexed, Kelly faced him, squinting in the sunlight. "Why was Matt so important to him? Didn't he hate everything to do with Delores?" She didn't have to clarify who she meant. Will was all she talked about with Randy. She was thirsty to know everything about the man she loved and couldn't have.

"He did. They never really met until later," Randy said. "Matt went to a Catholic school and the rest of us went to public. Matt and Will didn't meet until junior high and they hated each other on sight. No mystery there. But they were so alike. They both tried out for football. Will was like an Olympian, even back then. And Matt wasn't much weaker. Two strong bull-headed boys. They fought at tryouts, physically and verbally. It never would have worked."

"So what happened?"

Randy smiled. "Coach P. was a smart man. See, they tried out for football at the beginning of summer so the team would already be picked by the time school started. He cut them both. They were the two best players and he cut them both."

"Because they couldn't get along?"

He nodded. "And he told them they weren't man enough to play football. Hearing that at eleven? Talk about a low blow. So they took it literally, each of them going to the gym, pumping iron, running, jumping ropes."

Kelly saw it clearly. Will as a little boy lifting dumbbells with his scowl of concentration.

"It put them in the same place, every day. I think it was Matt who started it, but he told Will he was locking his arms when he bench pressed and would never get strong. Then Will told him he was doing lunges in the wrong form. They meant it as put-downs, but they were actually helping each other. So they bonded through weights and running. They were so alike, they had to be friends. They were inseparable."

Kelly nodded and paid attention to her toes in the sand.

"They had something important in common, too. Delores. She didn't love Will. She abandoned him. But she never loved Matt either. She portrayed the image of the perfect mom to the perfect son because image was all that mattered to her. And it ended up bonding the boys. They were so alike. Will valedictorian, Matt salut—"

"Will was top of his class?"

"Yeah."

Me too.

"They were both rebels and the best of friends. I used to envy how tight they were. They made their dreams, enlisted together, made it through boot camp at Parris Island, trained for SOC in

North Carolina. They walked in on a suicide bomb. Will carried him out."

They stood in silence save for the children squealing with delight in the water.

"You saw what he was like. It killed Will for Matt to die. He kept going because the memory of Matt. Why he's still like He-Man. Lifting and running even with his knee. It was their ritual, working out in the morning."

Kelly nodded, but still couldn't face Randy. Her heart squeezed painfully for Will.

"Kelly, what happened?" His voice was soft as he put his arm around her.

They must know. If Will didn't brag about it to his pals, then they could put one and two together and get three. Clay and Randy were there for her as friends, but she was appreciative they never asked.

"It was like he was human again. I know it pissed him off to smile again, but you made him—"

She shook her head.

"Kelly—" He squeezed her shoulder.

"He'll never love me." Her eyes burned with salty tears and Randy slipped into a fuzzy blurry image.

He pulled her in a hug.

On the public beach she knew her sobs had to attract the attention of the lot, but it felt too good to get the awful loneliness off her chest. "He'll never love me. It doesn't matter how much I do, he never will. I'm not good enough…" She lost the rest of it to sappy sniffles as Randy rubbed her back.

When he stepped back, he tipped her chin up to look at her closely. "It has nothing to do with you, Kelly."

She sniffed then cracked a laugh. "Right."

He smiled a little. "He has a hard time letting people in his life. Matt was the only person he ever trusted to take the risk on. His dad, Delores. He's used to people leaving him. And after Matt died, it's like a part of him died, too. It will be hard for him to ever take that risk again."

"Why would I leave him?" She blinked her moist eyes. "Why would anyone want to? He's such a great guy once you get to know him."

"He's lucky to have you." He pecked a chaste kiss on her forehead.

"He doesn't have me. He doesn't want me for anything but an easy lay."

"Maybe he'll come around."

"No. I'm not going to wait forever or try and change him. I can't compete with his past. And I can't handle putting myself in the vulnerable position to have him break my heart even more."

Randy watched her with a small smile and she finally sighed.

"What's with you Randy? You're so damn nice and considerate. Why aren't you married with a golden retriever and twins?"

He reddened and rubbed his neck. "Uh, I don't know. I'm still looking."

Kelly wiped at her tears, thankful for his embarrassment as a distraction from her sorrow. Randy was a good friend. Comfortable. Reassuring. She frowned, realizing he was probably never going to be able to come out in a small town like Churchston.

CHAPTER 25

Giddy with anticipation, Emily noted it was a short distance from the bowling alley to Randy's neat little house.

Good thing she opted for her concoction. The roofies wouldn't have had enough time to work in the short drive.

She had posed as a middle-aged woman at Alan's little bar while Randy had babbled about adding on to his kitchen. Kelly had referred to what someone named Sean said.

Sean? Was he Kelly's other lover? Emily didn't know of a Sean in Churchston. No matter. Kelly wanted Randy. Randy was the one. Randy was Forty-One. He had to be.

Scraping her finger over the worn patch on her steering wheel, she nodded at her confidence. This time, there could be no mistake.

Emily had seen them on the beach. Randy holding Kelly, soothing her, smiling at her. They had grinned at each other as he ate his dinner. Their fondness for each other could only reinforce Emily's conviction. Kelly and Randy. Couple of the year.

As she followed him home from the bowling alley, Emily remained alert for any sign of a witness, a noisy dog. She had watched the cops enough to know Fred would be off and Eric would be watching porn on his iPhone in the abandoned lot at the end of Main. It was almost too easy. She smiled as Randy's brake lights flashed vibrant red like an errant strobe as he zigzagged across lanes and sidewalks of the sleeping neighborhood.

Randy's car swerved over the curb, smashed the mailbox, and pulverized the bushes, finally stopping in the yard instead of the drive. With a final quick glance around, Emily exited her car, the bat ready in her gloved grip. She pulled him out of the car, his arms and legs heavy as deadweight.

With closed eyes, he groaned as she dragged him to the grass.

Slamming the bat with bottled-up fury, she beat him, breathing in harsh breaths at the strenuous effort to pound his flesh. Up and down, she swung the bat, enjoying the crunches of bone. Crunches like when she had killed Forty. She wished she could have had Randy conscious, a knowing Forty-One meeting his death with the knowledge that Kelly couldn't have him.

There would be no telling when someone would come.

As if her thought was a jinx, headlights shone at the corner of the intersection.

Careful to the take the bat with her, she ran off, thinking with satisfaction of the tears Kelly would cry when she saw her new lover dead.

Will's summon came from Clay, a rushed and frantic voicemail. As he processed the choppy details of the message, he remembered how he had watched from the garage as Randy held Kelly while she cried a couple days ago. Her crying had tugged at his heart. Was it because of her stupid ex? Still? The loser didn't deserve her tears. Or was she still hung up over the money bags who died on her? As he tore off his shirt for a clean one, he wondered if Clay had delivered the bad news to her yet.

He arrived at the hospital, his stomach knotted with bad memories. His shoulders tensed at the suffering he expected to see. The sweat from his recent run had dried from the wind on the bike, leaving a starchy sheen of cold on his skin, pricking goose bumps as he ran up the steps to the ER lobby.

Clay paced in the hallway. Daisy and Kendra huddled in a tearful hug on a waiting room loveseat. After the sliding doors swooshed shut, they acknowledged Will briefly. Eric leaned his elbows on the counter of the nurse's station, yawning as he nodded at the information the doctor provided.

Before Will could interrupt Clay from his pacing, Kelly arrived.

She wiped at her wet red eyes and Will wanted to hold her. He admired the no-nonsense aura she held, with a downturned mouth and the worried crinkle on her forehead. The opposite to the emotional wailing on the loveseat. She sniffled as she scanned the occupants of the room with a determined set of her jaw.

He wanted her to hold his hand. To be strong for him when he was scared for their friend. The nauseating fear crumbled his concentration as he fought back the memories of Matt in the base camp.

As though she sensed his suffering, she met his eyes for a second before focusing on the nurse's station.

She marched up to Eric. "What happened?"

His mouth twitched. "Looks like everyone's here for statements."

"What happened?" Kelly repeated, planting her feet in front of him.

"Easy, Miss Newland." Eric cast his gaze to the ceiling with a sigh.

"Eric, is he okay?" Daisy waved at Alyssa coming down the hallway.

"Tell me what happened," Kelly said.

"I'll divulge details as soon as I'm legally able—"

Kelly shoved him against the wall, erasing his smug look. He straightened his posture, chuckling lightly as though he wouldn't want anyone to imagine she had really maneuvered him. "Whoa."

She stepped closer. "Tell me what happened."

"Kelly—" Clay went for her.

"You better watch your temper, lady." Eric sidestepped Kelly. He met Will's eyes before facing her again. He leaned in to whisper and nodded his head to Will. "Don't let him rub off on you now. I've seen the way he looks at you."

"Scared of a girl, officer?" she said.

Will reached forward and pulled Kelly back. "Eric, tell us what the fuck happened."

"I ain't telling you shit, drunk."

Kelly shoved Eric back against the wall and Will and Clay both took her arms. She shook them free and turned to face Clay.

"Somebody better give me some goddamn answers. What happened? He was just eating at Alan's and said he was going to go home before the game came on." She leaned around them for a look at the nurse's station. "Where's the charge nurse? Where's the attending?"

Clay took a deep breath. "I was going to watch the game with him. Found him unconscious in his driveway. Someone beat the shit out of him."

"Who would hurt Randy?" Daisy whimpered and Kendra pulled her in for a hug. "He's so sweet."

Kelly faced Eric and licked her lips. "I saw you smoking dope behind the bowling alley. I'll take the security video from Alan. You give me details, and I don't tell my lawyer."

Eric frowned at her.

"Tell me what happened!"

He held his hands up. "Someone took a bat to him. No witnesses. Might have been wasted."

"I was with him at Alan's. Is he unconscious?"

"Hasn't woken up yet."

She faced Clay. "Was there any swelling or sign of head trauma? Was he conscious when you found him?"

Clay shook his head. "There was blood everywhere."

"Maybe he was unconscious from a concussion. Why does the doctor think he was intoxicated?"

Eric flipped open a notepad. "The doctor didn't say if he was intoxicated. *I* think he was high. Or drunk. He ran over his mailbox and parked on a shrub."

"He was drinking Pepsi. I know he was. Did you smell alcohol?"

"Did I *smell* alcohol?" Eric huffed.

"Are you even a real cop?" She sighed and massaged her forehead. "They'll detect alcohol in his blood, anyway."

"Look, I know you think he's all high and mighty but people don't swerve around like that sober. Maybe he hit up on the way home—"

"He left at six thirty. Clay, when'd you get there?"

"Six forty-five. We were going to watch the pre-game."

"He couldn't have hit up."

"Look here, Miss Newland. I'm the law here. I'm going to consider every possibility no matter how much you want to deny—"

"Mick talked to him in the parking lot as he was driving away and he didn't see him take anything. Randy's about one eighty, one ninety. If he took anything on the drive home, it wouldn't have been absorbed in his system in less than ten minutes. Any barbiturate, narcotic, stimulant. The substances couldn't have been digested and absorbed into his bloodstream that quickly. Not quickly enough to affect his CNS. And he had a full stomach. He had a burger and fries…"

Will watched her frown as her gaze followed two doctors striding down the hall. Impressed with her assessment, he was glad she came. Sharp and focused, she was in her element.

Eric clapped three times. "Well, thank you very much for the lecture. I'm sure the doctors will do whatever they think—"

"They need to run a tox screen," she said as a doctor came forward, heading for Eric.

"Officer—" the doctor began.

"Run a tox screen," Kelly insisted. "Blood and urine."

"Excuse me?" The doctor eyed her. "Who are you? Are you family?"

"No. But time is running out. I suspect GHB. There wouldn't have been enough time for flunitrazepam to take effect. He could have been slipped GHB at Alan's."

Eric chuckled. "Miss Newland, you can't run on with crazy ideas like this."

Kelly slapped his shoulder. "Shut up." She turned to the doctor. "Date-rape drugs don't remain in the body for long."

"Yes, ma'am, I am aware. We've had a couple cases of Rohypnol this summer. We've arranged for a blood screen."

"No. Blood and urine." She checked her watch. "It's already been two hours. It probably won't be detected in his circulatory system anymore, but it should show in urine."

As the doctor hesitated to reply, Will held up his hand. "I'm family. I'll pay if that's the case. I'll authorize it. Can't hurt, right? Save some from a bedpan."

Kelly shook her head. "Probably going to have to set up a cath if he's unconscious."

"We're going to do everything—"The doctor checked his pager at his hip. "I'll be back in a moment." He nodded to Eric as he left.

"Well, I'll be interested to know what he was drinking, or smoking, on his way home when he wakes up." Eric flicked a piece of dust from his uniform.

"You said he was beaten. Was he robbed?" Kelly said.

Eric sighed. "Fred said it looked like nothing was stolen. Wallet was on him. Nothing out of the ordinary except a hospital shoe in the grass."

"Shoe?" Clay asked.

"One of them paper things."

"You mean a surgical bootie?" Kelly brushed her hair back.

"Anyone ever tell you you're a pain in the ass, little woman?"

"Oh, so sorry I'm making you do your job, Eric."

"Every time I get a call, you're butting in the way. You taking charge about Roger's kid with the cottonmouth—"

"Adder," Will corrected.

"Whatever. Snake's a snake." Eric glared at him before jerking a thumb at Clay. "Then you show up to haul him home after he smashed the stop sign. Now this."

Will jabbed a finger at him. "Maybe if you wise up and act like a cop, she wouldn't need to."

Clay armed him away.

"Both of you need to mind your own. Let me do my job." Eric pointed at Will. "Don't tempt me to book you."

Kelly knocked his pointing hand away. "He didn't even do anything!"

"And you." Eric stepped back and shook his finger at her. "You quit being a know-it-all. I swear, ever since you came to town it's been one thing after another." After glancing at his phone on his belt, Eric cast them all a final glare and headed down the corridor.

Waiting for more news, they hogged the hallway. Jaycee came and the girls cried softly together while Clay resumed his pacing. Kelly darted from nurse to nurse, demanding information.

Will stood off to the side, too nervous to be social, questions germinating from Kelly's idea.

Why would anyone slip Randy a mickey?

CHAPTER 26

"Yes, ma'am, I will let you know if he—"

"What are you doing?" Kelly pointed at the nurse's hands. "Jesus Christ. You take the gloves off inside-out. It's the foundation of PPE. You contaminate your skin by removing your gloves like that—hey—hey!"

She kneaded her eyes with her palms as the nurse walked away. None of them would tell her shit. Probably because none of them knew anything. Randy's condition hadn't worsened or improved, that was why the nurses wouldn't tell her anything. They weren't giving her the polite blank replies nurses shared when they really wanted to tell visitors and family members to fuck off and let them do their jobs.

Leaning her head against the wall, she remembered her place. She was a visitor. Not a nurse. She couldn't bear the thought of Randy in pain and it was even harder to swallow the ache that she couldn't help him, as a visitor or as a nurse.

Too numb to cry anymore, she bottled her angry energy as she tapped her finger against her thigh. Sweet, responsible throat-clearing Randy. Mama's boy Randy. If it hadn't been a random act of violence, it made no sense. Eric seemed entirely incompetent, but he said nothing seemed stolen. Only thing out of place was a surgical bootie on the sidewalk.

How? Why? Who? Kelly couldn't think fast enough. She had been finishing her shift at Alan's when Randy came in for dinner. It had felt like he had been making a habit of checking on her, probably because he was so worried about her heartbreak over Will. She had talked with him some, mostly about sports. He wanted advice on adding on to his house and Kelly told him what her brother had suggested.

Between the bowling alley and his little suburb house, someone had drugged him. Beat him.

Who could hate Randy? Who could want to hurt such a caring and peaceful guy?

Was it a homophobic reaction? No one seemed to know he was gay.

It was the only motive any evil person could have against Randy, but Kelly dismissed it. Eric didn't comment on such an angle. From the number of times Clay had suggested Randy find a woman, Kelly assumed even Clay hadn't known he was gay. She bet there was only one other person in Churchston who might have figured out Randy was homosexual and kept it a secret.

And despite his temper, Will wouldn't hurt a fly.

She caught a glance of his poorly stifled fixation on her fidgeting finger. She stuck her hands in her pockets. She couldn't go to him.

He'd have to wait because this was about Randy. Randy was hurt. If she went to Will, she would have lost all of her control to keep distance from him. They were there together for Randy regardless of their problems with each other.

Randy stabilized and he would survive. That was the diagnosis they received. He didn't remember anything. There was no evidence. No weapon. No witnesses. Tidy violence. The last he recalled, he had left Alan's and felt dizzy and sick to his stomach as soon as he turned off Main.

Will's admiration of Kelly grew even more when they received word of positive screening results. Traces of the date-rape drugs had been found in his urine.

Not only was she courageous enough to behead a snake, she was smart enough to consider the possibility of GHB in Randy's attack.

How the hell had Randy made it all the way home before the GHB had hit? It felt like too precise of a timing to Will. Someone had known exactly what he was doing. Randy was still in the hospital. Broken collarbone, a concussion, fractured jaw, and busted femur. It had been a hell of a beating.

Most of all, why would someone want to target Randy?

Will visited him every day.

Kelly visited, too, judging by the get-well balloons and silly gag gifts only she could pull off. After Junior had his snake bite, she brought him about fifty cheesy get-well balloons, a monstrous plastic cloud of bright yellow Mylar filling the kayak hut. She had a stubborn way of making people smile when they were down. Probably an old habit from her nursing days.

It was a couple weeks after Randy's attack when Will brooded through a slow day at the garage. He tried his hardest not to think about her until a stranger came in. Clad in an impeccable suit, he was a tall striking man who oozed accomplishment from every pore.

"Do you know where I might find Kelly Newland?" he asked Will at the garage.

Will kept his face void of emotion as he took the flat tire the man was dropping off for a fix. He pointed to the kayak hut on the beach and the man grinned.

"Thanks. Could I come back in an hour or so for this?"

Will nodded. He didn't want to know what the man wanted to do with Kelly for an hour or so. After the man left, Will dropped the tire to the ground.

Everyone in Churchston knew where to find Kelly. So he had to be someone from Atlanta. *Probably the lucky dumb bastard ex-husband.*

Will leaned back at the workbench and drank water as the suit crossed the street toward the kayak hut. His heart clenched when Kelly looked up, shrieked, and threw herself into the man's arms.

"Oh my God! I can't believe you're here!" Kelly kissed the man's cheek.

"Missed you so much I had to see you for myself." He chuckled and set her down.

"Yo. Will." Clay's voice and the snap of his fingers broke Will's stare. He crushed the water bottle and threw it to the floor.

Kelly hugged him again, amazed he was there. "How'd you get away, Grant? Thought you had a bunch of projects lined up. Since you're a new Partner and all."

He messed with her hair in the way all the boys did. She slapped his hand away. "I always have time to see my baby sister."

"What's the occasion? I told Dad I was coming back to visit for his birthday."

"So this is home then, huh?"

"For now."

"Anyway, that's months away. I wanted to tell you as soon as I found out."

"What?" She matched her second oldest and busiest brother's mischievous grin.

"It finally happened."

She frowned.

"Tara's expecting."

She squealed and pulled him in for another hug.

Aside from the stress of Randy's attack, Kelly's heartbreak over Will was marginally lessened by Grant's visit and the news she would be an aunt. He wasn't likely to stay long, as his law firm always needed his constant attention in Atlanta, but she would make the most of the visit however long it lasted. She gave him a Churchston tour, complete with kayaking, swimming and bowling. She took him to meet Randy in the hospital, and they argued sports.

Kelly had forgotten Grant could be a snorer and she wished her couch was further away in the apartment. That was the thought she was smiling at as they had ice cream cones and sat on the beach after she was done at the bowling alley.

"Now there's a rare sight," Grant said.

She faced him, licking at ice cream melting down her hand. "Hmm?"

"You're smiling."

"I always smile."

"Something's bothering you, Kelly."

She quirked a brow at him. "Am I really so transparent?"

"Only to people who know you. What gives?"

She shrugged.

"Come on Kel. Do I need to beat someone up around here?"

She almost smiled. Men and their testosterone. Like a fight was the fix to all the bad things in her life. Something bothering little helpless Kelly, well her big old brothers will make it right. She sighed.

"Kel?"

She swallowed and sniffed. *Why am I such a baby?* "I'm still in love with him." She blinked back tears. "I try to stop thinking about him, but I can't. And I know he doesn't even deserve me. As much as I hate him, I want him back. But…it's—"

Grant laughed lightly and pulled her over to hug her next to him. "You've got too big of a damn heart."

"It's so annoying."

"And you're a tomboy."

"I know!"

"Last time I saw you cry was when we watched Bambi. Divorce is hard, kiddo."

"What?"

Grant lowered his ice cream. "What what?"

"Oh. No. Not John."

"You met someone?" Grant raised his brows.

Kelly crinkled her nose. Girl talk with her brothers had always been…well, weird. "Yeah. But he doesn't love me."

"Then he's a moron."

She smirked. "No. He's too damn smart."

"Want me to beat him up for you?"

She shook her head with a smile. "Not now. Besides, he was a Marine."

Grant pulled back, mocking a wounded chest. "You think I'm getting old or something?"

"I don't know…are you?" she teased.

He tickled her until she laughed. "Good to hear you laughing again." Grant hugged her to his side, one arm around her shoulders. "You seemed pretty beat about Norbert."

She nodded. "Not just him. All of it. It was an accumulation of all those years, all those patients, all the deaths I saw. I saw Dad in him. A lonely old man, no one at his bedside."

"Thought he had a girlfriend."

"Well, yeah. But she seemed more like a secretary. She was probably sleeping with him, but I only saw her when she tried to act on his living will. He'd never actually signed his papers. He'd actually never disowned his daughter. That's how we found her. The girlfriend brought in his copies of his will, but he'd forgotten to sign them. They weren't legit. So I had to hunt her down."

"Good thing you did."

"It took a whole day of cajoling her to come in and see him."

"Well, no one can stand a chance when you get set in your ways."

She smiled. "They really patched it up. I guess there's something about being on your deathbed to make you appreciate what really matters in life."

"They have you to thank."

Kelly considered his perspective. It was a nice alternative. She'd given Norbert and his daughter one last chance to be together. He'd lost his first daughter in a car accident years ago. But Kelly had facilitated his reunion with his estranged one. It was a prettier picture than the fact she gave her a false hope her father was going to be there for her.

"I doubt she would have said 'thanks', coming after me in the parking lot as she did. I'll never forget it, Grant. The look on her face, the tears. How crazed she was. Kept screaming about taking Norbert away from her, he was supposed to be hers."

"Whatever happened to her? You never did file a restraining order."

"She was admitted to a psych ward and I left town. No point to protect myself from someone who isn't a threat."

CHAPTER 27

In the darkness of the beach, Emily steadied her breath and listened for any approaching sounds. There was nothing. Only the waves sloshing at her feet. She was alone.

She had lost her temper earlier. Temper led to mistakes.

Randy was another mistake.

Emily had posed as a nurse at the hospital to eavesdrop when Clay had visited Randy. He had discussed his concerns about "Kel", worried about her being so sad and heartbroken. Said she needed someone to love her.

Randy had said she needed someone to love her, not that she had him loving her. Nothing about her being with him at all.

Emily clenched and released her fist. A scream tickled her throat as she remembered the conversation. Randy had talked about heartbroken Kelly. Heartbroken and sad from her damn divorce? Boo fucking hoo. The divorce was months ago and stupid-ass Kelly was still sad about it?

Emily snorted at the irony.

Recalculating, she crouched lower behind the rocks in front of her at the sound of someone nearing.

There was clearly another man in Kelly's life. Emily was positive this time. He had sat with precious heartbroken "Kel" on the moonlit beach. Hugged her. Teased her. He had even been staying the night at the townhouse with her.

Emily had watched him put his arm around her shoulder, heard him talking about having a baby. He had to be Forty-One. Had to be. No mistaking this time.

Kelly had moved on to the man in the suit. The man in the suit who was walking down the beach talking on his phone, oblivious to the stretched fish line Emily had tied between the rocks. Nothing left to chance this time. If he didn't bust his head open from the fall, she'd finish him off. She'd have to beat him in a different manner than she had Randy. No sense in letting the cops figure out a pattern. Eric wouldn't be smart enough to see a connection, but the older black guy, Fred, he might.

No one strolled the beach this far from town, the only visitors coming from the townhouse. The loner mechanic had already gone on his beach run in the morning. The ugly dog was preoccupied with the T-bone she had chucked in the backyard of the townhouse. Clay was off with his favorite bimbo. Kelly was reading a book.

Nothing could go wrong. Emily smiled with the delivery of justice she was going to serve Kelly. Finally, after so many mistakes, Kelly was going to learn her lesson.

Will's knee killed him with every footfall, but after seeing Kelly cozy with the flat-tire man on the beach on his way home, he needed the run.

Pumping his legs on the beach in the dark, he couldn't flush her from his thoughts. He debated whether he should lie to her and tell her he loved her and couldn't live without her. He winced at the idea of lying to her. And she seemed a bit too sharp. She'd probably detect his lie a mile away.

Maybe he couldn't live without her. Terrified at the notion, he ran harder to escape the grip she had on his mind. Deflated and incensed she was so stubborn and silly to push him out of her life, he dug his feet into the sand.

Suddenly, he drew up at the sight of a body half-submerged in the receding waves ahead.

He blinked and wiped his eyes. *I'm not in the war. This isn't a dream.*

Instinct took over and he flipped the body face-up, felt for a pulse. He administered CPR and patted the man on his back once he coughed up the lake water.

You've got to be shitting me. It was Kelly's ex. "You okay?" He couldn't help the roughness of his voice.

Sitting up, the man nodded and wheezed. "Thanks, man."

"What happened? Lose your balance?" No lingering odors of alcohol or weed. A quick look around told him they were alone with the lake. No voices. No footprints. Slick fish line on the sand captured his attention. He picked it up.

"What's that from?" the man asked after a raspy cough.

Will teased the thin plastic between his thumb and finger. Could have been new. Not pliant and weathered but stiff. "Fish line. Assholes are always leaving it all over."

The man shook his head and fingered his temple. With a harsh exclamation of pain, he looked down at his ankle. "Fuck. I must have tripped and twisted it."

"Hit your head too?"

"Like a motherfucker." The man struggled to stand and Will winced as he got to his feet to help him. Limping, they moved past the scattered rocks his head smashed on, trickles of blood smeared on the surface.

"You okay?" the man asked.

Isn't he the one who was drowning in the lake?
"Bad knee." Worse since he had knelt to give him CPR. He pointed to the man's ankle. "You might have sprained it."

The man grimaced and tested his weight on his foot. "Dammit. Now she'll be all fussy over me. She'll freak that I'm injured and overreact."

Will wedged his shoulder under his armpit and helped him toward the townhouse. "Your wife?" Will bit his cheek at the throbbing pain of his knee. *Well, she was his ex-wife...*

"Huh? No, my sister. She's staying at the house over there. I'm sure Tara will be worried, too. I've got to leave tomorrow. I hate to leave

Kelly when I know she's still sad, but I've got to get home." He groaned.

"You're her brother?"

"One of them. Grant Newland."

Will felt the weight of a thousand pounds lift from his chest. A brother. Not her ex. "Will Parker."

"Hey, is your knee really okay?" Grant frowned at their combined limping gait.

"It'll be fine. It's an old injury."

"Now she'll be worried I can't drive. And insist I stay to recover. She's always babied us. Even Dad. But she's too stubborn." He panted as they hobbled toward the building.

Will wearied from helping the man back to the townhouse, but stomached tenser anticipation of having to be near Kelly.

"How'd you hurt your knee?" Grant asked between breaths.

"War."

Grant raised his brows. "Oh yeah? How long did you serve?"

"Marines. Seven years."

"You were in the Marines?"

"What I said."

Grant nodded and save for their panting breaths, they remained silent for the rest of the trek. The twang of the screen door snapped sharply in the night, announcing Kelly's entrance to the porch.

"Thanks for finding me back there, man. You'll keep an eye out for her, right?" Grant said as they neared.

Will gulped a deep breath, confused her brother would think she needed a protector, least of all him. "Of course," he muttered before they reached her on the porch.

She slanted her lips. "What now?"

The flood light Will had asked Clay to install the day before highlighted her piercing blue-green scrutiny. He averted his gaze from their siren call.

"Oh, the compassion," Grant said. He hissed as Will helped him to the chair.

"What happened?" Kelly studied Will's swollen knee, then glanced up sharply at his face. How far had he supported her brother's 210-pound frame on that injury? She debated between chastising him and hugging him, but she held her tongue and her heart, as he would probably welcome neither.

"Found him face-down in the water. Twisted his ankle and fell in. Smacked his head on a rock."

"I thought Sean was supposed to be the clumsy one. C'mon, get inside." She held open the door and avoided eye contact with Will as he helped Grant inside.

CHAPTER 28

The next morning Will guessed Grant was either impervious to Kelly's fussy pampering, or she had discharged her sibling, because her brother waved to him as he left.

At the garage, Clay's giddy mood annoyed Will more than usual. Without Randy around, Clay was a bit much to handle. The doctors said Randy might be released the next day and Will considered who would pick him up from the hospital.

Probably Kelly. He hated himself for envying Randy for her attention.

As he closed up the garage that night, his cell phone beeped. Clay's number lit on the screen. Bone-tired and depressed, Will sat in his truck and leaned his head back against the headrest as he answered with his eyes closed. "Yeah?" He could hardly hear the other end with the background noise.

"Hey man, I need a favor."

Will waited, absentmindedly trying to remember if he had any more Hot Pockets in the freezer at home.

"Can you swing by the kayak hut and give Kelly a jump?"

He pulled his head up and opened his eyes to slits. Clay had the balls to ask him to help Kelly?

"Look, I know you guys got some kind of silent treatment going on, but I'm all the way out at Daisy's. Her birthday, man. Kendra and Alyssa made this surprise deal last minute. She needs a jump. You don't have to talk to her. I already told her I'd stop by but you're closer."

Will hung up and drove the short distance to the kayak hut, pulling onto the public beach. It was strange being out there in the dark of the night, with people gone and voices absent. Normally Kelly wouldn't have even been out there, he guessed, but there had been a full-moon special. Burns must have asked her to work late.

When he walked onto the docks, she was leaning over on the edge of the dock reaching for a kayak floating out of her reach. Admiring the slender curve of her back as she stretched out, he crushed the memories of how she had felt under his hands.

"Oh, come on." Her back to him, she begged the kayak closer.

He cleared his throat, and she screamed and fell forward into the river. Will planted his feet on the wooden planks, erased all trace of emotion from his face. Unsure of what else to do with them, he stuffed his hands in his pockets and watched her surface.

"What the hell are you doing?" She wiped the water from her eyes.

"You need a jump?" He frowned at her, sticking to his callous act because it was his comfortable default.

She spat the water out of her mouth and shot him a glare, then pulled herself onto the dock. "You scared me."

"You need a jump?" he repeated. *Jump? Didn't Clay get a new battery for her? Alternator must not be charging.*

He could hear fatigue in her sigh. "Yeah. I thought Clay was coming."

"He was too busy getting some."

She led him up the dock, squeezing the water from her ponytail.

"Why are they all over the place?" he asked of the kayaks randomly floating like elongated rubber ducks on the dark river.

"I don't know. Some punk cut the ropes when I made the last run," she said and pointed ahead. "I parked behind the hut."

He followed her, agitated at how hard it was to be near her. Damned hard. And damned if he wasn't getting hard. How could he not look? The clothes clung to her slim body. He recalled how she had looked when she fell asleep on his lap. The feisty woman all soft and serene. The best sex he ever… He slammed shut the memory.

She opened the hood and wrung more water from her hair.

Will looked in and frowned.

She didn't need a jump. She needed someone to stop tampering with her car. Concentrating, he put his fists on the frame and studied the cut wires. Someone who knew what they were doing.

Like Clay's brakes. *And coincidence that someone had cut the rope for the kayaks?*

He dropped the hood shut. "Jump's not going to help."

She slanted a brow at him.

"You need a new alternator," he lied. His stomach bubbled like it had on the boat when she fell off the skis. The same kind of gutsy turmoil he had shared with Matt many times in the war. *Danger?*

He dismissed the thought. Churchston, he reminded himself. Not Afghanistan. The paranoia and nervousness had waned with time, but he still had his moments. Still had to work at controlling his calm, remembering the world wasn't out to get him from behind every corner.

"Really? Damn." She hurried to follow him back down the dock.

Like when she fell off the skis. Will stood at the end of the docks and knew he wasn't letting her out of his sight, with her hating him or not. Something wasn't right. Paranoia or protectiveness. It didn't matter which, Will lived by 'better safe than sorry'. Probably a prank, but he still didn't like it.

"Well, let's herd them up." He lowered himself into a kayak.

"What?" She set her hands on her hips.

"I'm guessing you'll need a ride home now," he said and paddled off to retrieve another kayak. "May as well get this done."

"Oh." With a skeptical expression, she grabbed a kayak and chased after the liberated boats.

"What is it, you've got a hot date you're rushing for?"

Ahead of her, Will worked his jaw. "Yep," he lied again, more comfortable with her being annoyed at him than grateful for his help. "Let's hurry it up, would you?"

An hour later the kayaks were secured along a new line and Will led the way to his truck. Unable to resist staring at the wet clothes which clung to her body, he flung a towel at her.

She caught it in her face. With a swift thrust she threw it to the ground. "You know what? I'll walk."

Will chased after her. "It's miles away."

"I'm not afraid of the dark."

He paused for a second, watching her back as she stormed off. Like when she fell off the damn skis. She had shown enough common sense then. She knew she couldn't have swum all the way to the beach without help. This time, though, Will didn't doubt she could hoof it home. But he couldn't shake gut instinct that all the 'mishaps' weren't accidents. She might not be afraid of the dark, but Will was afraid for her.

"Come on." He trotted after her.

"As much as I appreciate you're reluctantly forcing yourself to give me a ride, I prefer my own company." She yanked her hand from his reach.

"Don't be a pain in the ass," he said and hustled after her again.

She stopped suddenly and he slammed into her back. They tumbled to the sand and he wrestled on top of her.

"*I'm* a pain in the ass?"

"Can't you get in the truck?"

"What's it to you? I don't have to put up with your attitude. I can walk fine. Go off on your damn date, Will. I'll pass on charity from a jerk every time."

He held his breath, fumbling for words. He couldn't tell her it didn't feel right. That he had a prickly itch of something bad in the air.

Churchston, not Afghanistan.

"I'll pick you up and carry you in there," he said. Maybe a physical challenge would work.

Her frown was pensive, not obedient. "What's it to you?"

He tongued his cheek again. "What if I say 'please'?"

She didn't answer but to turn her head on the sand, scanning their surroundings. With a doubtful smirk, she shoved at his arms to let her up.

It was a quiet ride home and when he pulled up to the townhouse, she reached into her pockets but failed to exit the cab of the truck.

"Um." She licked her lips in hesitation.

Will stared her down. *Please do not torture me.*

"My keys must have fallen out when I fell in."

He let his head fall back to the headrest. *So help me God.*

She glared at him. "Which wouldn't have happened if you hadn't scared me!"

He slammed the gearshift forward and drove for the stone house.

"Do you have an extra key?" she asked as they left the truck.

"Clay has it."

"And he's—"

"—out getting some."

Will flipped the lights on and went through the house as though she wasn't there. He paused in the hallway to toss blankets to the couch and then went to shower. Once he was clean and dressed, he found her sitting on the couch with the towel wrapped around her.

"Be back later," he said and slammed the front door behind him. He had no clue where he was going but he knew he couldn't sit there. Alone in his house. With her.

As he drove into town, he questioned the absurdity of his actions. Never before had anyone twisted up his motives and thoughts.

She's another ordinary woman. Another woman who wanted false promises of love so someday she could walk out on him. With the renewed frustration of not having her in his life, he vowed to find the hottest, most promiscuous woman at Elmer's.

"She's just another ordinary woman," he coached himself as he locked the truck on Main.

She's another ordinary woman. Right?

CHAPTER 29

By the time Will came home, he had a migraine, his knee was bothering him, and he never wanted to talk to another person again for as long as he lived. Better yet, never even think about *wanting* a woman again.

Instead of going to bed, he sat on the edge of the coffee table and watched Kelly sleep on the couch. It was torture as he followed the curves and shadows of her sleeping face. Committed her every detail to memory.

He thought about her car tampered with, the kayaks all over, the boat running over her. He tucked back a strand of hair from her face and studied her closer. How could she come to matter in so short a period of a time? As if looking at her would give him answers. All it did was test his self-control.

In the morning, after his run and shower, Will stood in the kitchen drinking water when Clay tapped on the front door.

"Hey man." He came in and ran his hand through his hair. "You go jump her car last night? It's still at Burns."

"Wouldn't start." Will still didn't know how to explain what he had seen.

"Well, where is she?" They looked to the couch as Kelly sat up with drowsy face. "Kelly—" Clay came forward and she snapped awake.

"What is it?" she said, alarm on her face as she eyed both men.

"Come on," Clay said and grabbed her shirt sleeve, hurrying her to the door.

They ran for the townhouse to find Eddie wheezing on the front yard.

"Eddie boy." Her voice cracked as she went to the dog and touched his face, checking his body for what could have hurt him.

"I came home a few minutes ago and found him out here." Clay said.

"Eddie," Kelly whispered and probed at his throat, his chest. "What happened to you, buddy?"

Will crumbled at her tender voice. Kelly had been at his place all night and Clay must have partied all night if he had just gotten home. "How'd he get out here?" he asked. He crouched to inspect the dog, but only saw Kelly's eyes concerned and alarmed. His attention was always riveted on her.

"Probably the dog door," Clay answered. "We cut one out for him a few weeks ago. Kelly, we'll take him to the vet. I'll drive you out there. It's not too far."

She nodded and caressed her dog's head.

Will went inside to get a towel to help move the dog in some kind of a sling, but stopped still at her apartment door. Ignoring his knee, he lowered himself to the square flap cutout on Kelly's door. Touching it gingerly, he removed a piece of black neoprene fabric that had been ripped off and stuck in the hinge. *Probably part of the dog collar.*

Outside, they loaded Eddie in the bed and Will told Clay he'd see him at the garage later. Will frowned at Eddie's bright blue nylon collar. Not black neoprene. Kelly wiped at her eyes as she climbed into the truck bed to ride with Eddie. Will rubbed at the back of his neck as they left, and as soon as they were out of sight, he searched the townhouse and yard for anything else suspicious.

"Maybe he ate something," Clay said to Kelly through the rear window of the cab.

"Maybe." She felt again for Eddie's pulse.

Downtown, they stalled in traffic and she looked around. "What's taking so long?" *Traffic in Churchston?* What an oxymoron. There weren't enough residents to *cause* traffic.

Clay sped around the car in front of them. "I don't know. There's a tractor up the road taking something to the beach."

At the animal clinic, the vet warned he couldn't perform miracles but promised to work as fast as he could. After the technicians pumped Eddie's stomach and announced he was stable and resting, Clay drove Kelly to the kayak hut on his way to the garage.

"So what happened with your car?" Clay said.

"I don't know. Will said I needed a new alternator."

Clay shook his head. "I checked it when I put the battery in. Worked fine. It wasn't very old."

She sighed, exhausted from the adrenaline rush of fear first thing in the morning.

"I'll check it out later," he said as she got out on the beach.

She spent the slow day tossing a ball against the wall of the hut, trying not to think about Eddie. But when she wasn't worrying about Eddie, she was missing Will.

She remembered Randy should have been discharged that morning. She had planned to make a cake and host a little celebration.

Scratch those plans. No car. Alternator? She anticipated Clay would procrastinate fixing it for her. In the meantime, it had to be back to bumming Burns' truck. And routine snake-checking.

Twitching her mouth, she looked at the perfect summer day on the beach. Blue sky. Puffy white clouds. Not too hot. She bet she wasn't busy because of whatever was going down at the other end of the public beach, where the tractor had been earlier. There had been a band playing, too. What was all *that* about? Community festival?

Woo hoo. Party hard, Churchston.

Lost in her solitude, her thoughts ranged from what to do later since Alan had given her the night off, or if Grant and Tara were going to have a girl or a boy.

"Kelly."

She frowned at Clay as he rushed up to the hut. What was it now? He could hardly catch his breath.

"Clay, calm down," she said.

Randy hobbled on crutches after Clay. He gasped for air as he bent over, hands on knees.

"Hey, look who's back." She tipped her lips into the first smile of the day. "Clay, stand up straight if you're trying to get air in your lungs. For all the exercise you do in every woman's bed I'm surprised you're out of shape to run across the damn—"

He shook his head. "Kelly, you've got to go to him."

Randy seemed to have an equally worried expression on his face.

"Spill it, Randy. He's freaking me out. What's going on?"

"Will. He left," Clay said as he caught his breath.

"What do you mean?" She came around to stand outside the hut and glanced at the garage, the three wide doors open to show it was empty.

"It's a fucking memorial. A memorial for Matt," Clay said.

"Delores had a granite memorial made for Matt," Randy explained. "This morning she had it delivered to the town square fountain on the beach down there by the marina. It's the anniversary of his death."

"Will went down there. Wanted to see," Clay went on. "She saw him and told him to leave. He was banned from ever stepping foot there."

"She can't do that." Kelly pinched at the bridge of her nose.

"She said he had no right to be there. He didn't deserve a memory of Matt. It was his fault Matt went to the war. His fault Matt died. He had betrayed him and didn't even try to save him from the bomb."

"She seriously needs some fucking medication," Kelly said.

"She kept screaming at him. Going on and on," Randy said.

"I've never seen him like that before. He shut down. Nothing. He walked away, came back for his truck and left," Clay said and stood up. "I've never believed the crap about him being suicidal, but I've never seen him react so freakishly."

She opened her mouth and shut it.

"I'll watch the hut," Randy offered. Clay thrust his keys forward and she took off.

Kelly found Will sitting on the couch with his face in his hands and his elbows on his knees. With no idea where to go, she had started at the stone house. If he heard her enter, he didn't move.

"Will?" Her heart ached at seeing him in pain and she closed the sliding door. Dropping the keys to the floor, she ran and squeezed herself onto his lap, cupped his jaw and gazed at him. "Will." He blinked and met her gaze, still hunched over and deadly silent and blank.

She clung to him, wrapping her arms around his neck and burrowing her face next to his. Strapped to him like a koala, she held him. After what felt like eternity, his arms went around her to

pull her to him, and his silent tears dampened her
shoulder.

CHAPTER 30

Will woke up in the dark and he glanced at the clock on the cable TV box. Seven in the morning or night? Kelly made a noise as she slept on his lap, in his arms, and it came back to him.

The memorial. Delores. The pain.

Then there was Kelly.

He smoothed her hair from her face to see her closer and he took a deep breath of contentment.

Isn't it easier when you're mad at me instead of missing Matt?

He smiled at the memory of Kelly's words in his office. He gave up the madness because it wasn't easy. She was such a stubborn damn woman. It was taking him a while, but he was learning he didn't like being mad at her if it meant she wasn't there. Mad, sad, angry, happy, teasing, bored. He'd gladly get lost in her eyes no matter what the mood was. As long as she was there with him.

Easing to his side, he pulled her to lie on the couch with him, facing the sweet pout she had when she slept. After watching her for a moment, he found her hand and laced her fingers with his before he closed his eyes again.

Kelly woke with a start and blinked the sleep away until she could see him clearly. Her hand jerked, and she treasured the feel of his fingers secured between hers. *Did I do that, or did he?* A small shy smile of wonder spread her lips, and she wanted to touch him, too nervous to disturb his peace. But looking at him and feeling what she did for him, she couldn't resist. Leaning closer, she brought her lips close to his.

"I love you," she whispered and then kissed him.

He responded instantly.

She leaned back and found him gazing at her with the intense heat which was theirs and theirs alone. Kelly doubted he had heard her in his sleep, and she kissed him again. It was still gentle, but urgent, too.

She pulled his face closer and kissed him, hoping with her lips she could ease some of his pain, to show him he wasn't alone.

He closed the gap between their bodies and pulled her to him at the waist and they kissed until breathing became irrelevant.

Will sat up abruptly and stood, stupefying her until he bent down to pick her up and carry her. Everything was familiar, the kisses, the touches, her sitting in his lap, him carrying her. But this time it was slow. She had faced him willingly on his lap, and he carried her in front of him, not over his shoulder.

Afraid to break the spell, she said nothing as he lowered her onto the bed, kissing her deeply. Clothes came off and heat soared. This time, there was no hurry and he didn't seem in the mood to let her be in charge. Will leaned up and took an eyeful of her naked skin, a steaming sear over every inch he saw. She reached up to pull his face to hers for a kiss and they made love.

Will woke up in a foggy limbo between sleep and consciousness, and he hesitated to open his eyes. He couldn't handle it if Kelly ran away again. He squinted them open, then jumped, widening his eyes in startled surprise. Kelly wore one of his shirts as she sat crossed-legged next to him. Her chin in her hands, she stared at him.

Her close study intimidated him. It was too direct of exposure for a man who tucked everything personal under lock and key and let very few close.

How long has she been staring and what the hell does she see?

She smiled the little lift of her lips which he found so sexy. He raised his brows.

"I like looking at you."

Will snorted a single laugh of amusement and crossed his arms behind his head. Lying there looking up at her, he realized he liked the heat in her gaze. Then she crinkled her nose.

"You don't like me watching you, do you? I know you value your privacy."

They were butt naked. Any privacy was long gone between them.

He reached for the shirt and yanked her down to him. "Yeah. Actually, I do like it. Now watch this."

They recovered an hour later. Will had never felt so satisfied, so tired and calm. With his thumb, he stroked her back as she curled to his side. Gazing at the ceiling and listening to her soft breaths, he relaxed. She slid her fingers down to touch him and he gently removed her hand.

"You're killing me. I'm exhausted."

She leaned up on an elbow to smile at him. "How old are you?"

He pinched her butt. "Not that old."

She gave him a pained expression.

"Thirty-three." He hooked his arms behind his head. "With the exception of you"—he paused and counted back in time—"I haven't had sex in four years."

Her lips parted in surprise. "I have a hard time believing you."

"We were in Afghanistan for two years. We were on the move, paranoid, and alert. There wasn't any time for sex. Besides, there wasn't anything over there that would've appealed to me. After the bomb…" He cleared his throat. "I wasn't the same."

"Um, was it, were you…damaged?" She reached to stroke gently.

His dick? Should have known she'd interpret his words anatomically. He felt his cheeks burn but figured he didn't need to be so guarded with her.

"No. I kind of shut down altogether. No spirit. I guess my dick lost his personality, too."

"It seems pretty outgoing now."

"No. With you it's *ingoing*." He grinned as she faked a laugh at his cheesy joke.

Later, at dawn, Will woke again and caressed her jaw.

She kissed his palm. Leaning to squint at the clock on the wall, she sighed. "Time to run?"

He frowned at her.

"Don't you always run before you go to work?"

He opened his mouth to answer.

"It's your time. Keep it." She kissed his forehead and climbed out of the bed over him. He appreciated her understanding.

"How'd you get here?" he asked.

"Clay's truck." She dressed in front of him.

Indulging himself, he sat and watched her.

"How does a girl get an alternator fixed in this town?"

And with that question, his comfortable la-la land vanished, and he was back to reality. Will got up and looked for clean shorts. "It was tampered with."

Kelly straightened sharply with one leg in her shorts. "What?"

"Wires were cut."

"Could they have been old?"

He shook his head and pulled on a sweatshirt. "If there were any old wires, Clay would have replaced them when he put your battery in. They were fresh cuts. No rust yet. Got any enemies in town?"

"None I know of."

"Where was the car all day?" He headed out of the room.

Kelly followed him to the living room. "Where we found it. Anyone could have gone up to it. I was making a lot of runs in the truck because of the guided nature rides all day and night."

Will didn't want to scare her with the explanation it couldn't have been anyone. This was deliberate. Precise. She beat him to it.

"Are you thinking it could be the same person who cut Clay's brakes?"

"It's not hard to do. Anyone could look it up online."

"Maybe it was the same person who pulled the prank and let the boats go free. A bored teenager," she said and tied back her hair into a messy ponytail. Will reached out suddenly and pulled her into a tight hug.

Maybe someone had been trying to strand her out there. And maybe he'd never stop jumping to conclusions. "I'll push it to the garage and fix it. I'm sure Clay can get around if you borrow his truck. I don't want you to risk another snake in Burns' truck." He nuzzled her neck and felt her smile. A few too many kisses later, she giggled and walked away. Snatching her Braves hat on her way out, she blew him a kiss.

CHAPTER 31

Kelly's morning was too busy to allow time to remonstrate about what she had done...with Will...for hours. *Frigid? I don't think so.* Instead of cringing and doubting and letting her low confidence and self-esteem get the better of her, she stopped at her apartment, showered and then drove to the kayak hut.

She didn't have time to think about him much. Everyone wanted a kayak. The vet called and made her day with good news. Eddie was recovering well and she could get him the next day. With the diagnosis of an overdose of Benadryl, she assumed her silly mutt must have gotten into the garbage. Three of her brothers called to check on her. Heather texted, but had to leave for her shift.

Clay stopped by and assured her she could use his truck until her car was ready. It had to be handy how there was always a collection of vehicles to use at the garage.

In the absence of mischievous smiles from Clay, she figured Will wasn't the kiss-and-tell type. Later, Randy came by, and to her relief, he didn't ask about Will either. She would have grinned like a damn fool at the first question. She smiled at the thought of him. Tender and rough all in one.

That was the thing about being one of the guys. With the lines clearly crossed, it posed a potential for some awkwardness. With her brothers' friends—who simply had been more brothers once removed—she had never had the problem of sleeping with one of the guys. She had always filed friends of her brothers into an off-limits category. But what she was doing with Will… *What* am *I doing with Will?*

Uneasy regrets squirmed into her thoughts as she headed for the bowling alley after her shift at the kayak hut. She noted Alan's was as busy as Burns' had been because there were not one, not two, but three children's birthday parties scheduled. Bumper bowling was such a pain in the ass to set up. Kelly wasn't one to preach, but she thought the mothers should really monitor their imps' caffeine intake. Or Alan should disassemble the pop machine.

Only when she was tired at the end of her shift did the doubts and worries monopolize her thoughts. *I love him. He'll never love me. That spells DOOM.* But like an ostrich with her head under the sand, she opted for the stupid path to pretend it wasn't so and enjoy the bliss in the present.

Armed with food because she hadn't eaten all day, she drove Clay's truck to the garage and wished for more confidence.

AMABEL DANIELS

What if the sex was because he was sad and vulnerable? What if he's lost all interest since I've comforted him?

Do I seriously have no self-confidence?

"Thanks a lot, Johnny boy," she said to herself. The burn of infidelity had scarred her deeply and she doubted if she would ever forget it.

With such enlightening thoughts, she came in the garage and looked for the mechanics. Will was the only worker present. She found him leaning over a hood, wrench in hand, and she tapped his shoulder with the sub box.

"Hungry?"

He turned and sighed at her.

"Long day?" She sat on the edge of the car.

Will cracked his neck and nodded. He set the sub down on the workbench. "Thanks."

It was like when they had first met. Curt, monotone answers. With a heavy heart, she got the message and stared at an oil stain on the floor.

I am an idiot.

"Yup," she said.

He came back over and elbowed her to get off the car. At the finality in the slam of the hood, she felt like ten thousand morons. He had gotten what he wanted and it was over. Again.

"My knee's been killing me all day. I'm not used to much extracurricular activity," he said as he moved around to clean up.

So not only am I discarded, I'm the cause for your damn knee, too. She nodded and tried to smile at him. Walking off, she felt like crying. *Used? Yep.* She had known what she was getting into. The blame could only be on her.

"What did you ask me?" His voice stopped her and she turned to him.

"What?"

"When you came in."

She grit her teeth. *Yeah, of course he hadn't even been paying attention.* "If you were hungry. I brought you food."

He nodded to himself then hooked a finger for her to come over. She put her hands on her hips, never one to take orders well. He walked up to her. In his dirty jeans and the greasy shirt which couldn't contain his muscles, he looked every bit the rough bad-boy, the powerful man she couldn't resist.

"Do you have any idea how long it took you to get here?"

"Oh! So sorry I couldn't expedite food any faster. We were busy. And you didn't even order it! I—"

"Ten hours and thirty-two minutes."

Kelly blushed. He had counted down the time since he saw her?

"And you come in here and ask me if I'm hungry? That's my greeting?"

She didn't want to meet his eyes. "I didn't know if you'd want me around."

He shook his head in disbelief. "I'll go insane if you're not around me in two minutes."

Well that's descriptive.

"Why wouldn't I want you?" he asked.

Because I love you and you don't love me.

"I thought maybe you got me out of your system. And, and, yesterday, you were vulnerable and so sad about Matt and I was there. Maybe I was a convenient distraction. And—"

He held his hand up. "Look around. There's you. And here's me. We're it. And you want to know if I'm *hungry*?"

Kelly smiled a little and nodded.

He kissed her quickly and carried her to the hood of the car. They didn't really manage to remove many clothes and they were too needy to bother with foreplay.

A short time later, Kelly sat on the hood in her bra and shoes and ate her sub, while Will lounged back in his shirt and socks and ate his. "Whose car is this?" she asked around the food in her mouth.

His grin charmed her. "Father Ronaldson's."

"Oh." She swallowed the un-chewed lump of food. Narrowing her eyes at him, she took a drink from his water bottle. "You are a bad-boy."

He put his pants on and Kelly was relieved they had privacy. Except for the row of rectangular windows cut into the three doors, the garage was virtually closed off from the world. It put an adventurous edge to being naked with him. Not that it wasn't exciting enough to begin with.

With an arm on each side of her, he leaned his fists onto the hood while she sat on the edge. She hesitated to face him.

"When it's you and me, that's it. I'd want you anywhere and anytime. Forget Matt, the psycho bitch who was my mom, your ex, the dog, everything. Do it for me. Because when we come together, we're all that matters."

It wasn't 'I love you', but it chased away her vulnerability. She leaned in for a long kiss.

He pulled back. "Hell no. On the hood again? I can't do it to my knee. Let's get out of here."

CHAPTER 32

Kelly returned Clay's truck four days later. It had taken Will so long to fix her SUV, and she gathered he had deliberately stalled on fixing it until she had persistently asked about it. He had given vague evasive answers about why it was taking so long. With a little leverage and equal stubbornness, she had gotten him to confess he had procrastinated because he wanted her to have a reason for stopping by the garage every night on the way home.

As if she needed one.

Since she had yet to figure out the dynamics of whatever she had with Will, she always went to the stone house. She was sure Will would have left the stone house and come to the townhouse, but she preferred even the minimal distance. With Clay next door, they never could have had true privacy at her apartment.

It was confusing at first because they couldn't get enough of each other's company, but she didn't know what she was to him.

Is he familiar with the concept of 'girlfriend'?

The absence of public displays of affection perplexed her. When they were alone, Will was to her what lighter fluid was to a campfire. And she guessed he was either a shy loner in public, or grudged and ashamed from the biases of Churchston. With his blunt attitude, she bet he was plain sick of the drama. She understood and accepted it. It was who he was, but at the same time, it lowered her self-worth, as though she was a naughty secret sex toy he had to hide.

He had his own issues to deal with, but she didn't understand why it had to feel like a game of hide and seek. She didn't care if everyone in the country knew she was with Will.

Later that week, they both stopped to get gas at the station at the end of Main. At the sight of him, she couldn't hide her smile. He acknowledged her with a brief glance. The lines of his forehead deepened the scowl and he avoided her eyes. His cold shoulder stung, but as the gas station door opened and Delores exited, Kelly had her answer.

Delores strode for her car to fill up. She shot Will a sneer. As she opened her gas tank flap, she turned to Kelly and distorted her lips as though she had stepped in fecal matter.

Kelly leaned back against her SUV to wait for her gas tank to fill. She flipped Delores the finger.

Will walked over after he finished filling up his bike. Without a word, without a glance at her, he reached in to unlock the hood and lifted it. He set his hands on the edge and looked at her engine, not her face. "Baby, I don't want her to know."

Baby? I qualify for an endearment?

She stood next to him and checked under the hood, confused if he was even looking at anything or pretending. "Know what?"

"You and me. She's—" He cracked his neck. "She's evil. If she knows how much you matter to me, she'll use you to hurt me. To hurt us."

Kelly bit her lip. "You think I'm such an idiot or a coward to let her—"

"I don't want her to ruin anything. She's wanted to ruin everything that's ever mattered to me. She tried every day to make Matt hate me. To keep him from being my friend. She doesn't want me ever to be happy. And you make me happy. I don't want her to know."

Kelly was both elated and peeved. *I matter! I make him happy! So who cares about her?* "I get it. You hate her guts. I don't blame you for avoiding her. But this is ridiculous. She can't control your life, and she sure as hell can't control mine. She could never manipulate me to hurt you—"

"You matter too much to me."

"So I'm the closet—I'm your—" Kelly's voice faded. *His what?*

"You're the reason I want to wake up every morning."

She crossed her arms to suppress the urge to turn and hug him. "Let me get this straight. We matter to each other. We make each other happy. And you want to hide because of her."

He faced her. "Please do this for me."

"But it's unnecessary. Consider me impervious. There is no way on Earth she could change the way I feel about you. Look, I'll go over to her mansion right now. I'll show my foot to her—"

"If she can't change the way you feel about me then it shouldn't matter if we keep what we have to ourselves." He paused with a small smile. "You told me to cut my losses, remember? I can. And I have. She doesn't have a spot in my life, but you do. And she will only try to ruin it. I know how she operates."

Kelly studied the serious pleading in his eyes. She lowered her arms and opened her mouth to argue, but he continued.

"I was going to graduate second of my class. Matt was ahead by one exam. He knew I needed top scores to get a scholarship for tech college. So he flunked his final. I know he did. And she did, too. She gave the president of the college a check for half a million. Matt said she claimed it was for an addition to the auditorium, but he'd found her emails stating the money was only good if I didn't attend. If I was rejected from the program."

"I've got nothing, Will. She can't touch me. I'm not malleable—"

"She already tried."

"How?"

He sighed. "Right after the day she saw us on the beach. When you tripped me on the sidewalk. And we found Junior with the snake bite. You gave him an EpiPen. Eric came by the garage afterward, trying to get me to sign a statement that I saw you give him a drug without parental consent. Some bullshit about how you had been fired from your last job, must have lost your license, and you were abusing power giving him a shot—"

"An EpiPen can be bought by anyone! Online! How could I be abusing my power? I don't have any power. I'm not a nurse. I'm not hired to provide medical care. You and I were bystanders. And since I *do* still have an active nursing license, I am bound by Hippocratic Oath to—"

"See what I mean?"

Kelly caught her breath.

"It's how she works. She's a sick, twisted woman."

"She's going to regret messing with me."

"Forget it, Kelly. I'm making a point. Eric's always been her pawn. I called Fred to get him out of my garage. He came by and tore up the papers. In the meantime, Clay must have called Roger about the commotion and he came to the shop, threatening Eric with a lawsuit about police brutality. No one blames you for anything you did."

"I don't care. I know I'm innocent and it's all that matters. But I'll be damned if she thinks she can—" Kelly gasped. "You asked me if I have any enemies in town. Do you think she could have cut the wires on my car?"

"I doubt it. Not her style. She's more focused on power. Psychological warfare."

"She could have sent Eric to do it."

Will shook his head. "Even with the help of the Internet, he couldn't have figured it out."

"Little bitch—"

"Don't worry about her. I won't let her hurt you. But do you get my point? Our time together is our time. But around everyone else… I don't want to risk anything. They'll always think I'm the black sheep. I've been condemned and criticized since I was a kid. I can take it, but I don't want anything to taint you. Or what we have."

What do we have?

The conversation struck a juvenile chord. It wasn't as though she had to brand him hers, announce it to the world. W.P and K.N. scratched into tree bark. For all the time she had been worrying about what she had with Will, she had forgotten to appreciate it for what it was. After John, she had been label-less. No man to define who she was any longer. And now here she was, trying to define what she could be to Will. "I don't like it, but it's doable."

They remained there for a moment. His knuckles whitened at his grip on the SUV's frame.

"You okay?"

He sighed. "You're still wearing your bikini under that scrap of shirt."

She checked. *Oh, yeah. Nipples.* She hugged her arms over her chest. "You're such a man."

He almost smiled then concentrated as he shut the hood gently. "No, I'm *your* man. You still need a serpentine belt."

"Hmmm. Looks like I'll have to find a mechanic around here."

CHAPTER 33

Will was relieved Kelly hadn't been annoyed or hurt by his wish to keep their relationship under wraps.

He dropped the oil filter.

Relationship.

The noun was alien to his vocabulary and it weighed heavily in his mind.

Is that what this is?

He'd had friendships with Matt and the guys, but he had never had a 'relationship' with a woman. He'd been under the lifelong assumption they had been created to correspond to a penis. But he couldn't imagine not being with Kelly, even in the moments when they didn't have their hands on each other.

Relationship?

It was surreal to roll the word on his tongue and he shook his head to try to concentrate on work.

If it wasn't a relationship by dictionary terms, every day with her was a grand and novel adventure. There were many firsts. She had started to teach him how to cook—baking still seemed too feminine, but the results had been good. He had showered with her, another new experience. He taught her how to change her brake pads.

She had discovered a way to massage his knee and it felt like the best therapy he ever had.

He learned how to tickle her in the right spot.

She had explained to him, albeit it felt like a lecture, how goose bumps were formed.

He had beaten her at Scrabble more than half the times they played.

Will had never relaxed on the couch and watched a whole baseball game with a woman next to him, without having to explain anything. He'd never had a woman sit on his lap and do a crossword puzzle while he watched the sun set from the back deck with a cold beer. He'd never had a woman watch him lift weights on the back patio, and he'd never seen a woman twist and bend in that crap they call yoga.

Sometimes, the memories of little things were better than the intimacy he bottled up, waiting for the workday to be over. It was damned hard to hide smiles in public. He had been grinning so much he was certain it was screwing with his face. It was a peeving instinct to bite his lip to hide it at the very thought of her name.

He suspected Clay and Randy might have caught on. Sometimes he caught them watching him with measuring stares. They were smart enough not to say anything or ask, and Will appreciated how his pals could give him space to figure it out.

And if they weren't giving him space, they were probably speechless. He'd never had a girlfriend before.

Whoa. She's a girlfriend, then?

He didn't see why she had to *be* something. She was just her. She was natural to him, natural with him. No nagging, fussing or irrational demanding. They were so mutually stubborn it felt like a perfect fit. He'd never known that down-to-earth women lived on the planet.

"You're sleeping with Kendra, too?" Daisy screamed in the background of the garage, jolting Will from his thoughts.

It wore him out, doing all the work while they waited for Clay's cast to come off. If Clay had been able-bodied to do his job, there would have been less downtime for all his bedmates to chat and linger at the garage.

"We never said we'd be exclusive. You keep hanging out with Brent."

"What! Are you saying I'm a slut?"

Will shook his head under the car. *Common knowledge, Daisy.*

"Don't get hung up about it."

"I can't believe you've been fucking Kendra behind my back!"

"What!"

"She said you were being aggressive. You wouldn't stop begging her to come over and—"

"She came on to me like a bitch in heat. We only fooled around a couple times a few weeks ago."

Will slid out from under the car and went into the store room for the correct filter. The front door slammed in Daisy's wake.

At least I managed to find a woman who doesn't recycle.

The oil filter slipped to the ground.

A monogamous relationship? Girlfriend?

He wiped at his face and scolded himself to slow down. There was no point to count the chickens before the eggs hatched, because for all he knew, she could leave him. Like everyone else had.

CHAPTER 34

With each day, she fell more and more in love with him, with every little detail. It was like a speeding car pursuit she had no control over. But the hiding nature of their relationship started to feel less like a thrilling forbidden love, and more like pathetic cowardice. It grated on her nerves, and she wasn't the only one getting cranky. There were moments where he seemed irritable and annoyed when she'd finally get to see him after work at the bowling alley. Quieter, subdued, more sensitive. The walls they had torn down seemed to be building back up.

Is he tiring of me already?

After skinny dipping late one night, they dressed and sat on the sand of the public beach in their damp clothes. It was peaceful except for the constant glances Will tossed at the opposite end of the beach.

Matt's memorial. She bit her lip, her anger at Delores renewed with fresh blood. Will's deep sigh was loud in the quiet of the night, and she couldn't stand his agitation.

"It's pretty ugly," she said.

"What the hell is it supposed to be?"

"An anorexic whale?"

He glanced in its direction again.

"I think it's some form of abstract art." She stood and held her hand out to him. "Come on."

"What?"

"Let's go look and see if we can figure out what it is."

He stared at the water.

"She can't ban you from the fricking *public* beach!"

He cursed to himself but got up. They held hands as they walked to the memorial. She swore he must be struggling with every foot, trying not to look over his shoulder as though he was going to be told he wasn't welcome.

I absolutely hate that woman.

They stood in front of it, their fingers laced together. Kelly cocked her head side to side, trying to figure it out. Will gave it a blank stare and stuffed his other hand in his pocket. Giving up, Kelly sat on the sand, and with his hand still in hers, he plopped down next to her.

"How the fuck is this supposed to represent him?" he asked.

"Did he ever say he wished to be reincarnated as a bug with blubber?"

"It looks like an elephant with antlers."

A faint noise sounded behind them and he moved to get up. Probably a raccoon.

"Will. I'm going to kick you if you scramble away. It's an ugly statue. You can look at it all you want. Don't let Delores control your life. She pisses me off."

He twisted his mouth and looked off to the water.

"You're not a damn sissy. It's past time you write her off and move on with it."

He turned to face her.

She stood. "I know you're the bigger person, Will. You don't have to take cover from her. I've got your back." She cupped her hands at her mouth to yell at the night sky. "Hey Delores! I'm on the beach with Will. The memorial looks like shit! And you don't deserve him, anyway. So you can kiss my—"

He yanked her hand to sit her down. With a small smile he pulled her to his side. "I shouldn't be here. How can I sit here and look at this thing? I let him die, Kelly. I should have saved him."

She swallowed the lump in her throat. *My bad.* He wasn't self-conscious because of his mommy issues, but the grief of losing his best friend. She had predicted he would never talk about Matt. It still had to be hard. She tucked her hand in his. "You can only do so much."

No answer.

"Do you know how many damn people I couldn't save? How many people I had to help into body bags? And I'm a bleeding-heart baby! I only talk tough. I quit my job because I couldn't handle the stress of Norbert dying. And his daughter hating me for letting it happen. Do you know how many threatening letters I got from his campaign staffers, saying I shouldn't work at the hospital if I can't do my job—"

"They threatened you? Is that why your brother asked me to look out for you?"

"When did Grant say…? Oh, when he tripped by the lake?"

"They threatened you?"

"Not really. I mean, I guess. His daughter was the only real threat. Physical at least. They told me she was straight-jacketed away."

"Are you always this naïve? Someone left a snake in the truck you were driving. Someone ran over you with a boat—"

"Will, settle down. Don't get far-fetched. I blame alcohol for the boat deal. And the snake? Don't you think that'd be bit extreme? It was back in Atlanta. The hospital took the letters seriously. Cops checked it out. Grant was all over the legal aspects of it. They were vague threats. Not about killing me, really. They were dumping blame, wanting me fired. Besides, they've been busy moving on to a new candidate to market."

His chest rose with a deep breath. "I should have talked him out of enlisting."

"You never wanted to go in the Marines?" She recalled Junior's clarification. It had been Matt's idea, but she assumed Will must have warmed to the ambition.

"I'm as patriotic as the next guy, but no, I never wanted to go. It was almost a week after I'd gotten out of college. I wanted to add on to the garage, expand clientele. Clay and I talked about subbing out the routine crap and setting up a specialty shop for ourselves. Classics and rebuilding antiques."

He laced his fingers in her hand. "He'd just gotten done with his carpentry program. The pole barn behind the townhouse? He was going to make it his studio and workshop. And she hated it. She wanted him to go into politics, not slave away working with his hands. So she shipped out his girlfriend. Made up some bullshit about him cheating on her. She broke up her son's fucking relationship. That's why he did it."

"Matt enlisted to get away from Delores?"

"He enlisted to get back at her. She abhorred the military. That, too, wasn't fit for *her* son." He shook his head. "I tried to talk him out of it. Let's dodge town. Move. Start up shop somewhere new. But he knew how much I wanted my garage. He thought going in the Marines, defying her, getting away for a while...he thought it'd be a way to teach her. To show her she can't control him. I had to go. I couldn't let him go without having his back. But it was his hand on the door handle that triggered the bomb. Not mine."

Kelly wiped a tear from his cheek. "The hardest thing about my job was telling the family to move on, to accept it. But it's true. Life's too short otherwise."

He nodded.

"What do you think Matt would want you to do? How do you think he'd want you spend the rest of your life?"

Will studied the concern in her gaze.

What would Matt want me to do?

He opened his eyes wider.

What should I do on the night-fallen beach, alone with an amazing, generous, beautiful woman, in front of the ugliest chunk of stone I've ever seen?

He leaned over to kiss her, lowering her to the ground.

"Mmm." She smiled as they kissed. She pulled his shirt off, running her palms over his chest. "I like the way Matt thinks."

He smiled into her lips and slipped her shirt off, turning to nuzzle her neck.

With a fast roll, she moved him to his back. "I like it on top."

He laughed lightly as he helped her slide his pants off. As suddenly as she had moved, he rolled her back under him on the sand. "I like it on top, too."

She threaded her fingers through his hair as he eased her shorts off. "And I like you—"

"Hey!"

"Shit." Will sat up, blocking her face from the light that flashed after the yell from the road.

"Eek!" Kelly smiled coyly as though she was mocking guilt.

"Hey! I see you over there! What's going on?" By the bounce of the flashlight in the sand, Eric had to be running.

Will checked over his shoulder as he helped Kelly up. She was laughing too hard to cooperate. "Fuck." Laughs slipped from his lips as he hurried. "Come on!"

"Hey! Will Parker! I saw you! Stop. That's public indecency, you good-for-nothing asshole! Who's with you?"

They took off on the beach, their clothes in their hands. Will scooped her up and carried her over his shoulder. She tucked her face into his neck, but couldn't stop laughing as he ran for the other end of the beach.

"Will!" Eric's voice wasn't far off.

Will ran toward the kayak hut and sprinted down the dock.

"The canoes." Kelly pointed and he rushed for one. After he lowered her into it, she fixed the paddles on the sides as he freed the rope.

Floating in the middle of the river, the riparian brush blocked them from Eric's sight. Alone again, they resumed what had been interrupted. Afterward, Kelly lay next to him with her head on his chest, watching the stars. Will thought about what she had said.

How would Matt want him to spend the rest of his life? Will didn't know. But he was getting a sinking idea he knew *who* he wanted for the rest of his life and it scared the hell out of him.

CHAPTER 35

Burns was out of town the next day so it was Junior who called Kelly to collect the kayaks at the shallow end of the river behind his house. In the game of tag which was their job, he had driven the van of people back to the beach. Around noon she pulled off the side of the road to check the straps on the kayaks she had loaded. Tires crunched on the roadside berm as a car slowed to a stop.

Ready for a dumbass tourist to cruise by and yell out something about her ass, she sighed and tightened the loose ratchet strap. No obscenities were shouted, no directions were sought, but the car hadn't left. With the next kayak secured, she peeked through the cracks of the boats. Plastic domes covered the red and blue inactivated lights on top of the car.

Eric must have seen them last night after all. She winced.

"What do you want, Eric? I'm busy." She concentrated on the next ratchet strap, giving Eric all the attention she felt he ever deserved. While she was a smartass, she had no problem respecting the law when they seemed competent.

Eric, however, had failed to impress her.

She headed around the kayaks, checking the trailer lights were blinking the four ways, and the license plate was affixed with its single screw. She wasn't going to give Eric the satisfaction of actually finding something wrong.

"Kelly?" Gannon stepped from his car, his hands in his pockets. A truck roared by on the road.

He hadn't changed a bit. Still reminded her of an Irish version of her Uncle Gavin, wearing a suit two sizes too big.

"You lost?" She smiled.

"What the hell are you doing? Boats? You're renting boats?" He shook his head. "People need smartasses like you in hospitals, not getting sunburnt renting out boats."

She set her hands on her hips. "You came all the way out here to tell me that?"

He sighed as he walked closer, shook his head. "Good to see you, too," he said as he hugged her. "Actually, I came by to talk to you about something else."

Another truck roared by, the drone of sound complete with the driver honking the "Me man, me see young lady" honk.

His grave expression worried her. "Here? Why don't you meet me back at the hut in town? You can follow."

Despite her familiarity with Gannon, she didn't like not knowing the reason for his visit. She had him follow her back to the kayak hut, stalling as her mind raced at what an FBI agent could possibly want with her.

Norbert and Betsy were closed cases. He died of a medical accident—she, suicide.

Fumbling through her purse as she drove, she checked her cell. Had something happened to Will? The boys? Dad? Why would a detective come down to tell her?

Ten missed calls from Heather. Three from Dad. Many more from her brothers. Her phone had been in her purse all morning. She pulled up at the hut before she could call or listen to the voicemails.

Gannon exited the car and walked toward the hut. With a swipe, she scanned her texts. They were long, too many to process. Only one caught her attention.

Grant's. "Don't say anything," she read.

Don't say anything about what? Her mind foggy with a charged mixture of curiosity and dread, she jumped out of the truck.

"Let me unlock it and open the window," she said.

"You got someone to cover for you while we talk?" Gannon asked.

"No. This will do. It hasn't been busy today. What's going on? You're freaking me out."

"Kelly, APD located the body of your ex-husband three days ago. Decaying in his freezer."

She dropped her phone. "Excuse me?"

She listened to the brief, official, and objective summary. In between words, she detected a hint of sincere sympathy, probably in case she was bereaved. Mostly, she sensed he was legitimately probing for answers to serious questions, and likely wondering at her potential involvement. They might be chummy, but she suspected underneath his laid-back manner, he was all business.

The shock settled in. It wasn't expected news, but she remained logical. "Why did you drive all the way down here to tell me? Phone call couldn't work?"

What does he want from me?

"When I saw your name, I thought it'd be a kind gesture to let you know personally."

"When you saw my name? What, in his obit?" she said. If there had been an obituary for John, she would have heard much sooner. Heather, Dad, her brothers. Any of them would have told her.

"No. In his file."

"File? This is a federal case?"

He sighed. "It wouldn't have been except for a couple details."

He offered her a scanned copy of John's scratchy penmanship. In a letter which had been addressed to her, he had penned some weighty news. He'd missed her. He'd made a mistake. He still loved her, needed her, wanted her back. She read it quickly and turned it over to see if there was more.

"Where did this come from?"

"It was found next to the body. There was an opened envelope addressed to you in Atlanta."

Kelly checked the scanned image of the envelope. "That's Dad's house. After the divorce, I stayed there until I decided to move."

Gannon pocketed it. "It was never sent. Someone opened the envelope before it was dropped in the mail. Stamp's on it, but it wasn't mailed."

She shook her head, trying to make sense of it.

"Were you aware he was trying to mend the marriage?" he asked.

"Mend what marriage? We were already divorced. That means 'it's over'."

"He never mentioned regrets to you?"

"No. The last time I spoke to him was when I signed the house over to him. Last I saw, he was with his lover. I caught him cheating on me with her."

"A Miss Jones?"

Kelly shrugged. "Maybe. I don't know. It was a while ago. I wasn't dwelling on the little details. Kind of busy being depressed and humiliated and betrayed. Divorce sorts of fun."

"Did you ever meet her?"

She looked around, aware of the stares which meant *everyone* was watching on the beach. "No. I saw her in the bed when they were screwing. First and last time I saw her or knew she existed."

"He never said anything about her?"

"When I called him the day after I caught him cheating he said her name. Sasha. He'd met her at a strip club."

"Remember which club?"

She shook her head.

Gannon scribbled on a notepad. "No one has seen her since the time of his death. It seems she used an alias. We've checked with his family and they don't recall her."

"John was an only child and seldom spoke to his family," Kelly said. "Doesn't surprise me."

"Friends and coworkers don't remember much other than her name. We have no idea who she was. She's gone."

"Gone as in dead? Was she killed with him?"

"There was only one body in the condo. One blood type."

Kelly inhaled shakily as her calm shattered. "Who would have killed him? I mean, how? Was it some punk robbing him? What—"

"No sign of robbery. It's odd about the girlfriend, but we've hit a dead end with her. She might have been gone before he died. People vaguely remember her at the condo. What I have gathered is they fought a lot."

"No one from John's office remembers her?"

"Oh, they do. From what we've heard, she was a looker. But there's no name to tie to her. We have a little video of her from the office lobby but nothing conclusive."

"What about his new job?"

Gannon knit his brows. "How'd you know about that?"

She explained the small world of Heather's brother working at John's company. When he remained quiet, she continued. "I remember thinking it odd."

"Why?"

"Denver? John hated anything higher up than a ladder. If he was relocating, the Mile High City is the last place to come to mind."

"The email was sent roughly the same time of his death. Given the extent of decay of the corpse, it's difficult to determine exactly what day he died."

Waves and beach-play noise deafened the roar in her head as she tried to think.

"As you've relocated some time ago, APD didn't include you for immediate consideration for questioning. They've already spoken to his family, his coworkers, his clients. Any enemies you think he might have had? Anything, anyone?"

"No."

Forensically, it was a nasty but clean murder. Tidy by means of the lack of evidence, nasty in regards to the violence and blood. Suicide, they said, seemed out of the question. His neck had been snapped by force before he had been mauled with a crowbar. Consensus was it seemed like a personal killing, the body beaten both before and after death.

"Normally in a case like this the spouse is one of the first to look to."

Business was business, but his question still stung. "Am I some kind of a suspect then?" She recalled Grant's text. "And I'm not his spouse. I'm his ex-spouse."

How can anyone think I killed John?

She hadn't seen him since the day they met at Grant's office to review the lease for their house they were renting out. At least more than four months ago. It felt like decades ago. John had been in his rented condo, decaying for months. She shuddered.

"No. It seems you were absent prior to his death. Divorce seemed amicable in paper. Neither of you made out with any money."

"I kept what was mine and he kept what was his. We both wanted out of the marriage."

"He have any money problems? His records indicate he was conservative with his finances."

She coughed rudely. *Conservative?* He was a stickler. A tyrannical saver. It had always annoyed her. They had made good money, after all. "No. We were secure. We both had good jobs."

"Drugs? Mistresses?"

She deadpanned at him. "Only the one I found him with as far as I know. I never saw any signs of drugs. I think I would have noticed something. He'd come home hung-over sometimes, but I didn't see him much. Our schedules didn't really line up."

No prints. No suspects. No answers. Decaying in—

"Wait, you found him in the freezer?"

"Yes. The landlord had been paid for three months upfront. He'd gone out of town for some time. When he returned, he followed up on complaints of a smell and found him in there."

"Decaying in the freezer? How? If he was on ice, he wouldn't have been decaying."

"Power went out," Gannon said. "Way back in the beginning of the year, we'd had a big storm. Blew the circuit and he began decaying."

"In the freezer? How can a body fit in…"

He tilted his head to the side with a grimace. "The coroner believes he must have been put in the freezer close to his time of death. Before the limbs stiffened."

John. Dead.

"I'm sorry, Kelly."

She nodded. "I am, too. I mean, it's a gruesome way to go."

Gannon checked his phone, then stepped away for a moment. She tried to let the news settle in her mind.

"You remember my last phone call?" he said as he returned.

"Vaguely. You found the name of some friend in Betsy's car."

"No. I said they had found a name. Not a friend. Denner."

"Yeah."

"That's what caught me, Kelly. APD contacted us because of the circumstances of the crime. They're thinking it might be a serial job. Lack of evidence motivated them for help, too. Once I saw your name on the envelope, I was intrigued. But when I started to read through the reports, it's the name that got me. They found a partial print on the freezer door."

"Whose was it? Denner's?"

He nodded. "It wasn't a very good print, but that's one of the hits."

Odd. No wonder it piqued Gannon's interest. Kelly swallowed thickly. "Does this Denner person have a record?"

"No. Only reason she showed up in the database was because she worked as a secretary in a prison in Salt Lake City."

"Maybe it's a print from the last person in the condo."

"Since it's a partial print, it's difficult to consider with weight." He scratched his chin. "But the name triggered me. We're gonna stay in touch, alright? I might not have the time to drive out here again, but I'm keeping my eye out for you, kid. You impressed me back in the city. You cared more about doing the right thing for Norbert than technicalities of whose shift it was and who gave him the meds. Your kind of compassion is a rare breed. And I know if you think of anything, no matter how small it seems, you'll call me. If I don't answer, leave a message. Right?"

"Of course." She followed him to his car. "Hey, wait. Do you know when the funeral is?"

CHAPTER 36

Will spent the day running errands. It was busywork which really needed to be done, driving around outer towns picking up parts and items. While it would have made more sense to have One Arm Clay to play fetch, Will had wanted to be mobile and out of Churchston, in case Eric wanted to play funny business with him for catching him on the beach with Kelly.

Sometime in bootcamp, Will had learned to appreciate rules. Laws were laws for good reasons. Technically, it had been public indecency. But they were alone.

When he came to the garage, Clay informed him an officer had talked to Kelly earlier. Checking across the street, he saw Junior manning the hut. He sped home, with his mind full of worry and his gut twisting with fear. First he looked at the townhouse. Then his stone house. He found her sitting on the beach, staring at the waves.

"Kelly." He ran toward her, thankful she was in one piece. Her face didn't show lines of pain or sadness, only that she was lost in thought. Her concentration could be just as worrisome. Eddie wagged as he came close and she stood to face him. "What happened?" He wrapped her in a hug and she sighed into him.

Hand in hand, they walked back to his house as she told him the news from the detective. She rambled on, explaining what Heather thought, what her brothers were asking, what she didn't understand herself. Questions and worries spilled from her mouth.

Caressing her knuckles, he led her inside and didn't know where he stood.

Is she missing this guy?

Does she regret not being there with him?

He was torn with unease. At the lack of tears, she didn't seem sad. He hated how the jealousy in him had him relieved at that. But the hints of confusion and worry on her face, the idea of her big heart bleeding at the thought of someone in pain, those thoughts had him sympathizing with her.

"I'm going back for the funeral."

Will nodded, letting the weight of her statement shift until it found its spot in his head.

"I'll drive up tomorrow and maybe stay a couple days."

"You want your old life back."

Kelly narrowed her eyes.

He twitched his mouth. She was leaving. He had known the day would come. She'd want to go home. This had only been a temporary change of scenery.

"You miss him."

"He's dead, Will. There is nothing to want back. Dead or alive."

He avoided her eyes. Maybe she didn't *miss* the idiot, per se. But she'd go home and realize it was where she belonged. With her family. With people who weren't afraid to tell her they loved her.

Like a magician's incredible shrinking man, he scolded himself for thinking she belonged here on the lake with him. She always talked about her brothers, her dad, some Heather woman. She was loyal to her family. She'd never stay away from them for good.

For good. He looked at her with a lump in his throat. *Kelly for good. Forever.* How had she gotten under his skin? And she was leaving him.

"Why do you need to go then?"

Begging? I'm pleading?

"I *was* married to him. He *was* family. I'd be a bitch if I didn't. It's like how people sneeze and still say 'God bless you'. I'd like to think everyone knows it started from the superstition that you sneezed your soul out or whatever. Everyone knows it's not true, but they still say it because it's polite."

"You're going to the funeral to say Gesundheit?"

"Something like that."

Quiet filled the living room.

She took a deep breath. "Will. I need to tell you something."

Christ, it's over. Whatever magic they had, it was fucking over. *I knew it.* He clenched his jaw, readying for the blow.

"I know you don't want to hear this, but it's not fair. To either of us. You can accept it or fight it, but I have to do this."

Shoot me now. Will stared into her warm blue-green eyes. "Don't."

She shook her head and her eyes moistened as she cupped his chin. "I love you. I know you won't reciprocate. I know you don't believe in it. But I do. I want you to know. I love you and I'll probably always love you. I want—" She inhaled shakily and he put his hands on her shoulders.

"I wanted to make sure I told you. John was only thirty and his life is over. Done. Just like that. You and I, we're so young, but life is so damn short. I can't take it for granted. I don't want another day to go by without you knowing I love you."

Will let out the breath he had been holding. He took her hands. "Kelly, I—"

She kissed him.

He allowed a small smile at her lips as he kissed her back. It was tender and slow and telling. Because when he held her like this, he wondered how she didn't catch on to his lie. As he kissed her, he showed her he reciprocated every and any kind of love he knew.

CHAPTER 37

On the drive back to Atlanta, it seemed like every median dash was a cumulative tally mark for the void that had grown in her heart. Kelly had told Heather, almost a year ago, that she left home because she had been lost. Back in her hometown for John's funeral, she felt lost, but empty, too.

Seeing her friends and family again lifted her spirits. Heather stuck to her side like glue. Wade was the only brother who wasn't there, but he called. Grant reported his ankle was fine. Finn interrogated her about "this Will character" Grant had mentioned. Sean asked how long she was staying in Churchston.

Still, even surrounded by people she loved and had truly missed, she couldn't shake the emptiness.

At the funeral home, she felt as though she was on display. Kelly had always been civil and fond of her in-laws, but she never liked them. She caught people staring. Some glared and whispered. She assumed they figured she was connected to John's death or somehow at fault, regardless of her alibi. Some wrapped her in teary-eyed hugs and murmured condolences. She had a guilt trip for depriving them of the mourning, loving, weeping act.

It wasn't that she didn't mourn. John's death was bad news. Especially the way he was killed. But having witnessed enough death, she was hardened to it. She couldn't weep. Dry-eyed and sober, she had attended the services because she knew she should.

John's death fell under the same category of the hundreds of patients she had seen at the hospital. Strangers. Acquaintances. How could her grief be heartfelt if John never had her heart? Not like Matt's death for Will.

It was almost easier to accept John's death than Norbert's. She hadn't been in control of John's health, his life. It had taken a while for her to bound back from the betrayal and humiliation of rejection, but sometime on the lake in Churchston, she had accepted it. There was no love between her and John when they divorced and she had suspected there never had been any real love for the man she had married. Not the real kind. Not the physical kind which had her missing Will every second she was gone.

Kelly sat in the back with her family and studied John's picture on the prayer card in Heather's hand.

Irony overwhelmed her. Not for the divorce. Not for being unable to appease his desire to get her back, but regret he had never gotten to experience the kind of bond she had with Will. She hoped everyone got the chance. It was a rare gift.

"She's not here," Heather whispered.

Kelly knew who. She had wondered if she would come face to face with the bitch she had found in her master suite. If 'Sasha'—or whatever her name was— would come to say good-bye. Kelly glimpsed Gannon standing at the door. He was probably wondering the same thing.

Since she had been his most recent companion, Kelly garnered Sasha had to know something about John's death. The timing said everything: the woman came and had left with no trace. And John had been killed.

Coincidences are crap.

The night after Kelly left, Will went to Elmer's and tried to drink himself stupid. Easier said than done. Every time he lifted the glass to his lips, he saw Kelly's face in the reflection of the glass, her smirk keeping the whiskey away from his lips. Exhausted, he leaned his head to the counter.

Kendra came in and purred to him until he snapped at her. With a roll of her eyes, she stalked off. Later, Jaycee tried and Will nearly yelled. She got the point, too.

Randy hobbled in on his crutches and, with a graceless slump, took the stool next to Will. They didn't speak in companionable silence. Will flinched when a glass fell and broke behind the bar. *Goddamn post-trauma.* He preoccupied himself with visions of Kelly in his head.

"She'll be back," Randy said without turning from the TV overhead.

Will shook his head. He opened and closed his mouth, with no clue how to express what was going on in his head. Randy patted his back and ordered a beer. His company was little comfort.

I'm not completely *alone, after all.*

But Randy would find a nice, polite, responsible girl someday, and he'd get married. Clay was probably already on his way to fatherhood and eventually, reluctantly, to husbandry. Matt, well, he was gone.

Panic pricked him as he considered a life without Kelly.

He traced the rim of his glass with his forefinger, the whiskey still untouched. He would lose Kelly, there was no question about it. She would go home to her family and realize she was loved. But he loved her, too. Surrendering the walls to his heart brought a lot of grimaces, but she was worth it. He did love her, but he could only win her for good, forever, if he took the risk and really let her in.

It would be a tough fight. The brothers and dad she worshipped like heroes, or him, a gloomy, scarred, pissed-off veteran no one had ever thought was good enough.

She'd never leave her family for me. Not forever.

But what if she had family here? It would be a fight on a level playing field. He swallowed, guessing he was either suckered, stupid, or smarter than he realized.

I'll make her my family. And try every damn day of my life to make sure she won't want to leave.

They had good times, right? Sure they fought, but they were loving fights, not like Clay fought with women. Debates. Not arguments. And they always made up even when it was unnecessary.

He straightened abruptly.

Randy quirked a brow at him. "You alright?"

It was simple. He'd get a ring and she'd stay. She said she loved him and always would. "When does Kelly's lease expire?"

Randy jumped at Will's unexpected question. "Uh, she paid upfront for the next two months, why?"

Settled. And he was watching Eddie for her. She had to come back for the dog. He clapped Randy on the back and took off. While he had the guts to follow through with such an ill-planned idea, he intended to ride on the momentum. Kind of like how Matt had decided they should go into the Marines.

One, two, three, do it.

CHAPTER 38

After the funeral, Heather helped Kelly make broccoli chicken alfredo and German chocolate cake to tease Dad. It was the supposedly foolproof meal he had burned when she was six years old— when she had decided it was time for *her* to do the cooking in the household.

Afterward, they retired to shoot hoops in the driveway. Once it was too dark to see, and Grant grew crabby since he couldn't play because of his ankle, they went in and started a board game.

Finn frowned at her. "You're cheating."

"Am not." She had always won at Clue. Not only did she use deductive reasoning, Kelly watched when her brothers wrote down a clue on their lists. She couldn't see what they were writing, which *would* have been cheating, but she could tell if they were writing at the top, middle or bottom of their lists, telling her which of the clues they asked had been granted. Not cheating. Sharp.

"What happened to your leg, honey?"

Kelly followed Dad's gaze to her calf. "Oh." The cut was nothing but a pinkish red slash of new skin. "Fell off a boat."

"On the same lake he tripped into?" he asked of Grant. "Sounds like a dangerous place."

Kelly dismissed him with a wave. She didn't want to face the gazillion questions he would have asked. Reminded again of the incident, she hosted a renewed angry question mark at which idiot was driving. "Accidents happen."

Lesson learned: don't play with drunks on boats.

Knocks sounded at the door and Grant got up to answer. Gannon entered the dining room.

Kelly assured him whatever he wanted to talk about, her family could hear. Finn offered his seat to Gannon, but he opted to stand.

"When was the last time you spoke to your ex-husband?" Gannon began.

She lifted a brow. They had covered this when they talked at the kayak hut. "I told you. At Grant's office when we finalized the house papers."

Grant confirmed since he had been the one who wrote the lease for them.

"Did you speak to him between when you found him this with Miss Jones and the divorce?"

Kelly shook her head. "No. It took me about half a day to call him and tell him I wanted the divorce. I don't think I saw him except to sign papers."

"He was agreeable to the divorce?"

"Yes. In the short time we discussed divorce, he was degrading and accusatory, saying he wanted me out of his life. He tried to make it sound as though he had asked for the divorce, not that I wasn't going to if he hadn't. Heather told me he moved in with Sasha when he quit his job."

Gannon reached in his pocket and pulled out a recorder. "He made several phone calls to you after you moved out of the house."

"I'm telling you, I didn't talk to him—"

"He called your old number. It took me a while to get the messages since you had shut off your phone, but he called the number you had before."

She relaxed. "Oh. It was a joint account. I canceled the phone and got a new one when I moved out and started my own account."

"I understand. It was a bit of luck I even got this message," Gannon said. "Someone bought a phone for his elderly mother and she couldn't figure out how to use it. John didn't know your number had been recycled. I'd like you to listen to this last message. The call was probably made around the time of his death."

Probably. They couldn't know for sure how long he had been dead from the advanced decay of his remains. And the body could have been maintained in the freezer before the power had gone out.

Kelly swallowed and nodded. It was eerie, listening to John's slightly nasal voice in the room, as though he was back from the dead.

"I know you hate me, Kelly. And I don't blame you. I screwed up. I think we should give it another chance. Maybe we could meet for coffee, you know? It's not… I'm not the same man now. I realize what I lost. She's not you, Kelly. She's not at all like you and I miss you. Sure we drifted apart but we'll work on it. I promise. I told Lisa I couldn't see her anymore either."

Kelly rolled her eyes. Not one, but two mistresses. *My, he was a busy man.*

"And Sasha…she's crazy. I want you. We'll make it work. I know you spend more money than you can save and you can be kind of paranoid sometimes and you'll always be a slob, but I can overlook your faults."

She bit her lip and glared at the recorder. *I'm not an overspending paranoid slob!*

She knew he had been stringent about finances because of his job the same as she was slightly germaphobic because of hers. And unorganized did not equal sloppy. She had always kept the kitchen and bathroom excessively clean. *Who cares if my bra sits on the floor for a couple days before I chuck it in the washer?*

"I don't want her. I want you—"

The sound of a door slamming shut came in his pause.

"What are you doing here? I never want to see you again—" His tone rang of anger and urgency. Scuffling noises took over speech and then the call ended.

Kelly stared at the recorder. *Was that when he died? Was that the sound of his neck breaking?* She had a hard time swallowing, imagining the grisly attack.

"You had no idea?"

Inhaling deeply, she looked up at Gannon. "No. But it wouldn't have mattered if I did, it was beyond over to me. I'm sorry about how this happened and I hope justice is served, but I don't see how I can have any answers for you. I don't see how I'm related to this."

Am I related to this?

She tried to clear her throat. "Do you think I'm involved—"

"Kelly—" Grant warned, ever the lawyer.

She held a hand up to him and continued. "Do you think I'm in any kind of danger? I wasn't even here. We divorced. I didn't matter to him. I moved away. I have a new job, a new life—"

"Deep breaths, Kel." Heather rubbed her back.

Gannon put the recorder back in his pocket. "Like you said, there is nothing to connect you to his death. Other than his attempts to mend the marriage—"

"There was no more marriage! We divorced!"

"Other than his attempts to reconnect with you, there is nothing to tie you to him. From his phone records and your relocation, there's no reason to think he had any hope you'd come back. It seems he didn't even know you'd left town. He did call you around the time of his death. It's a fact I can't overlook."

No one spoke.

Gannon cleared his throat. "I'm looking at every angle, Kelly. There's little else to go on at the moment. I don't see how you should be worried personally. Maybe he was in trouble with something you weren't aware of. Maybe he pissed off the wrong person. Maybe he made a mistake and wanted your forgiveness before things got worse. I won't know unless I ask."

"What's the date of the phone call?" Kelly asked. "Is it before or after he sent the email about quitting his job?"

Gannon took a deep breath before answering. "He made the call an hour before the email was sent."

Then whoever killed him had to have sent the email. Covering tracks.

Some minutes later, with a mutual agreement to stay in touch, Kelly saw the detective out the door.

Clue seemed like an ironically ill-fitting way to spend the rest of the night. Instead, they tossed ideas and speculations about the way John had died. The brothers departed one by one for the night and Heather stayed with Kelly in the kitchen over the last of the cake.

"You really love him." Heather's comment pulled her from scheming 'what ifs'.

Kelly straightened from her chocolate galore and groaned. "No. My God, I came back for the damn funeral because it seemed appropriate. I don't love him and I don't think I ever really did. For one kind gesture of respect for the dead—"

Heather smacked Kelly's forehead lightly as she stood up and poked in the freezer. "I meant Will. Is there still ice cream in here?"

"Oh." Kelly sighed. She had left Atlanta defending her explanation she had needed space, and she had come back to Atlanta defending her statement she wasn't mourning her true love. "I think so. I thought you were watching your cholesterol."

Heather shrugged and sat down with the tub and a spoon. "It's the real thing. It was like you were listening to a weather report or the stock market closing. The whole thing about missing you, it didn't even make you smile."

Because she had been busy craning her ears for a clue or a ninja noise. Some sound, some whisper, something to tell her who did it. The rest, in one ear and out the other.

"This is the kind of stuff that happens in movies, Heather." Her voice was shakier than she wanted it to be. She had seen all kinds of people maimed and dead in the ER. But she never knew any of them personally. It had made her world particularly safe in a philosophical way.

"I never realized how unhappy you were. The whole marriage."

Kelly pulled the ice cream toward herself for a bite. "I didn't either. I settled and thought I should tell my doubts to shut up and be happy with what I had."

"And Will? He makes you happy?"

Kelly smiled around the lump of Rocky Road in her mouth, amused the ice cream still felt so cold with the heat on her cheeks.

At night before she went to bed in the room she had used when she was a little girl, Kelly called the garage, simply to hear his voice.

"He's not here."

Kelly smiled at Clay's greeting.

"He left a couple hours ago to help Randy with some kind of mold."

"Someone's house flooded?"

"No. I don't know. Some kind of crown mold. Must be some kinda bug."

Crown molding. She smiled at the thought of Will getting closer to his pals.

"He's at Randy's, then?"

"Should be. Hey, gotta go. I'll see you when you get back."

Next, she called Randy's, but he said Will had already left. He also told her Will was acting really strange and irritable, something she could take with a grain of salt. Randy thought he seemed to be ignoring everyone who crossed his path. And when Randy said he'd never seen Will's temper so short, she wanted to believe it was because he was miserable missing her.

She tried the stone house and his cell phone, but still couldn't reach him. She'd told Burns and Alan she would be back late the next day, but she couldn't wait to see Will. Calling herself every kind of a dependent sissy-needy-clingy-helpless woman, she backed out of her dad's driveway at one in the morning.

And she did so with a smile.

CHAPTER 39

The excitement of seeing Will again kept Kelly alert on her drive back to Churchston. With her early return, she hoped she might be able to surprise him in the shower or in bed. He had given her a key to the stone house before she had left.

It felt so thrilling yet perfectly natural when he had given it to her. They had been practically living together in the stone house. Even Eddie had his preferred spot on the loveseat.

When they made love before she had left, she had felt it. Sensed it. *Will cares about me. He really does.*

It was no mystery to her he had a hard time with his feelings. It didn't seem fair, but she realized she was battling an old war and it would take time for him to break down his guardedness. Even if he couldn't say it, his actions had spoken loud and clear whether he wanted them to or not.

Smiling, she tortured herself with ridiculous ideas of a future. She'd definitely clean up the other rooms in the stone house. One would make a great library. And they'd have to do something about the kitchen. It was clean and orderly, the way Will did everything, but the stove was ancient. And it'd be nice to have a little breakfast bar so she could watch him lift on the back patio while she sipped her coffee every morning. Speaking of which, he definitely needed a newer coffee maker.

Her abstract thoughts turned to a list of things *they* needed for *their* house. It reminded her of how she had scanned the items for her bridal shower. John had not wanted anything to do with choosing the items, too busy and hectic at the almighty office, even then.

Thinking of the wedding registry had her thinking about marriage. Slight melancholy itched at her as she realized she was planning a future with Will when her ex had been buried the day before.

She didn't waste time worrying if she was really being rude with such thoughts because fear sharpened her questions.

What if I had been there?

What if John had done something stupid at the office and was bookkeeping for the Mafia?

I would have been with him as his wife in our jointly-owned house—and probably killed, too.

Or what if he had had a secret drug-smuggling operation and I was caught in the violence as a bystander?

"What are you doing here? I never want to see you again—"

Driving along in the dark, Kelly replayed John's words in her mind. Who had gone to the condo? Who hadn't he ever wanted to see again?

Gannon said the security camera in the condo lobby showed no visitors who stood out. And the condo owner had reused the feed, only going back in recordings three months.

A friend? Another lover? A pissed-off Mr. Nikki kind of cheated-upon husband? A Medusa? John sounded surprised at the visitor's arrival. But she rationalized by his words that he had known the person, had dealt with the person before…

"I never want to see you again."

He yelled those precise words to Kelly when they divorced, ousting her from his life as he started his new one with Sasha.

And what ever happened to Sasha?

Kelly recounted the memory of the recording in her mind and connected the dots. Sasha must have been gone already. Dumped.

"I told Lisa I couldn't see her anymore either."

The 'either' likely meant Sasha had already gotten the boot.

Sunlight crept over the horizon of the lake when Kelly arrived at the townhouse. She parked on her half of the driveway, tossed her dirty clothes into her apartment, and walked to the stone house.

Will wasn't there, and neither was Eddie, so she sat on the couch and flipped through early morning infomercials, waiting for him to come back, probably from his daily run. Fidgeting with boredom and anticipation to see Will, she took a shower and went to make pancakes and coffee.

Will returned from his run physically beat but mentally awake. *One more day. She'll be home in one more day.* He imagined the little box which sat in his dresser and he winced as though he had an ulcer. Rubbing his stomach with one hand, he patted his thigh for Eddie to follow, the dog's tongue lolling from the exercise. They neared the sliding door and Eddie whined to get in the house.

Will found her inside at the stove, wearing nothing but one of his old t-shirts.

That's promising.

She probably hadn't heard his entrance because she had the Drifters on too loud. She stood with her back to him, her hair still messy and damp from a shower. She rubbed her foot against the outside of her calf and he guessed the scar was itching.

Staring at her felt like a dream, not quite unlike the dreams he had of her every night since she left. He blinked the sweat from his eyes.

I dream of Kelly. Not Matt. Not cries from the dead. Not the blast of the bomb. Could Kelly be his future, leaving his dark past in the past? Again, he thought of the damn little box in his dresser.

Is she sad? Still confused? Will her blue-green eyes be warm and feisty and loving or deep in thought with worry?

He swallowed. Why does love have to hurt? *Does she still want me? Does she still love me?* He knew he wasn't worthy. He dropped his keys to the coffee table and she turned.

She matched his gaze for an intense moment and he was too terrified to move.

"What the hell did you do to the eggs? There was a whole dozen when I left." She looked back at the stove to check on the food. She turned her head to her side to see him and gave him the shy small smile he had missed so much.

"You hungry?"

"You're asking me if *I'm hungry*?"

Kelly turned to face him, biting her lip on a smile. Then she ran to him as he walked toward her. She giggled a little and jumped into his arms. Kissing her as urgently as she was him, Will took a deep desperate breath. He'd needed her like he needed air.

They didn't waste time speaking as he carried her to the bedroom and they lost their clothes. Before they could proceed, Kelly shrieked and ran into the kitchen. "The pancakes!"

Smiling, Will came into the kitchen and scooped her in his arms while she finished swatting at the pancake fire. As soon as the food flames were gone, they moved their heated touches to the bedroom. After a marathon of a shower, they dressed and had an alternative breakfast.

"So, how did everything go?" he said.

She twitched her mouth. "Grant thinks they're having a boy. His ankle's fine now, by the way."

He raised his brows.

"Wade's not sure if he wants to do the marathon in Colorado next week but if I call him a sissy enough, I'm sure he will."

He waited still.

"Sean and Finn are thinking about getting Dad a new grill for his birthday."

He nodded and scratched at his chin. "Uh huh."

"And Heather is thinking about moving back to nights because there's a hot doctor she's after." She glanced at him. He held his hand on his knee to resist tapping his foot on the floor.

She cleared her throat. "Dad's kind of annoyed with me, though. He doesn't like to travel much, but since I'm the one who makes the stupid turkey, they'll have to come down here for Thanksgiving. Maybe we can turn the room next to the kitchen into a guest room."

He dropped his fork on the plate as she spun to face the dishes.

It was bait. Her sneaky smartass way of saying something but meaning a whole hell of a lot more. *She sees herself in Churchston for the next couple months? In my house?* He wiped at the grin on his lips. She was staying, at least for now. It was a start, and for now, a start was good. It was perfect.

He shot to his feet and went for her. She blinked after he assaulted her lips with a long kiss. After he pulled back, he whispered, "There's no way in hell you're talking me into painting it pink."

"Argh!" She slapped his shoulder, tried to squirm away. "It's maroon!"

"It's pink," he insisted as he gathered the rest of the dishes.

Kelly huffed out a breath. "Maroon."

Will was sure she'd never hear the end of it. Randy had asked for her help and she explained her color choice would make his living room scholarly, like a den.

"It looks like a fermented raspberry."

"Your artistic flair stuns me," she said and resumed washing the dishes.

"It's pink. I've got to get going." He stopped in his step.

Could this sound any more like a sitcom from the fifties? Kiss the lady good-bye and come home singing, "Honey, I'm home"?

The idea of kissing her good-bye as he left for work seemed alarmingly domesticated. His gut tightened at the threat of so much commitment. And so much to lay on the line that she could abandon.

But because she was wearing only a shirt, the good-bye kiss he gave her was longer than he had intended. As soon as she slipped her arms around his neck, letting him slant his lips harder on hers, his fear of commitment waned. Kissing Kelly was something he'd do anyhow and anywhere in the world.

"Aren't you going to be late?" she asked on the floor some minutes later. He pulled his pants back on and grinned.

"Good thing I'm the boss, huh?"

CHAPTER 40

The entire first week back in Churchston, Kelly couldn't stop thinking about John's death, not of missing him, but the mystery surrounding it. She was an ordinary middle-class woman. Those kinds of things didn't happen in her life.

In the midst of her thoughts, her daily routines of work continued in town. One morning, her shift at the kayak hut was cut short because Junior was trying to earn some extra money. Lacking any better plans, she agreed to meet Randy for lunch.

Without any explanations, the guys had seemed to understand she was with Will. They must have respected her privacy, because none of them ever asked for details. Even Clay. His endearments of 'baby' had suddenly vanished, and he'd stopped flirting, not that his persistence had ever seemed sincere.

If they knew, they weren't broadcasting the news as gossip.

She sat across from Randy and gave him her most confident, encouraging smile. He was complaining about sales. They had been declining because he was still in his cast and sticking to paperwork instead of showing houses. Femurs took a while to heal, after all.

"There are four houses for sale on my street now."

"So?" She took a bite of her taco and waved when Clay and Will came in. "Hey."

"So, they've been for sale for half a year," Randy said. "Nothing's going to sell in the area after what happened to me. No one wants to live around crime."

Kelly dismissed him with a wave. "It's not the end of the world. Crime happens. People know it does."

"This is Churchston. Crime happens because it's a tourist town. There are petty thieves and drunken fools. That's the kind of crime we get around here, and Eric looks away. Eric and Fred haven't even figured out what happened to me. Not only is it a crime in the neighborhood, it's an unsolved one."

Unsolved.

It caught her. Staring at the napkin box of the diner, she concentrated.

Unsolved, like John? The similarities were striking. Two violent attacks. No witnesses. No useful evidence. No clues. John dead and Randy left for dead.

Red pepper and tortilla churned in her stomach. *But John was in Atlanta and had to have done something bad to deserve it. Randy's in Churchston and is like an altar boy who wouldn't hurt a fly.* The events seemed so alike, but the people were so different. *Besides, John was there and Randy is here. What could John and Randy have in common?*

"What's up with you?" Will asked her in the gruff, blank, indifferent tone he used with everyone—not the soft, sometimes goofy voice he relaxed to when he was with her. She found it strange how he seemed to be able to detect her slightest worry the same way she could guess the instant his knee was bothering him.

"Hmm? Nothing. Just thinking."

Junior seemed to be saving up for a new phone or getting Allison a present, because two days later, Kelly once again had rare free time between the kayak hut and the bowling alley. Instead of spending money on food in town, she drove home to have lunch on the beach with Eddie.

Rocking to Van Halen on the way, she cruised along the road, too carefree to worry about her speedometer.

After she passed the patrol car, she grimaced and checked how fast she was going. Eric wasted no time pulling her over. She tapped to the music with her driver's license and registration in her lap as he slowly walked up to her car.

Going too fast? Yep. Write the ticket so I can get back to it.

He scratched on the ticket pad and Kelly stared back at him.

"You been drinking today?" he said around the toothpick in his teeth.

It was ten in the morning.

"Yep. It's so roomy in the kayak hut I like to keep a fridge in there for all my margaritas. And then I've gotta have space to smoke my joint and relax with my underage lovers."

He narrowed his eyes. "Say what, now?"

"Will you give me the ticket already?"

He tapped her driver's license on his ticket book. "Address says Atlanta."

"Really? I'll be damned."

"Law says you need to update the address of your permanent residence after—"

"Did I ever say I'm staying here for good?"

Eric switched the toothpick to the other side of his mouth. "I saw the fed talking with you a couple weeks ago."

"My goodness! You must have twenty-twenty vision! First you can read my driver's license"— she snatched her card back—"and then you saw me speaking to a real cop."

"What's he interested in you for?"

"Give me one reason why I should tell you, you nosy son of a—"

"Merely asking. Seems like funny business is all. You quit your fancy job in the big city and move to our little old town. You get all uppity like you're a know-it-all about cottonmouths—"

"Adder."

"Whatever. Then you get all sassy about Randy's attack. What's next, Miss Newland? Every time I get a call, you're in the thick of it."

"Is there a point to this conversation?"

"Just saying. Churchston was a quiet little town before you showed up. Sure as hell never had the feds poking around."

"Eric, let me give you a little advice. Until I do something wrong, keep your nose out of my business and pretend to be a real cop, okay?"

Will sped by in his garage truck. Twenty yards up road, he braked then reversed. He stormed out of the cab with a glare at Eric. "What the hell are you doing?"

"What's it to you, drunk?" Eric ripped the ticket off the pad and handed it to Kelly.

"What are you doing with her?" Will's fists clenched as he came closer.

"A speeding ticket to frame and hang on the wall." Kelly waved it in the air and started the car.

"Why? What the hell are you bothering her for?"

Christ, it's a speeding ticket. Talk about an overreaction.

"I'm not bothering her." Eric stabbed a finger at Will's chest. "I'm doing my job."

"Leave her alone."

"Will, he gave me a ticket," she said.

"You're harassing her." Will looked at her as though he was making sure she wasn't bleeding.

If he still cares about keeping it under the down-low, he's really blowing it. "He's not harassing me, it's a stupid ticket."

"He's picking on you."

"She was speeding so I gave her a ticket. Why do you care if she gets a ticket, anyway?"

"I'm sick of you acting like you can harass anyone you want."

"She was speeding."

"Yeah, right."

"Will, I was going damn near eighty." Kelly furrowed her brows, not appreciating his concern. It was possessive, as though she was fragile and couldn't handle it herself perfectly well.

"When's the last time your radar was calibrated?"

She groaned. Will's macho-fierce-warrior-protector act was getting old. She could take her own fights. And she didn't intend to argue the ticket. She had been flying.

She ground her teeth as Eric left with a warning to stay out of trouble.

Will set his hands on his hips and studied the road before meeting her eyes.

She raised her brows. *What the hell was that about?*

CHAPTER 41

Will's behavior set her in a sour mood at the bowling alley. She didn't need his protector alpha male crap and his moody attitude. Since she had come back from the funeral he had seemed more distant, more pensive.

In public, yeah, she got it. She could respect his wishes for privacy. But he had seemed extra temperamental with her when they were together, like she was a pain in the ass. Well, she knew she was, but he was, too. It's why they fit together so perfectly. It made no sense to her, why he seemed to be building walls and getting jumpy at the same time he was more and more passionate and tender when they went to bed. Something seemed to be up his ass, and she imagined it had to be her.

It was like a bipolar intimacy.

But Eric's taunt stuck in the forefront of her attention. It did seem like she was stuck in a bit of a rerun. She had quit her job in Atlanta, but she still frequented a hospital. Junior's bite, Clay's accident, Randy's attack.

As she came back from the mechanical room after she reset a lane, a little boy tripped near the rack of bowling shoes. With the wobbly balance of a toddler, he tumbled down and smacked his head on the wall.

"Aw." She hurried over to him as he started crying. There would be a lump, but he'd be fine. "You're okay, buddy." Crouching, she tried to help him up, but he slumped to a sobbing sit. She glanced around for his parents.

"What'd you do to my son?"

Kelly checked over her shoulder as an angry mother bear came for her. She recognized her from the beach. Stella from the lemonade stand.

"He took a tumble," Kelly said and backed up as the woman snatched her child into her arms.

Shushing the boy, Stella held him tightly and rocked back and forth even though he had stopped crying and flailed his arms to be set down again. She turned to Kelly and pursed her lips. "You stay away from him! Don't you dare put your hands on him."

Kelly raised her brows and held her hands out in truce. "What the hell is your problem?"

"Don't touch my son, you filthy woman."

Kelly opened her mouth to say something, but had a total loss for words.

Stella patted her son's hair while he commenced screaming. Probably not from the fall, but to get back on his own feet. "Your mother would be ashamed. You go from man to man and toy with them. Nothing but another whore."

Kelly set her hands on her hips and pursed her lips, seeing a rational conversation would be useless. "Right."

"I see you out there." Stella stood, holding her son's head to her chest as though she thought Kelly was going to cast a spell on him. "In that teeny bikini, smiling at the men and using them as playthings."

Kelly shook her head. What was she, a disciple of Delores?

"First you flirt with the young boy. Roger's boy. Then you were all over the mechanic. The one who chases the women. Then Wanda's son, that sweetheart Randy. I saw you with a tall one too, in the suit."

Kelly stared at her and considered the list. Her playthings? Junior swapped SNL jokes with her when they were bored at the hut. Then Clay, he was her buddy. Randy was the shoulder she cried on. The suit? Grant? Her brother wasn't her plaything.

Kelly pinched the bridge of her nose. *Of all days to meet another delusional Churchston woman.*

"You don't even care. You strut out there for everyone to see. You should be ashamed of yourself. And your men should be ashamed, too!" She stomped off.

Kelly stared at her retreating form, too stunned to move. She caught Jaycee watching her with a smile, probably entertained with the drama.

She inhaled deeply to shake it off and resumed working.

That poor little boy.

She returned to the kitchen to pick up a delivery for the record store. Walking down Main, her attention fell on the public beach. The beginning shade of sunset cast over groups of the end-of-the-season tourists playing in the sand and sun. Beach balls, ice cream cones, and too much body fat pudged out from too-small bathing attire. There was a cluster of volleyball players, a mother smearing sunscreen on her impatient kid. Daisy appeared to be flirting with a college guy. Kendra paused checking her reflection in a compact as Kelly caught her eye. The teeny circle quickly showed a scowl.

Typical day at the beach.

Kelly never stopped to think about how public the kayak hut made her. Never had cared. She had impulsively stayed at Churchston with the impression of anonymity and indifference. It had been the beauty of a fresh start. She hadn't been Kelly the divorced woman. Or the Newlands' sister. Or the nurse who should have checked Norbert's medication as the next shift started. Just Kelly. The kayak girl. Alan's delivery girl.

On the return walk after handing off the sub, she realized her attitude hadn't changed since she arrived in the town.

Why should I care what any of these locals think of me?

She hadn't embraced that characteristic of the small-town atmosphere. The biases, the watching eyes, the gossip. It was why she hadn't hussed and fussed when Will wanted to maintain a private relationship with her. It was their business, not anyone else's.

For every time someone seemed to judge Will, she had wanted to scream, 'get a life'! But Stella's ranting had struck a nerve she couldn't calm.

"'My men'." She scoffed and counted the cracks of the sidewalk as she returned to the alley.

She had one man. And he was too scared to let the world know he was hers. Junior. Clay. Randy. Grant. *For God's sake, he's my brother!* And the rest were the next best things to real siblings. Well, Junior was a kid, but he wasn't so bad after he must have finally realized she was too old for him.

Her men. She passed the garage and peeked through the windows for *her man*. Will stood under a car pointing things out to an older man, no doubt busy, impatient and too blunt.

Clay waved at her with a grin. His cast was coming off the next week. Will would be happy about that too. It was childish, Clay teasing Randy he still had to wait to have his leg cast taken off. *Boys will be boys.*

Kelly stopped to tie her shoe outside the bowling alley.

Clay in a cast. Randy in a cast. Her fingers stopped moving.

Clay. Randy. Her men. Junior. Clay. Randy. Grant.

She gasped.

Jr. had been bitten by a snake. Clay's brakes had been cut. Randy, beaten senseless. Grant. She shook her head to clear her thoughts. He didn't fit in Stella's list.

"His ankle," she whispered. Grant had twisted his ankle. Her men. All of them hurt in one way or another.

In a daze, she returned to the bowling alley. Bypassing the counter in case another delivery was waiting for her, she went to hide in the mechanical room to think.

'My men' have all been hurt.

Coincidences were crap. There had to be explanations.

It wasn't *impossible* for a snake to crawl into the cab of the Burns' kayak truck and bite Junior. It could happen to anyone.

Clay had angered the wrong husband. It was a nasty write-off, but she had to think he had that coming.

Randy. She chewed on her lip. There was no answer for his attack. It seemed no one knew he was gay. She dismissed the possibility of a deranged homophobe.

Grant. It had to have been an accidental trip. One night Will had walked Eddie on the beach with her and had shown her where Grant took his spill. He looked for some old fishing line he guessed Grant had tripped over, but there wasn't any in sight. Line, no line, people tripped all the time.

But what happened to Randy?

She paced among the lane bins, pins clacking and crashing into the chutes. Kelly couldn't stop coming back to Randy. There was no answer.

Panting faster, she paced accordingly. She had a habit of worrying and a pastime of rambling. Always accused of a runaway imagination, she felt as though paranoia was getting to her.

"Kelly—"

She screamed and whipped around in a defensive pose. "Shit, Mick, you scared me."

He was cowered down with his arm over his head in a block. Slowly, he lowered his arm to show wide eyes. "Uh, Alan was looking for you. Delivery to the lifeguard post and the garage."

She nodded. Mick gave her a lingering look of disbelief before he left her in the mechanical hallway.

"Churchston was a quiet little town before you came here."

She had tuned out Eric's whine, attributing it to his lack of desire to do his job. He didn't seem intelligent enough to make a significant observation of the pattern of activity in town. And Gannon's presence probably excited him, having a real lawman, the FBI, on his sleepy territory.

But was there a connection? How? What could possibly connect Junior, Clay, Randy, and Grant to her?

She went to the counter and sorted the sub boxes. "Hey, Alan, you want anyone to pay for these or are the tabs up to date?" She flipped through the receipts in the pile under the cash register drawer. She typically collected payments on tabs at the end of the month.

"Eh, some of them paid up yesterday. Rest of them can wait," Alan called out. "You're all set."

Frowning at the stack of papers, she stilled her finger at the name on a receipt on the top of the pile.

Denner.

She tugged it free and peered at it.

A credit card receipt from a Denner. *Wasn't that the name they found in Betsy's car?*

"Alan, who paid this last one?"

He came to the counter, wiping his hands in his apron. "Kelly? Are you okay? You're awfully pale."

The receipt shook as she showed it to him. "Who paid this?"

He got his glasses out and studied the receipt. "Can't tell ya. I think Jaycee cashed it out."

CHAPTER 42

Armed with the subs as she walked onto Main moments later, Kelly tried to hide the worry on her face. Fumbling the boxes in one hand, she called Gannon on her cell.

No answer. She left a hasty message asking him how the name was spelled.

Lifeguards first. Daisy manned the stand. "What's with you? You pregnant or something?"

"Pregnant?" Kendra sauntered up to them in her perfect little bikini.

Kelly willed herself not to look at the stupid tramp stamp on her back.

Kendra crossed her arms. "I didn't know you were even getting laid."

Kelly faked a smile and walked away. *My life isn't any of your goddamn business.* Wrapped up in her thoughts, she dismissed the women's cattiness.

Denner? Denman. Dennison. Den-something?

She shook her head, walking away from the lifeguard stand. *I must have misread it. No one could have followed me down here because of what happened to Norbert. Denner was in*

Atlanta. Not Churchston. It had to be a fluke similarity of someone else's name. The string of events, those times when she'd been in the 'thick of it all', as Eric had said, those events had nothing to do with Atlanta. Her men had nothing to do with Atlanta…

As she passed the kayak hut, Junior waved her down. "Hey, you busy?"

"Making some deliveries."

"Can you take a break and watch the hut for a minute? My phone's dying and I left my charger at home."

"Yeah, yeah, go ahead." She waved him off and took the bar stool in the hut.

Checking her phone for a reply from Gannon, she jumped when a customer cleared his throat.

"Mr. Nikki. Medusa." She raised her brows at the unlikely couple.

He sneered at her. "I divorced that bitch. Nikki was a cheating cunt." He tightened his arm around Medusa, and she boosted a smug smile.

"Congrats," Kelly muttered and scribbled on the receipt for them. "Kayak?"

"Nah, we'll go for a canoe."

"Alrighty then." Kelly flipped for a different form and eyed them. *Seems like everything worked out for them.* "You moved on fast."

Mr. Nikki and Medusa. Weirder things happened.

"She wasn't worth the headache," he said.

"So you slashed Clay's tires for nothing?"

"I didn't slash no fucking tires." He slanted his lips at her. "She wants to sleep with that fleabag, she can go right ahead. She ain't mine anymore."

Kelly stilled the pen. "You didn't slash his tires?"

"No. I gotta watch it. Probation."

"You didn't slash his tires." She half-asked and half-stated it.

"Jus' said no. You hard of hearing? We want a damn boat."

Then who did? What were the odds of someone else being out there that night?

"Probably the asswipe in the Buick," he said as though he had read her mind.

"What?"

"The Buick. It was parked way up at the end of the drive. Some asswipe was sitting in there."

She swallowed. "Who was it?"

"Fuck if I know. Are you going to give us a canoe or what?"

Kelly picked up the pen, still riled. "Was it an older man or a younger guy?"

"I told you. I don't know. Little punk gave me a dirty look."

"So it was a man?"

"I don't know! It was dark. I had a few drinks. I didn't give a shit about who the hell was out there. I was looking for my woman!"

"What?" Medusa edged from his hold.

"My old woman. Baby, she doesn't matter no more. I chose you."

Medusa seemed placated and Kelly told them their boat number.

Doubts left her mind as fear cemented.

Someone was watching her at the kayak hut. Someone watched her at the townhouse.

This is real.

Adrenaline twisted her guts in knots.

Someone really was watching her. Threatening her. Playing with her. She cracked her knuckles, eying the people on the beach. Denner? Was that the name?

Is Denner stalking me?

CHAPTER 43

When Junior returned to the hut, Kelly continued to the garage, her thoughts scrambling like bouncy balls pinging off her skull.

Her friends, who could seem like lovers, had been hurt. Her men were hurt. Someone was watching her. What did Denner want? Denner's name was associated to all the recent death in her life. In Betsy's car. John's condo. What did it mean that Denner had followed her to Churchston?

Was Denner the one who hurt her men? Why? It made no connection to Betsy's suicide. Or John's death.

She gasped.

Not Betsy's suicide. But Norbert's death. Norbert hadn't been her friend, her man, her lover. Sure, he had been a charismatic older man, flirting with her like all the elderly men tried to. But Norbert hadn't been anything past a patient to her.

"John was my man," she whispered and covered her mouth.

John had been her man.

John was in Atlanta, not Churchston. Junior. Clay. Randy. Grant. John?

Okay, this is crazy exaggeration. She shook her head.

Fantasizing. Daydreaming what-ifs. John had always said she was paranoid. She still didn't think there was anything sinister to washing her hands constantly all day. *Germs, people.* There were germs everywhere. But she had never been the conspiracy-believing doomsday everyone's-out-to-get-me kind of paranoid.

Germs, those were real. Elvis, no, he's really dead.

"Whoa! Kelly!" Clay said as she stumbled into him.

She had walked into the garage absentmindedly and nearly slammed into the workbench behind him.

"Gotta look where you're going." He took the subs and she managed something of a smile.

"What's wrong?" His expression mirrored the one Mick had given her in the mechanical room.

With her thoughts racing, she barely heard him. "Huh? Oh, nothing."

She scratched her hair as itches tickled all over her skin. It reminded her of the time in fifth grade when she had taken a dare to steal a piece of candy from the corner store. Through her child's eyes those cameras had been looming large, all over, watching.

"Will!" Keeping a brow raised at her, Clay called, "Food's here!"

"About time," Will said and came toward the computer. As soon as he saw her, he frowned and hastened his step. "What happened?"

She grimaced. *I can't be that transparent.* "Nothing. Been thinking."

He was her man. The one who mattered the most. Sure, she loved Dad and her brothers, but Will really was *her* man.

He came closer and the grim line of his lips had her expecting another protective act.

"I'll catch you guys later." She left before he came close enough for her to be tempted to hug him.

Back at the bowling alley, Alan asked again if she was okay. She acknowledged him with a nod and went to the bathroom to lock herself in. She needed peace and quiet to think. Sitting on the counter, she focused.

Will was her man but he hadn't been on Stella's list. He couldn't have been because Stella only witnessed what the rest of the world saw. No one could have seen how Will was the man she was in love with. The only man who was her plaything and everything else she'd ever want and need from a man. Stella never saw Will hugging her at the kayak stand, kissing her, holding her hand.

The rest of them had been out there with her. Kelly envisioned it from Stella's perspective. Junior watching her with puppy eyes as they worked. Clay goofing off with her on his way to flirt with the lifeguards. Randy comforting her when she was upset about Will. Grant sitting on the beach with her while he gave her brotherly support.

She hugged her knees to her chest.

Someone is stalking me.

The timing of injuries made more sense. Randy had held her while she cried, something anyone could have mistaken for romance. Then he was attacked. Grant had been there hugging and teasing her. Then he *tripped*.

They were all connected to her. Her men.

"Oh God, oh God, oh God," she whispered a mantra of fear.

John had been her man and even though she hadn't known it, he wanted her back. He had wanted to be her man again.

"Is Will next?"

Her fingers shook as she pulled her phone from her pocket and called Gannon again. Still no answer.

"Ah!" She dropped the phone as it buzzed in her hand and it plopped into the toilet.

"Oh, son of a bitch." She got to her feet. With a wince, she retrieved it from the toilet.

Good thing it was empty.

She wiped the water off with toilet paper. At Junior's advice, she had gotten a waterproof case for it the first week she worked at the hut.

She narrowed her eyes at the phone, too riled to stress about the gazillion nasty things which resided in the toilet.

Missed call from Will.

He had to be concerned. Due to some kind of freakish phenomenon, he seemed to always know when she was worrying.

She paced, estimating one of two things could happen if she spoke to him about this.

He would tell her she was crazy and jumping to conclusions, things she could almost agree to at the moment. Or, he would go into the protective mode and try to solve her problems for her. Which would definitely *not* be on the down-low. And he was the single person who would be most in danger.

Someone was targeting any man she appeared to be with romantically. Norbert didn't fit, but she couldn't see any other reason why Denner, whoever was stalking her, would be connected to Norbert's death, John's murder, and her Churchston friends' injuries.

She dialed and left the contaminated phone on speaker. As she waited and prayed for Gannon to answer, she tried to rehearse what she would say, but no words came. At his voicemail she left a message and hoped it was coherent enough for him to understand.

Knocks sounded on the door.

Not like I can hide in the bathroom all night.

She pulled herself together and finished her shift. Alan checked on her often, asking if she was alright. She overheard her coworkers debating over her behavior. Mick insisted she was doped up, while Jaycee explained it as a pending period.

Instead of going to the garage to wait for Will to be done working like she usually did, she went home to the townhouse. She showered, hoping her funk and runaway imagination would rinse down the drain. No such luck.

She walked to Will's to make a simple dinner. When he came home, he fussed over her, paying no attention to the food. She couldn't help but feel like a deer in the headlights. His concern turned to frustration when she wouldn't talk and tell him what was wrong.

She didn't mean to shut him out, but she had to figure it out, had to know if he was going to be targeted.

Gannon still hadn't called back.

They made love, so slowly and agonizingly sweet. Kelly bit back the tears in her eyes.

He loved her. He couldn't say it, but he did.

She tried not to think of what her life would be like without him. Instead, she made a plan.

CHAPTER 44

I'm losing her.

Kelly had already left for work by the time Will came back from his run. He sensed the distance growing between them. She had avoided meeting his eyes. The blue-greens dark and worried as though she had been debating whether or not to leap off a high dive.

He was beside himself at the garage. He checked the little box was in his drawer. As if it was a magnet, he came to his office after every job to assure himself it was still there. It sat there, taunting him when he couldn't ask her.

Will. You. Marry. Me.

Four words. How hard could it be?

Or he'd be himself and go for two.

Marry. Me.

He guessed he was losing her because he was too guarded, too scared to chance her saying no. Too bruised to have her accept and someday leave. He brainstormed a proposal, even tried the three scariest words in his life.

I. Love…

He couldn't do it.

Cold memories of his childhood blurred his mind. He had never been good enough. Good for nothing. Unwanted.

The stress had him all thumbs at work. He couldn't turn the wrenches. Nuts and bolts slipped to the ground. Gaskets wouldn't line up.

I. Love…

Kelly sat on the deck of the boat which had almost killed her, acid tossing the breakfast in her stomach.

Had that been an accident? She narrowed her eyes as she focused through the binoculars.

Someone had been watching her. Someone had been targeting the people in her life.

Accident my ass.

The people on the boat the day she had fallen off the skis were all Churchston locals. She couldn't explain how someone from Churchston could have killed John in Atlanta. She couldn't let go of the Denner receipt showing up at Alan's.

Coincidences were crap. What were the odds the name could have shown up in Betsy's car, John's condo, and Alan's? From Atlanta to Churchston? She Googled the name last night. No known Denners in Churchston. The only connection she could figure, was herself.

Someone had been watching her, so from a distance on Randy's boat, she watched everyone.

All of the men in her life came to or near the public beach. It made sense to her since she frequented it so often for work.

She had paid Allison two hundred dollars to sit at the kayak hut with her Braves hat. As they had nearly the same hair color, she was a decent live decoy in the shade of the hut. Kelly had promised to buy Junior whatever phone he wanted if he would run the hut for the day.

Telescopically, she spied on the beachgoers, especially the ones who seemed interested in the kayak hut. She had no idea who she could be looking for, so she limited her attention to the people who had been on the boat the night she was ran over.

Stella checked the activity of the hut. Daisy and Kendra looked Allison's way. The lifeguard with freckles checked "her" out. Clay and Randy stopped by the hut, but Junior must have followed her directions explicitly and told them she wasn't there. Her excuse had been PMS, knowing the men wouldn't question such a topic.

She watched. Her fear eliminated the possibility of boredom as she sat and spied, but as she didn't have a focus, a target to follow, she fell to the habit of diagnosing.

With nurse's eyes, she clinically spied on the crowd. She was overweight. He had fake hair. She had been shooting up. He had a scar from ATC surgery. She had a mastectomy. He probably had a herniated disk. He had an open bypass. She had a third-degree sunburn.

Men, women, young, old. She watched them all. Hair. Randy had the same blond as Allison. Eyes. Daisy seemed as high as the girl who was hitting on Brent. Mouths. Clay smiled as often as Jared did at the ice cream stand. Tattoos. Kelly rolled her eyes at Kendra's tramp stamp. The solid black sun. It was asymmetrical. And trashy.

Her gaze roved over the people on the beach. One of them had been watching her, but who? Someone, other than Stella, had to have watched her with her friends. With her men.

I've got to be missing something. She checked face after face, focusing on the women, then the men. It could be either, she guessed. A man who had been angry she wasn't choosing him, or a woman who was…jealous?

Her phone rang beside her. Will again. She hoped he would stay away until she could save him.

CHAPTER 45

The next morning, Will made up his mind.

It's now or never.

He refused to accept the distance she was putting between them. She had barely looked him in the eyes last night.

He was going to ask her.

Delores. Eric. All of fucking Churchston. It wasn't important anymore. They had never wanted him. Too damn bad. He had a woman who did and he wasn't going to lose her. They'd move. He'd go up to Atlanta with her. Anywhere. As long as she was with him.

He had only come back to Churchston because he'd known no other place to go. But there wouldn't be any lost love if he left with Kelly.

When Matt died, half his soul had been lost. Kelly, she was his whole soul. He knew if she left him, he'd be one sorry pathetic man for the rest of his life. He was already so destitute for her warm love that he was willing to risk proposing.

"Here goes," he mumbled to himself and dropped the old oil filter in the pan. Dark liquid splashed up on his already dirty jeans and he checked his appearance.

Stained, grimy, dirty, calloused. It was still warm for the fall so he had sweated through his t-shirt.

He glanced across the street at the hut. She leaned at the counter, staring at the waves. He wanted to go home and shower, make himself more presentable, but he nixed the plan. It was too tantalizing. She was right there. Yards away.

She hadn't been the frilly kind to care about looks. She had seemed to love him no matter what, dirty, clean, clothed, or naked.

He wiped his hands on his jeans then washed them before he retrieved the damn little box in his desk.

On the phone, Clay glanced up at him as he strode out of the garage into the sunlight.

He clenched his teeth together with tense fear. He wasn't sure if he had ever been so intimidated before. Afghanistan came close. War had been life or death.

But so is Kelly.

The walk to the public beach felt like a hike through eternity, with the sun blasting down on him, everyone's gaze scorching him. As he approached, she faced him. Her mouth opened as though he had surprised her. She clamped her lips shut and frowned as she surveyed the beach.

"Will. What a surprise. What brings you out into the real world?"

What the fuck is he doing out here!

Kelly knew he had a stubbornly impatient streak. She loved that about him. It was no guess he was frustrated how she had been shutting him out, not sharing her mind.

Hadn't he bought the lie about PMS-ing?

His steely stare gave the impression of determination and fear.

What's he up to?

He gazed at her without a word. Gone was his usual stony expression of indifference.

Oh fuck. He was breaking it. He didn't want to hide their relationship anymore. How could he, if he came up to the hut and stared at her with such intensity?

"Will?"

She tried to watch the beach from the corner of her eye, not able to tear hers from his. Everyone watched. She didn't have to look to know.

The nearby quiet was tangible, as though respiration had suspended.

The good-for-nothing, sullen drunk crawled out of his hole to talk to her. They had the center stage.

He lowered to his good knee.

No. No. No. No.

She watched the strong cords in his neck stretch as he swallowed. Will looked at her with warmth in his eyes.

Oh my God. Tears burned. *He wants to—he wants me to—Will wants to…*

Sweat beaded and ran down her back.

"Kelly…" He paused.

She blinked quickly to stop the tears from starting. She cleared her throat. She couldn't let her voice crack. She forced away any trace of love as she asked, "What are you doing?"

They're watching. He. She. Someone. The person is watching. He can't blow his cover now!

He set his jaw. "What it looks like."

I can't let him do this. I can't lose him.

Her heart raced, but her mind was faster.

He didn't know it, but this was going to kill him. She didn't know why or who, either, but she knew it was dangerous. What she had to do would hurt him, crush him, scar him like his parents had. But she had to. There was no other choice. She couldn't let anyone know she loved him, or to know he was her man.

She didn't know if he'd forgive her, if he'd still want her after she rejected him in such a cruel and public way. But it couldn't matter. She would take him alive and hating her before she'd let anyone hurt him again.

"Get off your knee." She hoped she sounded every bit annoyed and flippant.

"Why?" He bore his gaze on her and she stiffened to stay strong.

"Because you've got a gross screwed-up leg."

He made a fist around the little white box that had been so tiny in his large strong hand.

In her peripheral vision, she saw Delores. Oh. How she hated to do this to him.

He'll never forgive me.

"Is there any point to even asking the question now?" His voice was like sandpaper. Lethal. Destroyed.

"No. No, I don't want to marry you. Are you kidding me? Where the hell did you ever get such an idea?"

He stood and glared at her. She wanted to cringe at the embarrassment in his eyes, the pain and hurt as he wiped his hand over his mouth and hung his head down.

"Why the hell would I want to marry you?" she asked. "You're the, the, um, the good-for-nothing town drunk! You've got to be kidding me!" She frowned more as he studied her, fearful he could read through her lies.

"You love me."

"Love you? I don't love you. What's there to love? No one loves you, Will. No one ever will." She put her hand on her hip as her knees weakened. *He's going to hate me forever.*

There was no way she could tell him he was in danger, that she was faking it, that she would love to marry him. There was no way she could tell the truth because as soon as he sensed danger, he would insist on taking over.

And how to even begin to explain…? She inhaled deeply as he rubbed the back of his neck.

"You're embarrassing me. You can take the ring. And. Rot. In. Hell."

People gasped. Someone whispered 'holy shit'. Soft snickers and laughter rose as Churchston absorbed every drip of the drama right in front of their faces.

Will left in a fast stride, his face blank and stony like the gargoyle he had been when she met him. She couldn't look. She couldn't watch him go back to the garage, her heart ripping in half, chunks crumbling with every step he took.

Under the scrutiny of the crowd, she rolled her eyes. She posed as an annoyed and peeved woman all the while her hands trembled and her knees shook. She crossed her arms to hide the physical effects of fear.

"What was he smoking?" she jeered loudly before she went back in the hut.

Delores had yet to walk away, and the lifeguards remained as a shocked audience. Stella mumbled at her lemonade stand. Jared shook his head over his ice cream freezers.

Fred cleared his throat as he walked through them. "Show's over, everybody." At his side, Eric chuckled, and Fred elbowed him.

Kelly bit the inside of her cheek to stop her trembling lips. She picked up the paperback Allison had left behind the day before, the words on the pages jack-hammering as she shook.

She needed to look up, she needed to check and see who was watching her. She waited until the tears ceased to soak the pages.

CHAPTER 46

Clay hung up the phone as Will came back to the garage.

Her words kept running in his mind like a broken record.

I don't love you. No one loves you.

He exploded in rage and hurt.

God, the pain.

"Will? Yo man, what—" Clay chased after him. "Will? You alright?"

What's there to love?

With a fierce kick, his boot sent his office door banging against the wall.

You're embarrassing me.

He picked up his chair and slammed it to the ground, splintering a leg off.

"Will!" Clay rushed in after him, restraining his arm.

Will shook him off. He clenched his fingers on the edge of the desk and hung his head down, breathing hoarsely.

Oh God, it hurt.

He opened his hand and set the damned little box on the center on his desk. Shocked with pain, he almost couldn't believe it.

She doesn't love me. No one does.

"Whoa," Clay whispered.

Will dragged his gaze up to his friend.

"Congrats?" Clay tried to smile.

Will snatched the box and ripped the drawer open. He threw it in and slammed the drawer shut hard enough to make the pens rattle in the coffee cup on top.

"Man, she's a headstrong one. Let her think on it," Clay said.

"She said she didn't want to marry me. Didn't know where I got the idea."

Clay winced as Will paced.

"She said she didn't love me. There's nothing to love about me."

Clay opened his mouth, but thought better.

"She told me to rot in hell!" Will yelled as Clay stood at the door.

"Hey man, she's probably—"

"She told me to rot in hell," Will repeated.

"Maybe she's on the rag or something. Women are strange—"

"She told me to rot in hell." Will lowered his voice, rolling the words through his memories.

"But I'm sure…"

Will ignored him, studying the door.

Kelly had leaned against that very door.

You know, scientifically, I don't think that's possible.

She wanted him to rot in hell. Told him so in front of everyone.

You could incinerate in hell if there is such a thing. But it doesn't sound as demeaning as rot in hell.

She wants me to rot in hell?

He heard the words from her mouth.

It sounds stupid. How about burn in hell? Has a nice ring to it.

"Bullshit," he said as he sank to the edge of his desk, unsure of his hesitation to accept her harsh rejection.

"Yeah, man, it is bullshit. But she can't—"

But she'd never tell him to rot in hell.

She had declared it sounded stupid. It hadn't been the real Kelly saying those words, the Kelly he knew and wanted forever. Those blue-greens weren't skilled at stealth. When she had argued with him on the porch, destroying Matt's railings, they sparked with challenge. When she scolded him on the beach, they flared with determination. When she curled next to him in bed, they melted with contentment.

When she had told him to rot in hell? They flashed with fear. Just like they had after the boat ran over her.

But did I ever really know her? Was it all a joke? No.

The Kelly he knew and wanted forever didn't exist. She had burned him.

Waves of raw emotions flooded him again.

Pain. Rejection. Humiliation. Anger. Kelly hadn't loved him. He was a fool. He should have remembered no one would love him.

He stood abruptly, feeling worse than he ever had in the aftermath of Matt's death.

Going to the middle bay, he walked past Clay, dismissing his rambling explanations and sympathies.

Shutting out the world, Will resumed working as he tried to lock away his thoughts.

I've been a fool.

Never again, he promised himself. *Never again.*

For the rest of the day, he took solace in work, keeping his hands busy in hopes to forget Kelly's rejection.

Seemed as though everyone dropped by the garage. Either everyone's vehicle had to have broken down, or Churchston had been entertained. Some presented legitimate car trouble, but others appeared blatantly nosy and spiteful, coming to stare at him as though he was an injured monster.

Kelly finally reached her brother on his cell phone. "Sean, do it!"

"Kelly, what the hell is wrong with you?"

"Okay, Ramon's gay. He's flaming gay. No one will ever think he's my lover."

"Yeah. Nice. But why the fuck do you want me to send my foreman down to your little beach town?"

Kelly inhaled. She needed help. It didn't kill her to admit it. But any person she asked for help would be at risk. She only had her guys. The guys in Churchston who were already hurt because of her. Heather was too sweet and innocent to involve. Her brothers?

Finn had boxed in his younger days.

No. If this asshole had already mistaken Grant for her lover, then he or she would do the same for the other brothers.

"I need his help. He's big, he's strong, he'll help me."

"Kelly!" Sean yelled before the background noise on his end quieted. He must have stepped into the onsite office at his construction site. "Help you what? Is someone threatening you?"

Threatening her, maybe? It seemed her pals were targeted, not her. She thought of the boat accident.

Okay. Maybe I am in danger.

But she was calling for Will. Will was the one in danger now.

"Is this about the old dude's daughter? The one who came after you at the hospital? I told you to get a restraining order against her!"

"Norbert's daughter? No. I don't think so." She frowned. What was her last name? It didn't start with a D... She shook her head. "No, she'd checked into a rehab place. In California or something."

"Did she check out?"

Jesus, *did* she check out? *I should have asked Gannon about her.* Kelly swallowed. What would Norbert's daughter have to do with John, though? It didn't make sense. "Sean, please."

"Kelly, you're crazy! It's a whole day of driving. And we're in the middle of a project uptown. I can't dispatch him to goof around with you. Tell me what's going on! Where's Will? Let me talk to that son of a bitch."

She hung up. It had been a feeble attempt, but she was scattered. She needed help. She didn't know who was targeting the men. She couldn't look out for Will because it would bring her closer to him.

Kelly focused and glanced at the garage across the street, fearing how much he hated her.

Maybe we could get a gun, take Eddie and float on Randy's boat. No one could reach us then. And I'd be there to protect him. He'd have my back and I'd have his.

The Hollywood perfect movie ending was unrealistic.

He'd never agree. He'd have to be the hero. And they couldn't float forever. Then when they came to shore, the person would still be waiting for them. Him. Her.

What the fuck do you want from me, Denner? Who are you, Denner?

Denner's name had shown up in Betsy's car. Denner had shown up in John's condo. Denner had shown up at Alan's.

Why? Who was Denner?

Kelly scanned the beach. *Was I convincing enough?*

It seemed as though Will's soul had crumbled to her feet. He had to hate her.

Now no one can possibly think I was ever in love with him.

But that conviction had her thinking of John. He had been killed after they divorced. She hadn't been with him and he had been killed because he wanted to be with her again.

It would be best for Will if he truly did hate her for all the world to see.

She dialed Gannon again, tapping her fingers on the counter as Junior came up to the hut with Allison. Her shift was over.

Oh, thank God.

"I need you to do me a favor," she told the teens as they came in.

Allison rolled her eyes.

"Double pay."

She widened them.

"I need you to tell me who goes in the garage and talks to Will."

Allison gasped. "So he really did—"

"Every time someone goes in there. You tell me."

She needed to know if Will was going to be mad and not let anyone near him for gossipy questions or consolation. Or, if he was going to be sad, hurt and heartbroken. Like John apparently had been. And therefore still in danger.

If she knew him as well as she imagined, Will was more likely to be angry and show it than sad and hide it. But it was a risk. It wasn't over by a long shot. Anyone who went to him to find out his worth and his potential love for Kelly would be the person she needed to watch.

"Why—"

"Do. It." She paced. "I need a fucking recorder. I need to know who asks him if he was sleeping with me."

Allison's jaw dropped. "You were doing it with him?"

"Oh, don't give me that naïve crap. I found the blue condom in here the day after his birthday." Kelly nodded her head at a very red Junior.

Allison blushed. "Why do you need to know who—"

She was involving them. Instinctively, she doubted they were involved. For one thing, they were kids.

How the hell would they have pulled it off? And why? First I plead for Ramon's help as a non-heterosexual bodyguard. Now I'm involving minors.

She was sure the guilt would catch up later.

"You have my number. Call me every time someone goes in there." Kelly got her keys and purse. "I'll be back in a little bit."

As she left, she thought through her impromptu plan to watch over Will. She wasn't safe anywhere. The townhouse, the stone house, the kayak hut, the bowling alley. Someone had breached her life like a virus.

Even her car would reveal her whereabouts.

She turned on the road, determined not to allow anything as an obstacle from protecting Will.

CHAPTER 47

All Will wanted to do was crawl in a hole and drink himself to sleep. Or beat the crap out of something. He appreciated how Clay gave him space, and he wished the women had done the same. All the way into the afternoon, they came and went, hopping around like skinned bunnies in their lifeguard bikinis. Chattering and giggling. Grating his nerves.

"Here you go, big boy." Jaycee waltzed in with sub boxes.

Will narrowed his gaze on her ridiculous grin. Who the hell ordered subs? Clay couldn't have been so stupid. Subs were a stark reminder of Kelly. As if he needed another one.

"Damn, I'm happy to see you, babe," Clay said. "I'm starving."

She winked. "All you wanna see me for?"

Clay grinned and took the food.

"I can't believe Kelly had the nerve to call off tonight. Now I gotta do her work and mine," she whined.

Will watched from the corner of his eye as she walked close to him and leaned over the fender of the car he was working on. She let the loose 'V' of her shirt drape low. "How are you doing, honey?"

Leave me the hell alone.

"I didn't even know you two were so serious." She slid a finger down his shirtsleeve.

Of course you didn't.

"I don't know what you saw in her," Jaycee said with a sigh. "Her husband probably left her because she was psycho. Remember how she freaked out on the boat?" She shook her head. "But it's okay. From now on, I'll be right here for you."

Will clenched his jaw.

"You want to come over tonight? We could have a drink and talk about it—"

"Clay!" Will massaged his temple as he waited for his mechanic to come to the bay. "Keep your damn social in the other bay."

Certain no one had followed her, Kelly turned the kayak truck onto Burns' driveway. She parked in the pole barn where he kept extra boats. On her drive over, the early evening sky had turned from beautiful sunny blue to an ominous overcast gray. Gray was good. She'd be less likely to encounter incoming traffic on the river.

She began a disguise with a wind jacket she'd taken from the hut's lost-and-found box. She rooted around the barn and found an old cowboy hat. It stunk like sweat from the eighties, and, on a normal day, she would have immediately assessed how much mold would be residing in it. Today, she stuck it on her head and tucked her hair into the collar of the windbreaker.

It was the best she could do on short notice. She carried a kayak to the bank and began to paddle her way back to town.

She didn't pass any kayakers, and she had never realized how windy and wavy the river could get in a pending storm. Especially against the current.

Her arm muscles burned from the exercise by the time she reached the dock for the kayak hut. Darkness had fallen, and with the looming clouds, the beach was almost deserted. Junior had been collecting the boats for closing time when she paddled close.

"Kelly?" He frowned.

"Shut up," she whispered as she climbed onto the dock. She checked for any watching eyes on the beach, but it seemed everyone had retired for the day. Good and bad news.

What if the person after me is gone, too?

Allison raised her brows as Kelly came in the hut. She slipped to the floor, out of sight under the counter, and sighed. "I told you to call me when people went in there." She rubbed at her shoulder.

"I tried. Kept going to voicemail."

Great. Ever since it had taken a dive in the toilet, her phone had been misbehaving. So much for the waterproof case.

"You said you were coming back, anyway." Allison handed her a piece of paper. "Here's a list."

Kelly scanned the names.

Randy in and out. Clay with Brent. Clay with a lifeguard. Jared. Edna from the diner. It went on. She squinted at the list of forty names as though it was a Magic Eye illusion and the answer would pop out. A lot of names didn't seem to matter but she had no way of knowing.

Jaycee had brought food.

"They ordered from the bowling alley?" Kelly glanced up at Allison on the stool. "Don't look down!"

The teen snapped her face to the lake and frowned. "Why can't I look at you?"

Kelly shook her head.

So smart, yet so stupid. "Then someone will know you're talking to someone on the floor. And then they'll know it's me and that I'm in here."

"Who's watching you?" Junior came in from the dock.

"I don't know."

"Everyone was," Allison said. "You ditched him in front of everyone!"

Kelly ignored the reminder. "They ordered food?"

Was that Will's way of trying to get me to come to him?

Allison shrugged. "Jaycee had two sub boxes. She was all over him."

Kelly stiffened.

"He didn't care," she added quickly. Kelly almost smiled at her loyalty.

"He didn't even talk to her," Junior said. "He's been yelling at everyone who gets in his way."

She inhaled with relief. They must have really been hawking on the activity at the garage. She peeked her head over the counter. All three garage doors were open as they often were on humid days. Wouldn't have been hard to watch the comings and goings from across the street.

So far so good. He does hate me. How could he not?

"How does he look?" she asked quietly.

"Pissed off." Allison leaned on the counter above and yawned. "Hasn't said but three words all day."

Kelly nodded. *All the better.*

CHAPTER 48

No sooner than Clay had removed Jaycee, the female presence seemed to triple.

For the second time in the hour, the lifeguards stopped by. Will gave them no attention and guessed they were restless from the coming storm. Otherwise, they'd probably take it out on the sidewalk. Clay had noticed them alright, goofing off and popping beers in the first bay. Will finished a tune-up as he tuned them out. Alyssa sung off-key with the radio.

It had to be a fucking Friday.

"Don't be so glum, Will. She doesn't deserve you." Daisy and her pals had come over to his bay. She patted his back. He walked away for a torque wrench.

"She's not worth it," Kendra said.

Thought I told him to—

"Come on, girls, leave him alone," Clay said as he trotted over to them.

"You're lucky she said 'no'. You wouldn't want to be married to a fat-ass for the rest of your life," Jaycee said. They all giggled.

Women and their stupid catty sneers. He loved Kelly's ass. Had loved. He grit his teeth.

"I thought she was a dyke. I had no idea she was even capable of attracting a man," Kendra said with a gleam in her eyes.

"Get the hell out of here!"

Daisy choked on her beer. "Hey, there's no reason to get crabby, Will—"

He slammed the wrench down. "Get the fuck out of here! Every one of you. Get the fuck out of my garage!"

"Aw, come on, Will…" Alyssa protested.

"Come on, leave him alone." Clay ushered them toward the front door. Will went to each of the three garage bays and slammed the doors down. He jabbed his hand on the locks, the metal rods bouncing back at the excess force.

The girls lingered at the entrance door, protesting and taking last sips of their beers.

"Everyone! I don't want one more fucking person to come in here!"

Clay closed the door after them and locked it.

Will wiped at his eyes and went back to work.

From the kayak hut, Kelly heard the rumble of Will's wrath. As she sat on the floor of the hut, she resorted to watching the garage with one of the toy periscopes Jared sold to little kids at his ice cream stand.

Kelly ignored Allison's raised brows.

It was the best she could do. Not like she had ever needed to spy on people before.

She paid close attention as the girls partied in the garage and Will lost his temper.

Darkness had nearly blanketed the street, and she rested easier with the knowledge that except for Clay, Will had shut the world out from his garage. It made it safer.

"You staying here all night like this?" Junior asked as he began to lock up for the night. The shutter swung closed on the counter, but the gap at the bottom allowed plenty of space for her to keep watching.

"Until he leaves."

"What are you so freaked about? You turned him down. Why do you care what happens to him?" Allison said.

Kelly bit her lip. "Tell you later. Lock the door after you go. No one will be able to see me. It's going to rain soon. No one will be around. I'll be fine."

Ha. Ha. Fine was light-years away. It probably would have freaked them out if she asked if their parents might have a gun to borrow. Not to mention she had absolutely no experience with weapons.

"Kelly, are you in trouble? Does this have something to do with the lady who came after you in Atlanta?" Junior asked.

"Look, the less you know—"

"Oh my God, what happened? What's going on?" Allison dropped to the floor and stared at her.

"Nothing. I can't explain it. Go home—"

"You want me to send Dad down here? He's got a gun," Junior said.

"Call Fred," Allison said. "Eric's a dumbass, but Fred's okay."

Yeah, tell Fred and Burns what, though? She couldn't explain her instinct how Will was in danger. "Please, go."

Junior jerked his bangs back and Allison shook her head.

Dammit, they're going to do something whether I want them to or not.

"It's too hard to explain. Here, text me. Text me every hour on the hour. If I don't respond…" She flailed her hand. "Hell, I don't know. Tell your dad to come to the hut."

Junior nodded and Allison flung her arms around Kelly's neck.

After they left, Kelly moved to the stool. Thankful for Roger's shabby craftsmanship, she gave up on the periscope and spied through the side crack of the shutter.

CHAPTER 49

"Hello?" Clay answered the phone.

Emily smiled. "Hi, big boy."

"Hey baby, what's up?"

"Nothing much. Seeing how you're doing. Is he still pissed off?"

Clay took a deep breath. "Leave him be. He's a little upset."

"A little upset?"

He chuckled.

"It's well, the worst timing."

"What?"

"If he hadn't gone berserk on us, I was going to see if I could bring my car in to have him look at it. The check engine light is going on and off."

"Let him cool down a little bit."

She snarled her lip as she faked a light laugh. "He locked up the whole shop. I'd ask you to do it to avoid him—"

"He'll cool down."

"When? You're still in a cast. I was going to drive upstate to my girlfriend's bachelorette party tomorrow at noon. Now I'm scared to drive it."

Clay sighed. "I can run the scanner on it in the morning."

"But how would I get it there? He locked the garage all up."

"I'll come pick it up. Randy's coming by with some food. He can run me over and I'll bring it to the shop. No biggie. I'll check it out in the morning."

"Thanks, Clay. Brent is coming by in a bit. We're going out for some drinks. I'll leave the key under the floor mat in case I'm gone when you come."

Emily hung up.

She waited in the trunk with her spare key in her hand until Clay came. It still reeked from the body she had stolen at the gas station—the sweet reminder of another successful identity change. She drew a full breath.

He called out something to Randy and she felt the vibration of the driver's door opening and closing. Rain pounded like BB pellets on the roof of the trunk, and she strained to listen.

The car stopped moving and the driver's door clanged again. He must have gotten out to open the garage door, because she rolled again as loud music replaced the rush of the rain.

"Will!" Clay called out.

Will sat at his desk in his office. The radio quieted enough for him to hear Clay's footsteps.

"There you are. Wondered if you left." Clay leaned into the room, hand on the doorframe.

Will tore his stare from the little box and faced him.

Clay hesitated. "Uh, Randy took me to pick up a car. I'll run the scan check on it in the morning. I put it in the first bay. I'm going to head home, alright?"

Will returned his attention to the little box.

Rot in hell? She never would have said it. Like he never would have imagined she would deny loving him. Why would she have said that? He couldn't shake the hunch she was afraid. He'd seen her hand shaking. But what had she been so scared of?

Clay left, but returned a moment later. He leaned over to pull Will to his chest and clapped a hand on his back. The straight man's hug. He left again.

Rain deluged as a car pulled up to the garage. Kelly hadn't caught any movement through the tiny windows since Will had gone in his office. When Randy pulled up thirty minutes ago, Clay seemed to have left for the night.

Who the hell is this?

Squinting, she strained to see who had opened the garage door. Someone who had disobeyed Will's order to stay out of his garage. It was damned hard to spy inside the garage with the limit of narrow rectangular windows.

"Goddammit." It was raining too hard to see anything. The car was in the garage, and she had no idea whose it was.

Emily waited in silence, checking she was alone in the garage with Will. She pushed the trunk open and stepped out. Will wasn't in the bay, but she spotted the shine of illumination from his office.

She smiled. Tiptoeing, she spun in a circle, surveying her surroundings, calculating what could be a threat, what could be evidence. She had noted before there were no cameras. No mirrors. No alarms. Nothing.

She stepped toward the office. He came out into the bay at the same time she tripped on an oil pan on the floor. He turned at the screech of metal on cement.

"What are you doing here?" Those had been the exact same words Forty had said. Her blood boiled.

The annoyance and irritation of her clumsiness countered the excitement of seeing him, the real Forty-One. Kelly's new man. Forty had been a steal for revenge. Revenge for Kelly screwing up Thirty-Nine. But Forty hadn't worked. She smiled at Will. Finally, she'd reap her revenge on Kelly. "I had to see you, Will."

He looked around, but kept her in his view. "How the fuck did you get in here?"

"I love you, Will. It doesn't matter if she doesn't. I do. I love you and I'll make you happy. Choose me, Will." She stepped forward, her heart ticking in controlled excitement.

It didn't matter anymore. Kelly would never win if she was dead. If Will was dead. It didn't matter if Will succumbed, if he faltered and said yes. Yes, I choose *you.*

It didn't matter if Will really did become Emily's Forty-First steal. If she couldn't steal Will from Kelly, she'd kill him so Kelly couldn't have him.

But she couldn't resist the temptation to try. She couldn't say no to the all-consuming need to be reconfirmed.

I will always win.

He will want me. He will choose me. Not Kelly. I am better than Kelly.

The manipulation she had managed over so many men, so many steals, had been an ongoing play of that game. The challenge in her life to ensure they would always choose her. She had given them exactly what they wanted. Attention, loving words, kinky sex, sentimental bullshit, praise and ego-boosting. Whatever her intended victims needed, she provided. And they always chose her.

Thirty-eight individuals had chosen her. Thirty-eight people, she had won over. Seduced, tricked, manipulated. Emily reigned in her ability to steal people. Until she met Kelly.

Will recalled how the women had taken stabs at Kelly earlier. They had all been so damn wrapped up in Kelly ditching him. Churchston needed a hobby, but the girls seemed so curious, overly excited.

What business was it of theirs? Why did they care about Kelly or what she did?

What he had thought were female scrimmages seemed like much more as he studied the neurotic expression on this woman's face.

Obsession.

"Get out of here." He reached one hand back to his waist, hoping his phone was in its holster.

"Do you love her, Will?" Her voice pitched in an eerie note.

"Get the hell out of here."

"Do you love her?" she screamed.

Why is she obsessed with Kelly?

She pulled a gun from the waistband under her shirt.

His throat went dry. *Fuck.*

"Do you love her?" she shrieked like a feral animal, distempered and wild-eyed. "Do you want her like she wants you? You think she's pretty? You think she's sexy? You think she can fuck you like I can?"

Will backed up, retreating through his garage as she approached him, screaming every step until she had him cornered.

Who's in the damn garage?

Kelly slid the latch for the shutter and jumped over the counter of the kayak hut. It was more like jumping into a whirlpool as the rain soaked her to the skin. She ran for the garage across the street, her shoes squishing as they suctioned into the sand.

She stopped, ran back to the hut and searched for some kind of defense. The cracked canoe oar had to do.

No one was in sight as she sprinted across Main. Businesses had closed for the night. Rain had chased people into their homes, distant from the commercial hub of the public beach area.

Alone.

Standing in front of the garage, under the hazy glow from a streetlamp, she hated how no one would have her back. Exposed, endangered and hunted, she stretched on her toes to press her face to the rectangle window and peered at the car.

Buick!

Mr. Nikki had seen a Buick at the end of the townhouse drive.

"Fuck." She stepped back from the door and spun, looking for someone, anyone, to help.

She pulled her phone from her pocket. Frozen. Shielding her eyes from the rain, she headed for the front door to the garage.

Never before had she missed payphones.

Burns? Eric? Gannon? She didn't know who she could call, even if she had a phone.

She tried the doorknob and it didn't give.

"Nooo."

CHAPTER 50

"She can't win." Emily held the gun at him as he backed into the far wall. She calmed as she took control.

I've got Kelly's man in the corner.

"You should have chosen me. I'm better."

It was her life. Her agenda. Her game. Years of floating through people, stealing men, manipulating them to choose her. As a mistress, a girlfriend, a substitute for their spouse. She'd say what they wanted to hear, tease them with the right fantasies, goad them with false praise, and lavish them with attention. Any relationship, she could break it.

They always choose me. They have to.

All the waiting. All those mistakes. Emily clenched her teeth.

"What do you want?" Will asked. Emily twisted her lips in a smile. She hadn't missed how he surveyed the room, likely hunting for a weapon. She tightened her fingers on the gun.

She recalled how Forty had cried when he said he missed his wife. John had sobbed about how great she was. How he had to have her back. The soulful love-lost sadness.

It sickened her. Emily had sought John as her fortieth steal to seek revenge on Kelly for screwing up Thirty-Nine. But no. When Emily had gotten John to choose Emily over his wife, he had wanted Kelly back. Now Will had chosen Kelly, too.

They must always choose me. That's how it's supposed to work.

But they hadn't. John hadn't. Will hadn't.

Kelly couldn't be allowed to have such power.

"I want Kelly to learn a lesson." Emily reached in her pocket for her Taser. She wanted Kelly to squirm, to cry, to plead. To apologize for screwing up Thirty-Nine, for making Forty want her back. To beg for forgiveness for stealing John out from under her.

Emily was going to make sure Kelly watched as she slaughtered her lover, her man. This fool who wanted her.

Emily would have to kill her afterward. She couldn't let her live. Kelly had stolen what Emily had stolen. Emily had taken John, and Kelly had made him want her back.

She shook with the anticipation of finally killing Kelly, frustrated from her failures. She should have killed her when she ran her over with the boat. She should have killed her when she had stranded her at the kayak dock.

It failed because he had come. Emily glared at Will. He had taken Kelly to his home.

How had I not seen that?

Trembling with rage, the gun quivered in her hand.

I'll take Will and use him as bait. Maybe Kelly will try to sacrifice herself to save Will.

She smiled. *No.* No.

Emily had to kill Will to show Kelly, to teach her she would take any man Kelly could ever want. It would be Kelly's last lesson on Earth.

"Don't hurt her. Kill me. I don't care," Will said.

She detected no anger, fear or worry from his tone. Calm and brave, so matter-of-fact. It snagged at her nerves.

Such love. Such dying fucking great admiring love.

Kelly had a power to make this man choose her and love her at the face of his own death?

Gritting her teeth, Emily aimed the Taser at him, satisfied when he fell against the rack of parts.

Kelly ran up and down the sidewalk, her eyes barely open from the river of rain. Jumping up to peek through the windows, she tried to see him, to see who had come in the Buick, but she saw no one.

A crash sounded in the garage, followed by metallic clangs on the cement floor.

Will?

With a gasp, she froze as she listened past the thunder in her ears. She glanced at the oar in her hand, then at the double-paned Plexiglas window on the entrance door. It snapped in half as she tried to break the window.

She ran to the hardware store three shops down the sidewalk.

Sledgehammer.

Stripping her shirt off, she wrapped it around her fist like Finn had taught her when they were kids. She punched the single layer display window. Glass shattered and she grimaced at the pain in her wrist. She knocked down shards of glass and crawled in, not giving a damn about the red flashing lights in the corner of the room.

Kelly went to crawl back out the window and saw a screwdriver in the aisle display. She doubled back and grabbed it. Weaponry.

The more, the better, right?

Will's window broke with the sledgehammer's force and Kelly reached inside to undo the lock on the handle. Stepping in, she held the screwdriver next to her head in a stance that reminded her of the first Nintendo's Mortal Kombat figures. She gripped the sledgehammer in her other hand, hanging it ready at her knee.

For all the classes she had taken, she couldn't recall a single move. Tae kwon do? Nothing doing. Never before had she needed to ambush. She had only learned how to protect herself when attacked.

She stepped slowly through the garage, cautious to keep her back to a wall. Her chest heaved in rapid bursts as she scanned the rooms.

Hail Mary, Mother of God...

She passed the Buick's open trunk. Sweet stagnant decay fumed from the lining.

...just so you know, I'm going to kill this fucking bastard...

Her feet sounded with soft wet squeaks, doused from the rainfall. She inched past the car, straining her ears.

Pray for us sinners...

A grunt sounded from the rear bay by the storeroom.

...even this sick demented person who's going to regret messing with me...

A scuffle of footsteps came from the other room.

Now until the hour of our death...

Her arms shook from nervousness. She squeezed her fingers on the handles of the screwdriver and sledgehammer as she came closer.

...because this creep is going to hurt Will over my DEAD BODY!

Will lay on the ground, eyes closed, as a woman wrapped rope around his ankles. A gun lay at the woman's side. Crouching over, the brunette's shirt had lifted to show a large black tattoo. Kelly focused on the black sun, not quite at the center of her back. She had seen that tattoo before. She had seen it on her old bed. It had been a flower then. A rose.

She raised the sledgehammer as though it was a bat, readying to take a swing as though the woman's head was on the tee. She dropped the screwdriver to bring both hands on the hammer.

As the tool clattered to the floor, the woman jumped to her feet, the gun ready in her hands.

Kelly narrowed her eyes. "Hello, Sasha. Or is it Kendra?" She checked Will's still form. No blood.

Her grin reminded Kelly of the little girl in *The Exorcist*. Possessed. Eerie.

The woman trained her eyes on the sledgehammer before her face. "Kelly. How nice of you to come. Saves me the trouble of bringing him to you."

"What are you doing?" Kelly pressed her lips together, not wanting to show how terrified she was.

CHAPTER 51

Kendra was Sasha. They were the same woman. She'd dyed her hair. Some surgery? Fatter. Boob job. Tattoo over the older one. But it was the same woman. The same gloating smile.

And some freaking fucked-up déjà vu.

"Teaching you a lesson." She turned the gun to Will's head and with her other hand, she targeted a Taser at Kelly. "Drop it or I shoot him."

Kelly glanced at Will again. No blood, but he was so still. The sledgehammer thudded to the floor without a bounce, the handle smacking down next to her foot.

"What'd you do to him?" Kelly held her hands up in surrender, staying in motion on her feet.

We're in a garage. There has to be some kind of a weapon.

Emily kicked his knee and he twisted in pain. "He's alive. I had to keep him alive for you to watch."

"Watch what?" Kelly ducked, but Sasha was faster.

Sasha smacked the gun upside her face and Kelly stumbled back. She fell to the floor, her head whirring, blood on her tongue.

Grunting, Sasha hurried over and pulled up the collar of Kelly's wet shirt, straddling her on her knees, pinning her to the ground as she spat words at her face.

"You have to learn, Kelly. You can't win. I win. Nothing, no one, is going to make me lose ever again. They always choose *me*. I never lose. Every man comes to me. They choose *me*!" Sasha inhaled sharply as though the air would calm her furious speech.

Kelly tested her legs, but she couldn't flip the woman off of her. No sledgehammer, no tool, no weapon. Naked without defense, she stalled as she listened.

"You're Denner."

Sasha laughed. "Denner? I was Mrs. Ruth Denner eight years ago. In Lauderdale." Her lips flattened to a stiff line. "Where did you hear that name?"

"You used a credit card at a gas station in Betsy's name. They found a print in John's condo." Kelly swallowed. "Someone paid a tab at Alan's under your, her…name."

Sasha jerked her head to the side in a stiff reaction. "Must have used the wrong card," she said to herself. "I've been getting so impatient, wanting to end this…."

"What did you do to Betsy?"

"Betsy?" Sasha reared back with a smile. "Betsy? The fat old hag in the hospital? I *was*

Betsy, you little bitch. I was the fucking nurse assistant."

"You—"

"I killed her to get in and slip him the heparin. I needed a way in the hospital. I was Betsy, you bitch. The same as I'm 'Kendra'." She stabbed herself in the chest. "Same as I was the old fart's fucking girlfriend for two long fucking years."

Kelly blinked. Sasha. Kendra. Betsy. Norbert's girlfriend? She couldn't keep up. Betsy had been an overweight older woman. Norbert's girlfriend was...an overweight older woman. Wigs, makeup, baggy clothes. It was possible they were all the same woman. She scraped the floor for the screwdriver as Will stirred in her peripheral vision.

Come on, Will, get up.

"Why?"

"Why?" Sasha sneered. "Because of you, that's why! He was worth millions. Lonely old man. Lost his wife and daughter years ago in a car accident. Sad, lonely workaholic with terminal cancer. I did my research. He was the perfect fucking steal. No family to get his money. No current girlfriend. It took months to get him to trust me. I started as his secretary. Then I started on his cock. He had months to live and he was going to leave his money to ME!"

Spittle shot to Kelly's face.

"He finally came around. Decided to make it legal. Let's get hitched, he said. Leave his money to me because he had no one else. But no. You had to fuck it up." Sasha grabbed Kelly's collar to pick her off the floor and slam her head back down.

"You. Perfectionist brilliant fucking hero Kelly. You had to feel sorry for the old bastard. You had to dig into his contacts. You had to find out he had an estranged doped-up daughter."

Kelly fingered a washer on the cement and flicked it to Will to rouse him. "And he forgave her."

"Thanks to you. You get Papa and daughter hugging again and there goes my money. There goes two long fucking years of getting him to choose me."

"But why did you kill him?"

"The old bastard? Too many loose ends. I hurried, hoping he might have already changed his papers to leave his money to me. But no. The fucking kid got it all. I lost it all because you screwed it up."

"But why did you kill—"

"John?" Sasha snorted. "Revenge. And he was such an easy steal. You needed to be punished for screwing up the old bastard. For throwing two years of my hard work down the drain. I stole him from you like I always take them. Every man decides I'm better and they choose me. They never want their wives and girlfriends because I'm better. But, no. He didn't want me anymore." She paused and slanted her head to the side in another stiff jerk. "He wanted *you*. He wanted *you* back. You won him back from me!"

As Sasha screamed on, Kelly spread her fingers on the ground, feeling for the Taser that wasn't in Sasha's hand.

Sasha shook her head. "You can't beat me, Kelly. I will steal who I want and you can't stop me." Her chest puffed between words. "So I need to make you understand. No man will want you over me. They'll want me."

She jabbed the gun at Kelly's temple, the cold metal stinging her skin.

"But you can't go on. You can't steal what I always win and walk away. So I had to follow you. I had to take every man you had. Every man you want, I can take. Any man you desire will want me more because I'll always be better!"

A faint groan came from Will and Kelly dared a glance at him. Sasha jerked her to pay attention.

"The others were mistakes. I thought they were your lovers so they had to be taken. Killed."

Sasha fisted her collar tighter with a shake. "It took so long. You have no idea how long I waited to find a man to steal from you. So long. But I found him. And now you'll watch me take him and kill him."

Kelly's heart thudded like a piston and she swallowed blood.

Sasha leaned up to train the gun on Will. "You can't have him. You can't have anyone. You see? This time, finally, you lose. Not me." She moved her finger to the trigger and grinned at her. "Say good—"

Will jerked up to throw a jack-stand at Sasha, and her head twisted back at an unnatural angle. A faint oomph of air shot out of her lips as she clumped to the side, off of Kelly.

Will slouched to the ground with a wince and crawled toward Kelly. She scrambled on hands and knees to him.

"Will." Her voice strained as he grabbed her and held her so fiercely she had to gasp for air.

He reached for the sledgehammer and she pulled back to check Sasha's still body on the ground. She clutched his shirt and rested her forehead on his chest.

Footsteps came in the front bay. "The drunk bastard's breaking in to stores now. Busting his own damn windows. He's going in. Drunk and disorderly." Eric's sniggering voice neared. "Where's that good-for-nothing—?"

"NO!"

Kelly spun her head from Will's protective embrace at Sasha's scream. She jerked up and turned the gun at Kelly's face.

Will pulled her to his chest as Fred and Eric came in the room.

Three shots roared in the garage like thunder.

CHAPTER 52

"What the hell were you thinking?" Will's question was a yell as he followed the stretcher to the ambulance on Main. Locals and tourists crowded the scene in front of the garage.

"Hey." Her voice didn't carry like his bellowing, but Kelly was tired of being talked over. Tired in general. *Damn that's a lot of blood.* "Hello! Hey!" She smacked the closest EMT on the shoulder.

"Easy ma'am, take it easy."

She gave the young EMT the finger and tried to sit up. *Goddammit, I'm a nurse. I've tended to more gunshots wounds than he has.*

"Hey!" She tried to get the EMT's attention again as they wheeled her away. "He's bleeding!"

Will's angry frown hovered over her as they directed the stretcher to the back. "What the hell were you thinking?" he demanded again.

"Oh, shut up," she said, swiping the gauze out of the EMT's hand just before he pressed it to her shoulder. "Here." She shoved it at Will. "Put it on your arm."

He narrowed his eyes at her as they wheeled her further.

"You're bleeding," she said.

He *was* bleeding. But she was the one who got hit. Twice.

Eric's a dead man.

"What the hell did you shove me down for?" He climbed in the back of the ambulance as they loaded her up.

Kelly pointed to the grazing on his arm, still nurturing him when *she* had been shot. He obeyed and held the gauze to the cut.

"Did he even go to an academy somewhere?" Kelly said, wincing.

Eric had come in, hopefully with the intent to disarm Kendra, but he had tripped on an oil pan and shot Kelly in the thigh instead.

And when Kendra aimed for Will's heart, Kelly had shoved him down, taking the bullet through her shoulder, slowing it down before it grazed his forearm.

The love stuff. Kelly sure didn't take it lightly.

"She shot you." Will hated how her face seemed so lined with fatigue.

"*He* shot me!" Kelly argued. "A cop, my ass."

Will's lungs couldn't catch up, and he was certain his heart never would.

He had thought he'd lost her. When Kendra sat up to shoot her, he had tucked her down to save her. Save her. No. Of course not. Not Kelly.

She takes the damn bullet for me.

"She shot you." He frowned at her.

Kelly's alive. Kelly's alive.

He spun the idea in his head, trying to calm down.

"No. She was aiming for you. *That*'s what I was thinking. I knew she wanted to kill you. I was trying to save you. Leave it to the goddamn cop to fuck it up." Kelly groaned and strained to inspect her shoulder.

Kelly relaxed back in the stretcher, replaying the blur of action in her frenzied mind. One shot, she felt a stab in her thigh. Another shot, she pushed Will down as fire burned her shoulder. Last shot, the gun fell out of Sasha's hand.

At least Fred knew how to keep his feet and hit a target.

As Will argued with her in the ambulance, she let his words in one ear, out the other. He was alive. She checked her shoulder. *I'm alive*.

It didn't escape her notice. As furiously as he argued and scolded her in the ambulance, he had yet to let go of her hand and lose the scared shitless expression that hid under his scowl.

Annoyed he couldn't save me? Probably.

"And if I push you out of harm's way then you obey—"

"Hey, Will?"

He faced her with his mouth still open mid-sentence.

"I love you." She tipped the corner of her mouth up in a grin as the EMT shoved an oxygen mask over her face.

Sasha-Kendra-Betsy-Denner, whoever, is dead. Will is safe.

His death grip on her hand gave her hope he could forgive her for the refusal on the beach. She rubbed her thumb over his trembling knuckles.

CHAPTER 53

Commotion was a mild way to describe Kelly's room at the hospital. At ten in the morning the day after Sasha had tried to teach her a lesson, the whole herd of her family had come. Heather had driven Dad down. Wade was trying to fly in from San Diego. Sean and Finn had flown in, and Grant had come in the middle of the night. They were the non-Churchston half. When Clay, Randy, and the Burns trooped in, Kelly protested and ousted them from her room.

Wanting explanations, she posted Grant as her sentinel. Only Will and Gannon were allowed in.

After receiving her voicemail, asking about the name Denner, the detective had driven back to Churchston—arriving an hour after Sasha had tried to kill Kelly and Will. She and Will had already given their statements. But it was too much to understand.

Her immediate worries were resolved. Her men were safe. After Fred had taken Eric's gun and badge, he'd secured the scene at the garage. A bloodied bat was found in the Buick's trunk, next to a single surgical bootie. An animal crate was found smashed in the back seat.

They found the person who had hurt her friends. But who that person was, remained ambiguous.

Kelly fingered the bandage on her shoulder. She couldn't wait for answers from the crazy woman she had known as Sasha, as Kendra, after she came out of surgery, in custody, of course. It seemed too unreal of a tale for one woman to change identities so often.

"So her real name was Ruth Denner?" Will asked Gannon.

He gulped back coffee before answering. "One of them. Eight years ago she had married Richard Denner. CEO from Salt Lake City. She filed divorce three days after the marriage. I suspect she was also Linda Grimes in Dallas twelve years ago. And five years ago, she might have been Wendy Smith."

"She legally married them? Bigamy?" Grant asked.

"Yes and no. Maybe. Denner, we have records of her divorcing him. Grimes, he was killed in a car accident. Smith... I think she pulled a disappearing act on him," Gannon said.

"She went from man to man, seducing them for money? And Kelly interfered with her plans to make big on this Norbert guy?" Will asked.

Kelly shook her head. Emily had screamed about power. About winning. It was the game of convincing people to choose her that motivated the sicko. "No. She said she 'stole John from me'.

John wasn't loaded. He had money, but no wealth."

Gannon nodded. "I think the money appealed to her. It was her income, if you would. We've found traces of this Denner money being used all over the country. It took a while to follow the pattern, but there were oddball slips in cold cases." He consulted his notepad. "First time she showed up in records was a child's thumbprint on a bloodied knife. Cold case from Tallahassee nineteen years ago. A prostitute by the name of Carmen Dunstan was killed in her apartment—she'd had a daughter by the name of Emily, but there was no further record of the girl. In school. Doctor appointments. Social Security Number. Nothing. Next, we've got her print on a gun in Miami. Drug dealer shot in his bed. It'll take some time to piece it together, all these little tips in old cases. At some point, she must have gotten smart, careful to leave fewer clues. There's a long gap where there aren't any leads to her. Until this Denner name pops up.

"She must have anticipated Norbert leaving his money to her—his girlfriend, fiancé, whatever she was. But when Kelly found his daughter and reunited them, he choose his daughter to love, not Emily. Since her plans were botched, she killed Betsy in order to get in and kill Norbert. All speculation—" Gannon took a deep breath. "But we should get some answers as soon as the doctor clears her for questioning."

"If John didn't have money, why did she go from Norbert to John?" Grant asked.

AMABEL DANIELS

"Revenge," Kelly said. "She wanted to get revenge at me. For spoiling her plans with Norbert."

"So she stole him," Will said. "She got him to cheat on you. She broke up your marriage. Why'd she come down here and—"

"Because she didn't really steal him," Kelly said. "He had wanted me back." Will must not have been listening to all of Emily's confessions in the garage. "I was a threat somehow. She manipulated John, but she never really got him."

Will glared at the tiles on the floor. "So every man you seemed to be with, she tried to take from you."

Kelly leaned her head back to the pillow with a sigh. Gannon peeked at his phone. "I'm needed down the hall."

"We'll be in touch?" she asked.

"Of course." He shook hands with Grant on the way to the door. "Where am I going to find you next? Atlanta? Here?"

Kelly wanted to shrug. She couldn't answer those questions yet.

"I'm going to go find Dad, Kel," Grant said as he moved to leave, passing Gannon at the door. "Get some rest."

Gannon glanced at Will, staring out the window, then back to her. With a smile, he rocked on his heels and stepped out of the room.

Kelly closed her eyes, too exhausted to work on an answer to Gannon's question. To her own. The only person to give her direction remained standing at the window.

"I know you're awake, Kelly," Will said.

Her smile turned to a frown as she opened her eyes. "I wouldn't be if you'd stop harassing me." She tested her shoulder.

"Why did you shove me down?" he demanded and set his huge hands on the bed.

For such a sharp man he could really be dense. "She was targeting any man I seemed involved with. You were the only one. I didn't want you to get shot."

"But you did!"

"Well, I can't explain Eric's piss-poor aim but I knew she was trying to kill you." She gave him a one-sided shrug. "You know, I figured you'd be happier than this."

"You could have died!"

"So could you. Goddammit, Will. I took the damn bullet for you. It doesn't mean you're less of a man!"

"You weren't supposed to take a bullet for me."

"Too bad."

"I'm supposed to protect you."

Like he was supposed to have protected Matt. It had to be hard for him. But she wasn't going to be a burden on him. "Be my guest. But it doesn't mean I won't have your back, too."

Guilt had taken a toll on his life and if they had a future to share, it was going to be with more than guilt and worry.

"You're a pain in the ass." He stood up to pace again and wiped his face. "You could have died back there and…"

"Heather out there?" Kelly looked around him at the closed door. "She was supposed to bring me ice cream two hours ago."

He stared at her speechlessly. Probably imagined she was dismissing him with her blunt dodge around the guilt trip he intended to ride through. "Yeah. She's out there." He moved for the door, and paused with a heavy breath. "Thanks for taking the bullet, Kelly."

"You're leaving?"

"*I* don't have any ice cream."

"Where's my ring?" She sat up more and watched the cords of his neck strain as he grit his teeth.

"What ring?"

"You don't want to marry me anymore? Oh, come on! Because I took the bullet for you?"

"Because you don't want to marry me." Will stormed back to the bed.

"I said no because I knew she was trying to kill you. Or me!"

His eyes steeled on her and she stuck her chin out. "You don't want to marry me anymore?"

He fidgeted.

It was an old game and her patience thinned.

Now or never, she waited.

"Fine." She looked out the window. "Nice knowing you, Will. See ya around."

The silence was heavy until he cleared his throat. He tossed the ring box onto the bed and his voice cracked. "Please don't scare me like that anymore."

She eyed the box. "What's this?"

"Your ring."

"You're tossing it to me?"

He rolled his eyes.

She whipped her focus back to the window and crossed her arms. "I changed my mind. I don't want to marry you."

"Yes, you do." He leaned his fists on the bed, caging her in.

"Nope." She refused to look at him, but the skyrocket of her pulse was likely to send one of the nurses in.

"Yes, you do." His voice melted to a softer husky tone.

"Why would I?" She met his gaze.

His lips curved in a little smile. "You love me."

You love me. Was he ever going to say it?

"Do you?" she asked.

Come on, Will, say it.

His lips twitched.

"You can't say it, can you?"

"Give me back that damn box." Will anted up to her yells. "Kelly, stop it—"

She tucked it further under the sheets. "Why do you want to marry me?" she insisted.

"Because you said you loved me."

"Oh, you're such a wimp!"

"Give me the box."

"You can't marry me if you don't love me."

"I do!" Will bellowed back.

"Wrong line. That's what you say when you're actually at the altar—"

He rubbed at the back of his neck. "You are the most—"

"You do what, Will?"

"I love you, dammit!"

"Was that so hard?"

"Oh, give me your hand. There. There's the ring." He slid it on. He lifted her hand to his lips and kissed her knuckles.

She smiled up at him. "You're going to make my life a living hell, aren't you?"

"Only as much as you'll make mine." He pushed the side bar of the bed down.

"Will. Stop. You can't fit up here."

"Hell I can't."

Kelly laughed. "Really, you can't fit up here. Hey." She quieted as he kissed her lips. "That's my nightgown."

"Mmm. It's my fiancée's nightgown and I say it goes."

She squirmed to make room for him. "Will, where *are* we going to go?"

He laced his fingers with hers and thumbed the ring. Kissing her uninjured shoulder, he said, "I think you'll have to stay another night."

She shook her head. "Do you want to stay here, Will? In Churchston? Do you want to leave? You could have a garage anywhere. But I'll start my EMS-1 classes online next week and—"

"Wherever you want to, Kelly. As long we go together."

ABOUT THE AUTHOR

Amabel Daniels lives in Northwest Ohio with her patient husband, adventurous toddler and a collection of too many cats and dogs. Although she holds a Master's degree in Ecology, her true love is finding a good book. When she isn't spending time outdoors, she's busy brewing up her next novel, usually as she lets her mind run off with the addictive words of "what if…"

For more information about Amabel's work, please stop by www.amabeldaniels.com